REGRESSION

CULLEN BUNN
STORY

DANNY LUCKERT
ART

MARIE ENGER
COLORS/LETTERS

JOEL ENOS
EDITOR

IMAGE COMICS, INC.

ROBERT KIRKMAN — CHIEF OPERATING OFFICER
ERIK LARSEN — CHIEF FINANCIAL OFFICER
TODD MCFARLANE — PRESIDENT
MARC SILVESTRI — CHIEF EXECUTIVE OFFICER
JIM VALENTINO — VICE PRESIDENT
ERIC STEPHENSON — PUBLISHER / CHIEF CREATIVE OFFICER
COREY HART — DIRECTOR OF SALES

JEFF BOISON — DIRECTOR OF PUBLISHING PLANNING & BOOK TRADE SALES
CHRIS ROSS — DIRECTOR OF DIGITAL SALES
JEFF STANG — DIRECTOR OF SPECIALTY SALES
KAT SALAZAR — DIRECTOR OF PR & MARKETING
DREW GILL — ART DIRECTOR
HEATHER DOORNINK — PRODUCTION DIRECTOR
NICOLE LAPALME — CONTROLLER

IMAGECOMICS.COM

ELEVEN

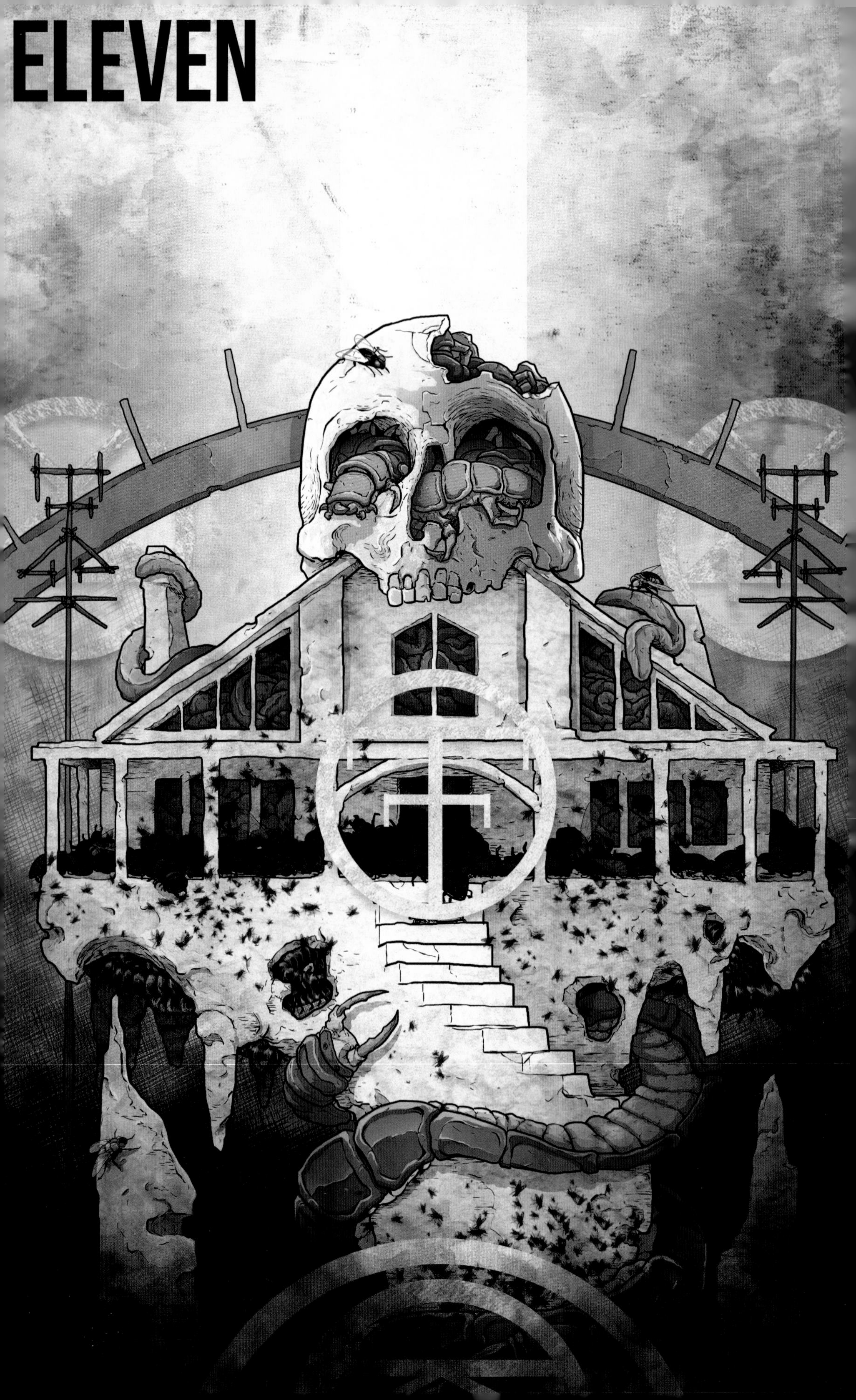

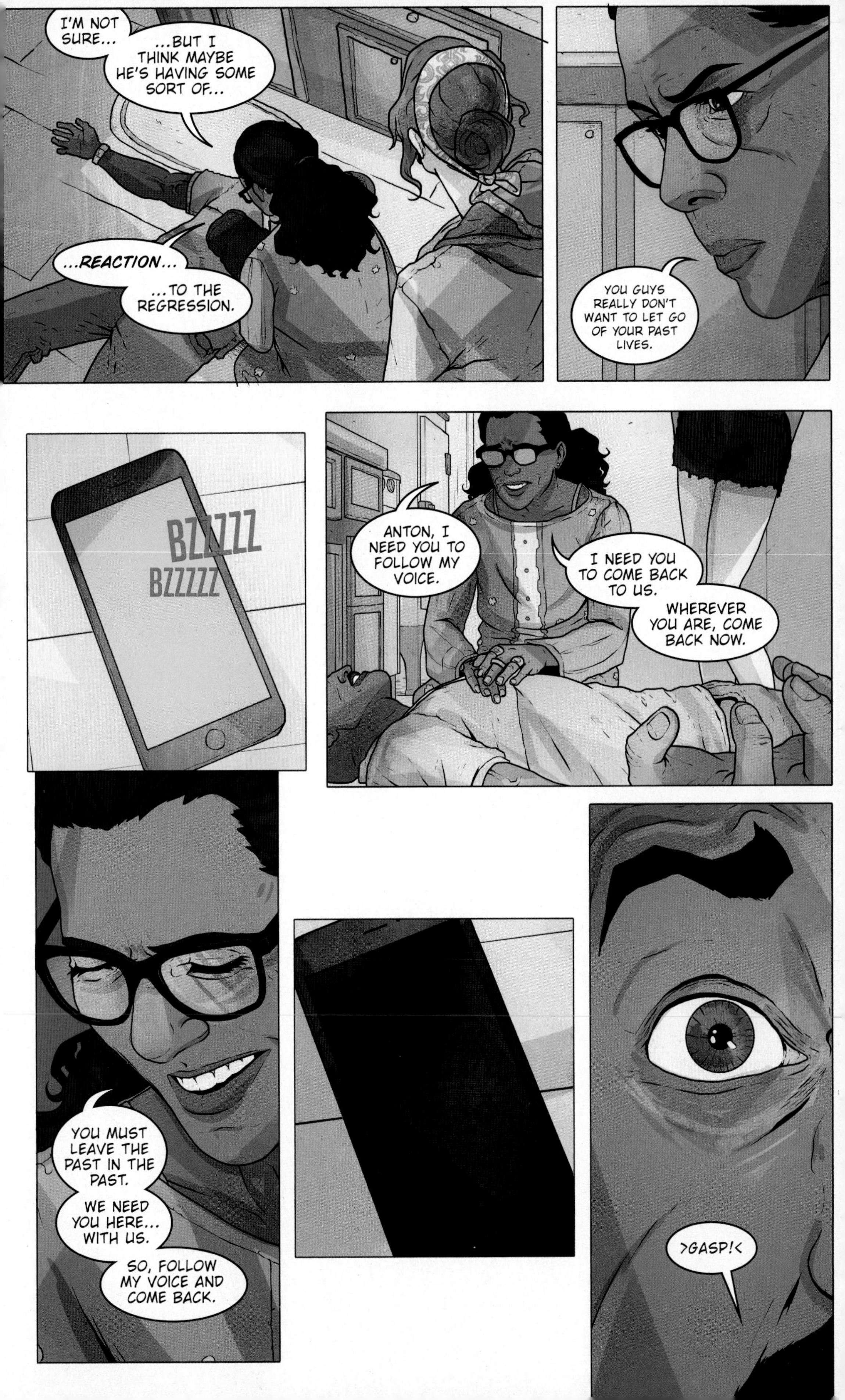

I'M NOT SURE...
...BUT I THINK MAYBE HE'S HAVING SOME SORT OF...
...REACTION...
...TO THE REGRESSION.
YOU GUYS REALLY DON'T WANT TO LET GO OF YOUR PAST LIVES.
BZZZZZ
BZZZZZ
ANTON, I NEED YOU TO FOLLOW MY VOICE.
I NEED YOU TO COME BACK TO US.
WHEREVER YOU ARE, COME BACK NOW.
YOU MUST LEAVE THE PAST IN THE PAST.
WE NEED YOU HERE... WITH US.
SO, FOLLOW MY VOICE AND COME BACK.
>GASP!<

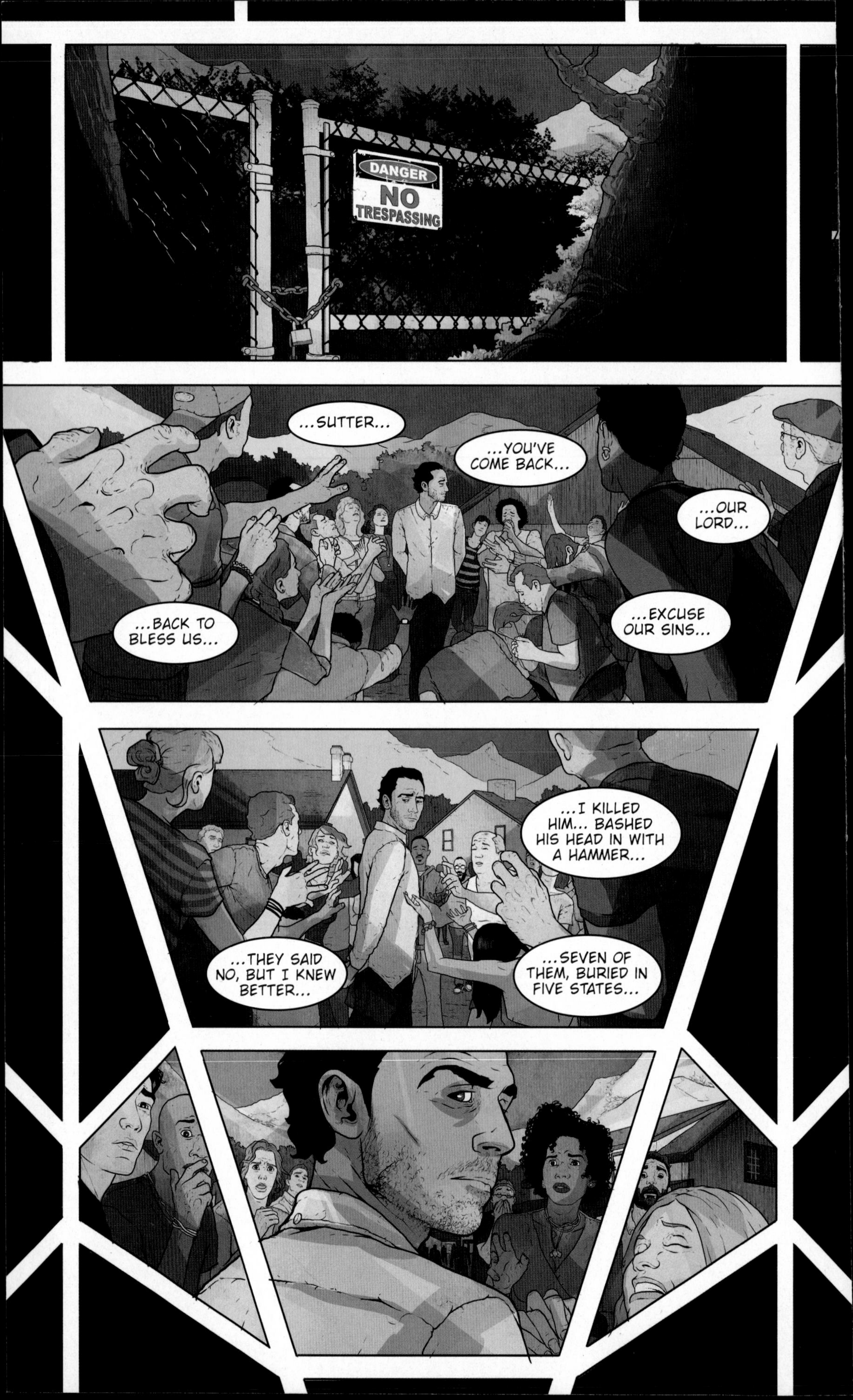
DANGER
NO
TRESPASSING
...SUTTER...
...YOU'VE COME BACK...
...OUR LORD...
...BACK TO BLESS US...
...EXCUSE OUR SINS...
...I KILLED HIM... BASHED HIS HEAD IN WITH A HAMMER...
...THEY SAID NO, BUT I KNEW BETTER...
...SEVEN OF THEM, BURIED IN FIVE STATES...

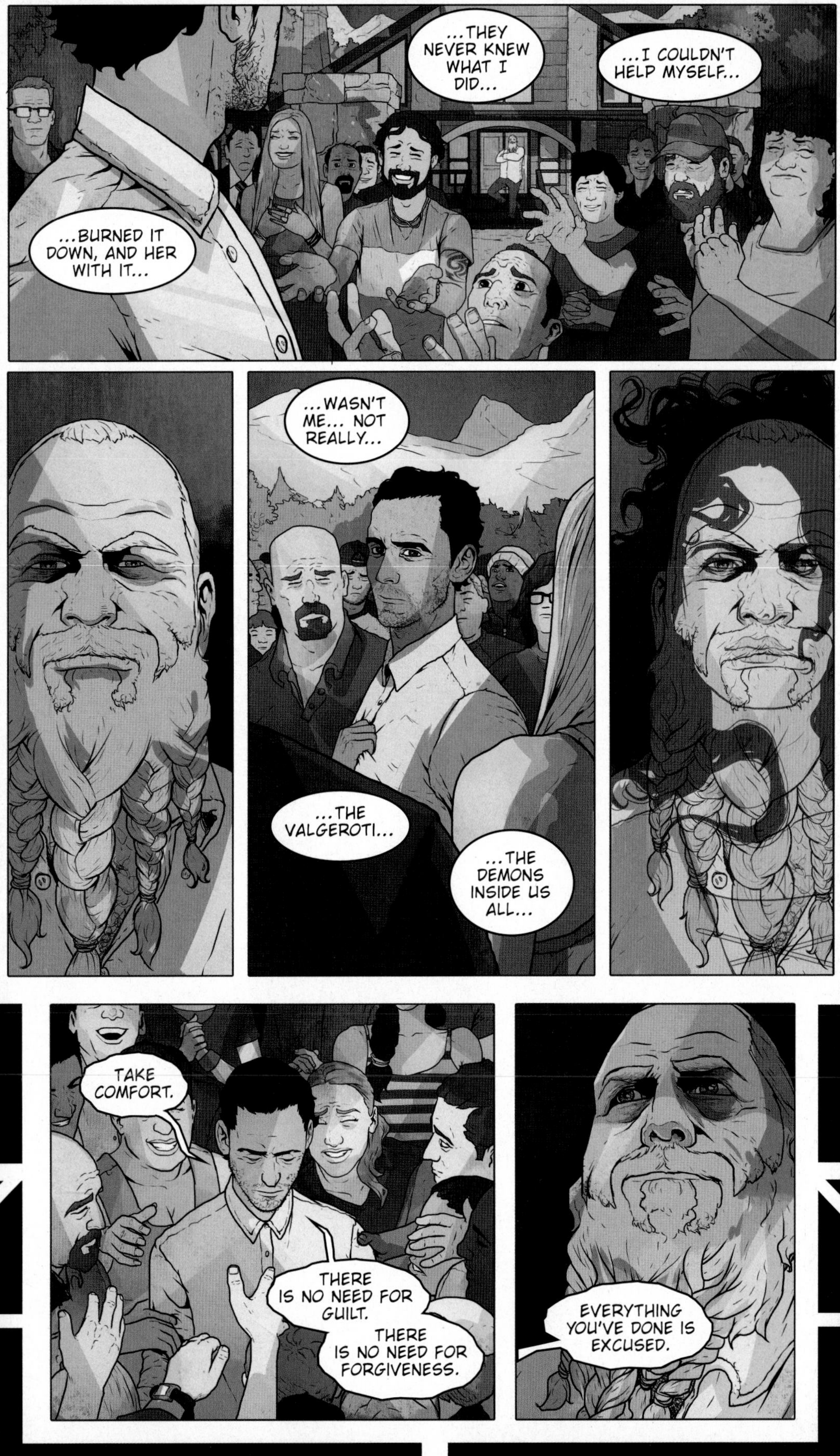
...THEY NEVER KNEW WHAT I DID...
...I COULDN'T HELP MYSELF...
...BURNED IT DOWN, AND HER WITH IT...
...WASN'T ME... NOT REALLY...
...THE VALGEROTI...
...THE DEMONS INSIDE US ALL...
TAKE COMFORT.
THERE IS NO NEED FOR GUILT.
THERE IS NO NEED FOR FORGIVENESS.
EVERYTHING YOU'VE DONE IS EXCUSED.

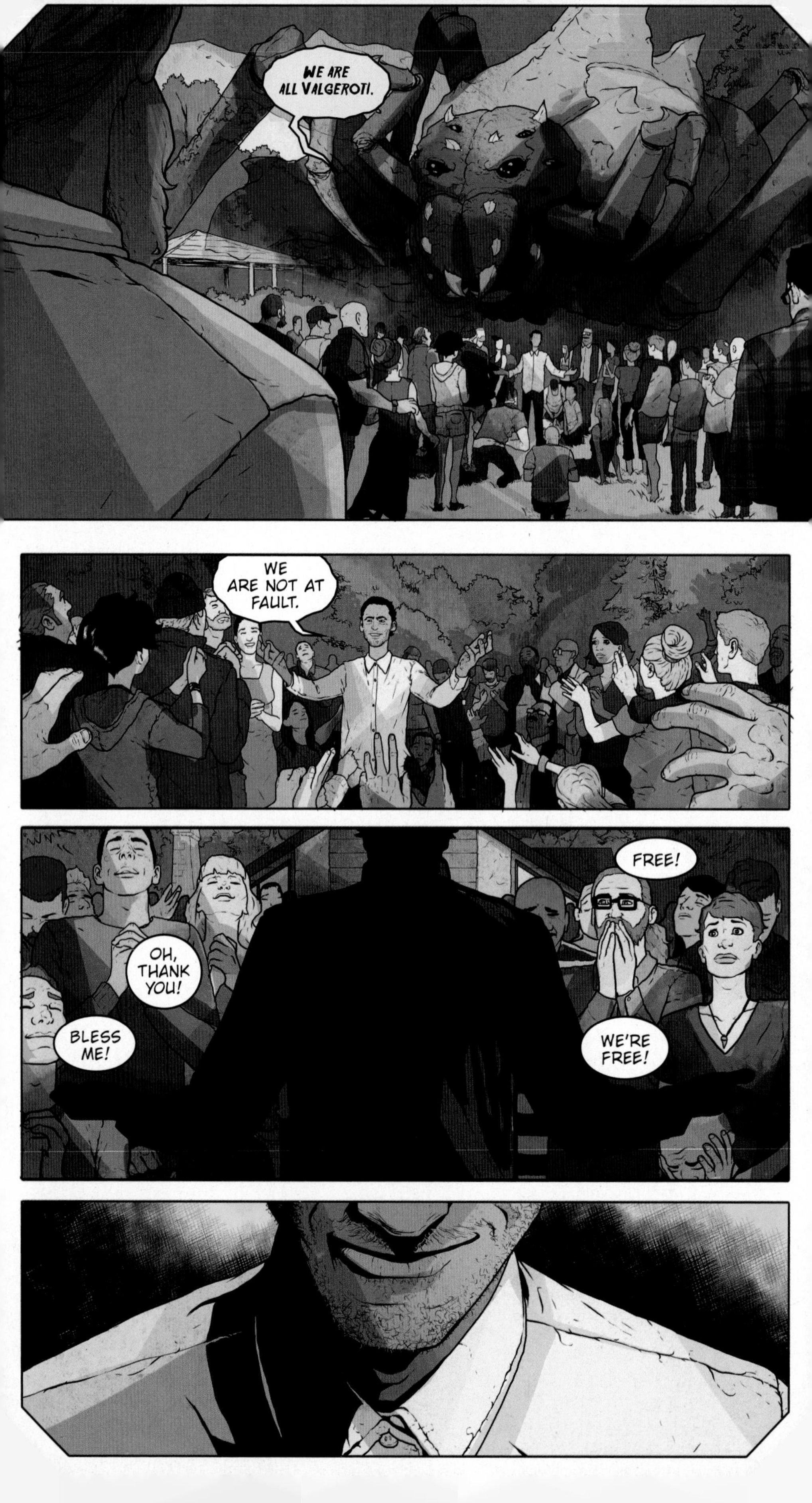
WE ARE ALL VALGEROTI.
WE ARE NOT AT FAULT.
OH, THANK YOU!
BLESS ME!
FREE!
WE'RE FREE!

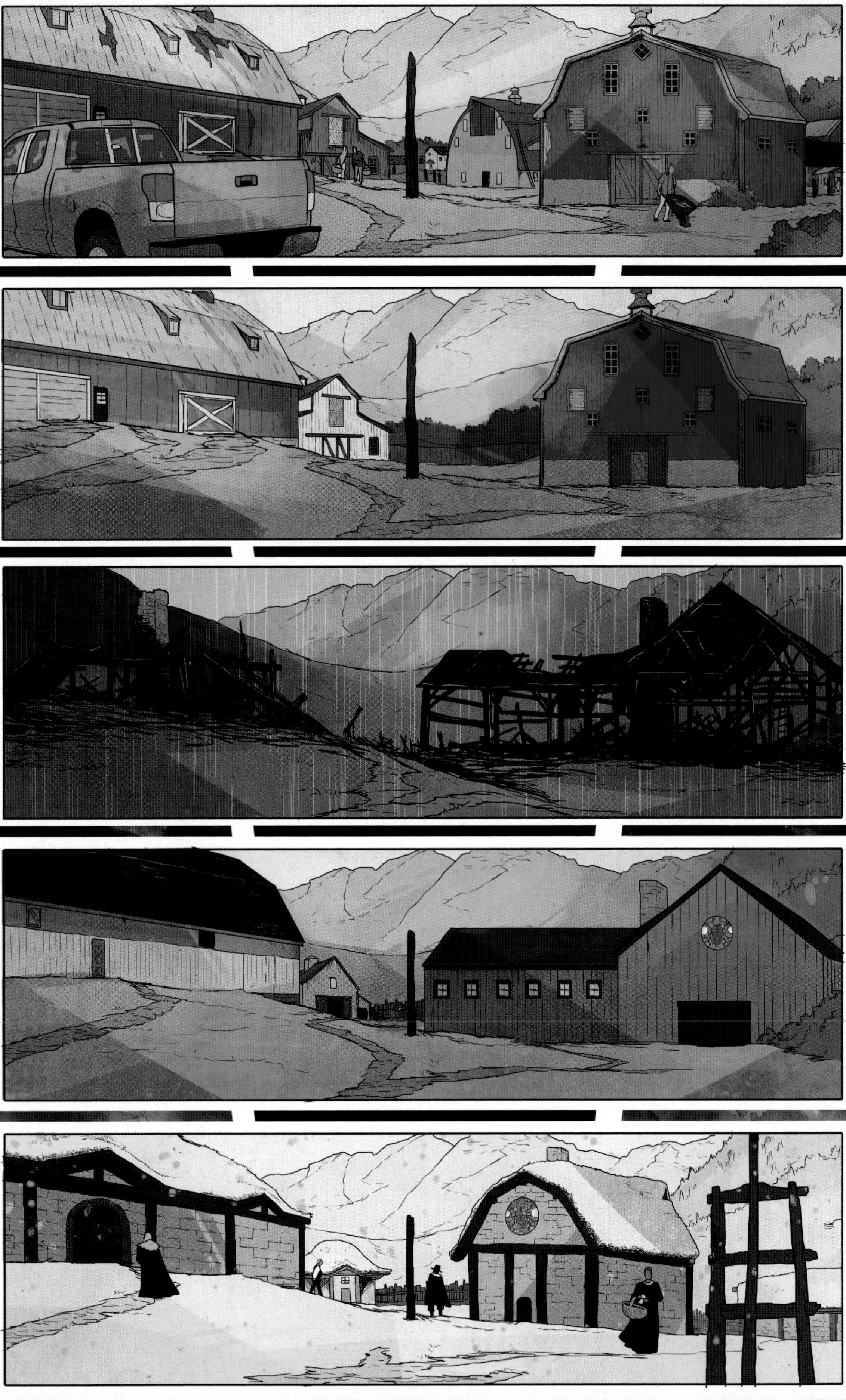

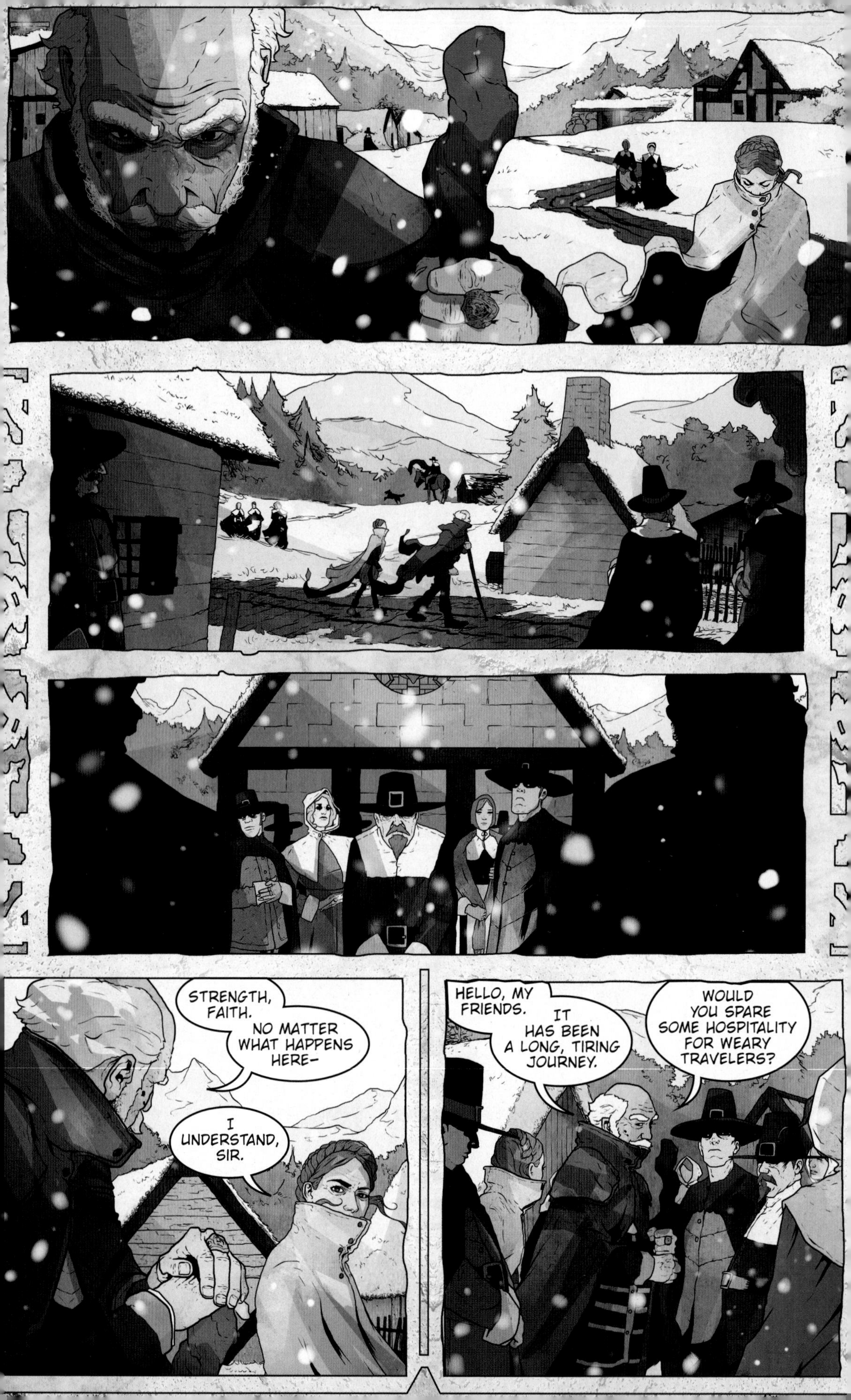
STRENGTH, FAITH.
NO MATTER WHAT HAPPENS HERE–
I UNDERSTAND, SIR.
HELLO, MY FRIENDS.
IT HAS BEEN A LONG, TIRING JOURNEY.
WOULD YOU SPARE SOME HOSPITALITY FOR WEARY TRAVELERS?

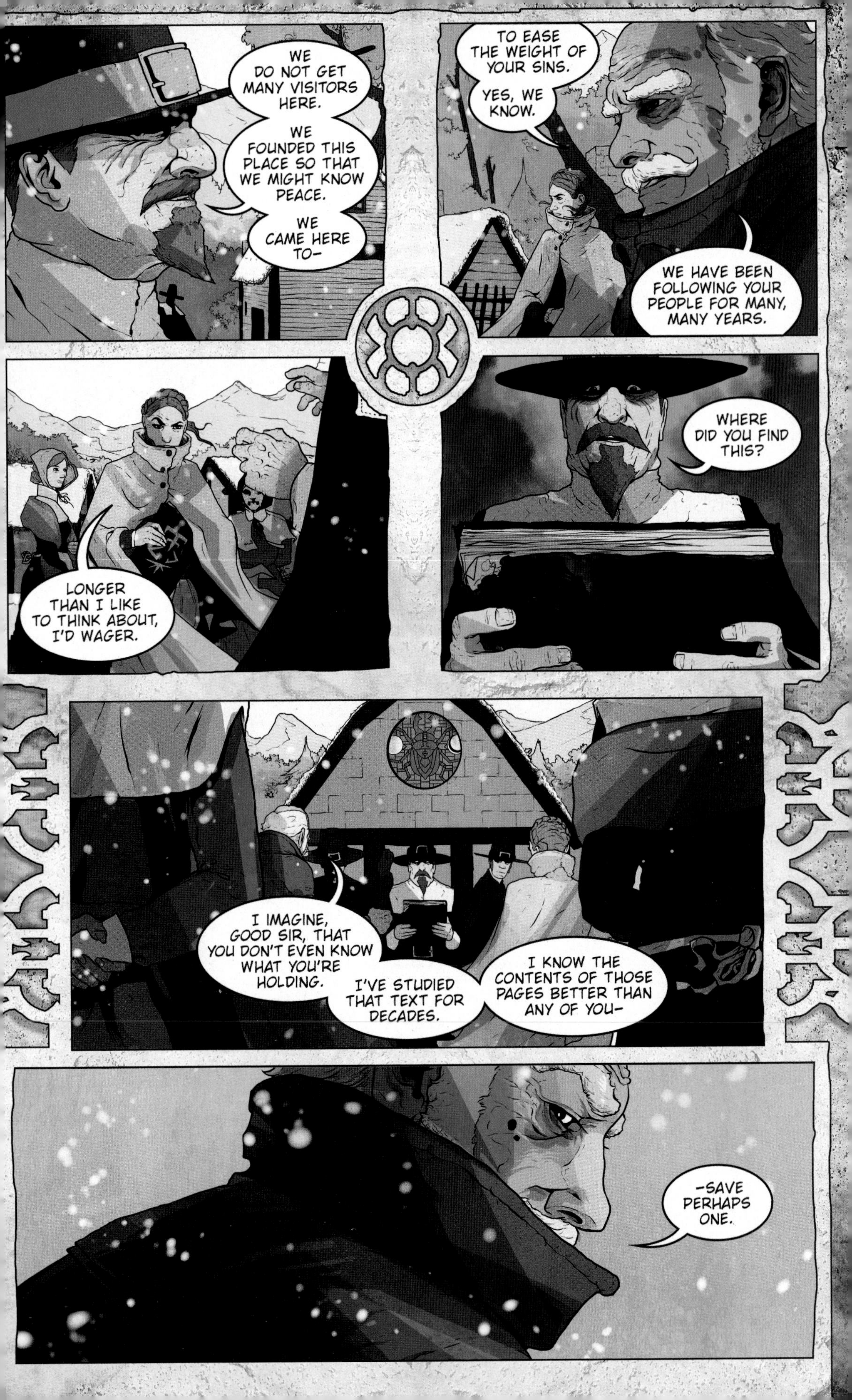
WE DO NOT GET MANY VISITORS HERE.
WE FOUNDED THIS PLACE SO THAT WE MIGHT KNOW PEACE.
WE CAME HERE TO—
TO EASE THE WEIGHT OF YOUR SINS.
YES, WE KNOW.
WE HAVE BEEN FOLLOWING YOUR PEOPLE FOR MANY, MANY YEARS.
LONGER THAN I LIKE TO THINK ABOUT, I'D WAGER.
WHERE DID YOU FIND THIS?
I IMAGINE, GOOD SIR, THAT YOU DON'T EVEN KNOW WHAT YOU'RE HOLDING.
I'VE STUDIED THAT TEXT FOR DECADES.
I KNOW THE CONTENTS OF THOSE PAGES BETTER THAN ANY OF YOU—
—SAVE PERHAPS ONE.

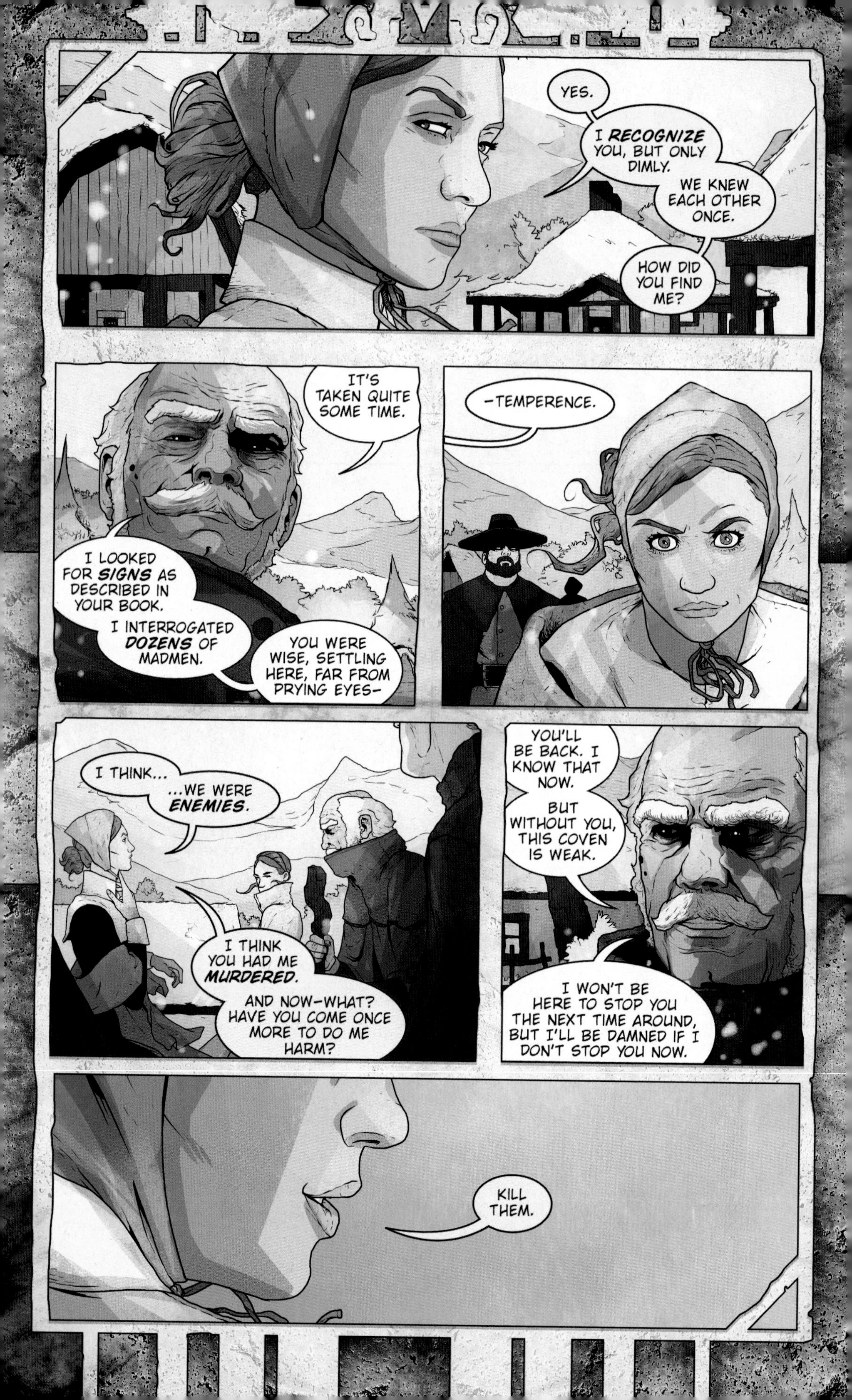
YES.
I RECOGNIZE YOU, BUT ONLY DIMLY.
WE KNEW EACH OTHER ONCE.
HOW DID YOU FIND ME?
IT'S TAKEN QUITE SOME TIME.
I LOOKED FOR SIGNS AS DESCRIBED IN YOUR BOOK.
I INTERROGATED DOZENS OF MADMEN.
YOU WERE WISE, SETTLING HERE, FAR FROM PRYING EYES-
-TEMPERENCE.
I THINK...
...WE WERE ENEMIES.
I THINK YOU HAD ME MURDERED.
AND NOW-WHAT? HAVE YOU COME ONCE MORE TO DO ME HARM?
YOU'LL BE BACK. I KNOW THAT NOW.
BUT WITHOUT YOU, THIS COVEN IS WEAK.
I WON'T BE HERE TO STOP YOU THE NEXT TIME AROUND, BUT I'LL BE DAMNED IF I DON'T STOP YOU NOW.
KILL THEM.

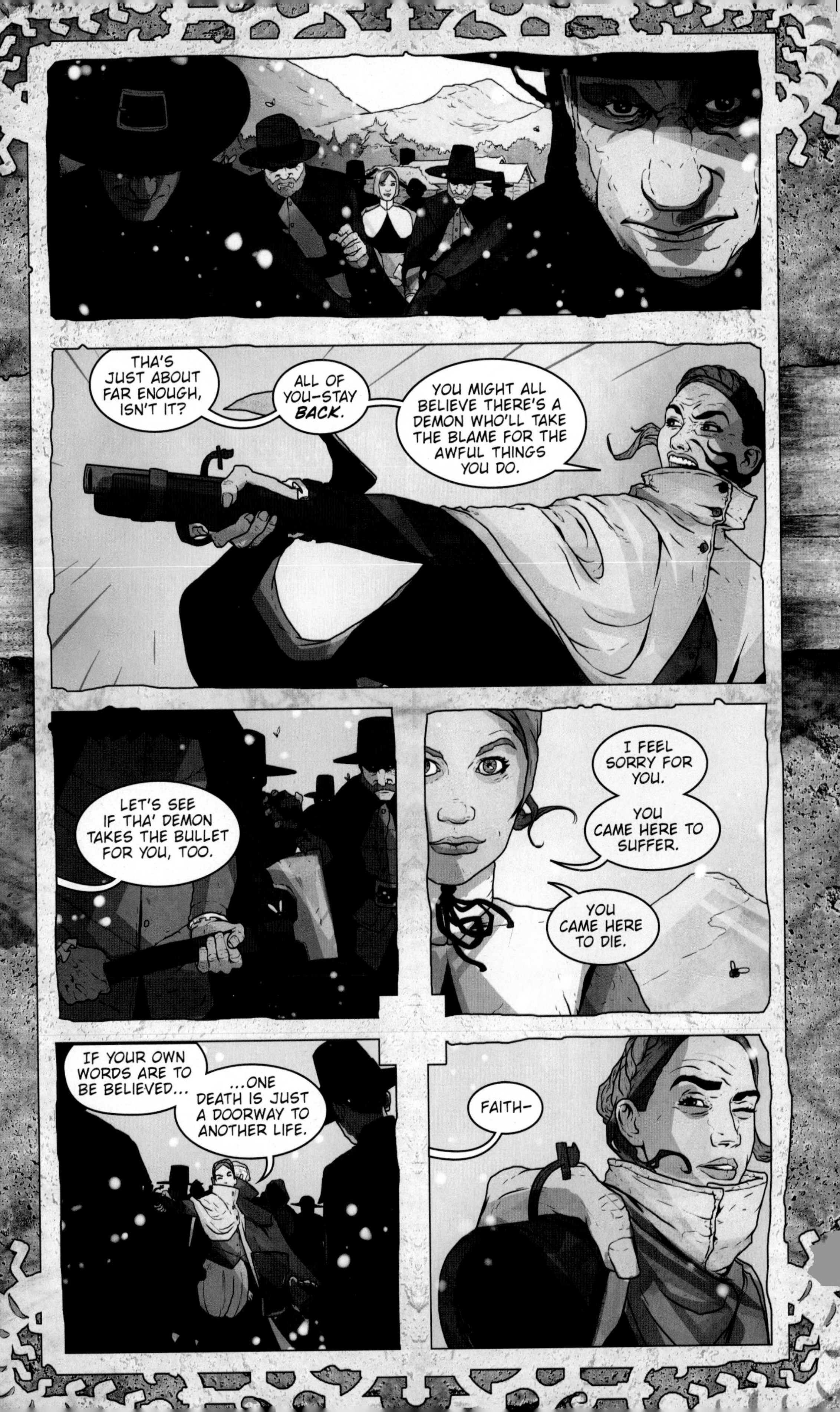
THA'S JUST ABOUT FAR ENOUGH, ISN'T IT?
ALL OF YOU—STAY *BACK*.
YOU MIGHT ALL BELIEVE THERE'S A DEMON WHO'LL TAKE THE BLAME FOR THE AWFUL THINGS YOU DO.
LET'S SEE IF THA' DEMON TAKES THE BULLET FOR YOU, TOO.
I FEEL SORRY FOR YOU.
YOU CAME HERE TO SUFFER.
YOU CAME HERE TO DIE.
IF YOUR OWN WORDS ARE TO BE BELIEVED...
...ONE DEATH IS JUST A DOORWAY TO ANOTHER LIFE.
FAITH—

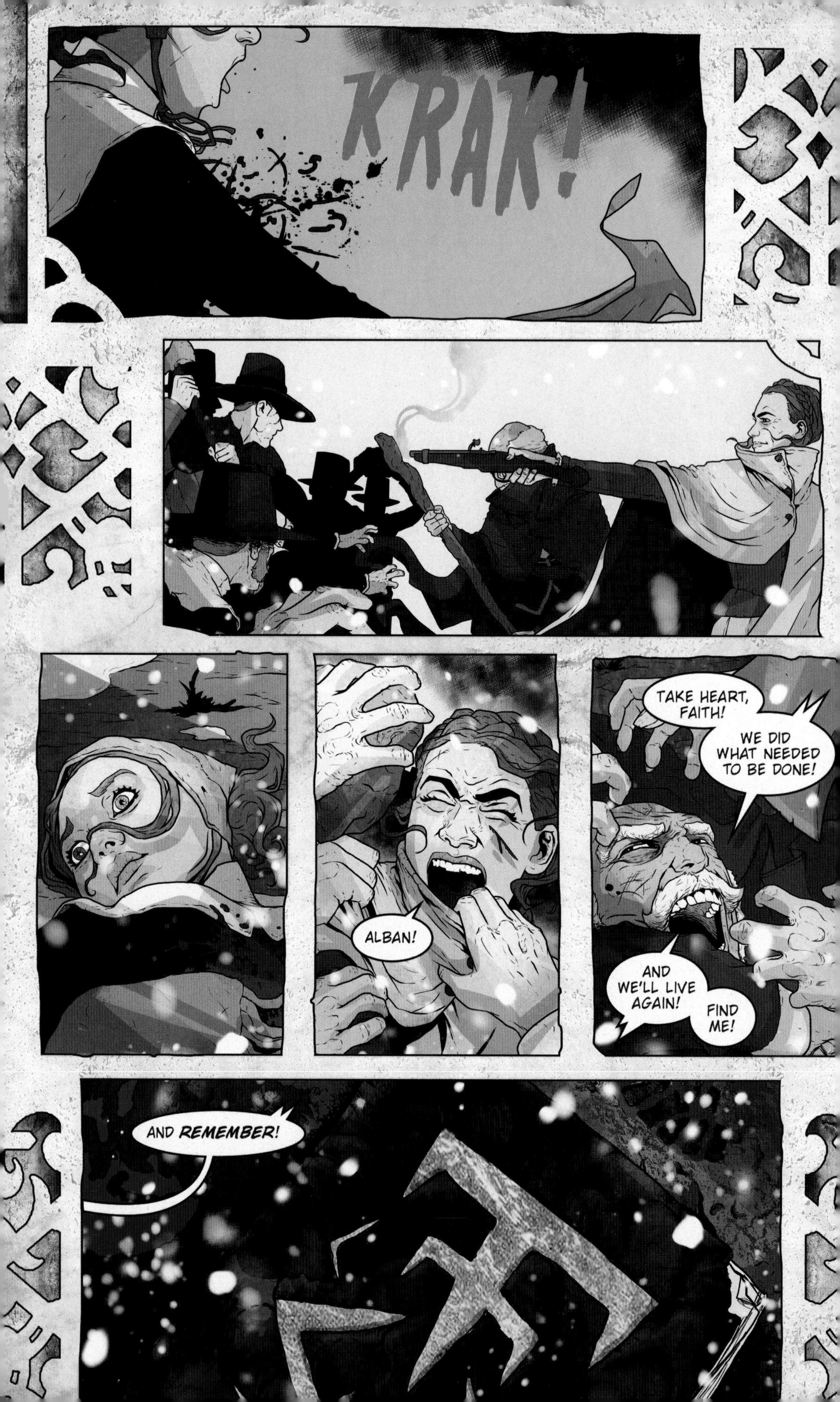
KRAK!
ALBAN!
TAKE HEART, FAITH!
WE DID WHAT NEEDED TO BE DONE!
AND WE'LL LIVE AGAIN!
FIND ME!
AND REMEMBER!

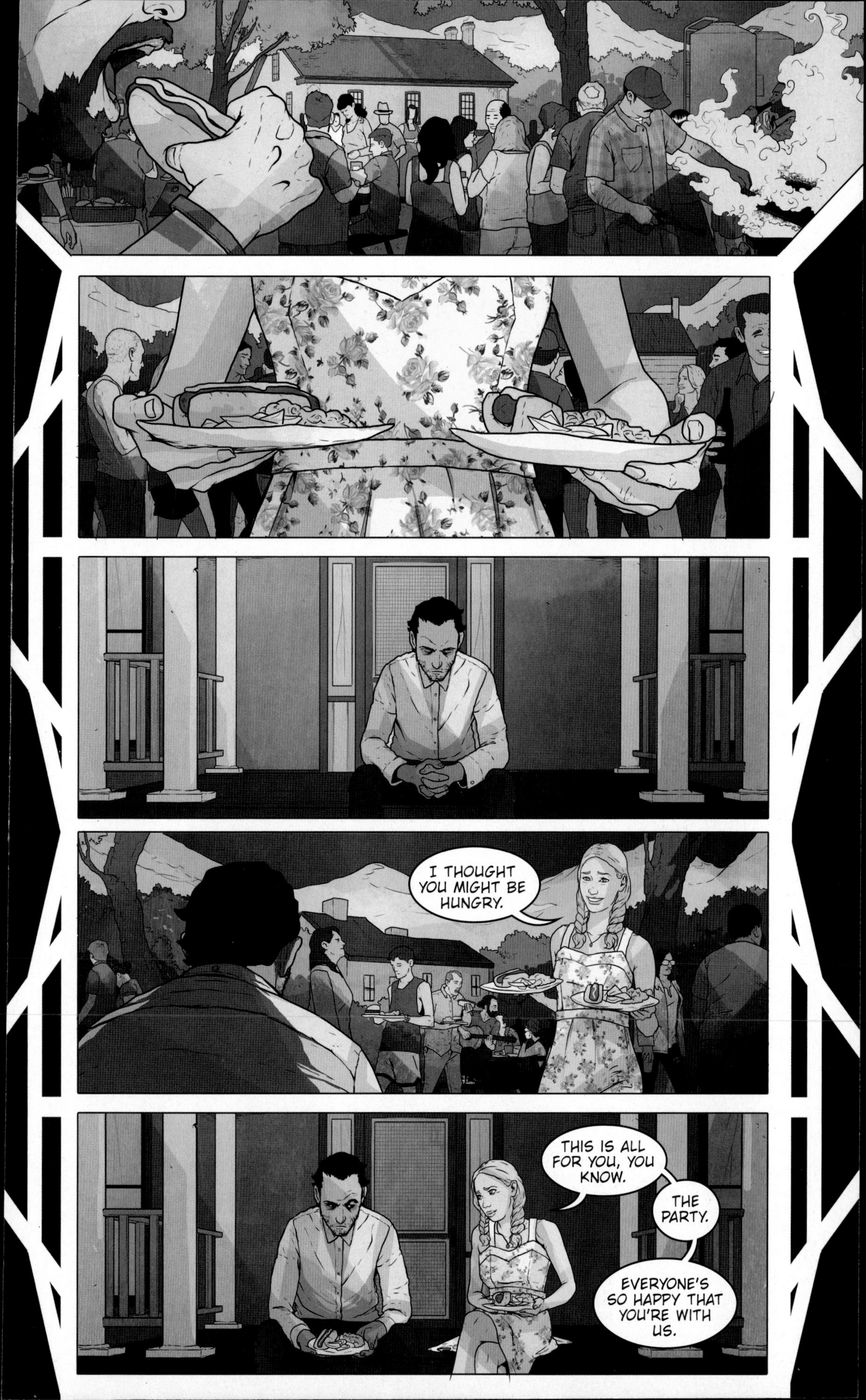
I THOUGHT YOU MIGHT BE HUNGRY.
THIS IS ALL FOR YOU, YOU KNOW.
THE PARTY.
EVERYONE'S SO HAPPY THAT YOU'RE WITH US.

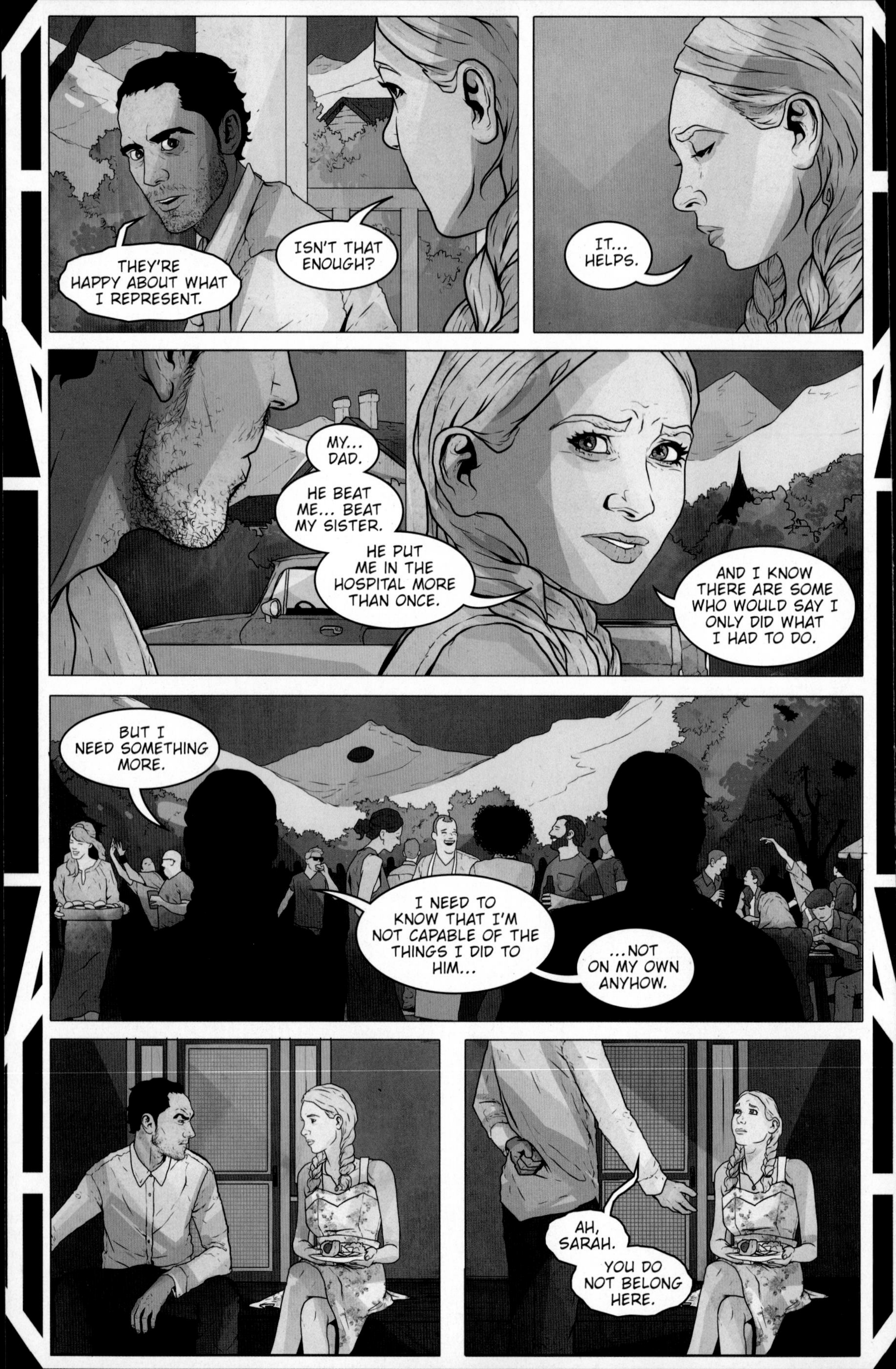
THEY'RE HAPPY ABOUT WHAT I REPRESENT.
ISN'T THAT ENOUGH?
IT... HELPS.
MY... DAD.
HE BEAT ME... BEAT MY SISTER.
HE PUT ME IN THE HOSPITAL MORE THAN ONCE.
AND I KNOW THERE ARE SOME WHO WOULD SAY I ONLY DID WHAT I HAD TO DO.
BUT I NEED SOMETHING MORE.
I NEED TO KNOW THAT I'M NOT CAPABLE OF THE THINGS I DID TO HIM...
...NOT ON MY OWN ANYHOW.
AH, SARAH.
YOU DO NOT BELONG HERE.

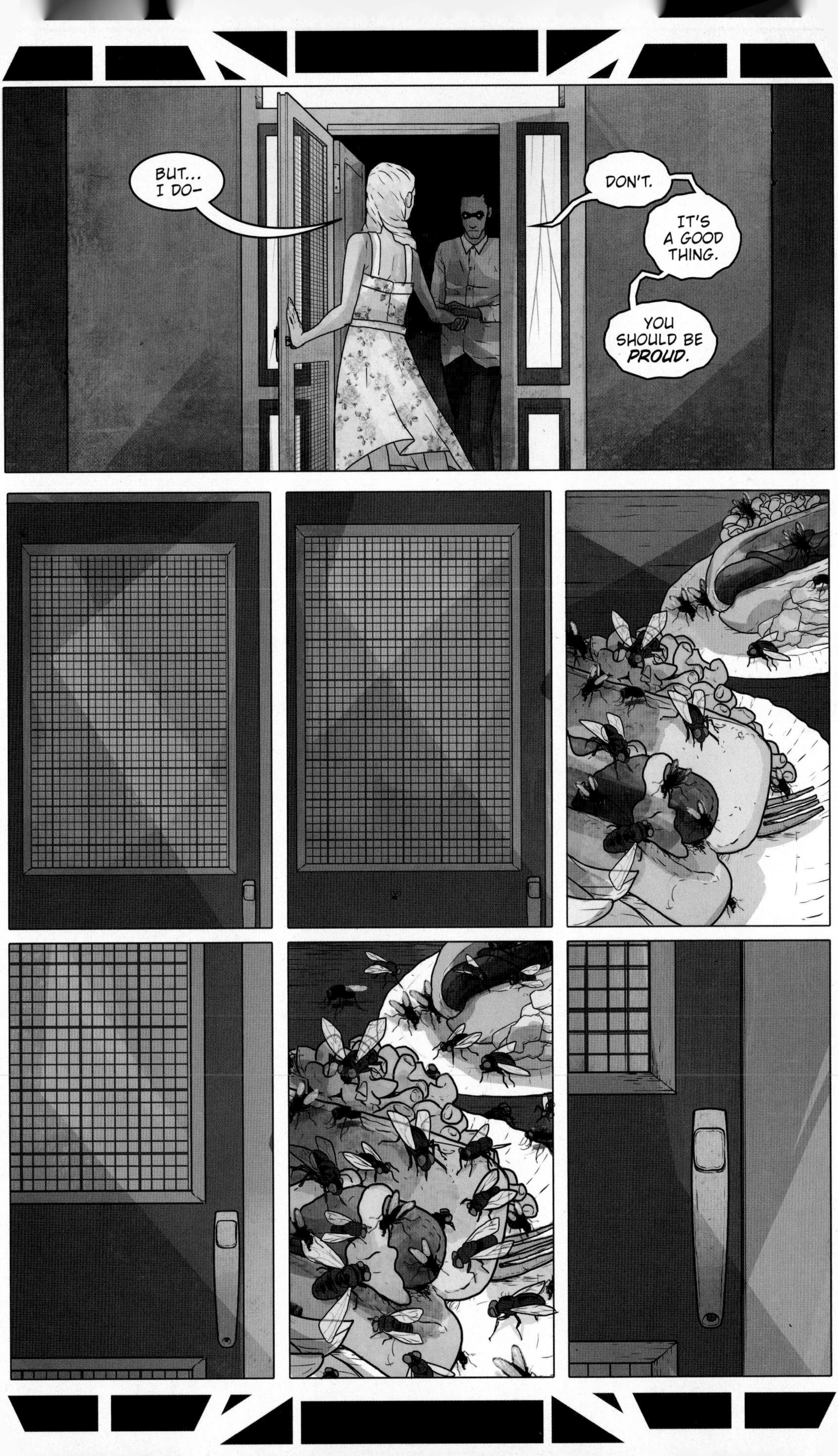
BUT... I DO-
DON'T.
IT'S A GOOD THING.
YOU SHOULD BE PROUD.

THERE WAS A WOMAN.

SHE HELPED THIS BODY.

SHE HELPED ADRIAN.

SHE TRIED TO LOCK ME AWAY.

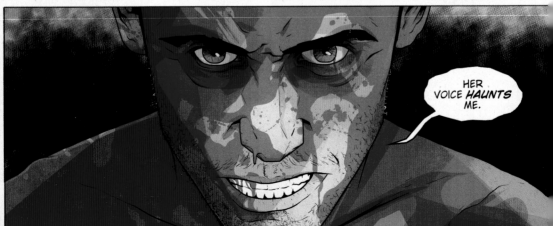

HER VOICE *HAUNTS* ME.

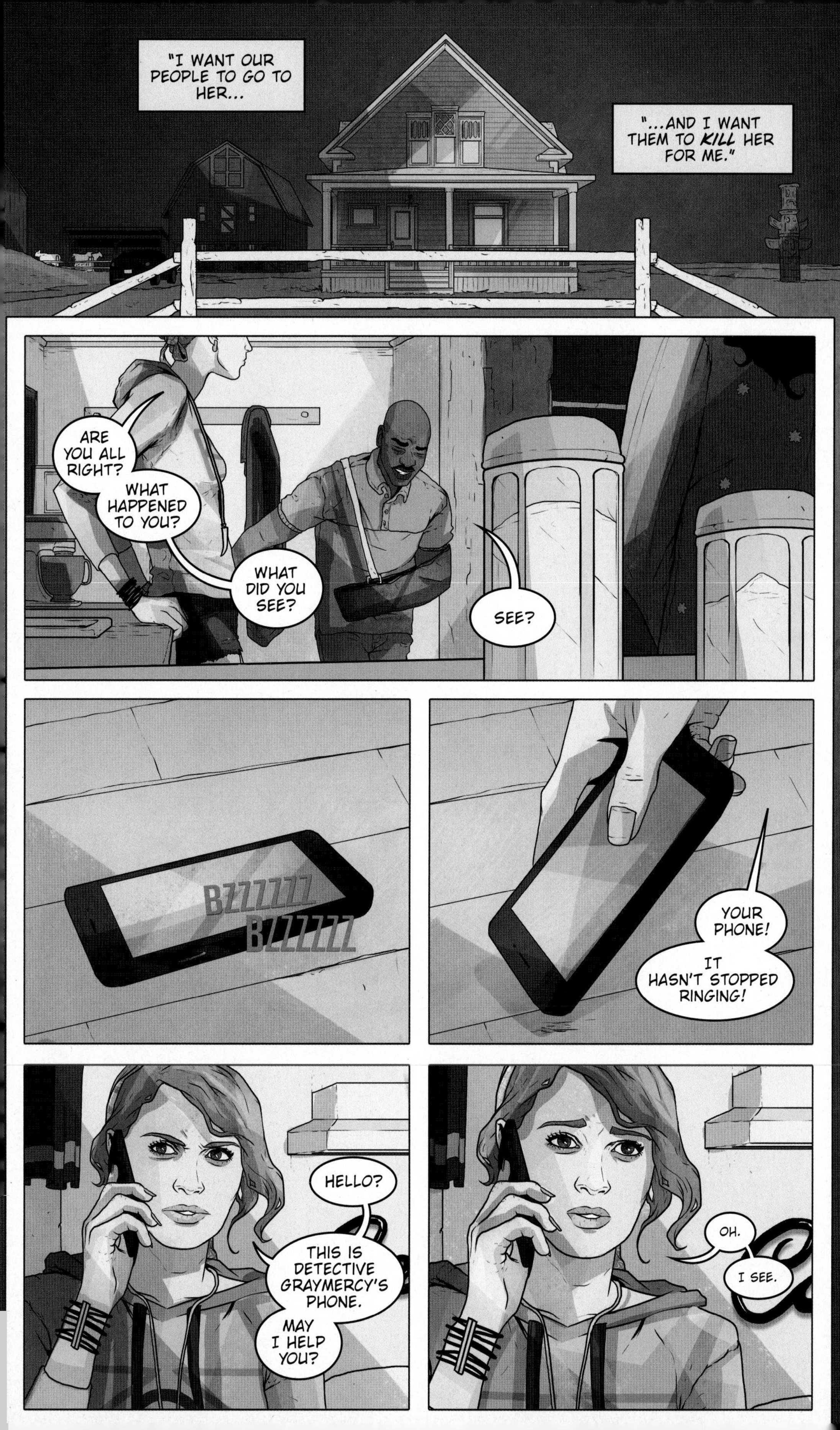
"I WANT OUR PEOPLE TO GO TO HER...
"...AND I WANT THEM TO KILL HER FOR ME."
ARE YOU ALL RIGHT?
WHAT HAPPENED TO YOU?
WHAT DID YOU SEE?
SEE?
BZZZZZZ
BZZZZZ
YOUR PHONE!
IT HASN'T STOPPED RINGING!
HELLO?
THIS IS DETECTIVE GRAYMERCY'S PHONE.
MAY I HELP YOU?
OH.
I SEE.

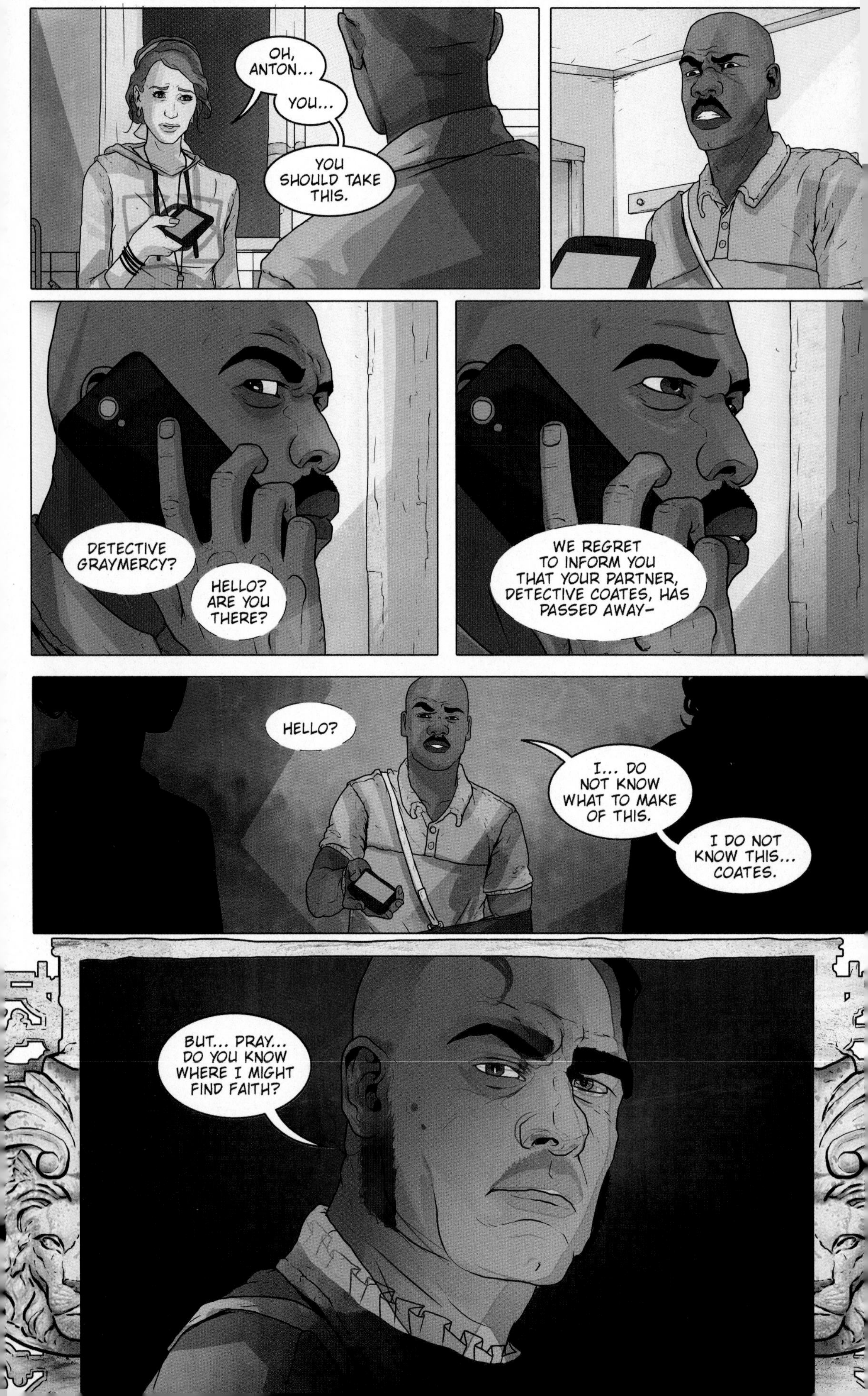
OH, ANTON...
YOU...
YOU SHOULD TAKE THIS.
DETECTIVE GRAYMERCY?
HELLO? ARE YOU THERE?
WE REGRET TO INFORM YOU THAT YOUR PARTNER, DETECTIVE COATES, HAS PASSED AWAY-
HELLO?
I... DO NOT KNOW WHAT TO MAKE OF THIS.
I DO NOT KNOW THIS... COATES.
BUT... PRAY... DO YOU KNOW WHERE I MIGHT FIND FAITH?

TWELVE

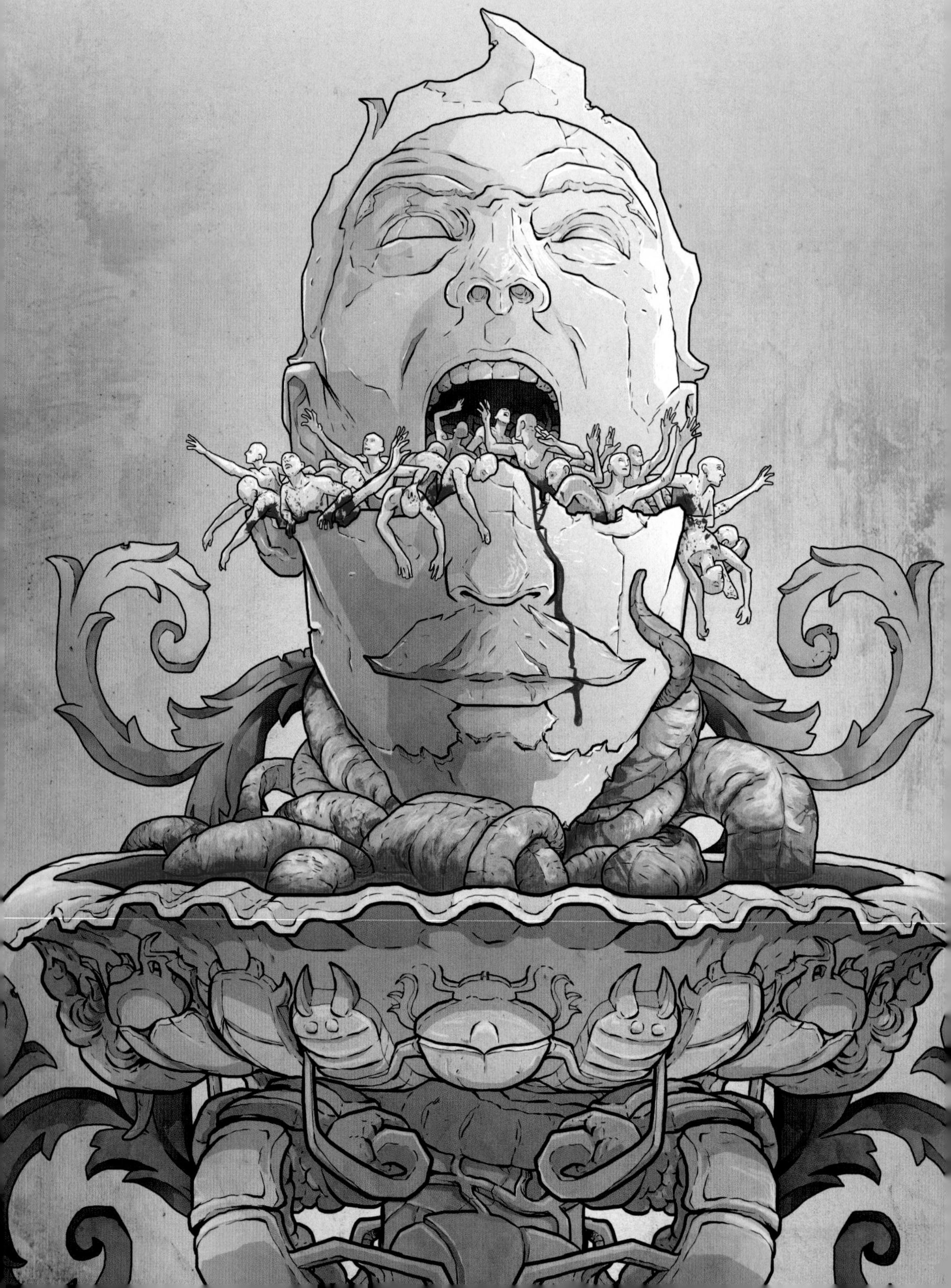

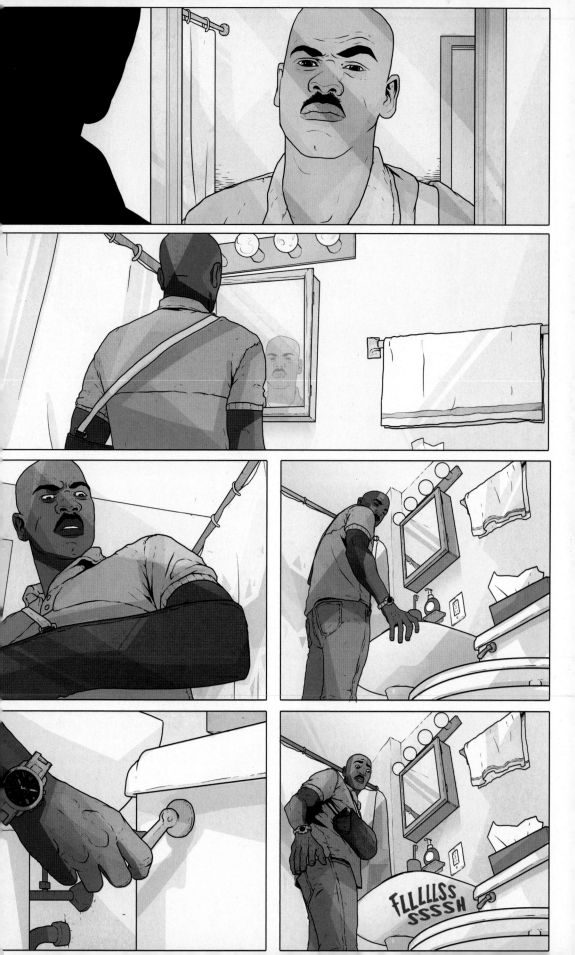

FLLLLLSS
SSSSH

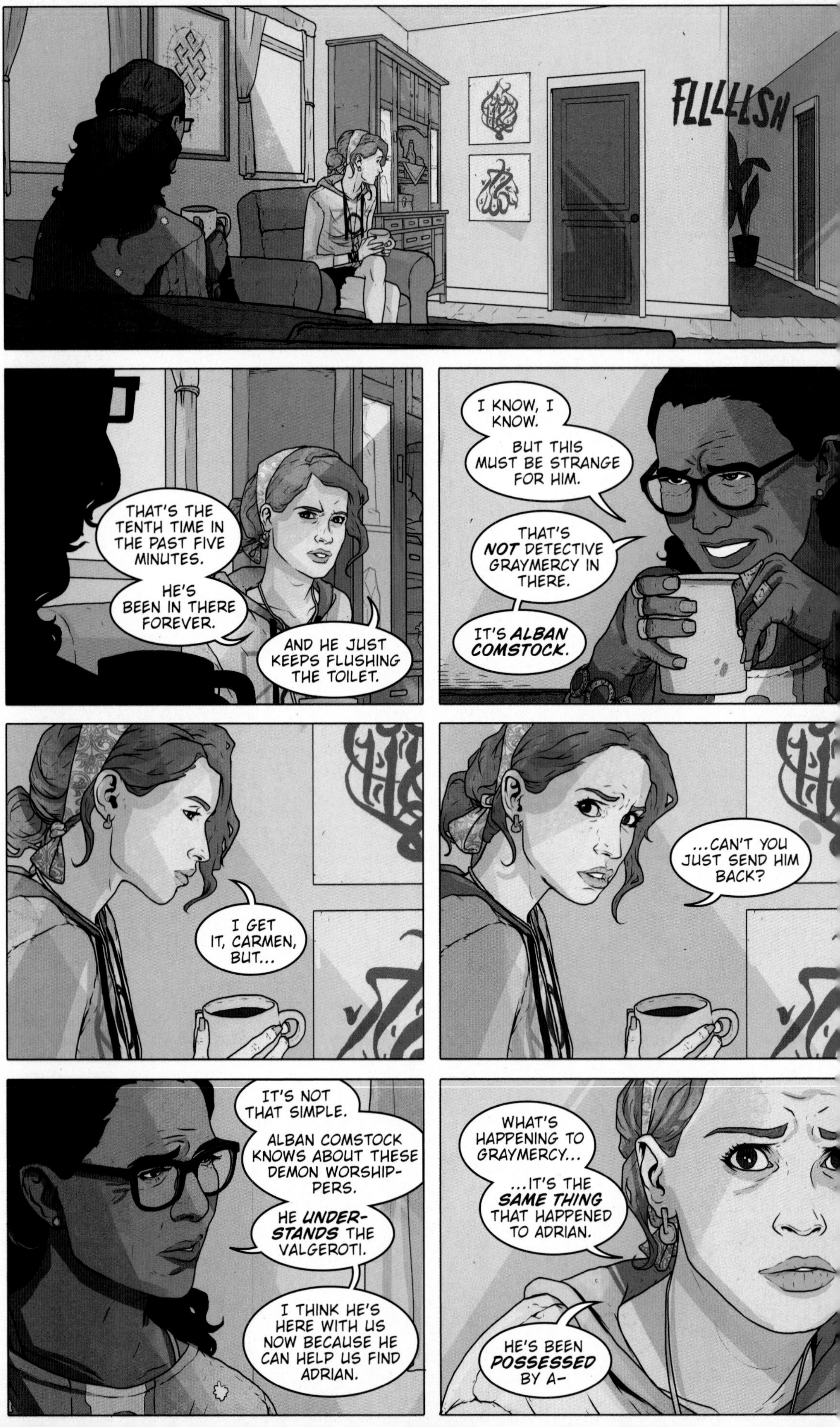

FLLLLLSH
THAT'S THE TENTH TIME IN THE PAST FIVE MINUTES.
HE'S BEEN IN THERE FOREVER.
AND HE JUST KEEPS FLUSHING THE TOILET.
I KNOW, I KNOW.
BUT THIS MUST BE STRANGE FOR HIM.
THAT'S *NOT* DETECTIVE GRAYMERCY IN THERE.
IT'S ***ALBAN COMSTOCK.***
I GET IT, CARMEN, BUT...
...CAN'T YOU JUST SEND HIM BACK?
IT'S NOT THAT SIMPLE.
ALBAN COMSTOCK KNOWS ABOUT THESE DEMON WORSHIP-PERS.
HE ***UNDER-STANDS*** THE VALGEROTI.
I THINK HE'S HERE WITH US NOW BECAUSE HE CAN HELP US FIND ADRIAN.
WHAT'S HAPPENING TO GRAYMERCY...
...IT'S THE ***SAME THING*** THAT HAPPENED TO ADRIAN.
HE'S BEEN ***POSSESSED*** BY A–

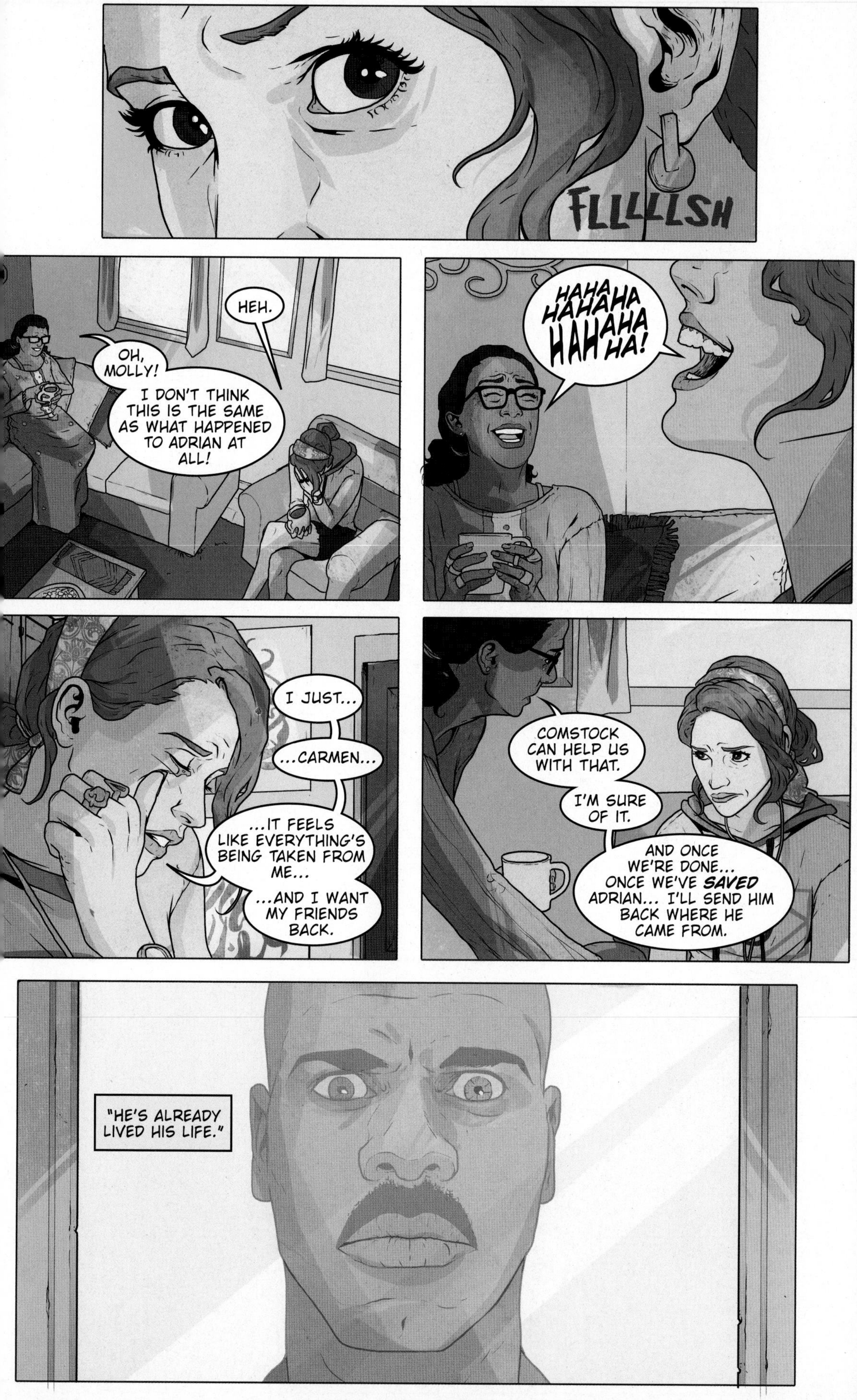
FLLLLLSH
OH, MOLLY!
I DON'T THINK THIS IS THE SAME AS WHAT HAPPENED TO ADRIAN AT ALL!
HEH.
HAHA HAHAHA HAHAHA HAH HA!
I JUST...
...CARMEN...
...IT FEELS LIKE EVERYTHING'S BEING TAKEN FROM ME...
...AND I WANT MY FRIENDS BACK.
COMSTOCK CAN HELP US WITH THAT.
I'M SURE OF IT.
AND ONCE WE'RE DONE... ONCE WE'VE SAVED ADRIAN... I'LL SEND HIM BACK WHERE HE CAME FROM.
"HE'S ALREADY LIVED HIS LIFE."

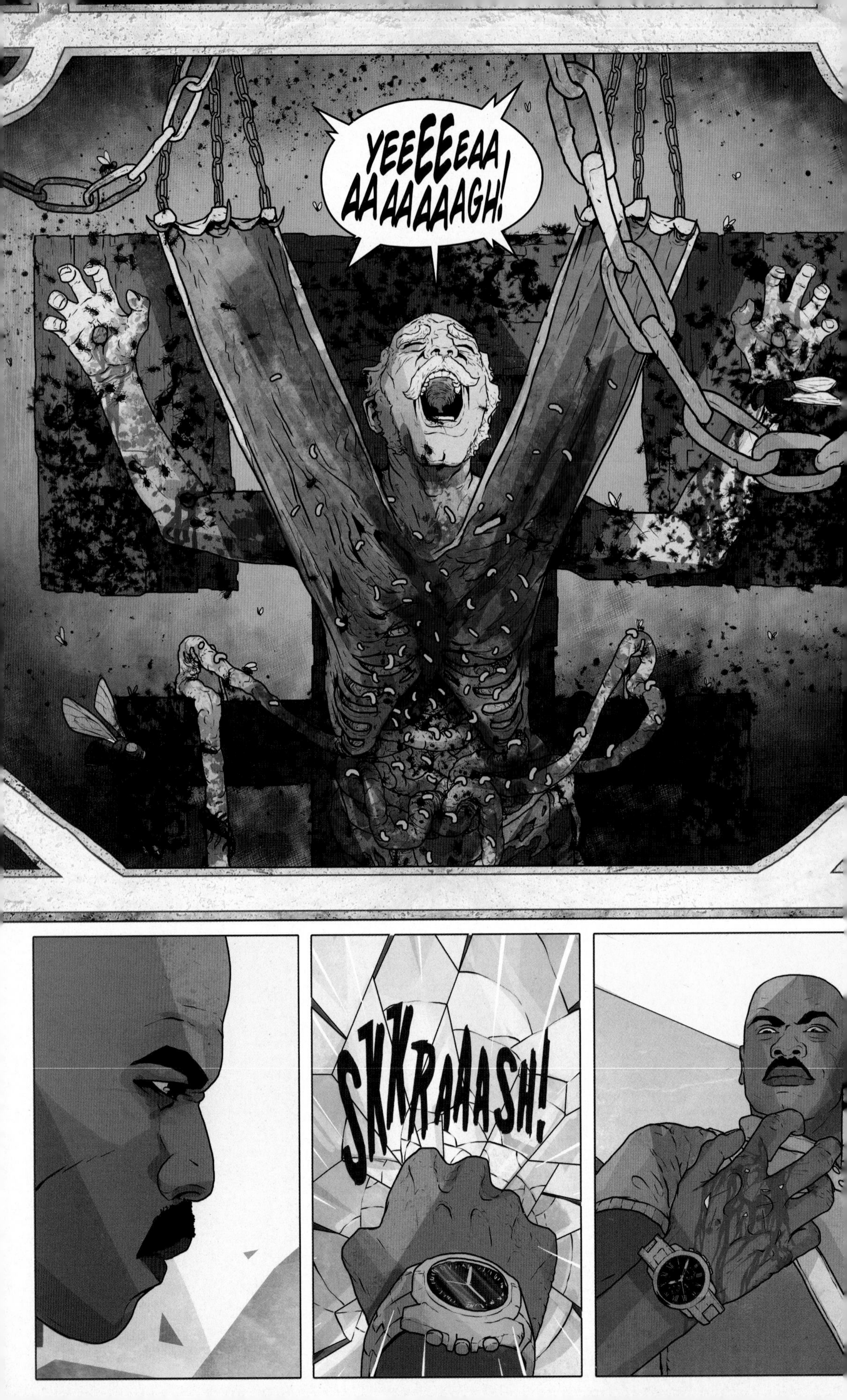
YEEEEEAA AAAAAAAGH!
SKKRAAASH!

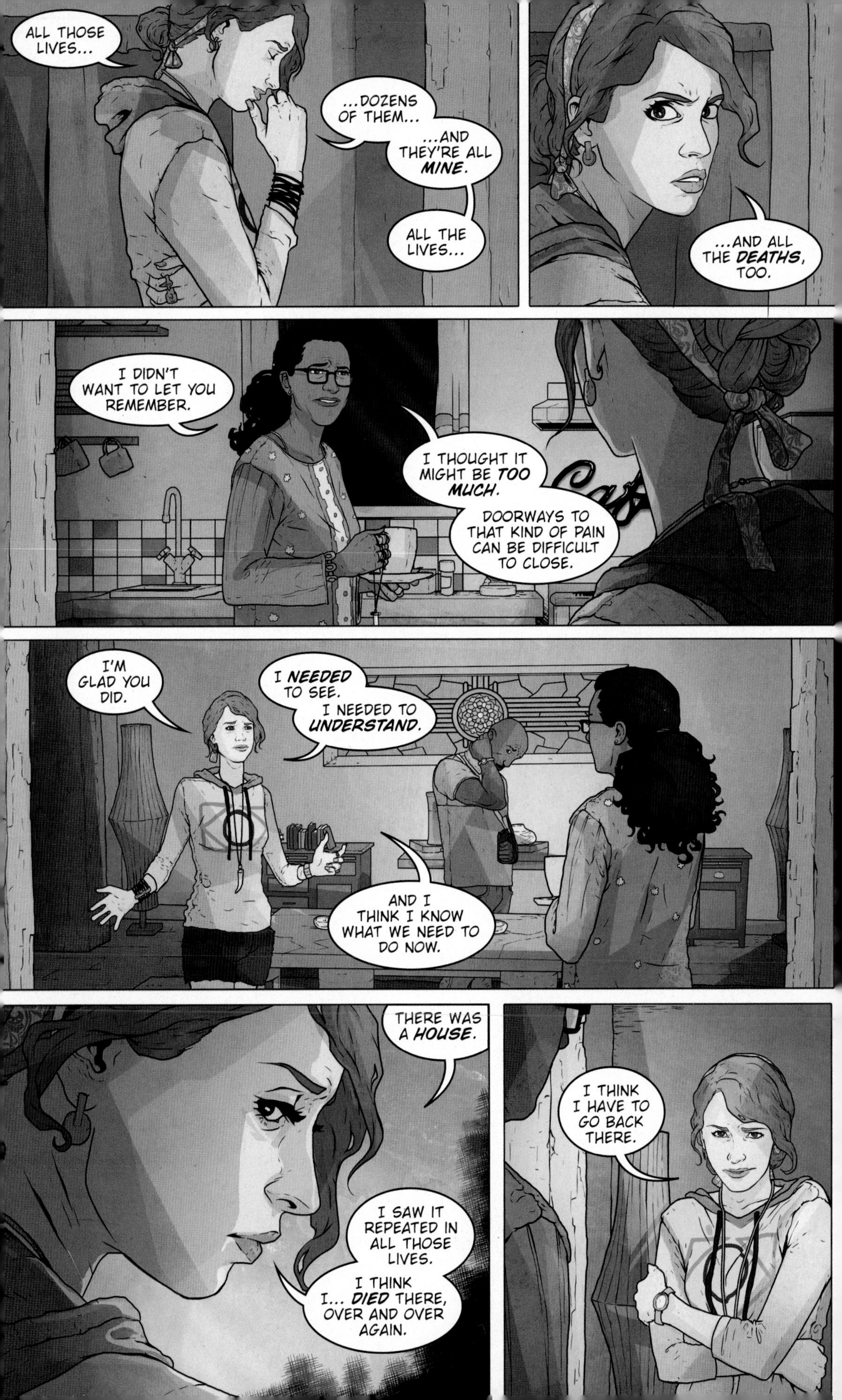
ALL THOSE LIVES...
...DOZENS OF THEM...
...AND THEY'RE ALL *MINE*.
ALL THE LIVES...
...AND ALL THE *DEATHS*, TOO.
I DIDN'T WANT TO LET YOU REMEMBER.
I THOUGHT IT MIGHT BE *TOO MUCH*.
DOORWAYS TO THAT KIND OF PAIN CAN BE DIFFICULT TO CLOSE.
I'M GLAD YOU DID.
I *NEEDED* TO SEE.
I NEEDED TO *UNDERSTAND*.
AND I THINK I KNOW WHAT WE NEED TO DO NOW.
THERE WAS A *HOUSE*.
I SAW IT REPEATED IN ALL THOSE LIVES.
I THINK I... *DIED* THERE, OVER AND OVER AGAIN.
I THINK I HAVE TO GO BACK THERE.

I DON'T THINK THAT'S A GOOD IDEA, MOLLY.

WHAT DO YOU MEAN?

FINDING SOME SORT OF CLUE AS TO THIS CULT'S WHEREABOUTS....

...FINDING ADRIAN...

...THAT'S WHY WE WENT THROUGH THIS IN THE FIRST PLACE.

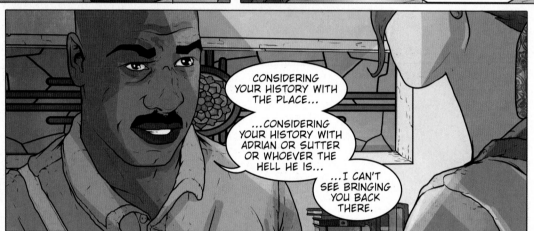

CONSIDERING YOUR HISTORY WITH THE PLACE...

...CONSIDERING YOUR HISTORY WITH ADRIAN OR SUTTER OR WHOEVER THE HELL HE IS... ...I CAN'T SEE BRINGING YOU BACK THERE.

I CAN *FEEL* ALL THOSE DEATHS.

EVERY BRUISE... EVERY BURN... EVERY CUT. I CAN FEEL... INSECTS *CRAWLING* UNDER MY SKIN.

I'M NOT GOING TO LET SOMETHING LIKE THAT HAPPEN TO ME AGAIN.

THIS IS SOMETHING I MUST DO.

AND EVEN IF IT WASN'T...

...IT'S NOT YOUR CALL AS TO WHETHER I GO OR NOT.

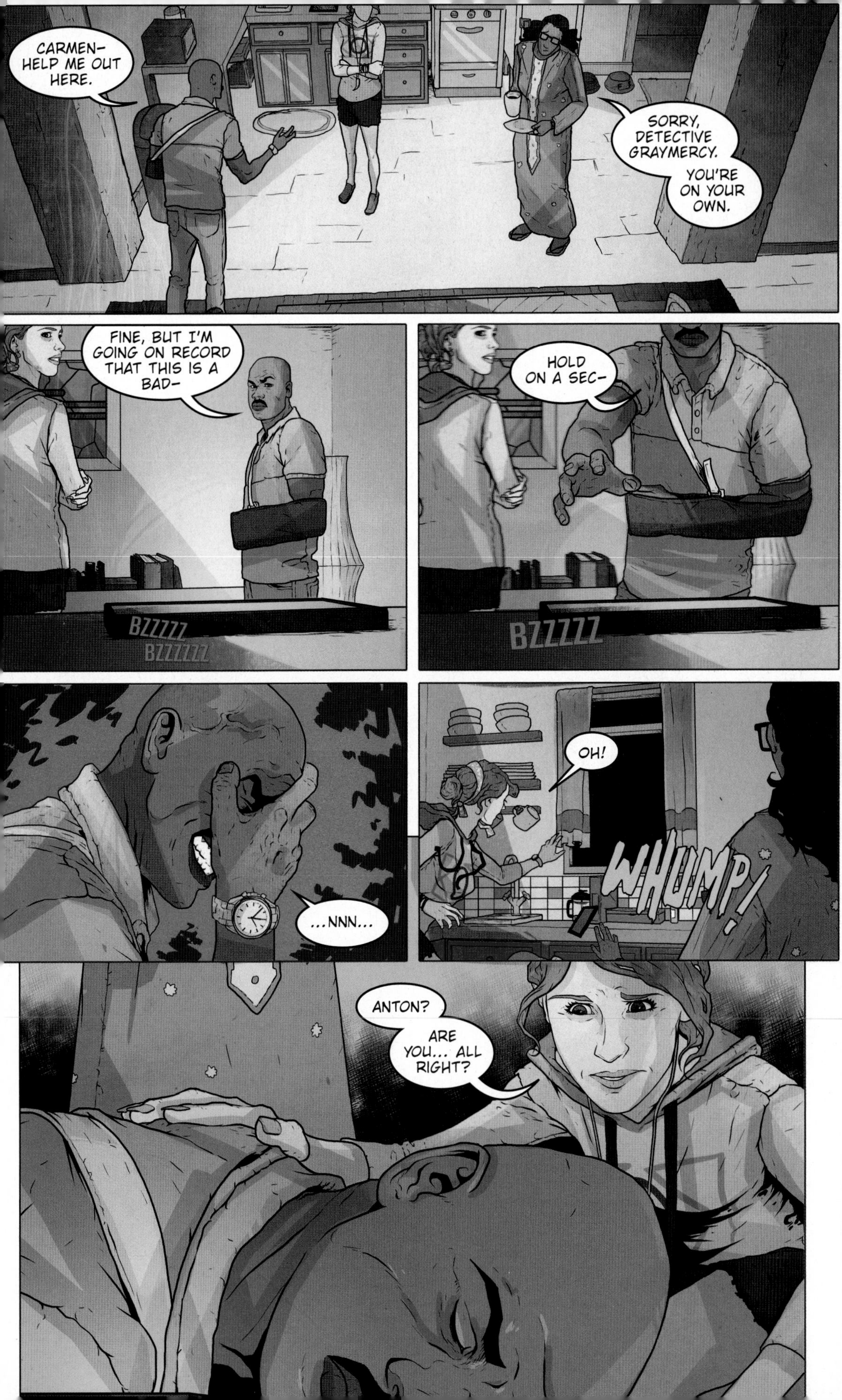
CARMEN-
HELP ME OUT
HERE.
SORRY,
DETECTIVE
GRAYMERCY.
YOU'RE
ON YOUR
OWN.
FINE, BUT I'M
GOING ON RECORD
THAT THIS IS A
BAD-
BZZZZZ
BZZZZZZ
HOLD
ON A SEC-
BZZZZZ
...NNN...
OH!
WHUMP!
ANTON?
ARE
YOU... ALL
RIGHT?

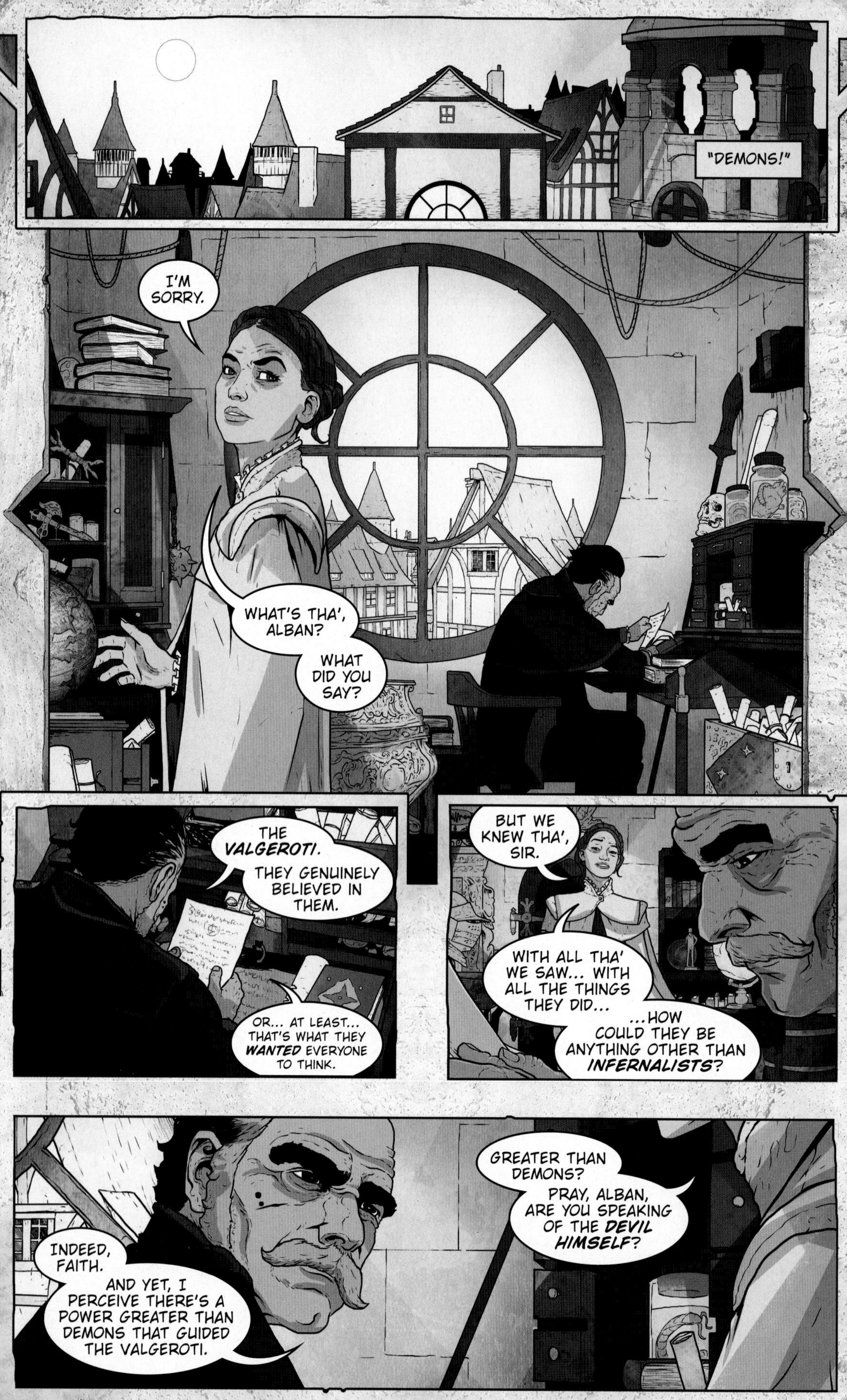
"DEMONS!"
I'M SORRY.
WHAT'S THA', ALBAN?
WHAT DID YOU SAY?
THE VALGEROTI.
THEY GENUINELY BELIEVED IN THEM.
OR... AT LEAST... THAT'S WHAT THEY WANTED EVERYONE TO THINK.
BUT WE KNEW THA', SIR.
WITH ALL THA' WE SAW... WITH ALL THE THINGS THEY DID...
...HOW COULD THEY BE ANYTHING OTHER THAN INFERNALISTS?
INDEED, FAITH.
AND YET, I PERCEIVE THERE'S A POWER GREATER THAN DEMONS THAT GUIDED THE VALGEROTI.
GREATER THAN DEMONS?
PRAY, ALBAN, ARE YOU SPEAKING OF THE DEVIL HIMSELF?

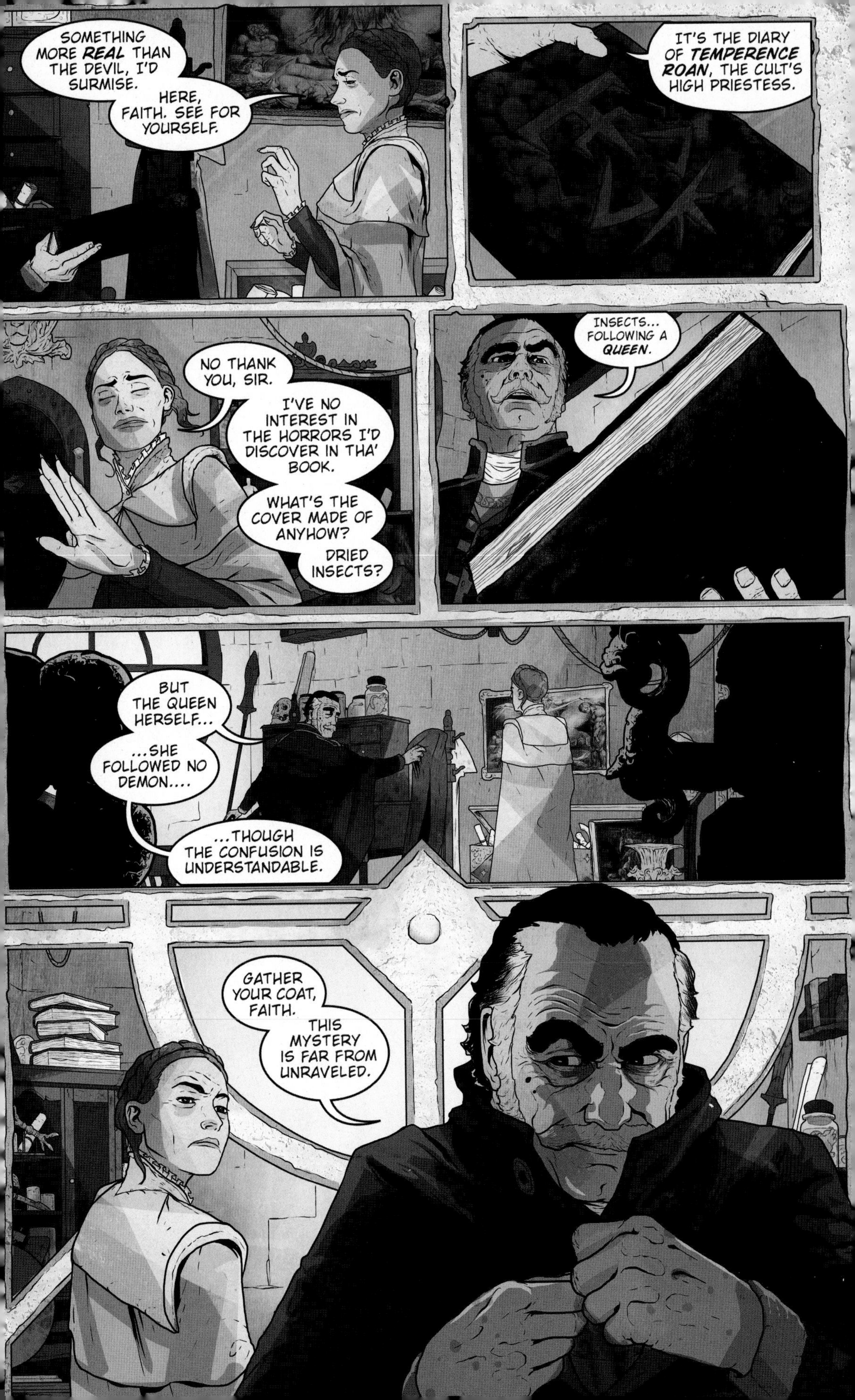
SOMETHING MORE REAL THAN THE DEVIL, I'D SURMISE.
HERE, FAITH. SEE FOR YOURSELF.
IT'S THE DIARY OF TEMPERENCE ROAN, THE CULT'S HIGH PRIESTESS.
NO THANK YOU, SIR.
I'VE NO INTEREST IN THE HORRORS I'D DISCOVER IN THA' BOOK.
WHAT'S THE COVER MADE OF ANYHOW?
DRIED INSECTS?
INSECTS... FOLLOWING A QUEEN.
BUT THE QUEEN HERSELF...
...SHE FOLLOWED NO DEMON....
...THOUGH THE CONFUSION IS UNDERSTANDABLE.
GATHER YOUR COAT, FAITH.
THIS MYSTERY IS FAR FROM UNRAVELED.

"AND BRING THE BOOK, WON'T YOU?"

BUT, SIR.

WE'VE STOPPED TEMPERENCE... STOPPED SUTTER.

THE THREAT THEY POSED... IT'S ENDED.

SURELY, WE'RE BETTER SERVED FOCUSING ON–

THE THREAT IS FAR FROM OVER, FAITH.

NOT IF THE IDEAS CONTAINED IN ROAN'S DIARY HOLD ANY TRUTH.

WHAT DOES THE BOOK SAY?

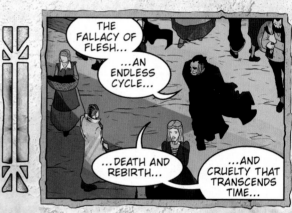

THE FALLACY OF FLESH...

...AN ENDLESS CYCLE...

...DEATH AND REBIRTH...

...AND CRUELTY THAT TRANSCENDS TIME...

THE VALGEROTI...

...THEY INDULGED IN THEIR EVERY CARNAL DESIRE...

...AND THEY BLAMED *DEMONS* FOR THE THINGS THEY'D DONE.

THAT'S HOW THEY GATHER THEIR WORSHIPPERS... NOT BY PROMISING ABSOLUTION... BUT BY GRANTING AN *EXCUSE* FOR THEIR INIQUITIES.

BUT I'M NOT SURE TEMPERENCE BELIEVED IN THOSE DEMONS HERSELF.

INSTEAD, WHAT SHE BELIEVED...

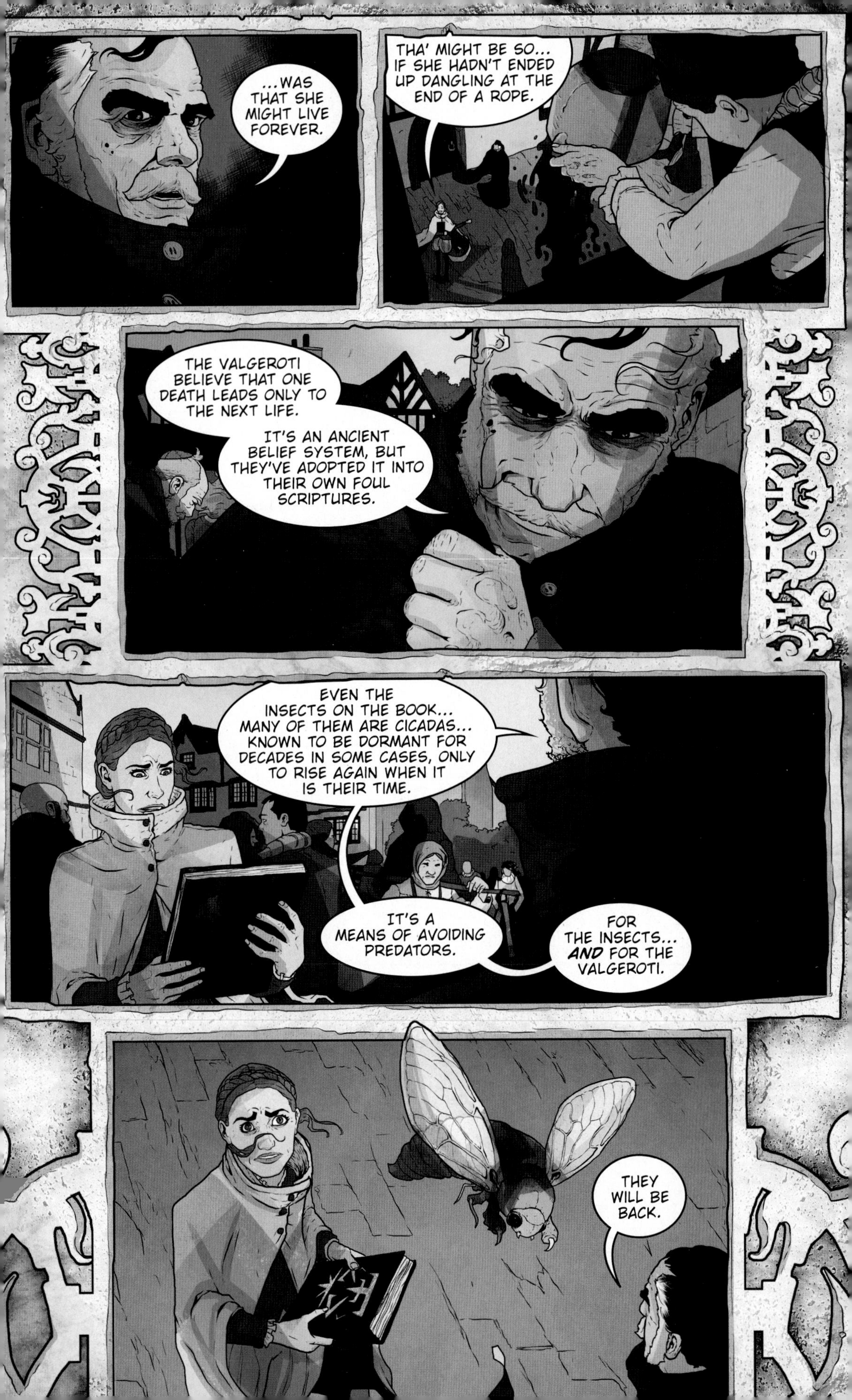
...WAS THAT SHE MIGHT LIVE FOREVER.
THA' MIGHT BE SO... IF SHE HADN'T ENDED UP DANGLING AT THE END OF A ROPE.
THE VALGEROTI BELIEVE THAT ONE DEATH LEADS ONLY TO THE NEXT LIFE.
IT'S AN ANCIENT BELIEF SYSTEM, BUT THEY'VE ADOPTED IT INTO THEIR OWN FOUL SCRIPTURES.
EVEN THE INSECTS ON THE BOOK... MANY OF THEM ARE CICADAS... KNOWN TO BE DORMANT FOR DECADES IN SOME CASES, ONLY TO RISE AGAIN WHEN IT IS THEIR TIME.
IT'S A MEANS OF AVOIDING PREDATORS.
FOR THE INSECTS... ***AND*** FOR THE VALGEROTI.
THEY WILL BE BACK.

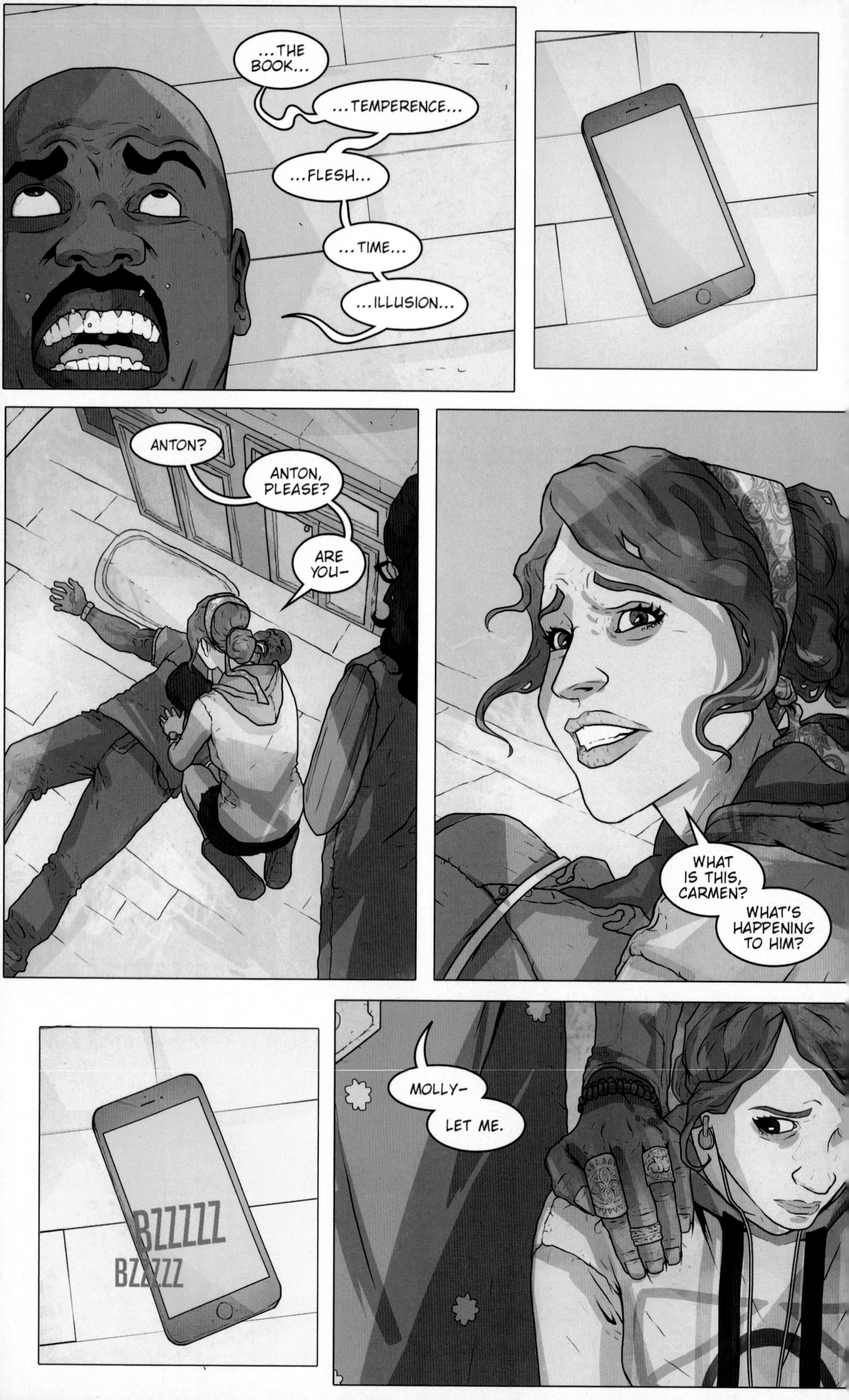
...THE BOOK...
...TEMPERENCE...
...FLESH...
...TIME...
...ILLUSION...
ANTON?
ANTON, PLEASE?
ARE YOU-
WHAT IS THIS, CARMEN?
WHAT'S HAPPENING TO HIM?
BZZZZZ
BZZZZZ
MOLLY-
LET ME.

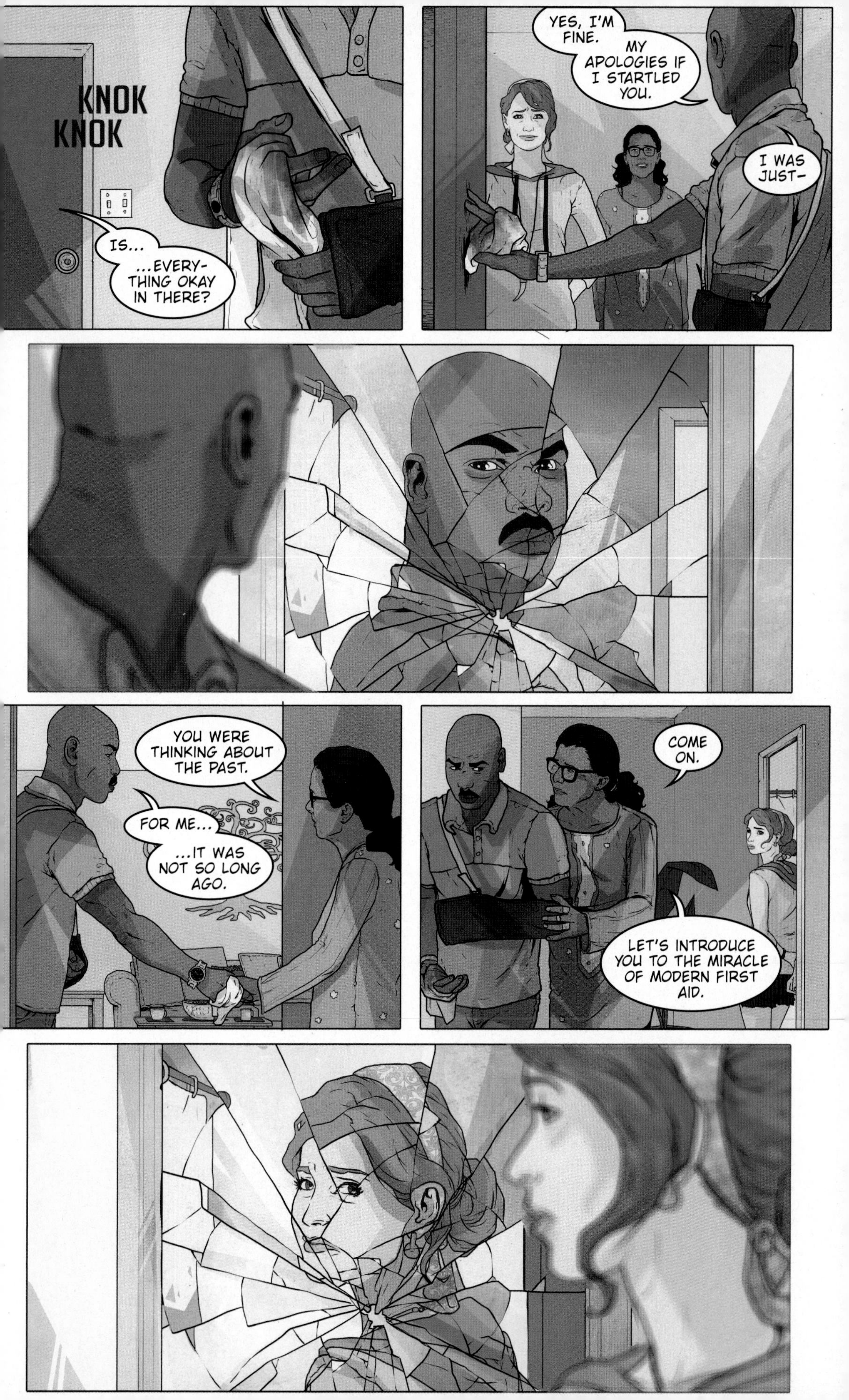
KNOK
KNOK
IS...
...EVERY-THING OKAY IN THERE?
YES, I'M FINE.
MY APOLOGIES IF I STARTLED YOU.
I WAS JUST-
YOU WERE THINKING ABOUT THE PAST.
FOR ME...
...IT WAS NOT SO LONG AGO.
COME ON.
LET'S INTRODUCE YOU TO THE MIRACLE OF MODERN FIRST AID.

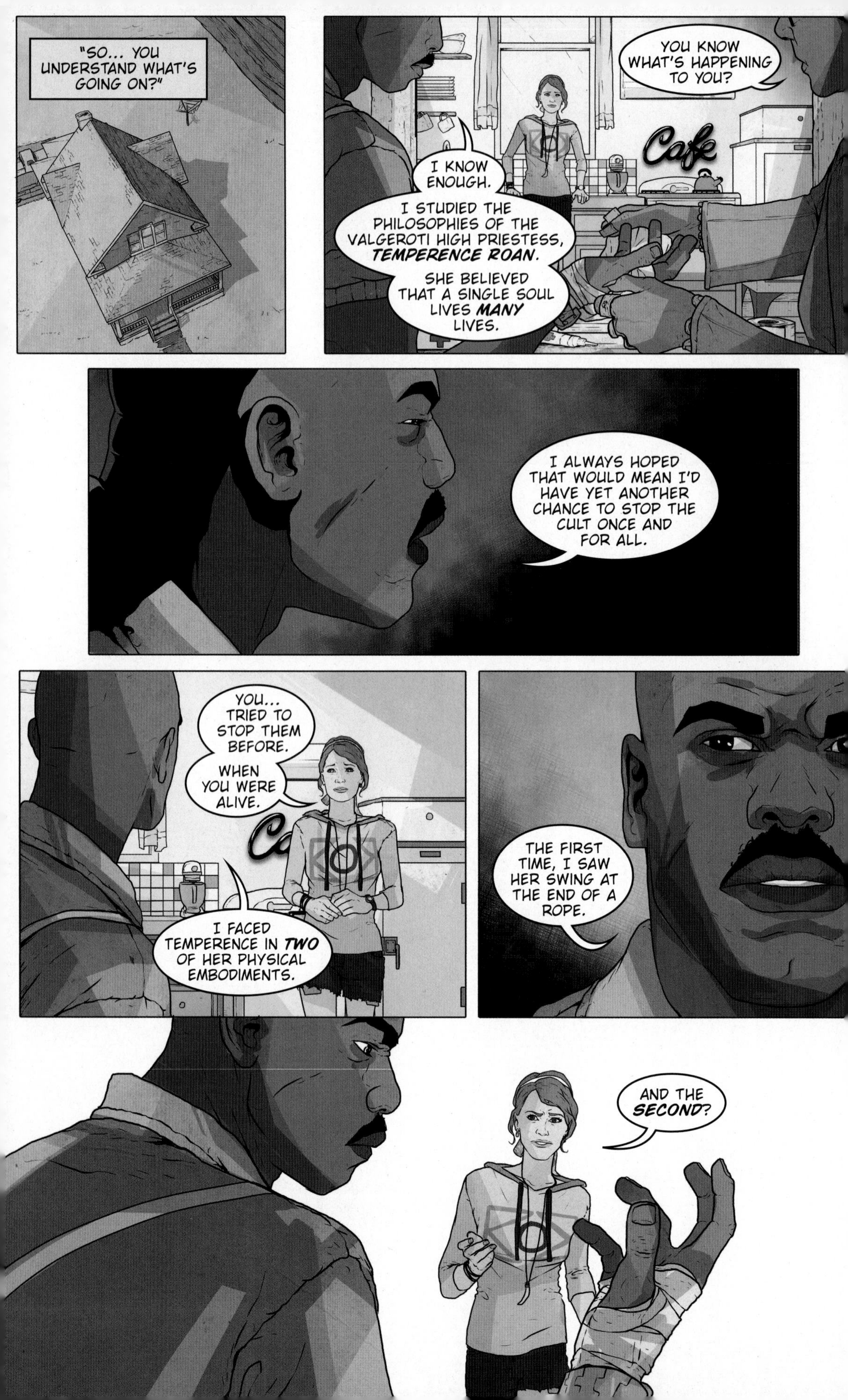
"SO... YOU UNDERSTAND WHAT'S GOING ON?"
YOU KNOW WHAT'S HAPPENING TO YOU?
I KNOW ENOUGH.
I STUDIED THE PHILOSOPHIES OF THE VALGEROTI HIGH PRIESTESS, TEMPERENCE ROAN.
SHE BELIEVED THAT A SINGLE SOUL LIVES MANY LIVES.
Cafe
I ALWAYS HOPED THAT WOULD MEAN I'D HAVE YET ANOTHER CHANCE TO STOP THE CULT ONCE AND FOR ALL.
YOU... TRIED TO STOP THEM BEFORE.
WHEN YOU WERE ALIVE.
I FACED TEMPERENCE IN TWO OF HER PHYSICAL EMBODIMENTS.
THE FIRST TIME, I SAW HER SWING AT THE END OF A ROPE.
AND THE SECOND?

YEEEEEAA AAAAAAGH!

NEITHER OF US SURVIVED THAT ENCOUNTER.

AND SHE'S BACK NOW.

TEMPERENCE IS BACK AGAIN.

AND SHE'S TIED TO THE PEOPLE WHO KIDNAPPED ADRIAN.

SHE'S CONNECTED TO THIS BUSINESS WITH SUTTER.

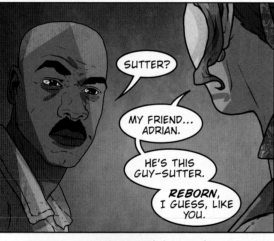

SUTTER?

MY FRIEND... ADRIAN.

HE'S THIS GUY-SUTTER.

REBORN, I GUESS, LIKE YOU.

SUTTER IS AS FOWL AS TEMPERENCE HERSELF. PERHAPS MORE SO.

THE VALGEROTI BELIEVED HIM TO PLAY HOST TO THE DEMON THEY WORSHIPPED.

IF HE HAS RETURNED—

SUTTER'S GONE.

I SENT HIM BACK TO THE PAST.

HE NO LONGER HAS A HOLD ON ADRIAN.

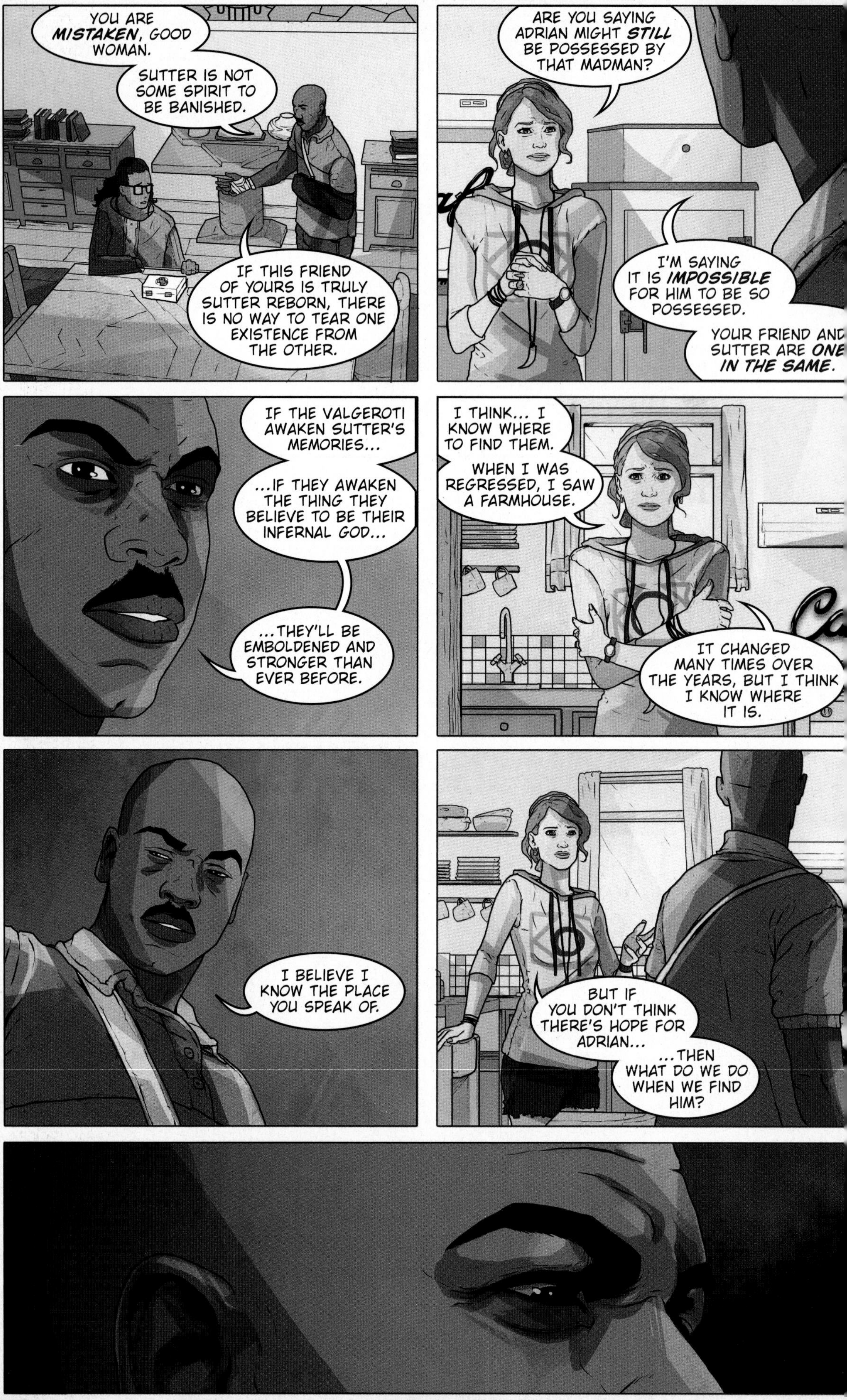

YOU ARE MISTAKEN, GOOD WOMAN.
SUTTER IS NOT SOME SPIRIT TO BE BANISHED.
IF THIS FRIEND OF YOURS IS TRULY SUTTER REBORN, THERE IS NO WAY TO TEAR ONE EXISTENCE FROM THE OTHER.
ARE YOU SAYING ADRIAN MIGHT STILL BE POSSESSED BY THAT MADMAN?
I'M SAYING IT IS IMPOSSIBLE FOR HIM TO BE SO POSSESSED.
YOUR FRIEND AND SUTTER ARE ONE IN THE SAME.
IF THE VALGEROTI AWAKEN SUTTER'S MEMORIES...
...IF THEY AWAKEN THE THING THEY BELIEVE TO BE THEIR INFERNAL GOD...
...THEY'LL BE EMBOLDENED AND STRONGER THAN EVER BEFORE.
I THINK... I KNOW WHERE TO FIND THEM.
WHEN I WAS REGRESSED, I SAW A FARMHOUSE.
IT CHANGED MANY TIMES OVER THE YEARS, BUT I THINK I KNOW WHERE IT IS.
I BELIEVE I KNOW THE PLACE YOU SPEAK OF.
BUT IF YOU DON'T THINK THERE'S HOPE FOR ADRIAN...
...THEN WHAT DO WE DO WHEN WE FIND HIM?

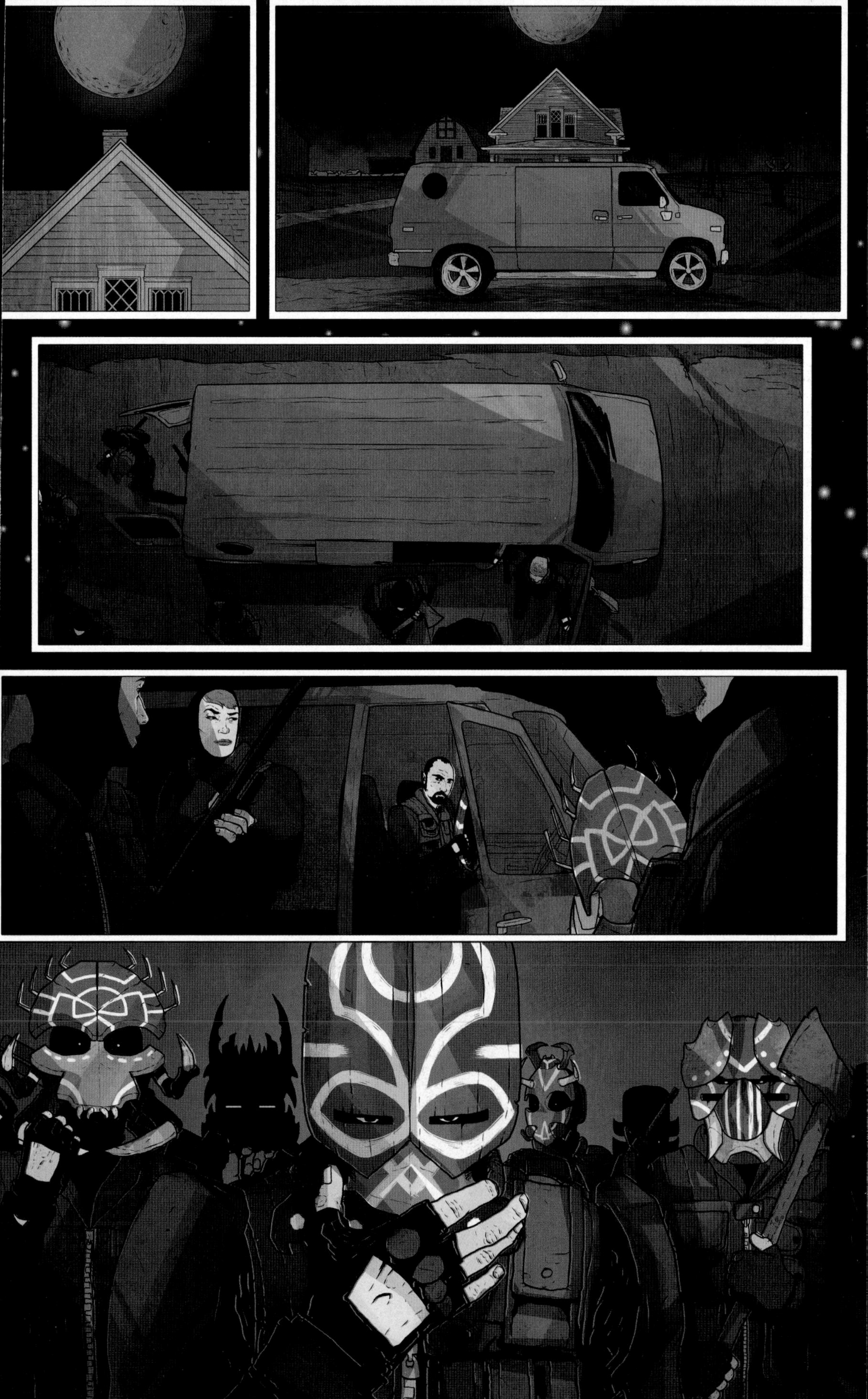

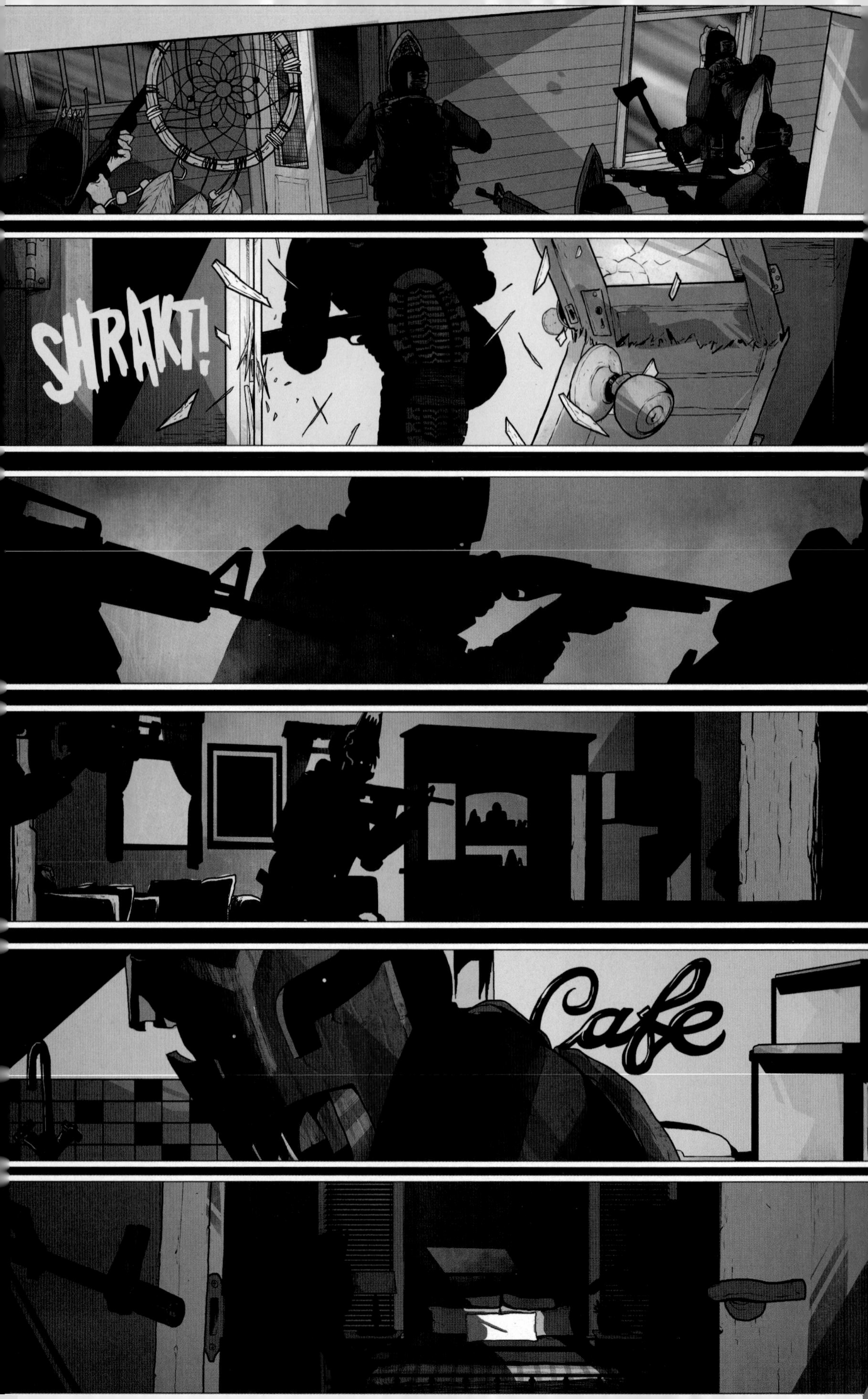
SHRAKT!
Cafe

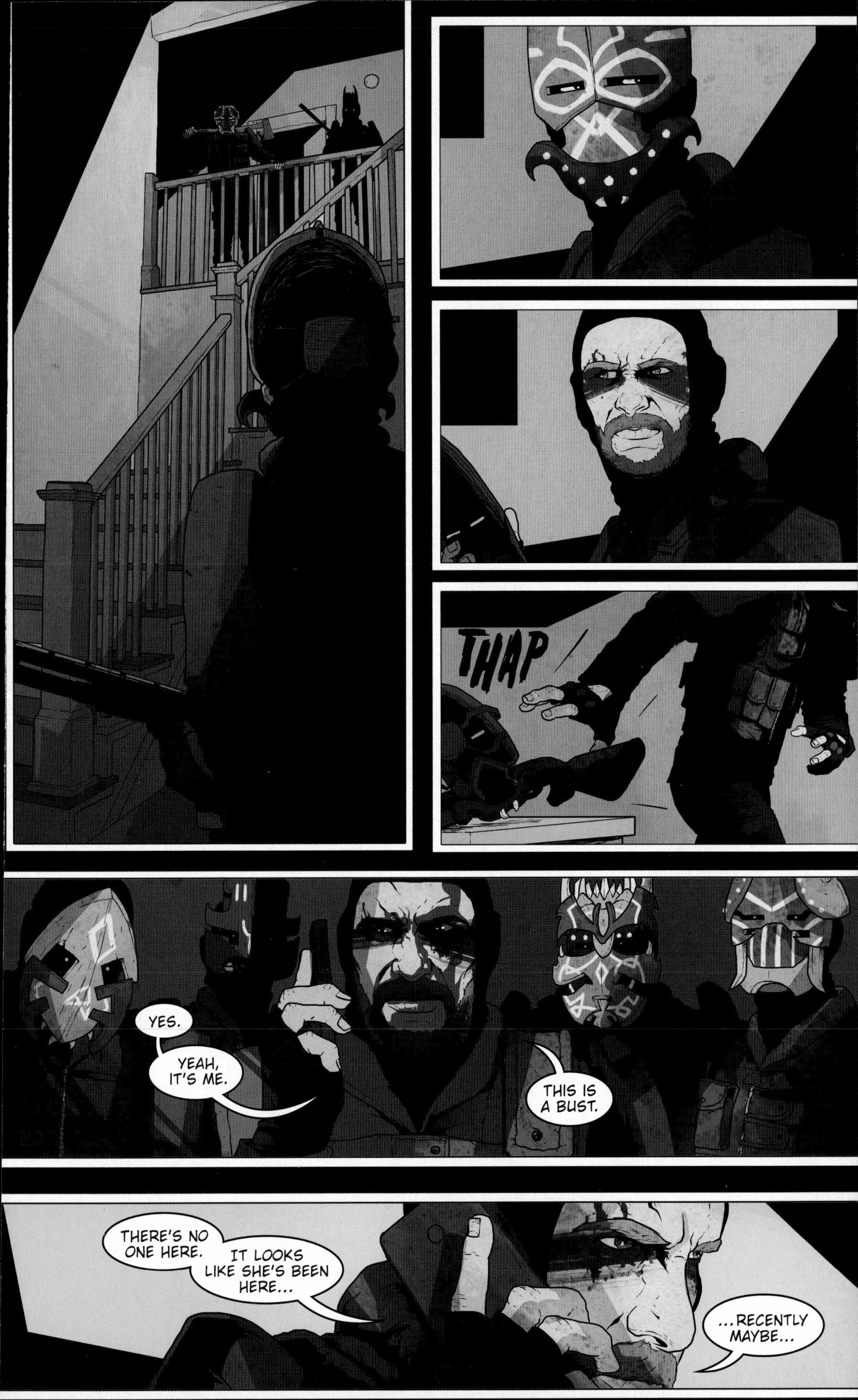
THAP
YES.
YEAH, IT'S ME.
THIS IS A BUST.
THERE'S NO ONE HERE.
IT LOOKS LIKE SHE'S BEEN HERE...
...RECENTLY MAYBE...

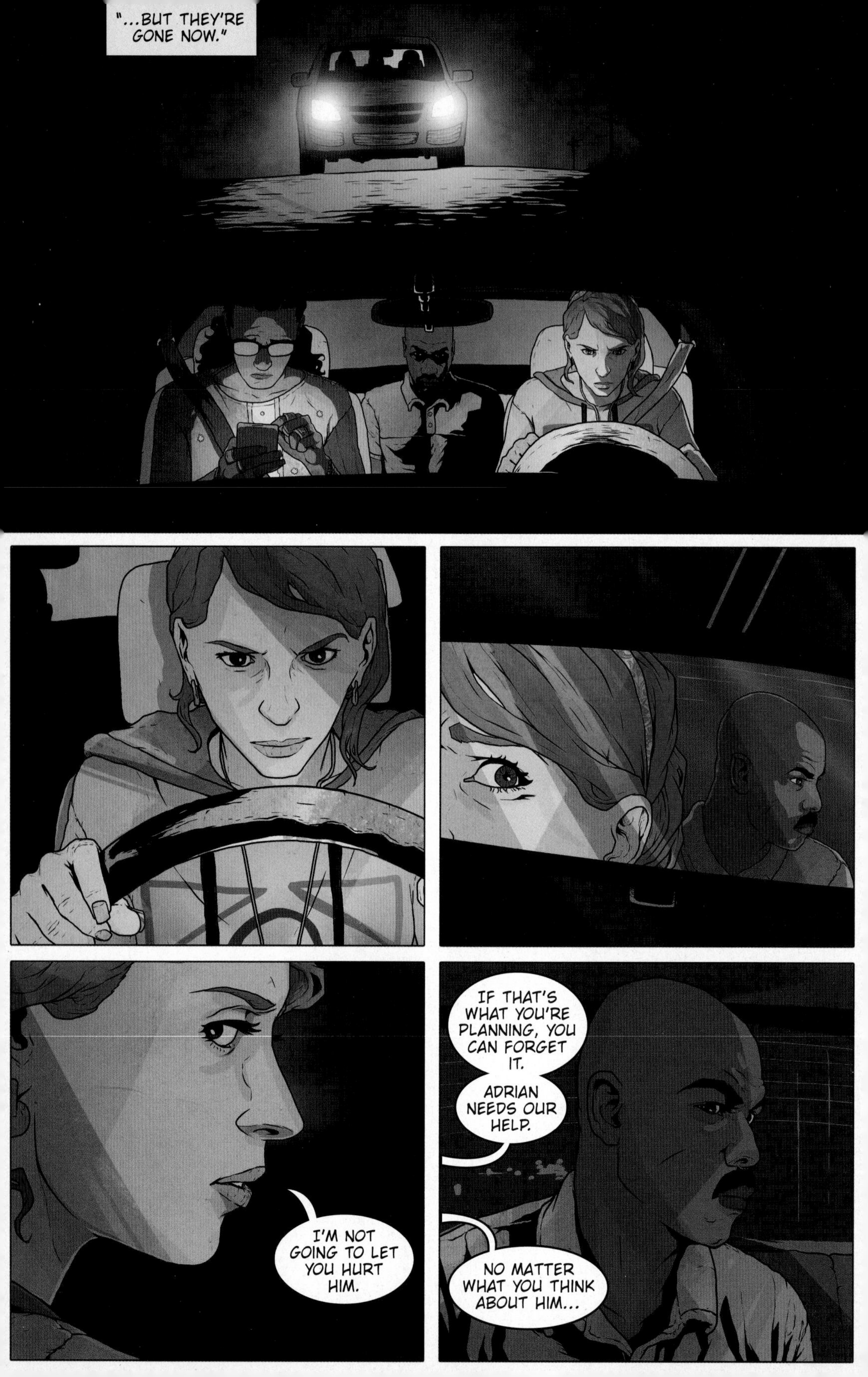
"...BUT THEY'RE GONE NOW."
I'M NOT GOING TO LET YOU HURT HIM.
IF THAT'S WHAT YOU'RE PLANNING, YOU CAN FORGET IT.
ADRIAN NEEDS OUR HELP.
NO MATTER WHAT YOU THINK ABOUT HIM...

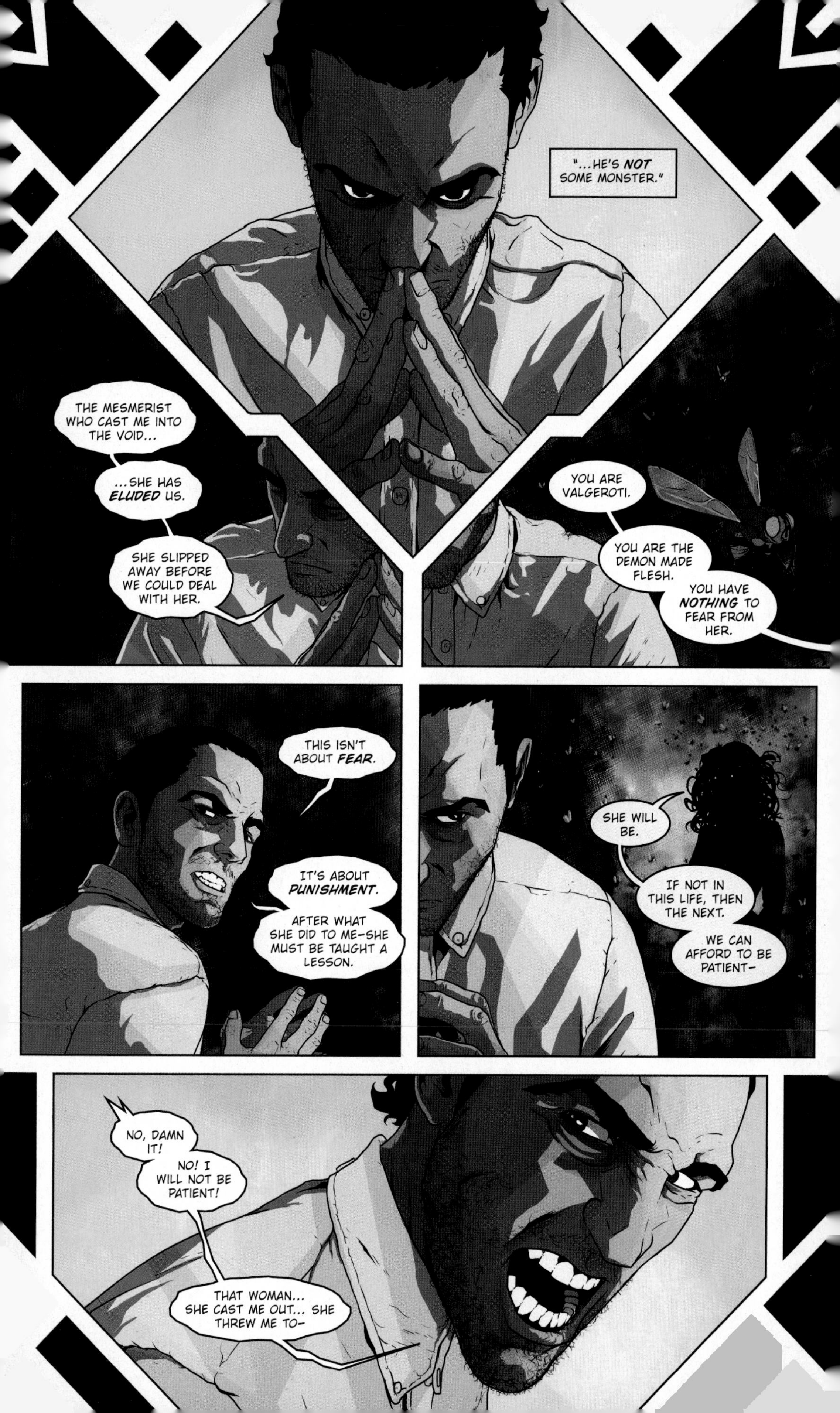
"...HE'S NOT SOME MONSTER."
THE MESMERIST WHO CAST ME INTO THE VOID...
...SHE HAS ELUDED US.
SHE SLIPPED AWAY BEFORE WE COULD DEAL WITH HER.
YOU ARE VALGEROTI.
YOU ARE THE DEMON MADE FLESH.
YOU HAVE NOTHING TO FEAR FROM HER.
THIS ISN'T ABOUT FEAR.
IT'S ABOUT PUNISHMENT.
AFTER WHAT SHE DID TO ME–SHE MUST BE TAUGHT A LESSON.
SHE WILL BE.
IF NOT IN THIS LIFE, THEN THE NEXT.
WE CAN AFFORD TO BE PATIENT–
NO, DAMN IT!
NO! I WILL NOT BE PATIENT!
THAT WOMAN... SHE CAST ME OUT... SHE THREW ME TO–

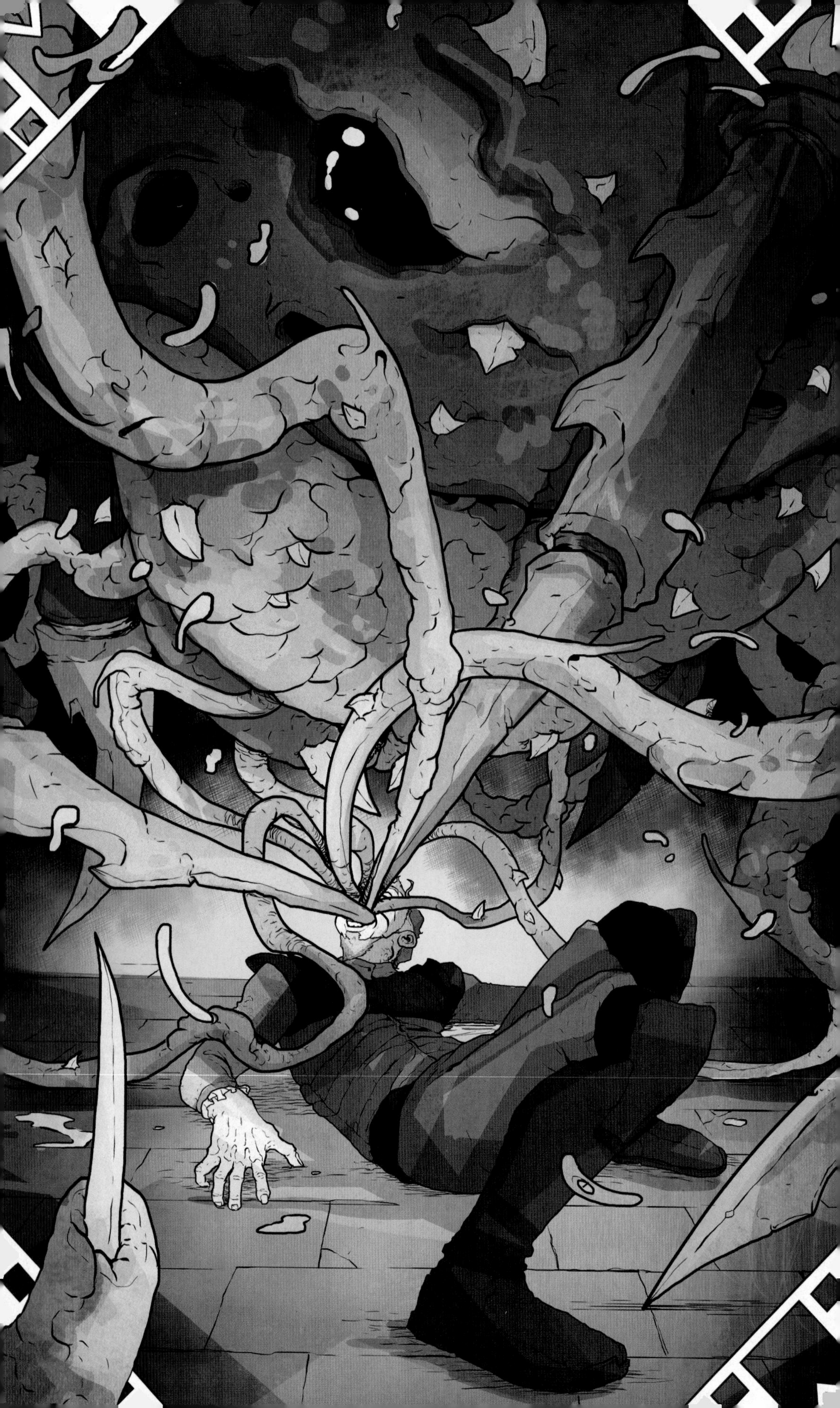

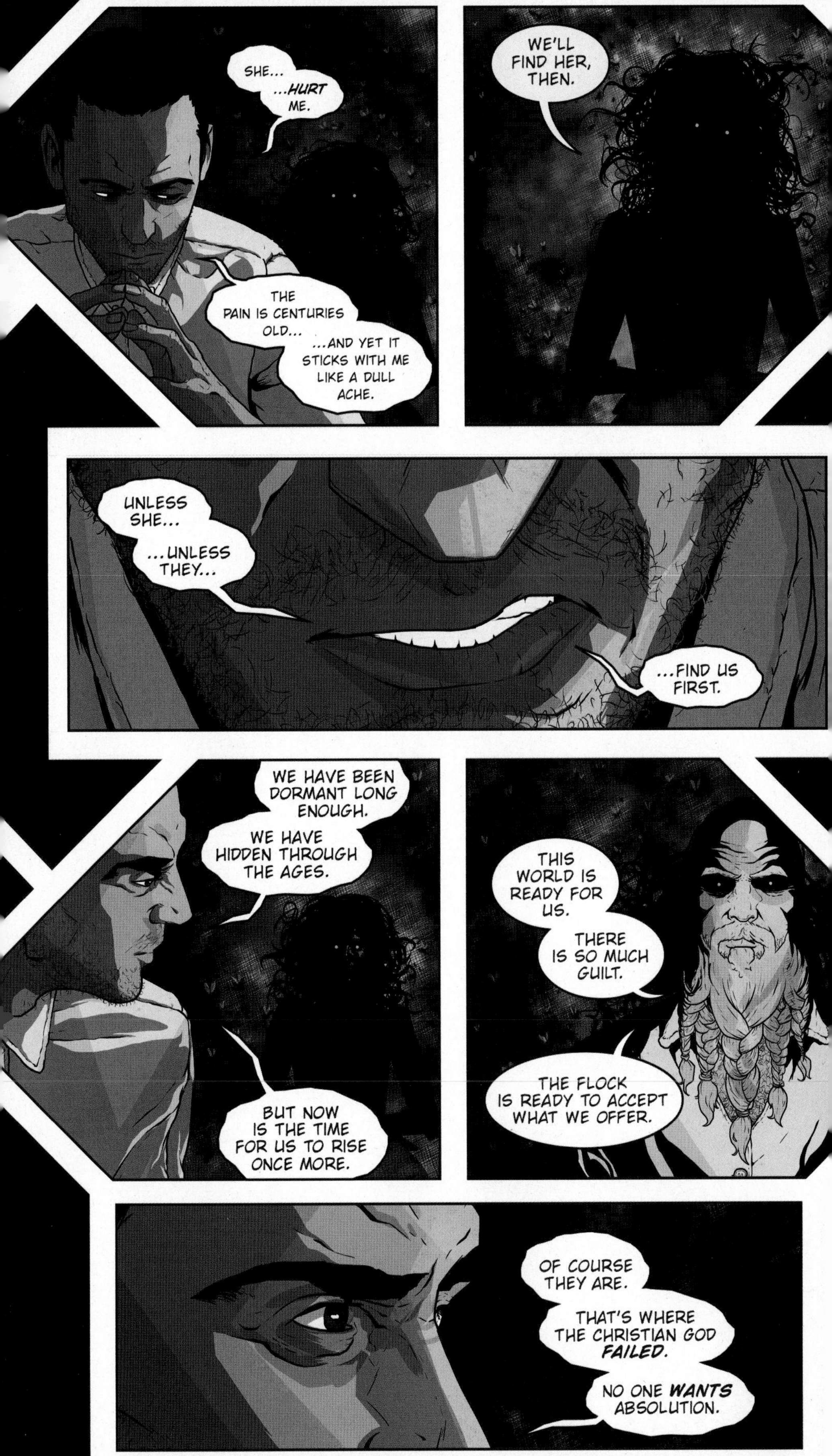
SHE... ...HURT ME.
THE PAIN IS CENTURIES OLD...
...AND YET IT STICKS WITH ME LIKE A DULL ACHE.
WE'LL FIND HER, THEN.
UNLESS SHE...
...UNLESS THEY...
...FIND US FIRST.
WE HAVE BEEN DORMANT LONG ENOUGH.
WE HAVE HIDDEN THROUGH THE AGES.
BUT NOW IS THE TIME FOR US TO RISE ONCE MORE.
THIS WORLD IS READY FOR US.
THERE IS SO MUCH GUILT.
THE FLOCK IS READY TO ACCEPT WHAT WE OFFER.
OF COURSE THEY ARE.
THAT'S WHERE THE CHRISTIAN GOD FAILED.
NO ONE WANTS ABSOLUTION.

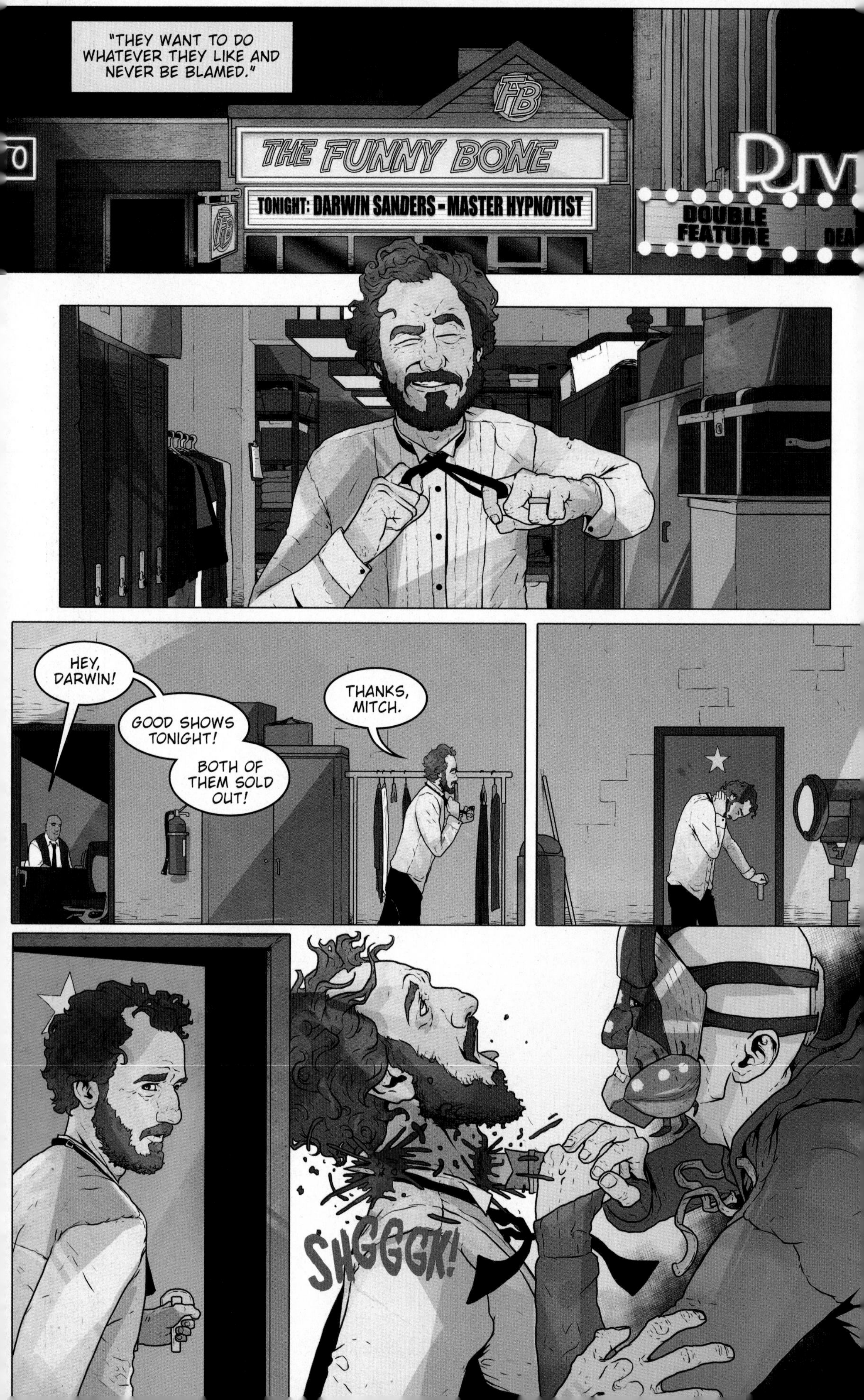
"THEY WANT TO DO WHATEVER THEY LIKE AND NEVER BE BLAMED."
THE FUNNY BONE
TONIGHT: DARWIN SANDERS - MASTER HYPNOTIST
DOUBLE FEATURE
HEY, DARWIN!
GOOD SHOWS TONIGHT!
BOTH OF THEM SOLD OUT!
THANKS, MITCH.
SHGGGK!

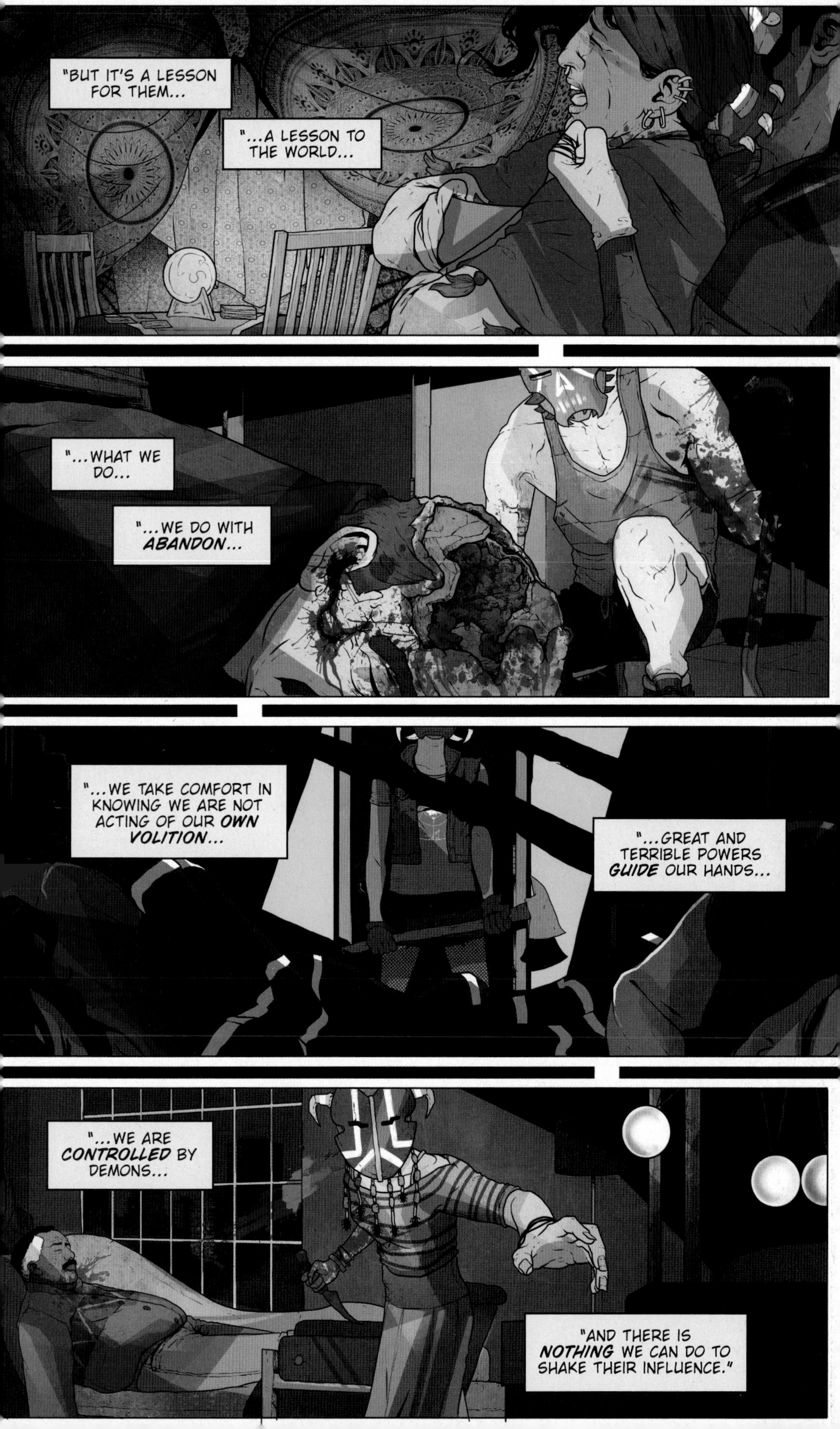
"BUT IT'S A LESSON FOR THEM...
"...A LESSON TO THE WORLD...
"...WHAT WE DO...
"...WE DO WITH *ABANDON*...
"...WE TAKE COMFORT IN KNOWING WE ARE NOT ACTING OF OUR *OWN VOLITION*...
"...GREAT AND TERRIBLE POWERS *GUIDE* OUR HANDS...
"...WE ARE *CONTROLLED* BY DEMONS...
"AND THERE IS *NOTHING* WE CAN DO TO SHAKE THEIR INFLUENCE."

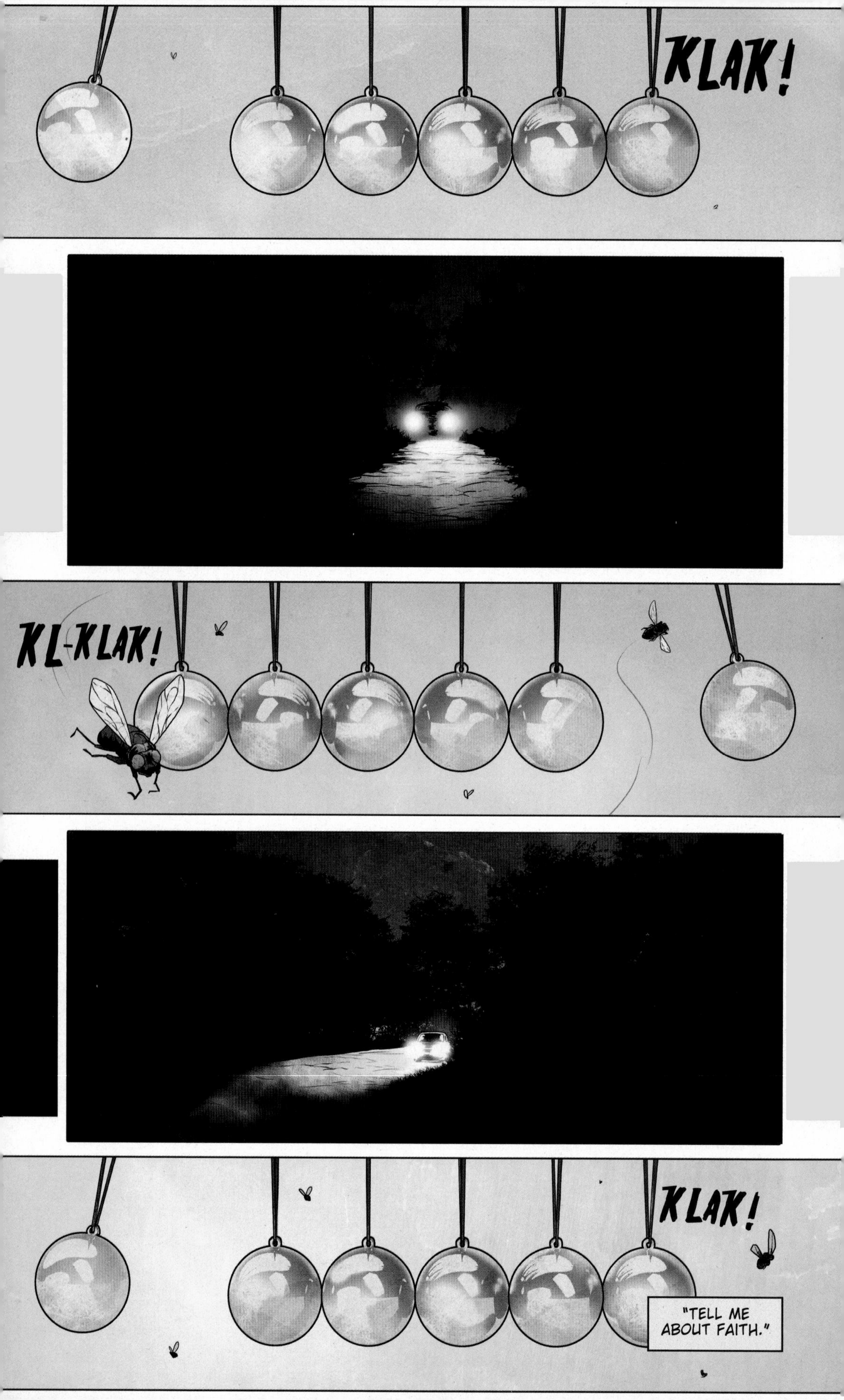
KLAK!
KL-KLAK!
KLAK!
"TELL ME ABOUT FAITH."

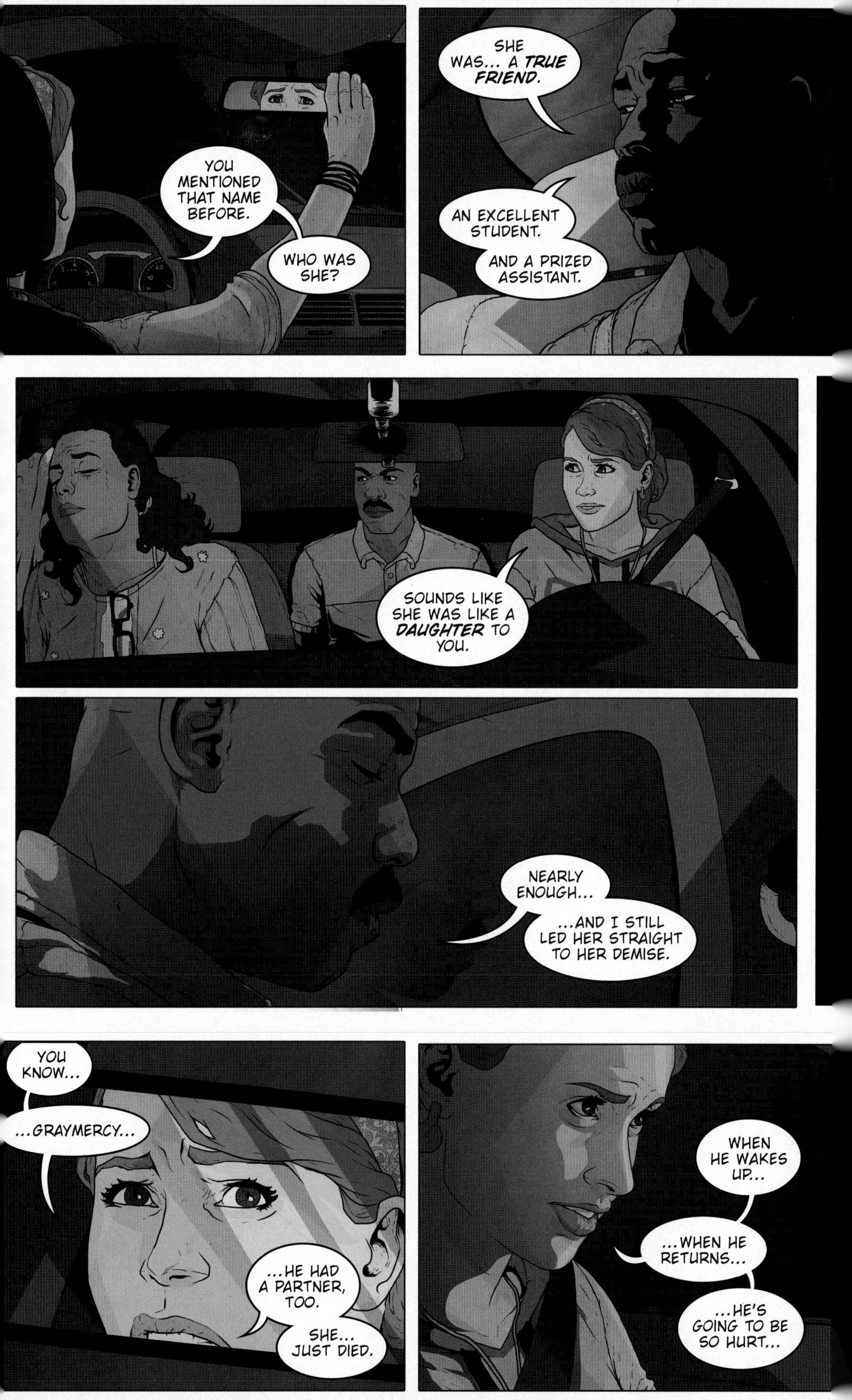
YOU MENTIONED THAT NAME BEFORE.
WHO WAS SHE?
SHE WAS... A TRUE FRIEND.
AN EXCELLENT STUDENT.
AND A PRIZED ASSISTANT.
SOUNDS LIKE SHE WAS LIKE A DAUGHTER TO YOU.
NEARLY ENOUGH...
...AND I STILL LED HER STRAIGHT TO HER DEMISE.
YOU KNOW...
...GRAYMERCY...
...HE HAD A PARTNER, TOO.
SHE... JUST DIED.
WHEN HE WAKES UP...
...WHEN HE RETURNS...
...HE'S GOING TO BE SO HURT...

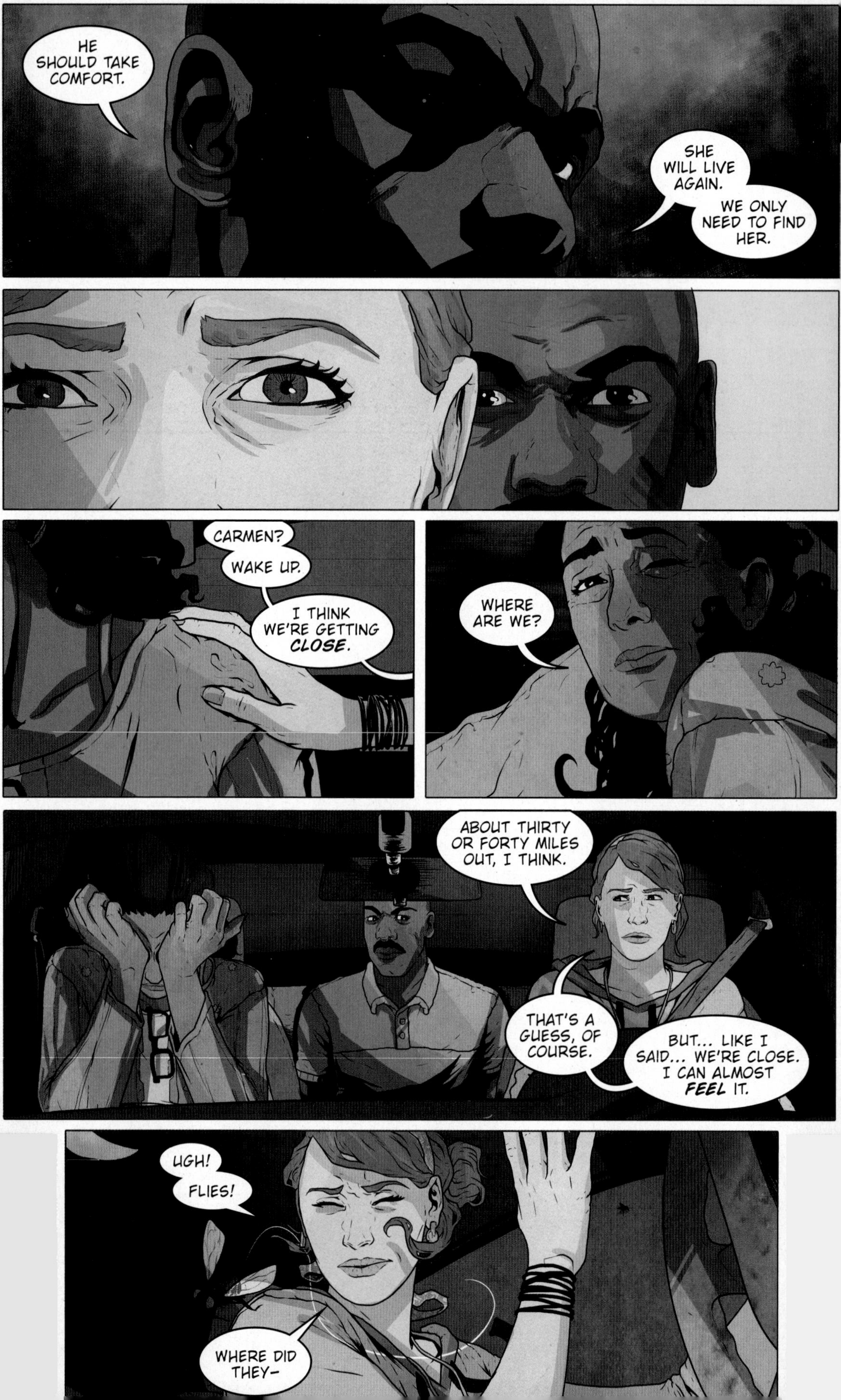
HE SHOULD TAKE COMFORT.
SHE WILL LIVE AGAIN.
WE ONLY NEED TO FIND HER.
CARMEN?
WAKE UP.
I THINK WE'RE GETTING CLOSE.
WHERE ARE WE?
ABOUT THIRTY OR FORTY MILES OUT, I THINK.
THAT'S A GUESS, OF COURSE.
BUT... LIKE I SAID... WE'RE CLOSE. I CAN ALMOST FEEL IT.
UGH!
FLIES!
WHERE DID THEY-

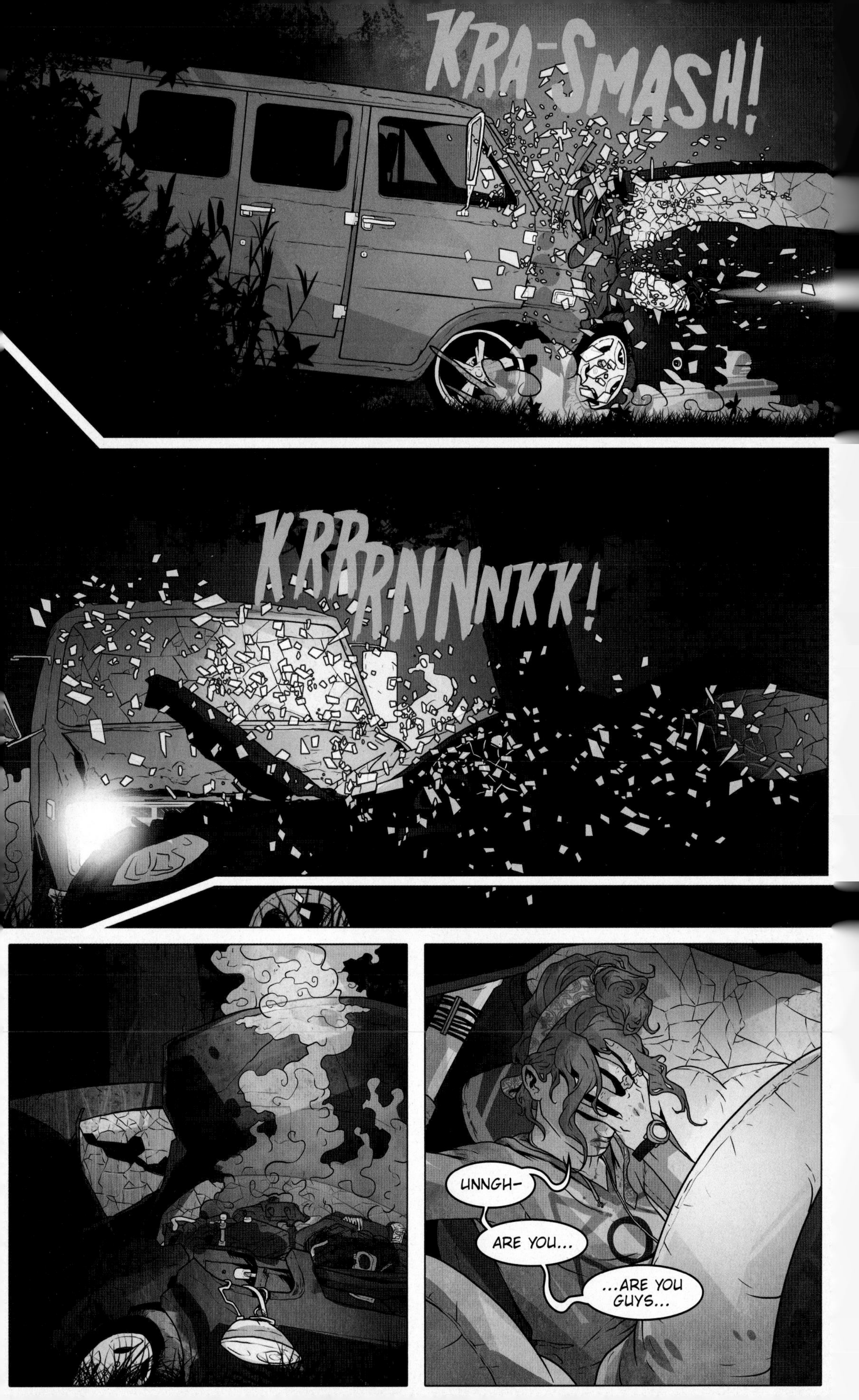
KRA-SMASH!
KRRRNNNKK!
UNNGH-
ARE YOU...
...ARE YOU GUYS...

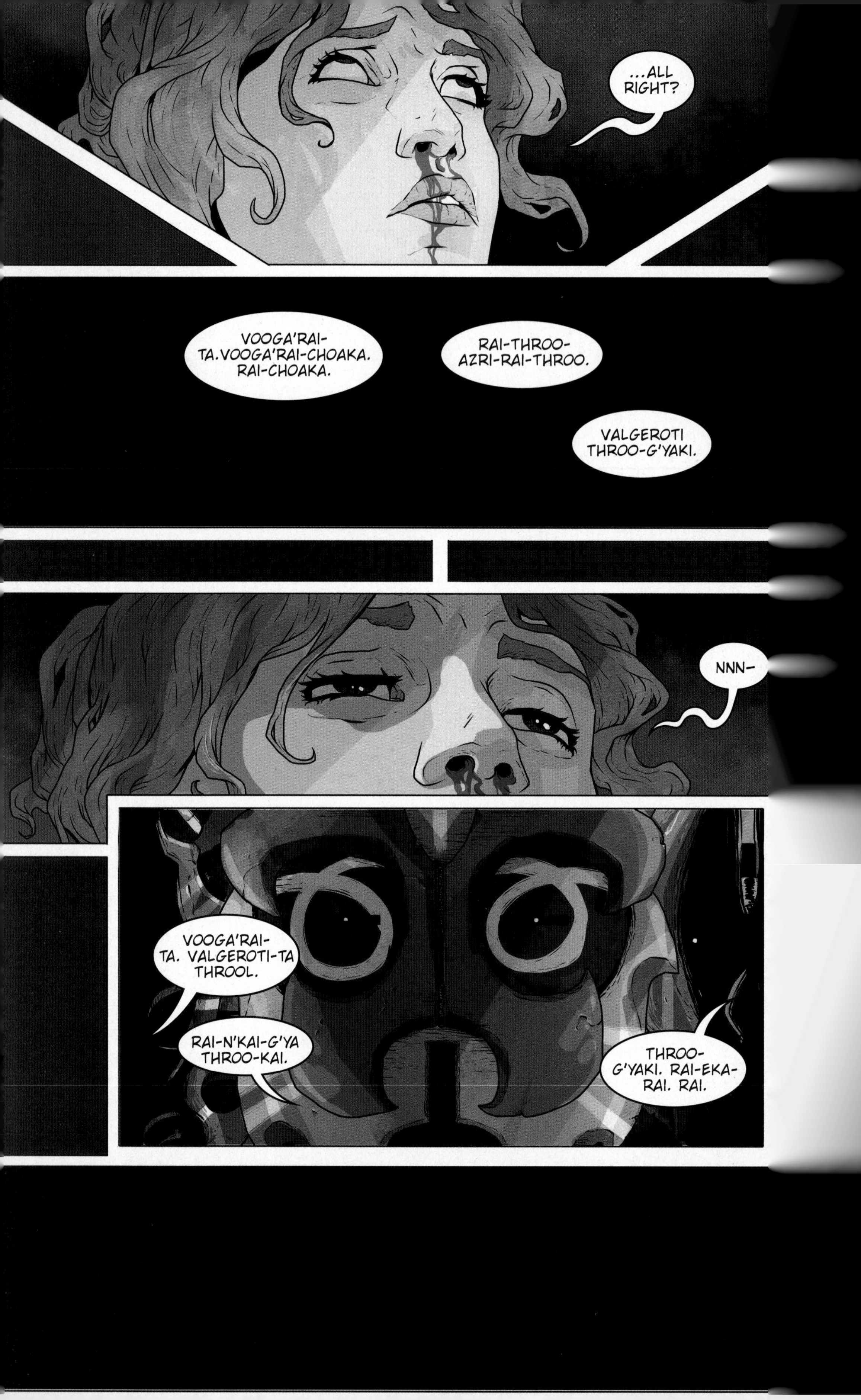
...ALL RIGHT?
VOOGA'RAI-TA. VOOGA'RAI-CHOAKA. RAI-CHOAKA.
RAI-THROO-AZRI-RAI-THROO.
VALGEROTI THROO-G'YAKI.
NNN-
VOOGA'RAI-TA. VALGEROTI-TA THROOL.
RAI-N'KAI-G'YA THROO-KAI.
THROO-G'YAKI. RAI-EKA-RAI. RAI.

THIRTEEN

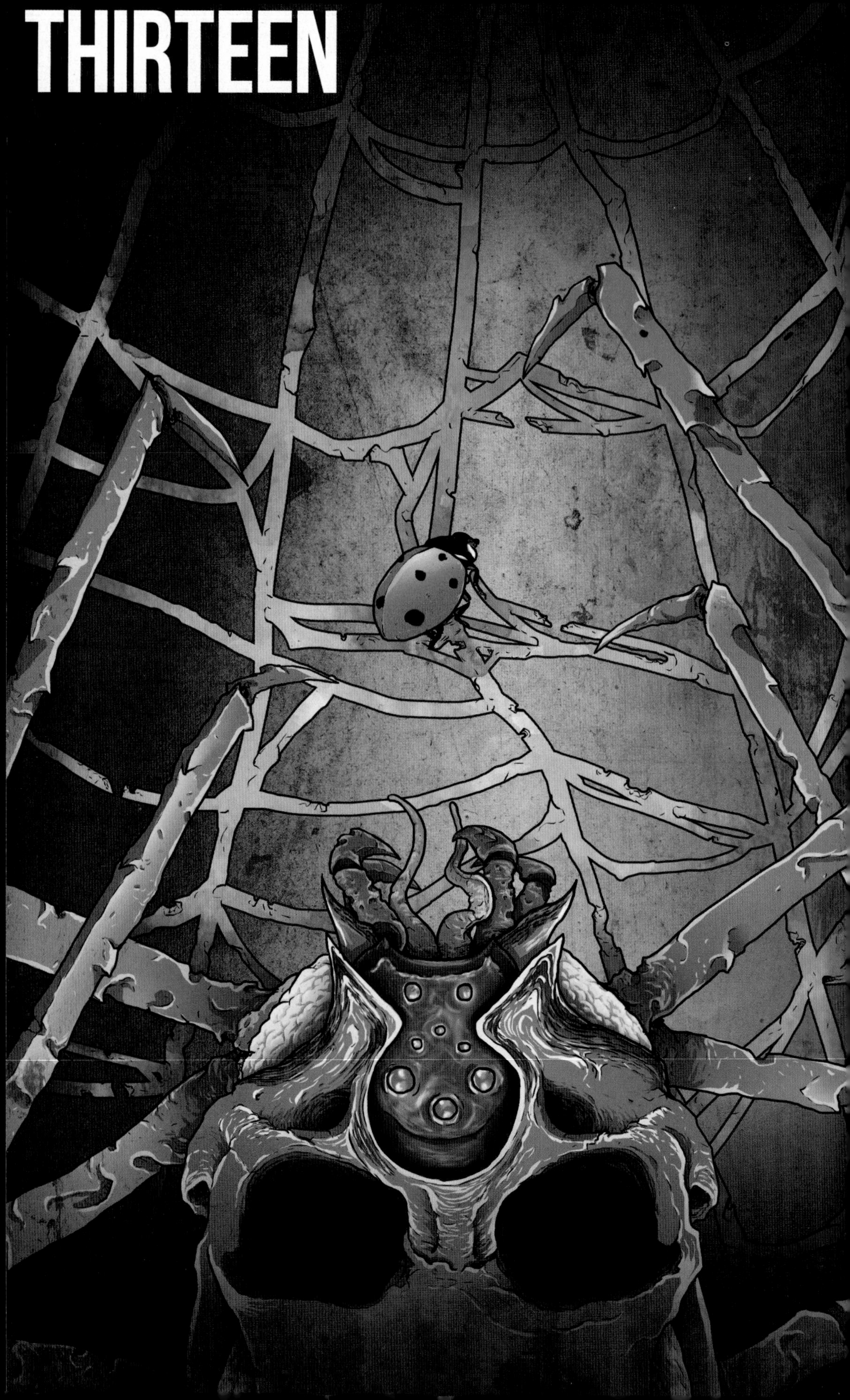

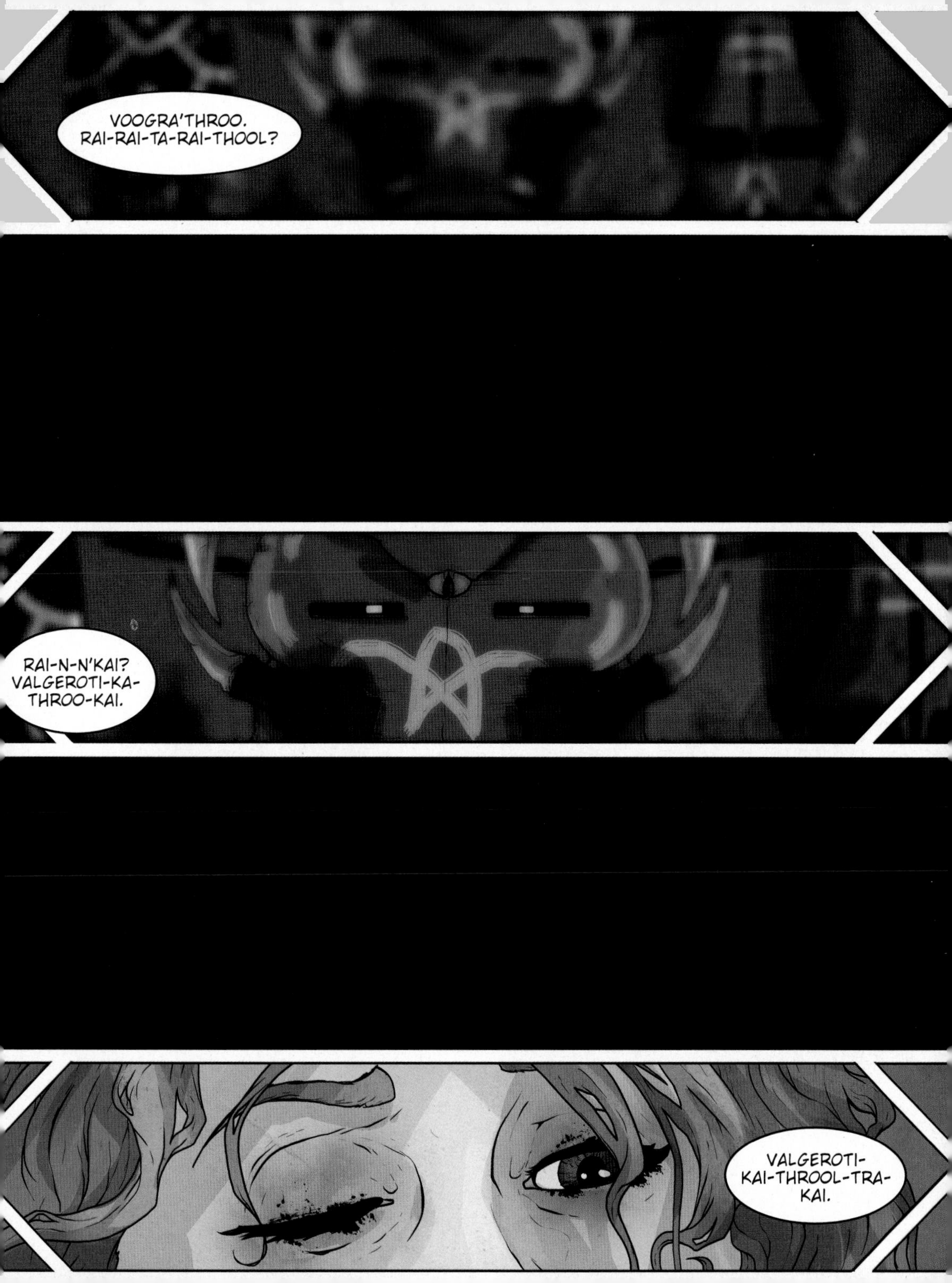
VOOGRA'THROO. RAI-RAI-TA-RAI-THOOL?
RAI-N-N'KAI? VALGEROTI-KA-THROO-KAI.
VALGEROTI-KAI-THROOL-TRA-KAI.

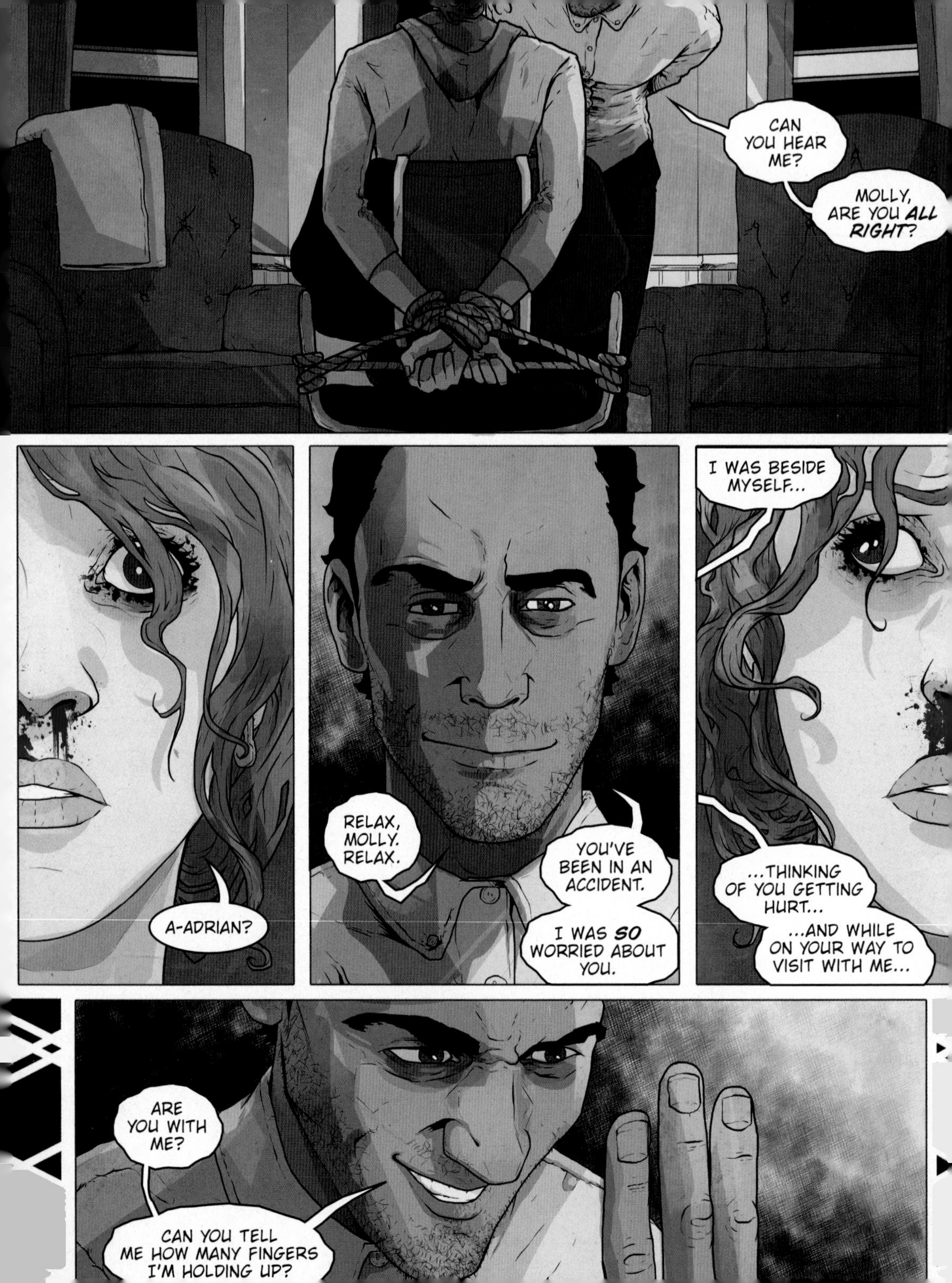
CAN YOU HEAR ME?
MOLLY, ARE YOU **ALL RIGHT**?
A-ADRIAN?
RELAX, MOLLY. RELAX.
YOU'VE BEEN IN AN ACCIDENT.
I WAS **SO** WORRIED ABOUT YOU.
I WAS BESIDE MYSELF...
...THINKING OF YOU GETTING HURT...
...AND WHILE ON YOUR WAY TO VISIT WITH ME...
ARE YOU WITH ME?
CAN YOU TELL ME HOW MANY FINGERS I'M HOLDING UP?

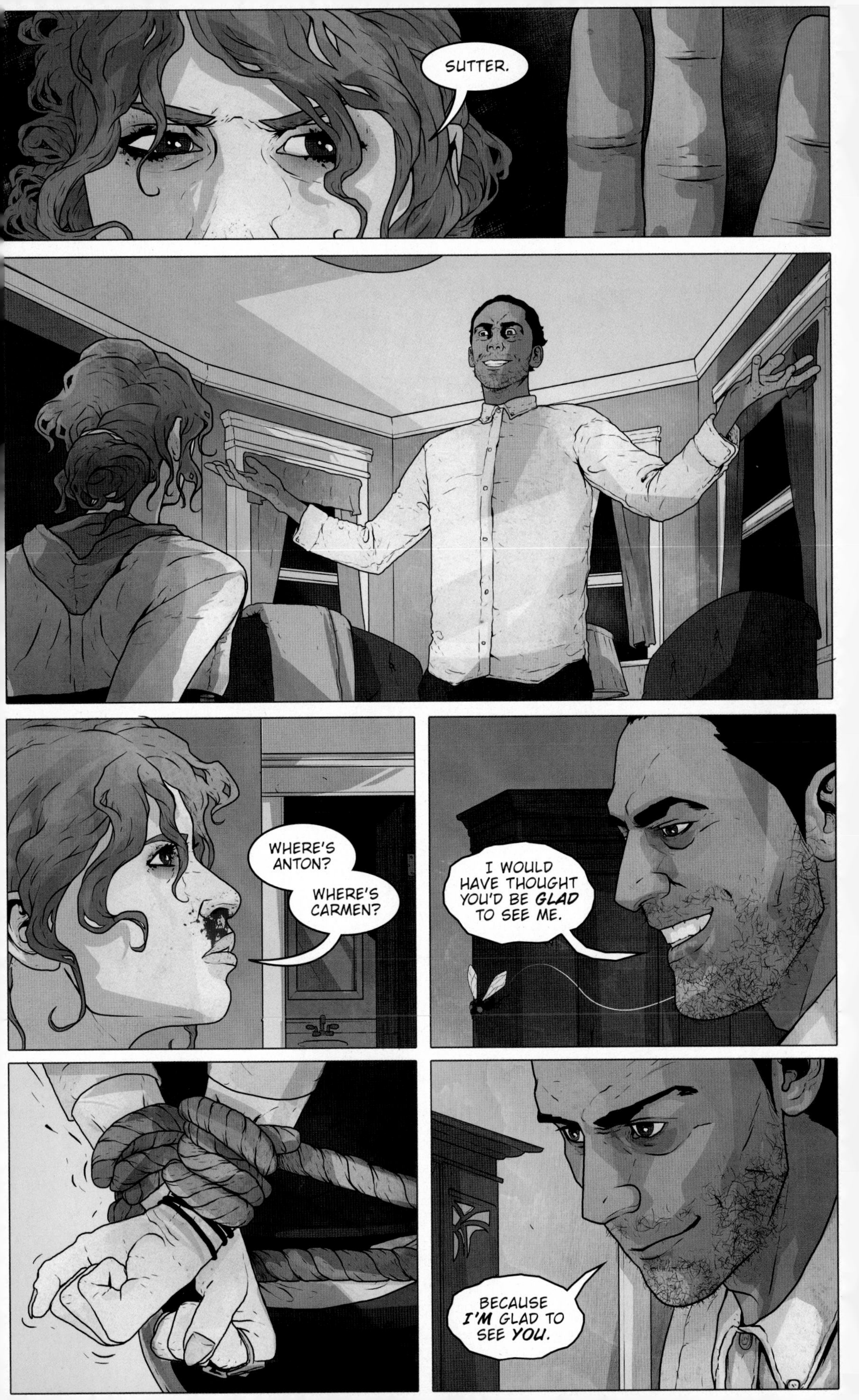
SUTTER.
WHERE'S ANTON?
WHERE'S CARMEN?
I WOULD HAVE THOUGHT YOU'D BE *GLAD* TO SEE ME.
BECAUSE *I'M* GLAD TO SEE *YOU*.

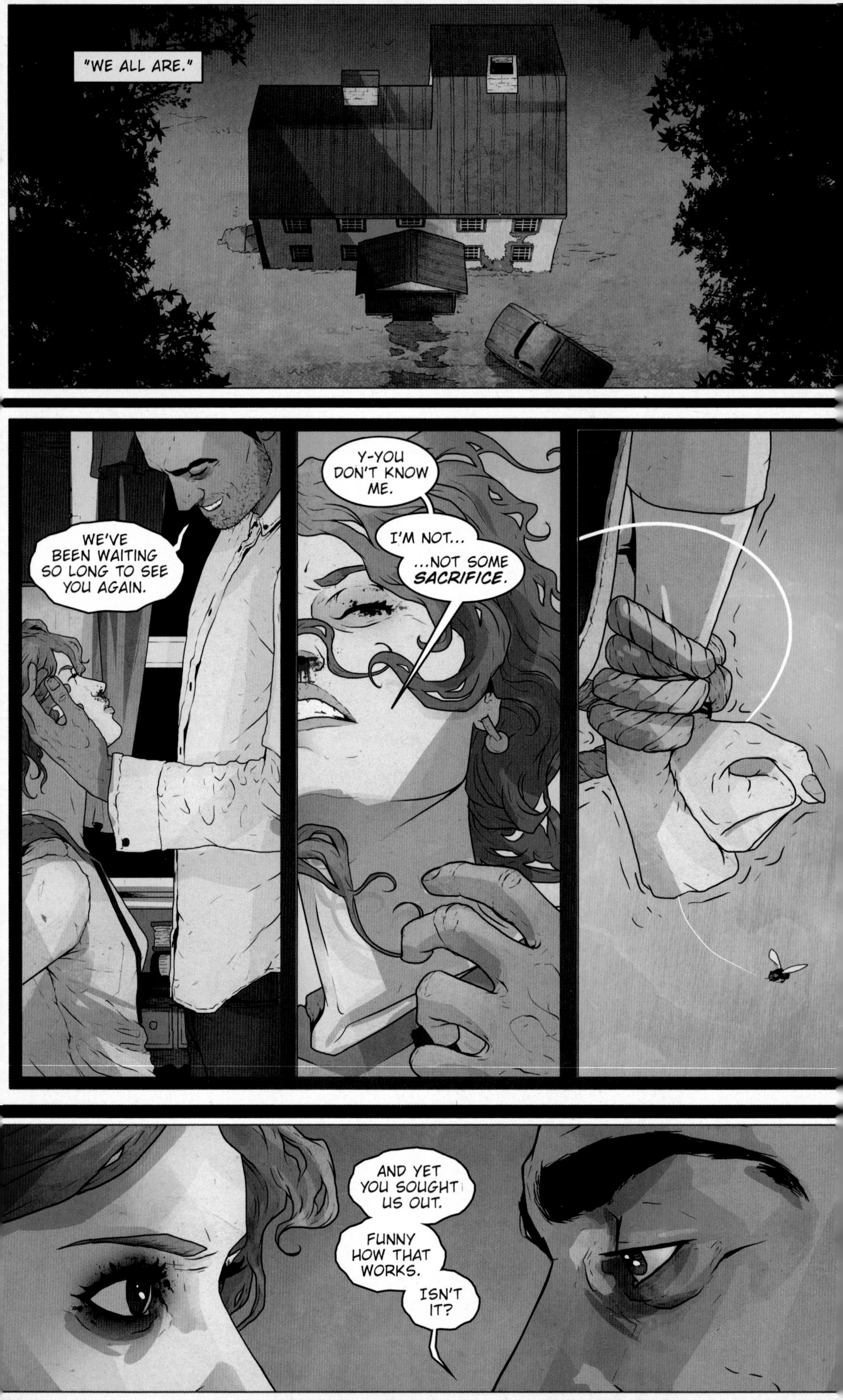
"WE ALL ARE."
WE'VE BEEN WAITING SO LONG TO SEE YOU AGAIN.
Y-YOU DON'T KNOW ME.
I'M NOT...
...NOT SOME *SACRIFICE*.
AND YET YOU SOUGHT US OUT.
FUNNY HOW THAT WORKS.
ISN'T IT?

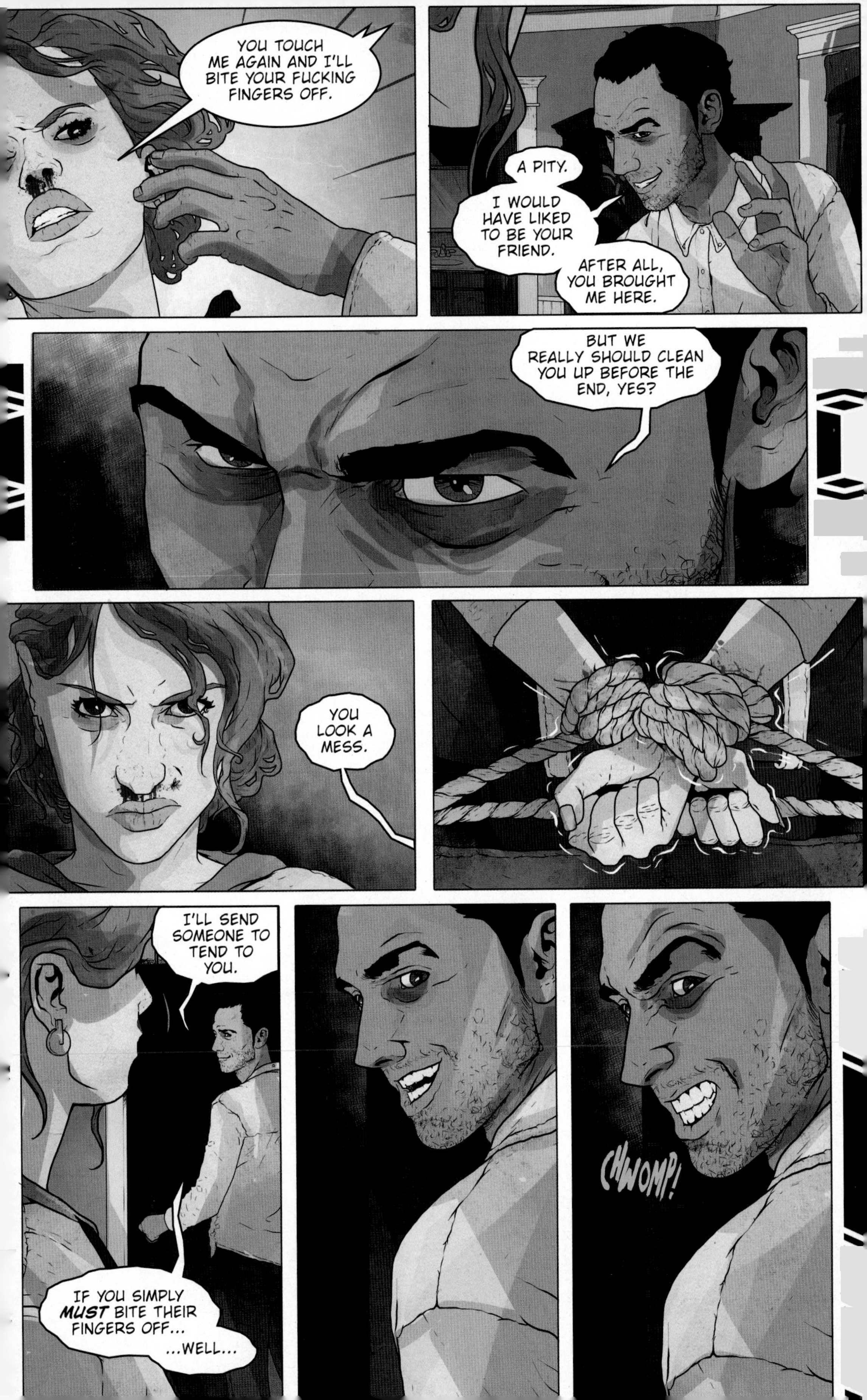
YOU TOUCH ME AGAIN AND I'LL BITE YOUR FUCKING FINGERS OFF.
A PITY.
I WOULD HAVE LIKED TO BE YOUR FRIEND.
AFTER ALL, YOU BROUGHT ME HERE.
BUT WE REALLY SHOULD CLEAN YOU UP BEFORE THE END, YES?
YOU LOOK A MESS.
I'LL SEND SOMEONE TO TEND TO YOU.
IF YOU SIMPLY MUST BITE THEIR FINGERS OFF...
...WELL...
CHWOMP!

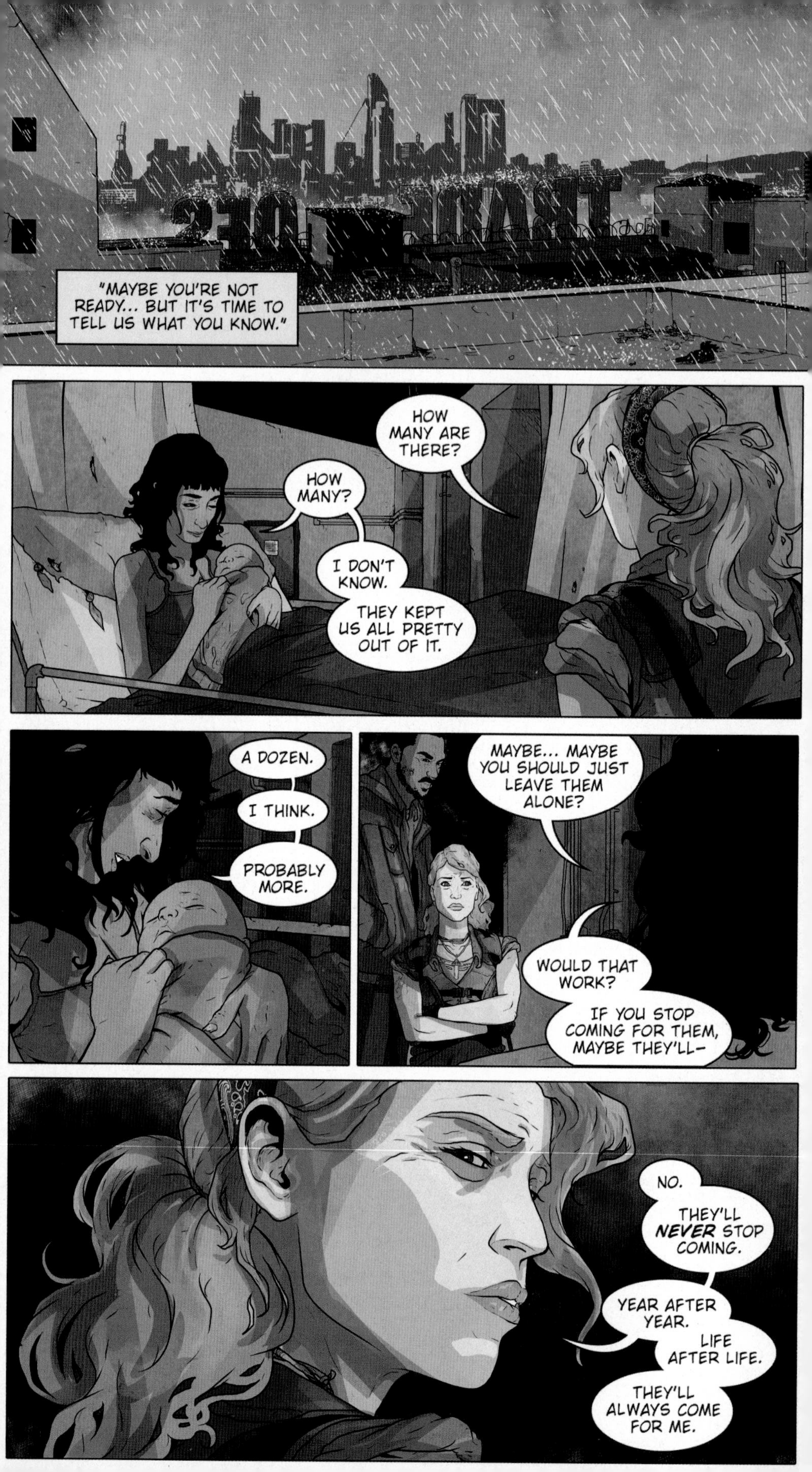
"MAYBE YOU'RE NOT READY... BUT IT'S TIME TO TELL US WHAT YOU KNOW."
HOW MANY ARE THERE?
HOW MANY?
I DON'T KNOW.
THEY KEPT US ALL PRETTY OUT OF IT.
A DOZEN.
I THINK.
PROBABLY MORE.
MAYBE... MAYBE YOU SHOULD JUST LEAVE THEM ALONE?
WOULD THAT WORK?
IF YOU STOP COMING FOR THEM, MAYBE THEY'LL-
NO.
THEY'LL ***NEVER*** STOP COMING.
YEAR AFTER YEAR.
LIFE AFTER LIFE.
THEY'LL ALWAYS COME FOR ME.

FOR YOU. NOT FOR ME.

NOT FOR ANY OF THESE OTHER PEOPLE.

YOU'VE RAISED A LITTLE ARMY TO PROTECT YOURSELF, BUT THIS ISN'T ABOUT ME.

YOU'RE RIGHT. THIS IS BIGGER THAN JUST YOU.

AND YOU SHOULD BE THANKFUL FOR WHAT MY MOM'S DONE FOR YOU—

HAL. IT'S ALL RIGHT.

HAL, COULD YOU GIVE ME A MINUTE ALONE WITH DARA?

MOM—

JUST A MINUTE, ALL RIGHT?

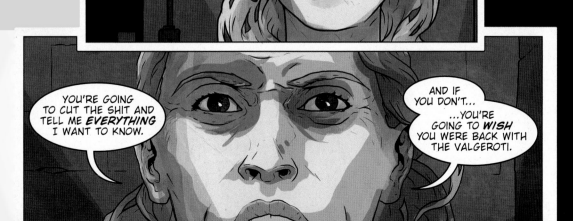

NOW.

YOU'RE GOING TO CUT THE SHIT AND TELL ME **EVERYTHING** I WANT TO KNOW.

AND IF YOU DON'T...

...YOU'RE GOING TO **WISH** YOU WERE BACK WITH THE VALGEROTI.

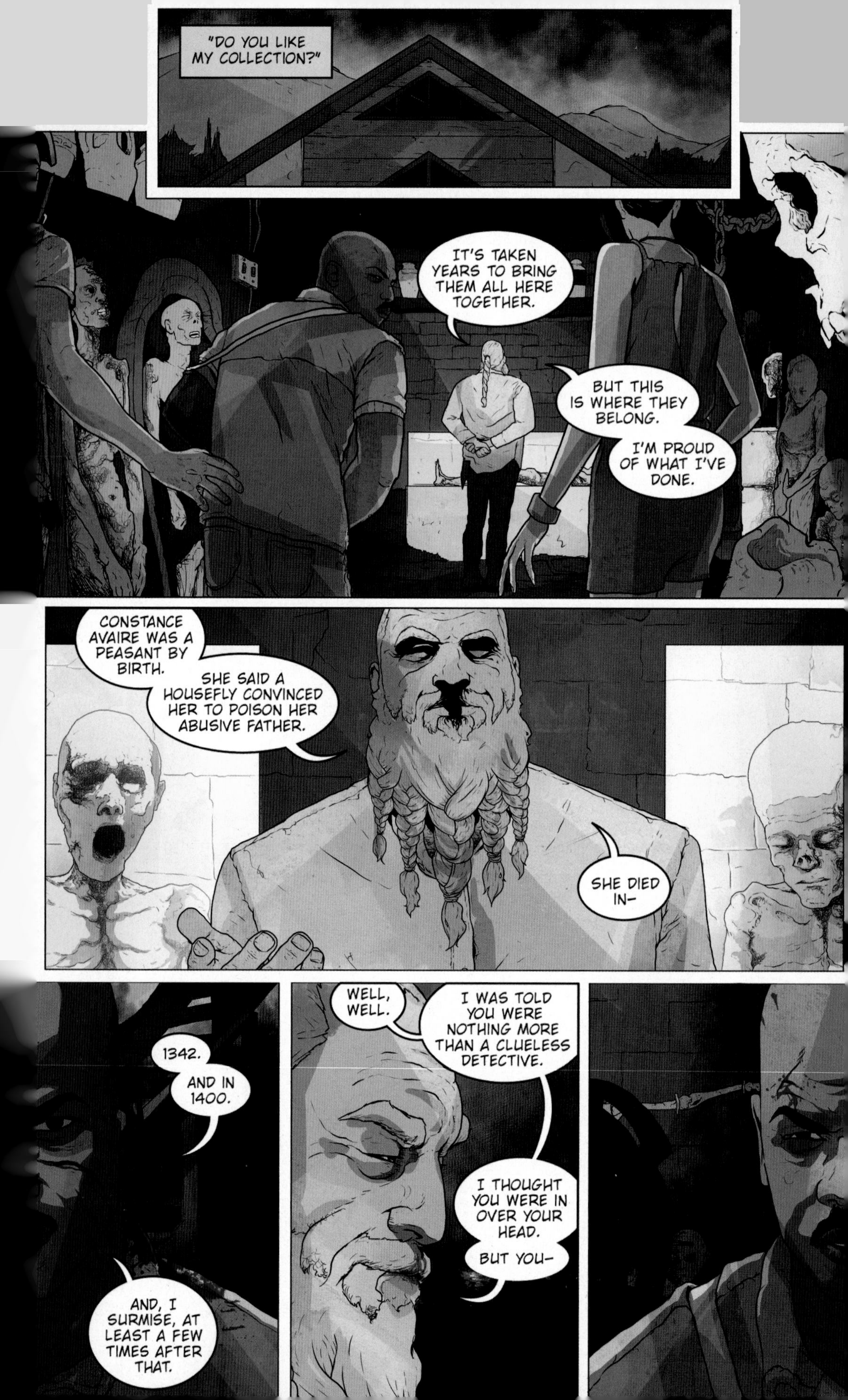
"DO YOU LIKE MY COLLECTION?"
IT'S TAKEN YEARS TO BRING THEM ALL HERE TOGETHER.
BUT THIS IS WHERE THEY BELONG.
I'M PROUD OF WHAT I'VE DONE.
CONSTANCE AVAIRE WAS A PEASANT BY BIRTH.
SHE SAID A HOUSEFLY CONVINCED HER TO POISON HER ABUSIVE FATHER.
SHE DIED IN–
1342.
AND IN 1400.
AND, I SURMISE, AT LEAST A FEW TIMES AFTER THAT.
WELL, WELL.
I WAS TOLD YOU WERE NOTHING MORE THAN A CLUELESS DETECTIVE.
I THOUGHT YOU WERE IN OVER YOUR HEAD.
BUT YOU–

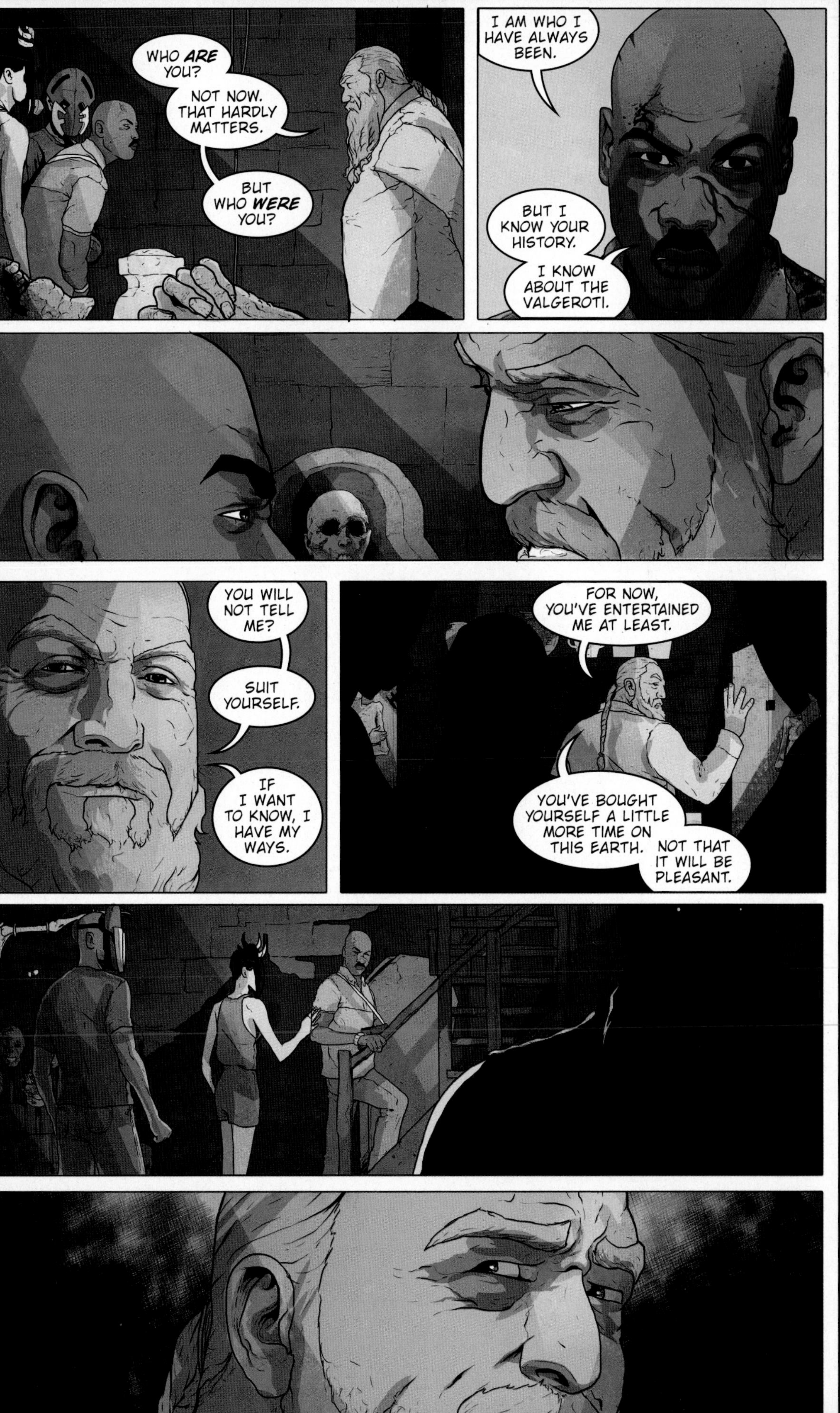
WHO *ARE* YOU?
NOT NOW. THAT HARDLY MATTERS.
BUT WHO *WERE* YOU?
I AM WHO I HAVE ALWAYS BEEN.
BUT I KNOW YOUR HISTORY.
I KNOW ABOUT THE VALGEROTI.
YOU WILL NOT TELL ME?
SUIT YOURSELF.
IF I WANT TO KNOW, I HAVE MY WAYS.
FOR NOW, YOU'VE ENTERTAINED ME AT LEAST.
YOU'VE BOUGHT YOURSELF A LITTLE MORE TIME ON THIS EARTH.
NOT THAT IT WILL BE PLEASANT.

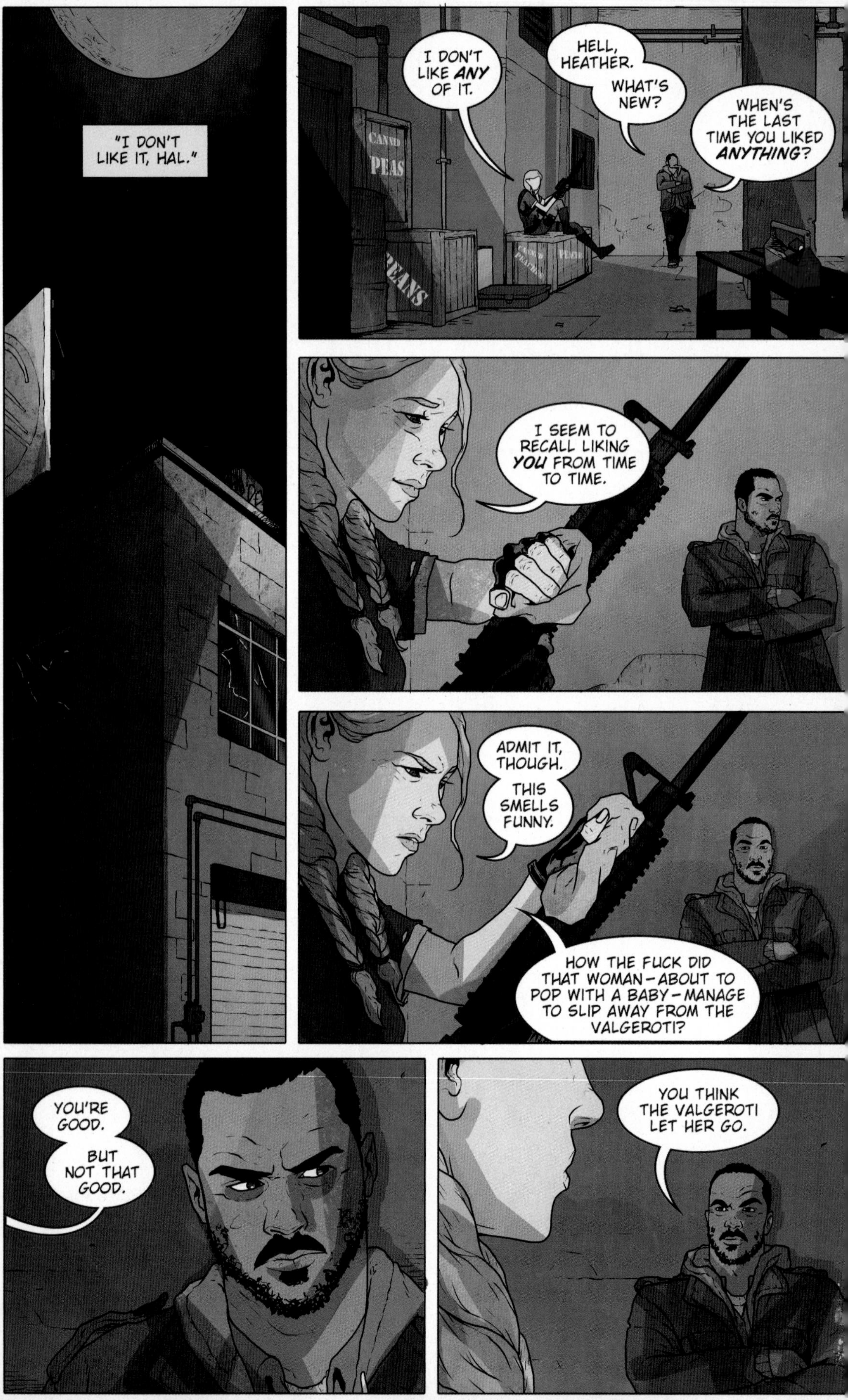
"I DON'T LIKE IT, HAL."
I DON'T LIKE ANY OF IT.
HELL, HEATHER.
WHAT'S NEW?
WHEN'S THE LAST TIME YOU LIKED ANYTHING?
I SEEM TO RECALL LIKING YOU FROM TIME TO TIME.
ADMIT IT, THOUGH.
THIS SMELLS FUNNY.
HOW THE FUCK DID THAT WOMAN—ABOUT TO POP WITH A BABY—MANAGE TO SLIP AWAY FROM THE VALGEROTI?
YOU'RE GOOD.
BUT NOT THAT GOOD.
YOU THINK THE VALGEROTI LET HER GO.

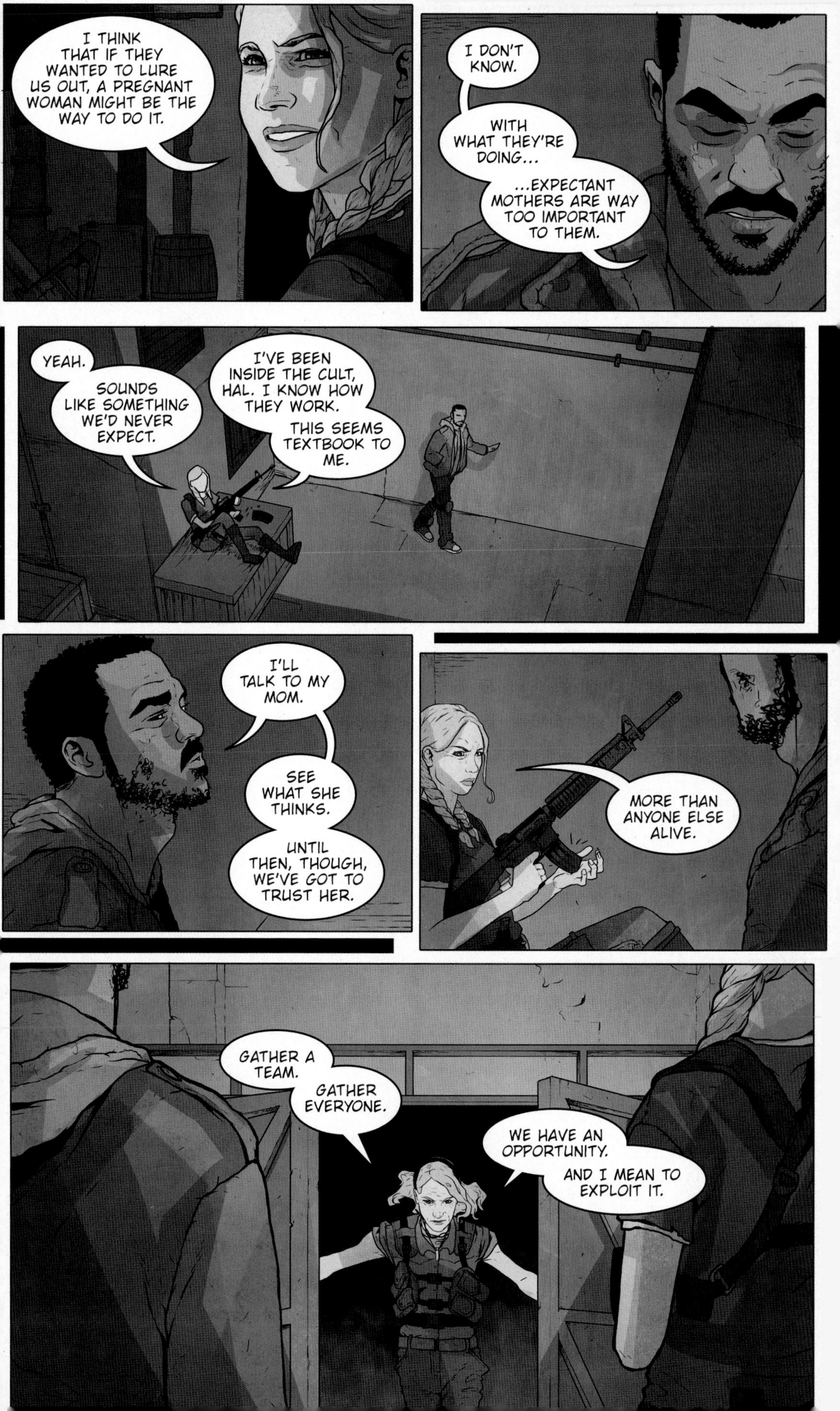
I THINK THAT IF THEY WANTED TO LURE US OUT, A PREGNANT WOMAN MIGHT BE THE WAY TO DO IT.
I DON'T KNOW.
WITH WHAT THEY'RE DOING...
...EXPECTANT MOTHERS ARE WAY TOO IMPORTANT TO THEM.
YEAH.
SOUNDS LIKE SOMETHING WE'D NEVER EXPECT.
I'VE BEEN INSIDE THE CULT, HAL. I KNOW HOW THEY WORK.
THIS SEEMS TEXTBOOK TO ME.
I'LL TALK TO MY MOM.
SEE WHAT SHE THINKS.
UNTIL THEN, THOUGH, WE'VE GOT TO TRUST HER.
MORE THAN ANYONE ELSE ALIVE.
GATHER A TEAM.
GATHER EVERYONE.
WE HAVE AN OPPORTUNITY.
AND I MEAN TO EXPLOIT IT.

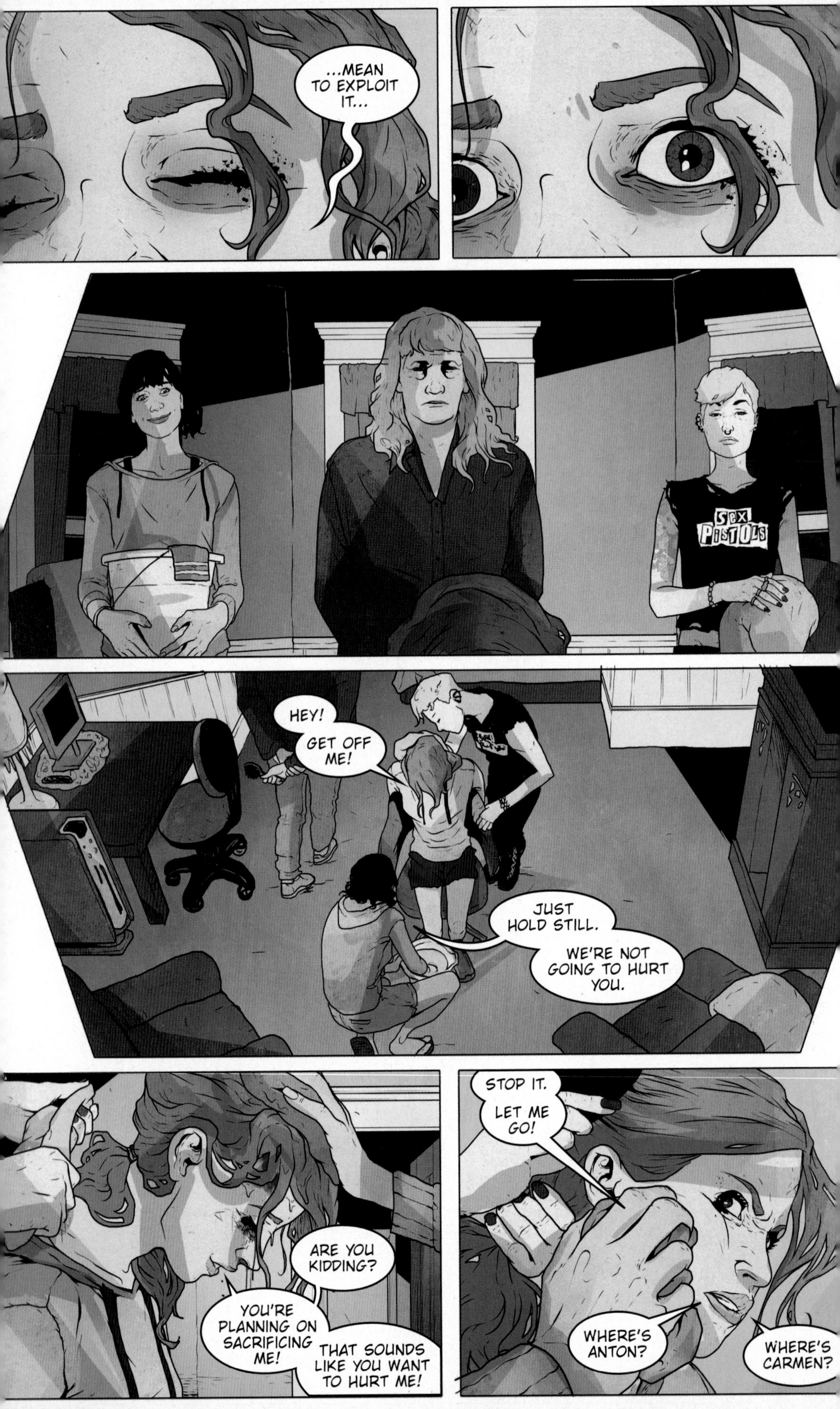
...MEAN TO EXPLOIT IT...
SEX PISTOLS
HEY!
GET OFF ME!
JUST HOLD STILL.
WE'RE NOT GOING TO HURT YOU.
ARE YOU KIDDING?
YOU'RE PLANNING ON SACRIFICING ME!
THAT SOUNDS LIKE YOU WANT TO HURT ME!
STOP IT.
LET ME GO!
WHERE'S ANTON?
WHERE'S CARMEN?

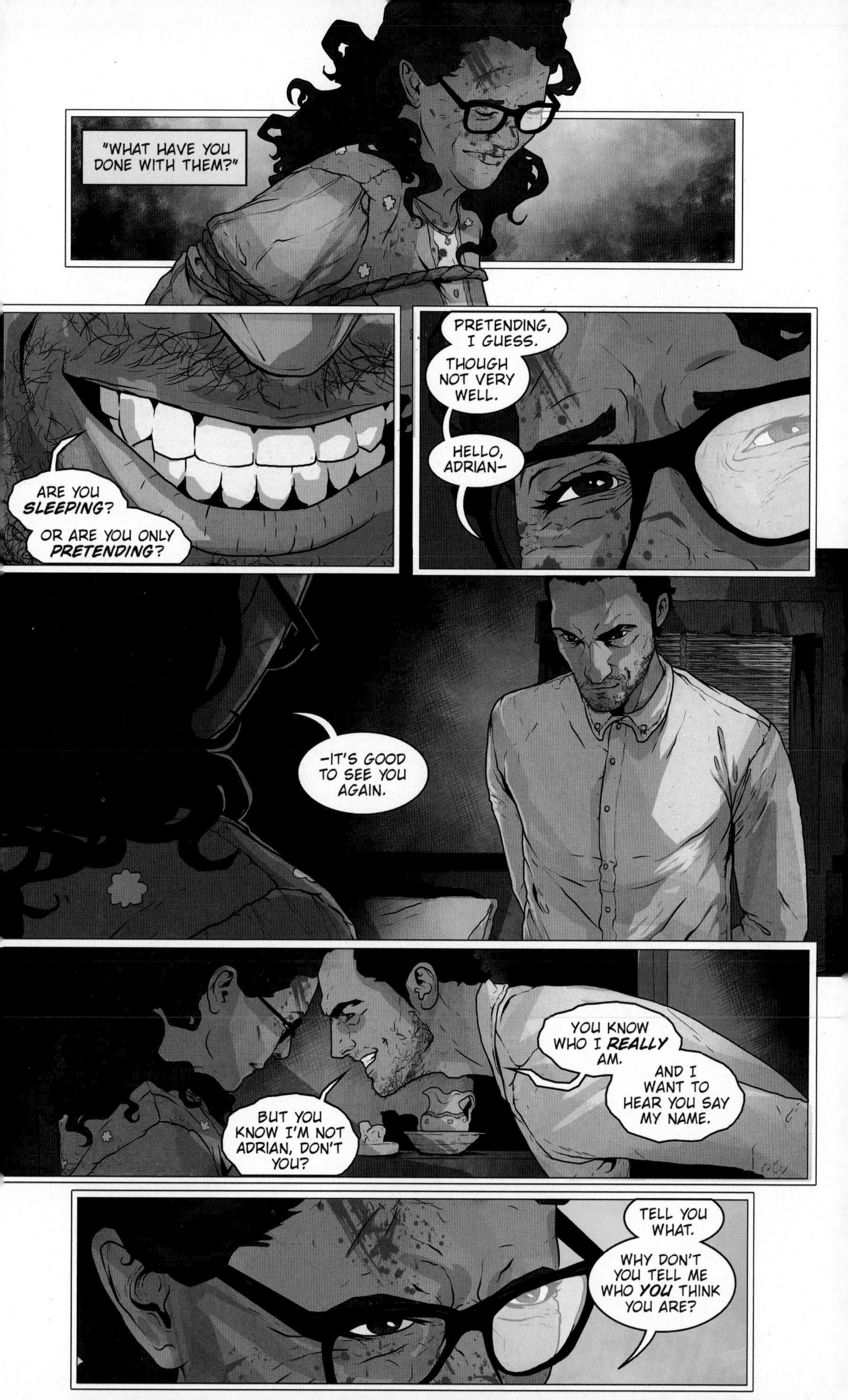
"WHAT HAVE YOU DONE WITH THEM?"
ARE YOU SLEEPING?
OR ARE YOU ONLY PRETENDING?
PRETENDING, I GUESS.
THOUGH NOT VERY WELL.
HELLO, ADRIAN–
–IT'S GOOD TO SEE YOU AGAIN.
BUT YOU KNOW I'M NOT ADRIAN, DON'T YOU?
YOU KNOW WHO I REALLY AM.
AND I WANT TO HEAR YOU SAY MY NAME.
TELL YOU WHAT.
WHY DON'T YOU TELL ME WHO YOU THINK YOU ARE?

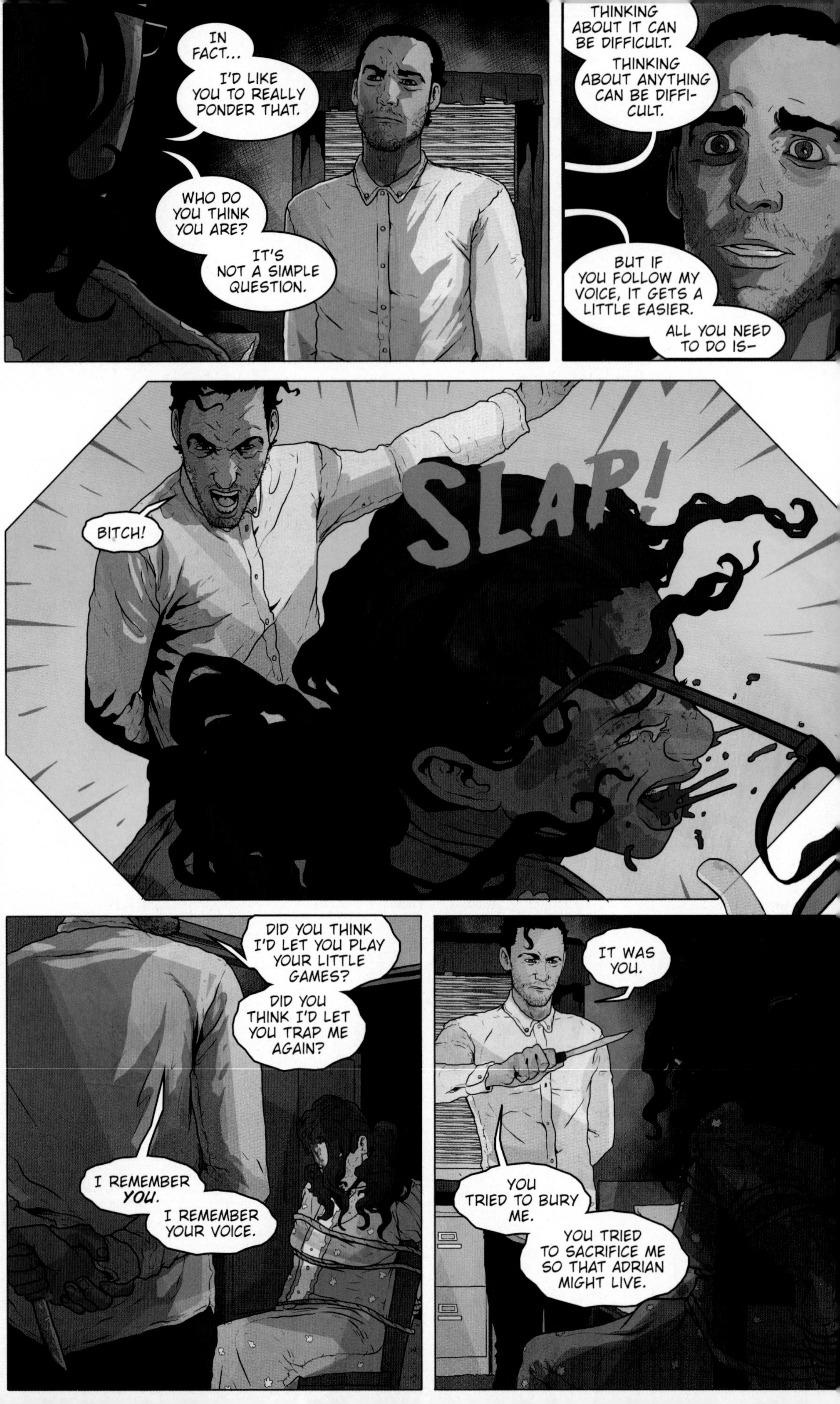

IN FACT...
I'D LIKE YOU TO REALLY PONDER THAT.
WHO DO YOU THINK YOU ARE?
IT'S NOT A SIMPLE QUESTION.
THINKING ABOUT IT CAN BE DIFFICULT.
THINKING ABOUT ANYTHING CAN BE DIFFI- CULT.
BUT IF YOU FOLLOW MY VOICE, IT GETS A LITTLE EASIER.
ALL YOU NEED TO DO IS-
BITCH!
SLAP!
DID YOU THINK I'D LET YOU PLAY YOUR LITTLE GAMES?
DID YOU THINK I'D LET YOU TRAP ME AGAIN?
I REMEMBER YOU.
I REMEMBER YOUR VOICE.
IT WAS YOU.
YOU TRIED TO BURY ME.
YOU TRIED TO SACRIFICE ME SO THAT ADRIAN MIGHT LIVE.

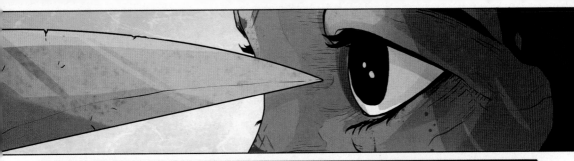

WAIT, GREGORY.

WAIT?

YOU WANT ME TO DELAY MY VENGEANCE FURTHER?

DO YOU KNOW WHAT THIS WOMAN HAS DONE TO ME?

I KNOW.

BUT I WORRY.

I WORRY THAT WE ARE ACTING TOO HASTILY.

WE HAVE NOTHING IF NOT TIME.

SHE CAST ME INTO THE VOID.

SHE SUBDUED ME.

SHE WAS ALMOST MY *UNDOING.*

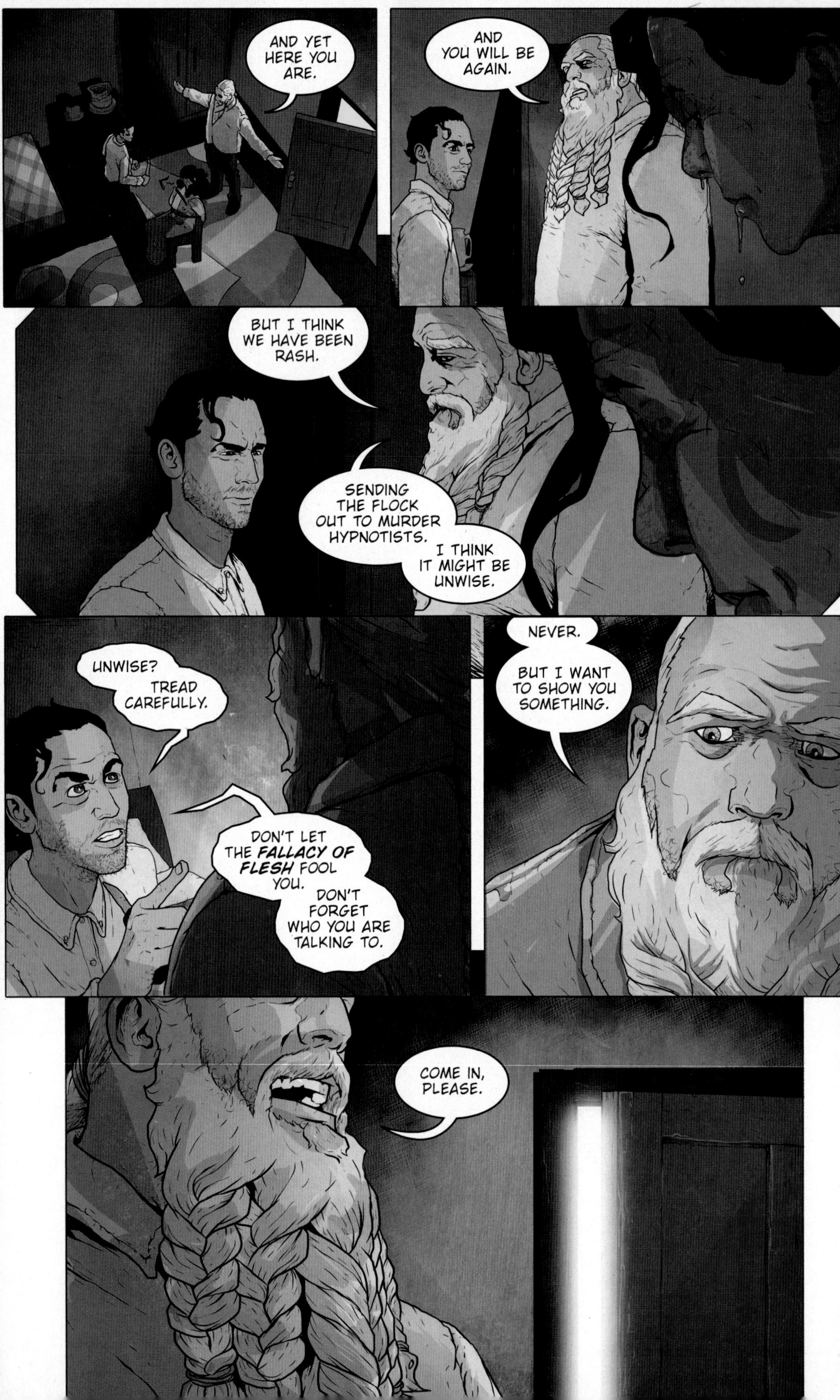
AND YET HERE YOU ARE.
AND YOU WILL BE AGAIN.
BUT I THINK WE HAVE BEEN RASH.
SENDING THE FLOCK OUT TO MURDER HYPNOTISTS.
I THINK IT MIGHT BE UNWISE.
UNWISE?
TREAD CAREFULLY.
DON'T LET THE **FALLACY OF FLESH** FOOL YOU.
DON'T FORGET WHO YOU ARE TALKING TO.
NEVER.
BUT I WANT TO SHOW YOU SOMETHING.
COME IN, PLEASE.

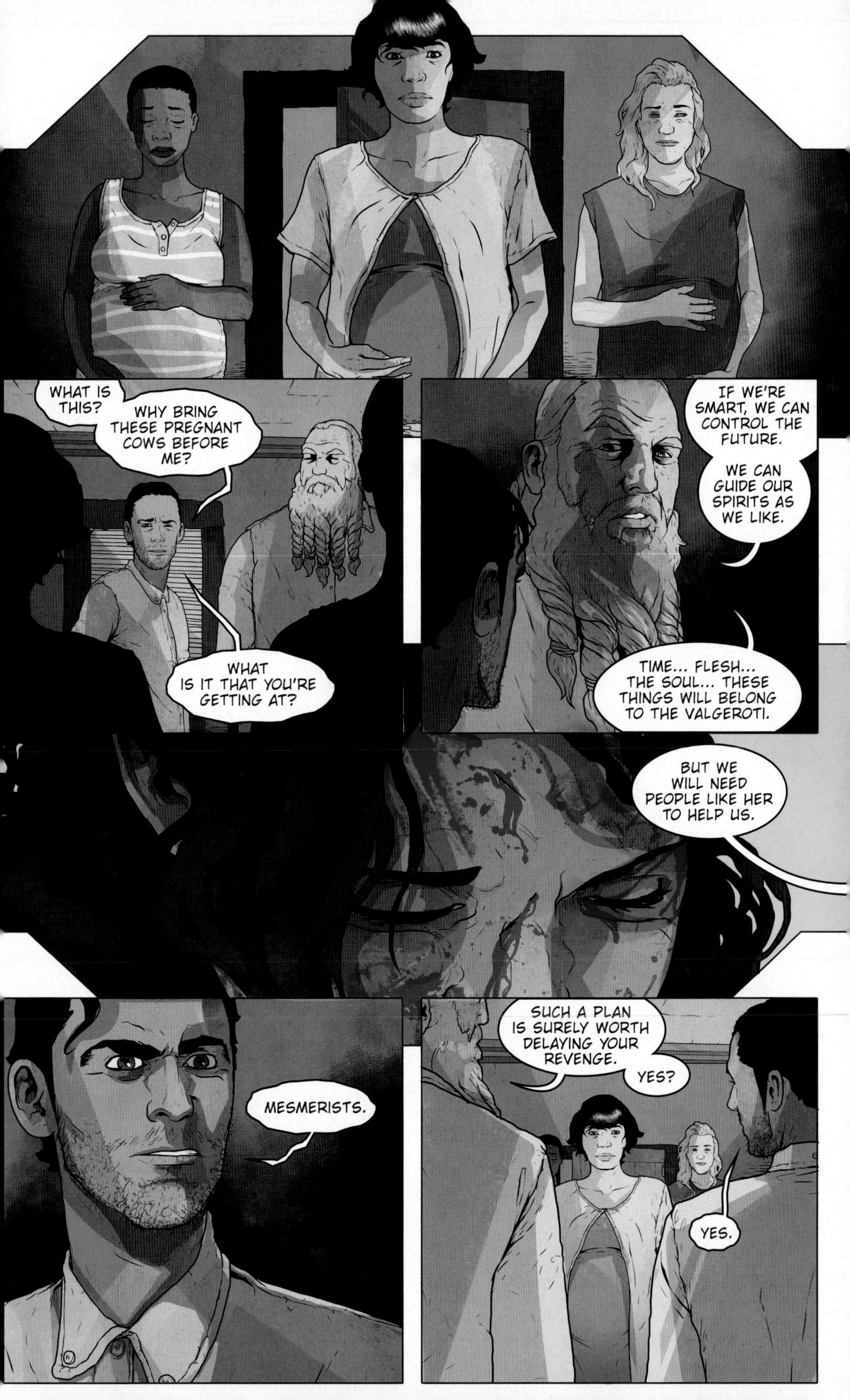
WHAT IS THIS?
WHY BRING THESE PREGNANT COWS BEFORE ME?
WHAT IS IT THAT YOU'RE GETTING AT?
IF WE'RE SMART, WE CAN CONTROL THE FUTURE.
WE CAN GUIDE OUR SPIRITS AS WE LIKE.
TIME... FLESH... THE SOUL... THESE THINGS WILL BELONG TO THE VALGEROTI.
BUT WE WILL NEED PEOPLE LIKE HER TO HELP US.
MESMERISTS.
SUCH A PLAN IS SURELY WORTH DELAYING YOUR REVENGE.
YES?
YES.

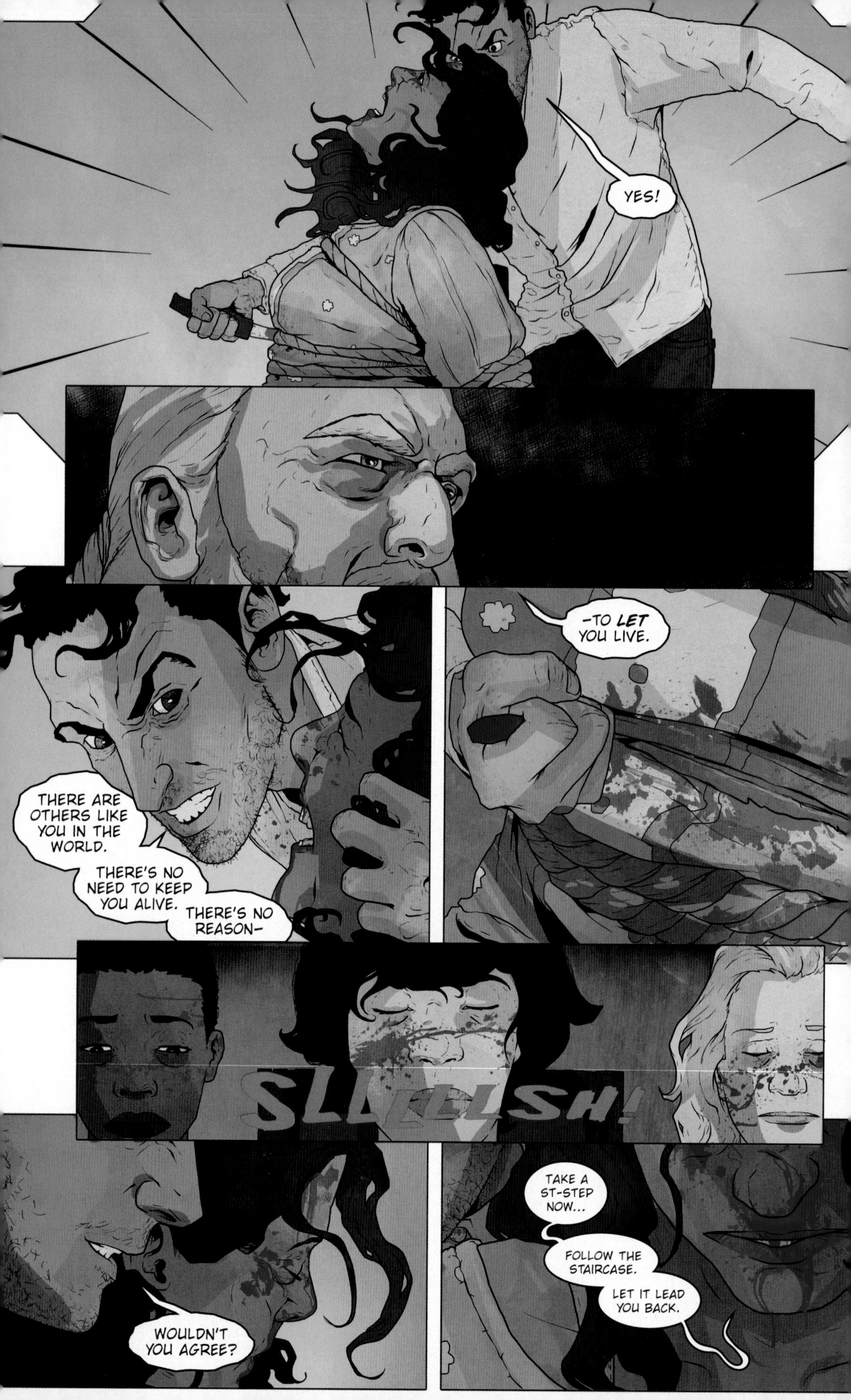
YES!
THERE ARE OTHERS LIKE YOU IN THE WORLD.
THERE'S NO NEED TO KEEP YOU ALIVE.
THERE'S NO REASON-
-TO LET YOU LIVE.
SLLLLSH!
WOULDN'T YOU AGREE?
TAKE A ST-STEP NOW...
FOLLOW THE STAIRCASE.
LET IT LEAD YOU BACK.

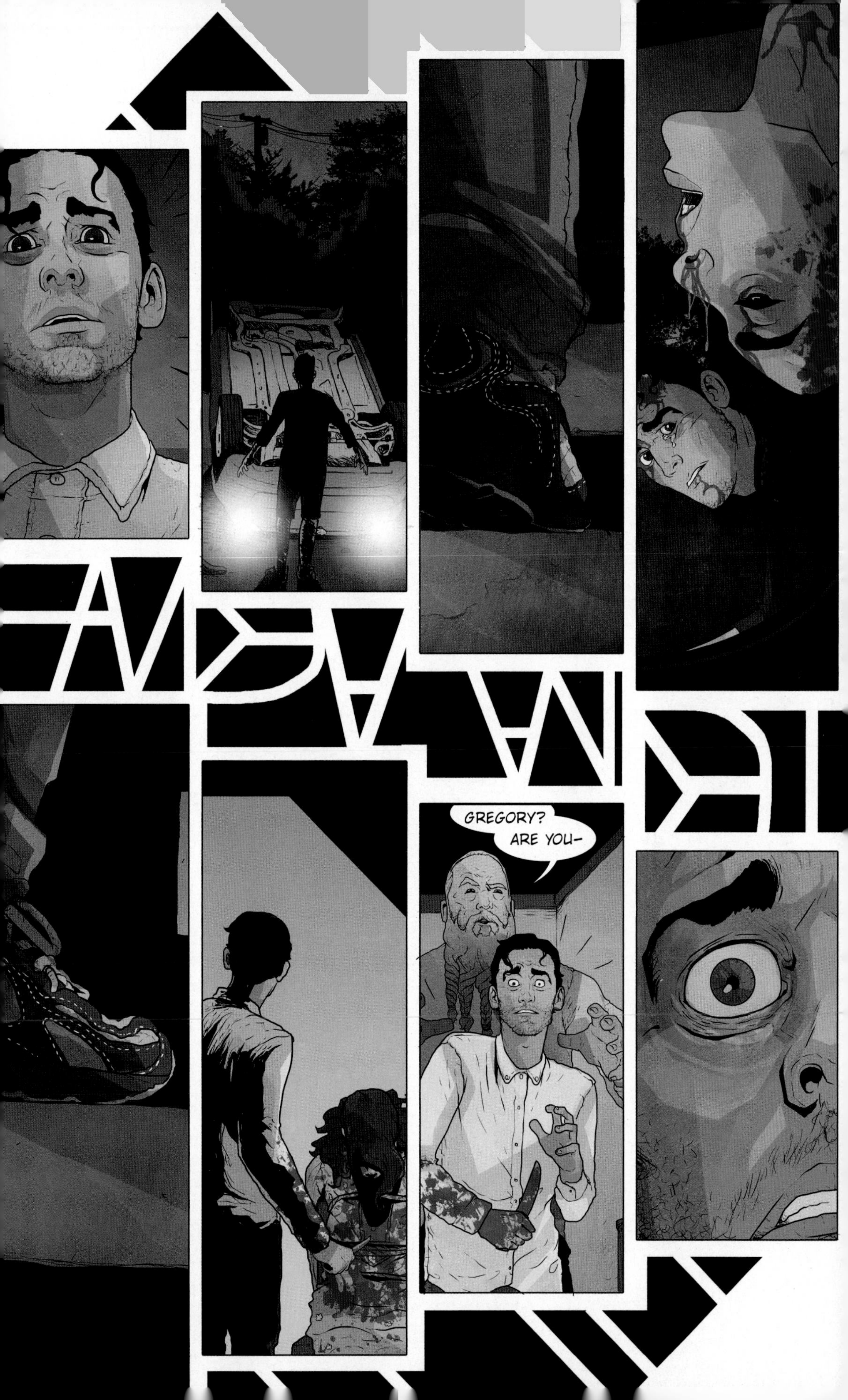
GREGORY?
ARE YOU-

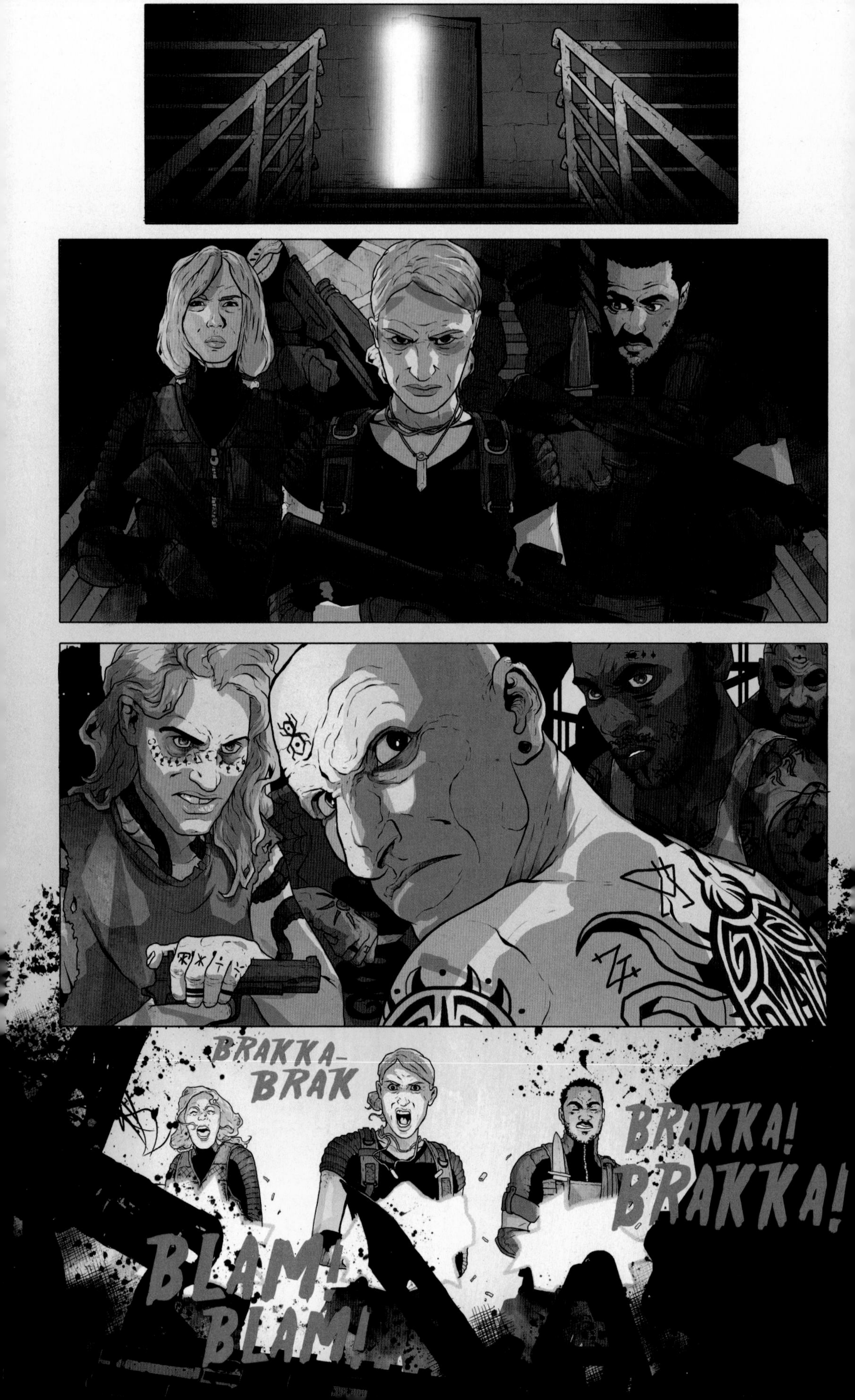
BRAKKA-
BRAK
BRAKKA!
BRAKKA!
BLAM!
BLAM!

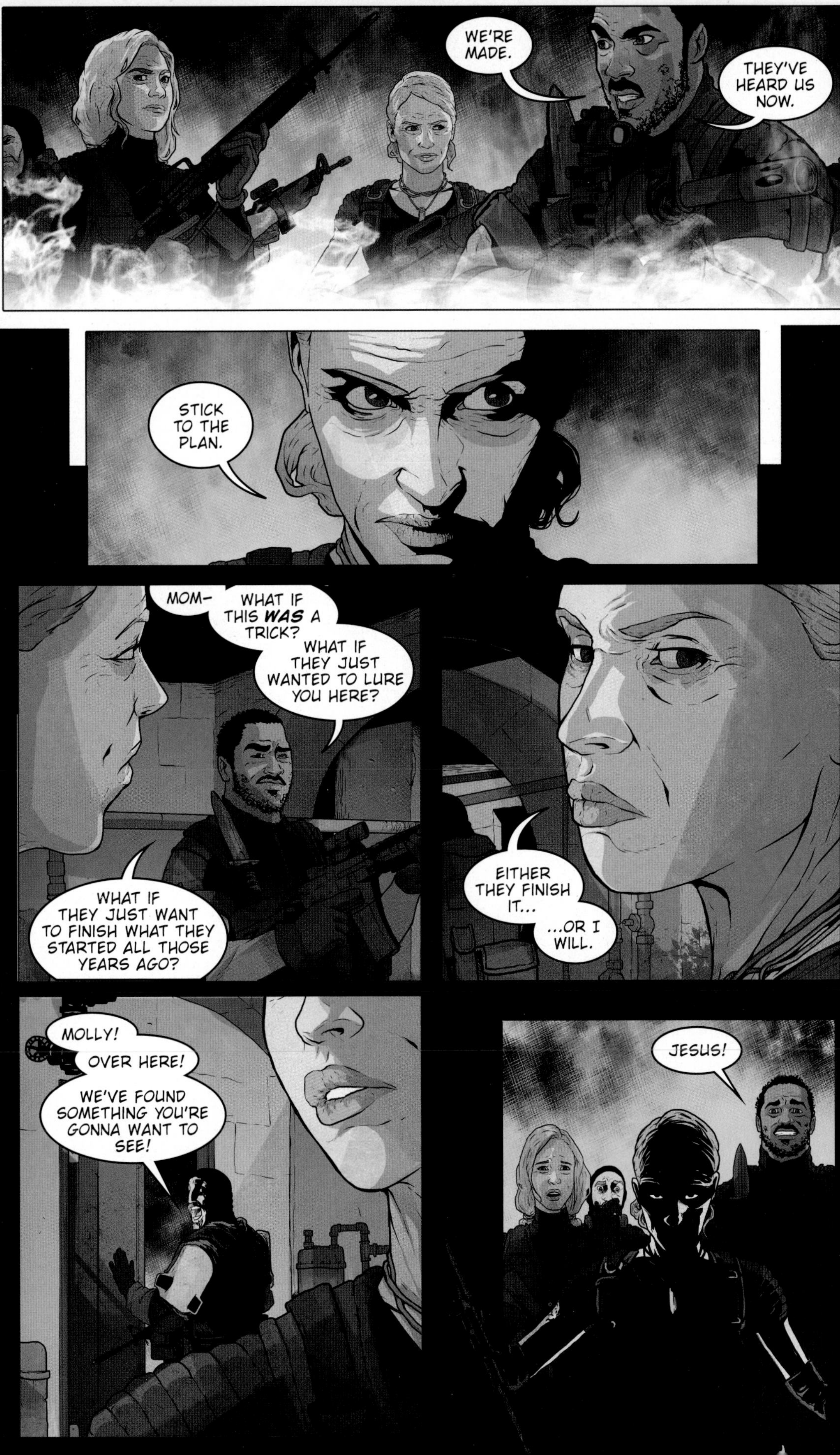
WE'RE MADE.
THEY'VE HEARD US NOW.
STICK TO THE PLAN.
MOM-
WHAT IF THIS WAS A TRICK?
WHAT IF THEY JUST WANTED TO LURE YOU HERE?
WHAT IF THEY JUST WANT TO FINISH WHAT THEY STARTED ALL THOSE YEARS AGO?
EITHER THEY FINISH IT...
...OR I WILL.
MOLLY!
OVER HERE!
WE'VE FOUND SOMETHING YOU'RE GONNA WANT TO SEE!
JESUS!

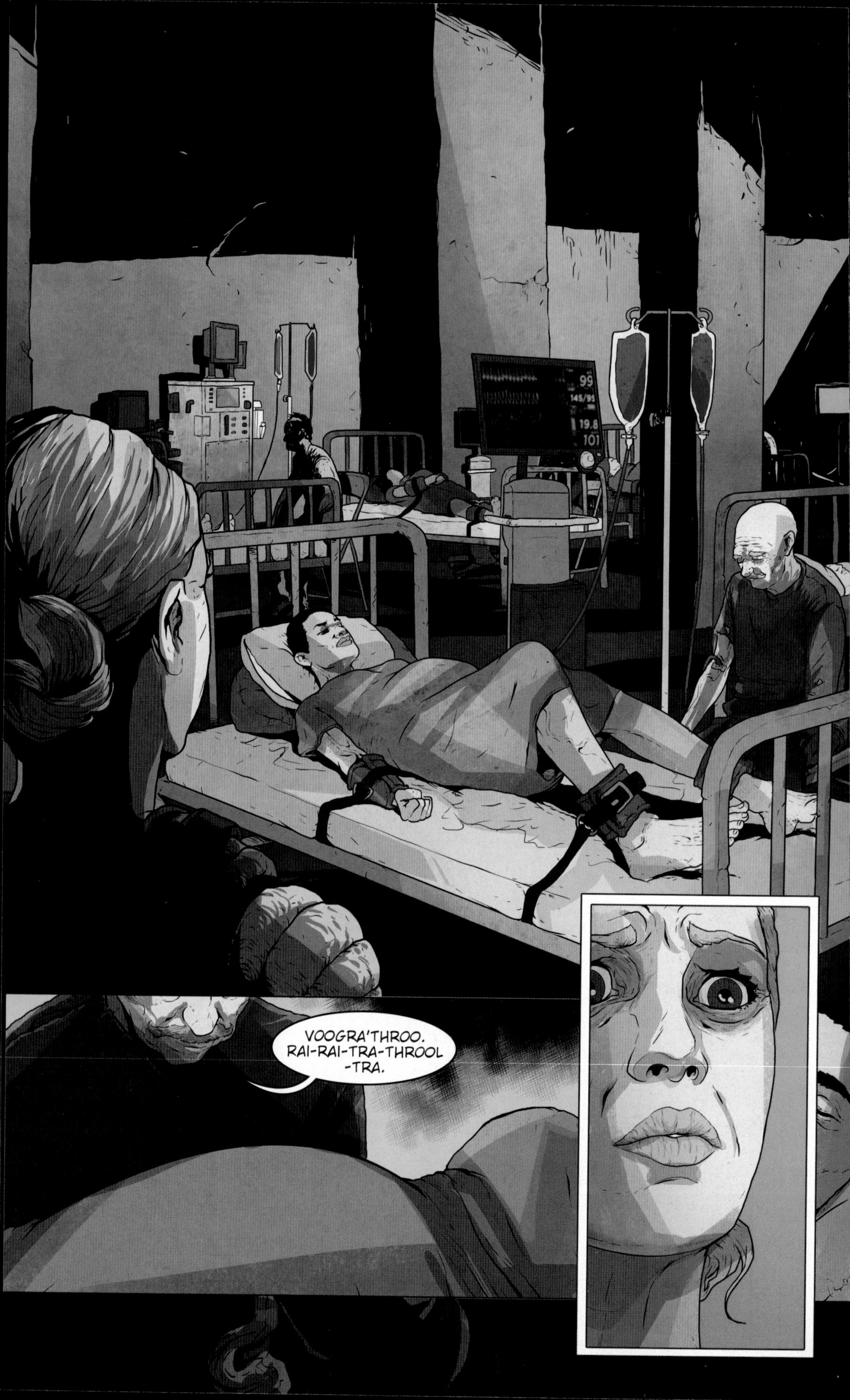
VOOGRA'THROO. RAI-RAI-TRA-THROOL -TRA.

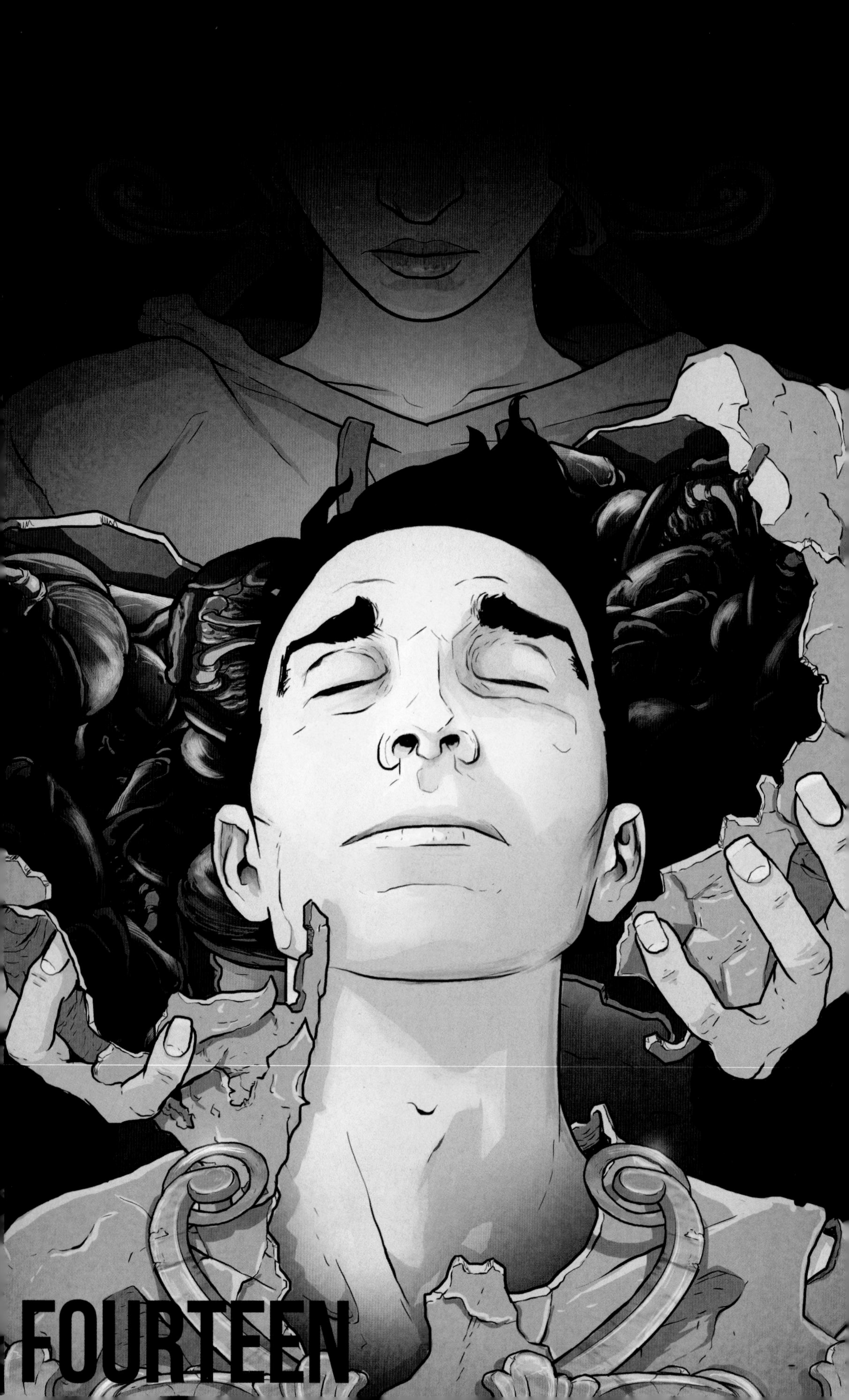
FOURTEEN

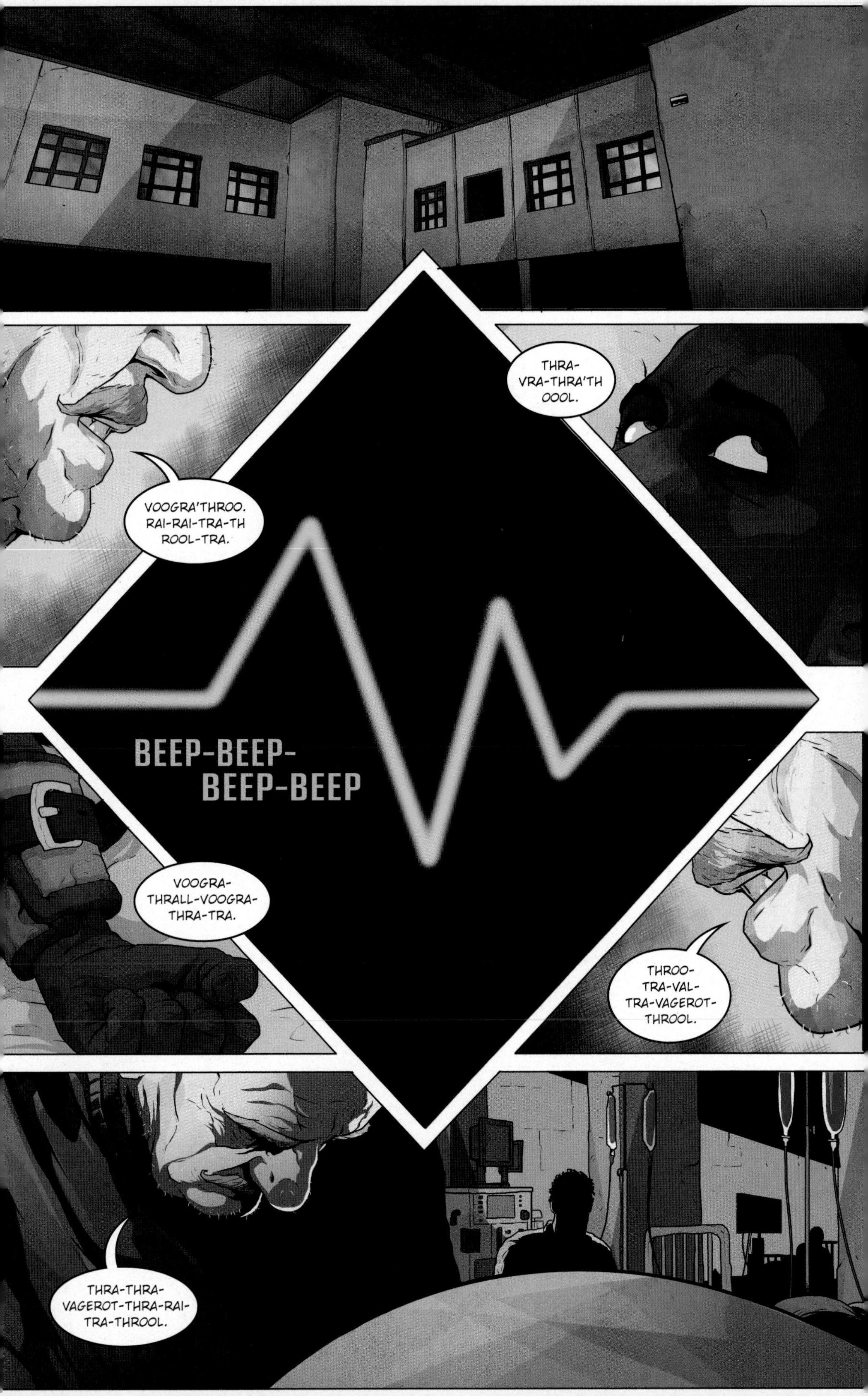
THRA-
VRA-THRA'TH
OOOL.
VOOGRA'THROO.
RAI-RAI-TRA-TH
ROOL-TRA.
BEEP-BEEP-
BEEP-BEEP
VOOGRA-
THRALL-VOOGRA-
THRA-TRA.
THROO-
TRA-VAL-
TRA-VAGEROT-
THROOL.
THRA-THRA-
VAGEROT-THRA-RAI-
TRA-THROOL.

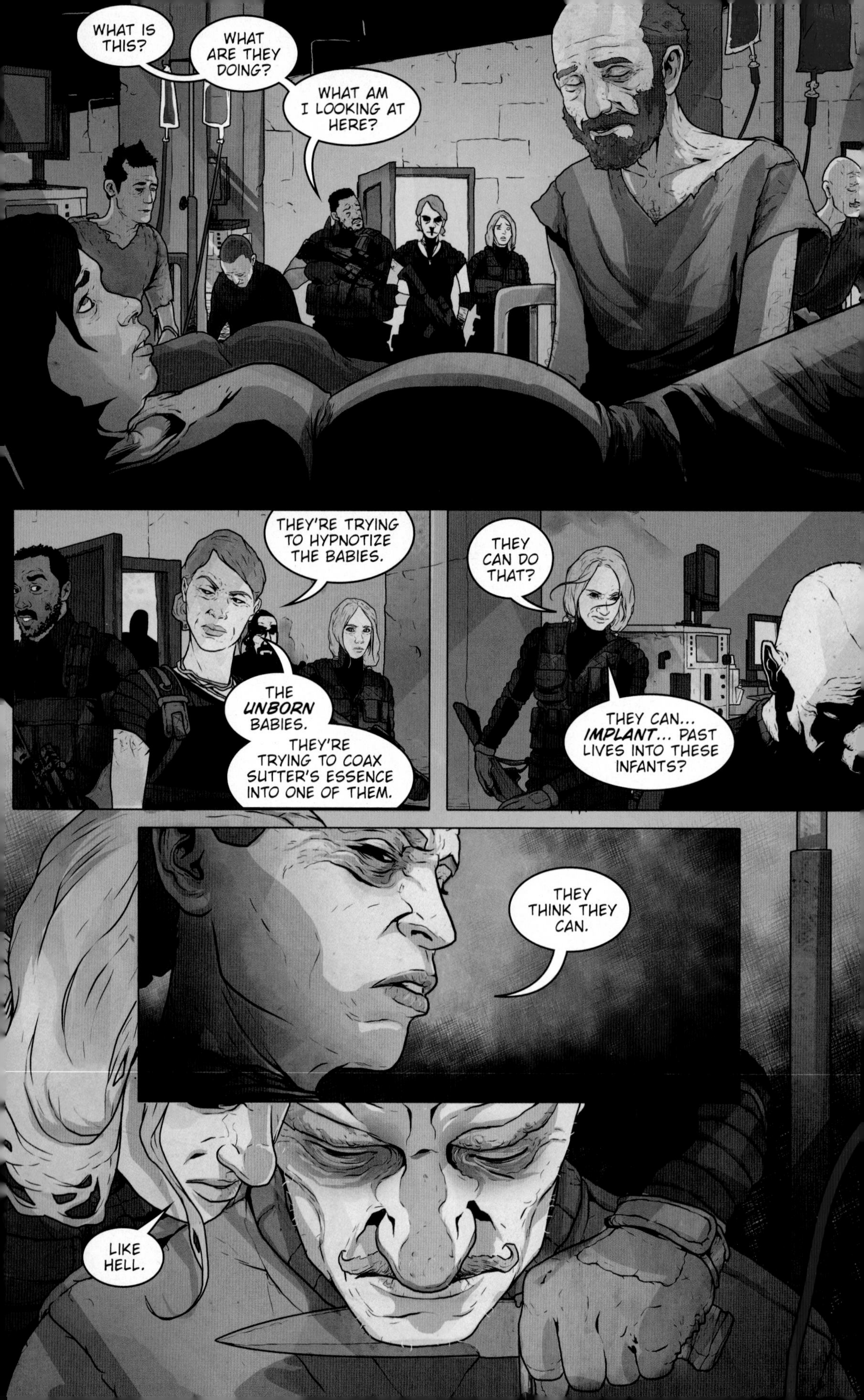
WHAT IS THIS?
WHAT ARE THEY DOING?
WHAT AM I LOOKING AT HERE?
THEY'RE TRYING TO HYPNOTIZE THE BABIES.
THE *UNBORN* BABIES.
THEY'RE TRYING TO COAX SUTTER'S ESSENCE INTO ONE OF THEM.
THEY CAN DO THAT?
THEY CAN... *IMPLANT*... PAST LIVES INTO THESE INFANTS?
THEY THINK THEY CAN.
LIKE HELL.

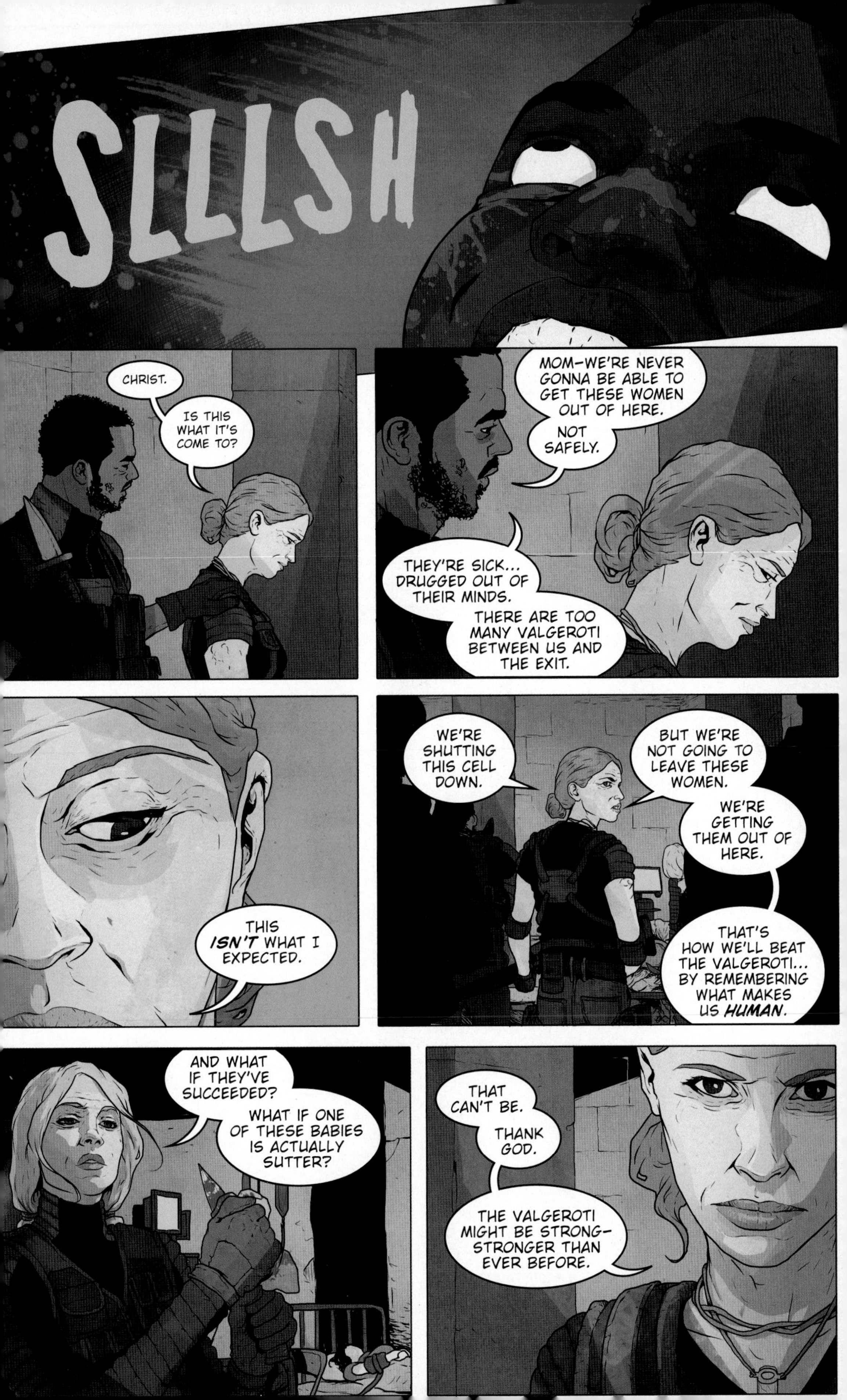
SLLSH
CHRIST.
IS THIS WHAT IT'S COME TO?
MOM—WE'RE NEVER GONNA BE ABLE TO GET THESE WOMEN OUT OF HERE.
NOT SAFELY.
THEY'RE SICK... DRUGGED OUT OF THEIR MINDS.
THERE ARE TOO MANY VALGEROTI BETWEEN US AND THE EXIT.
THIS *ISN'T* WHAT I EXPECTED.
WE'RE SHUTTING THIS CELL DOWN.
BUT WE'RE NOT GOING TO LEAVE THESE WOMEN.
WE'RE GETTING THEM OUT OF HERE.
THAT'S HOW WE'LL BEAT THE VALGEROTI... BY REMEMBERING WHAT MAKES US *HUMAN*.
AND WHAT IF THEY'VE SUCCEEDED?
WHAT IF ONE OF THESE BABIES IS ACTUALLY SUTTER?
THAT CAN'T BE.
THANK GOD.
THE VALGEROTI MIGHT BE STRONG-STRONGER THAN EVER BEFORE.

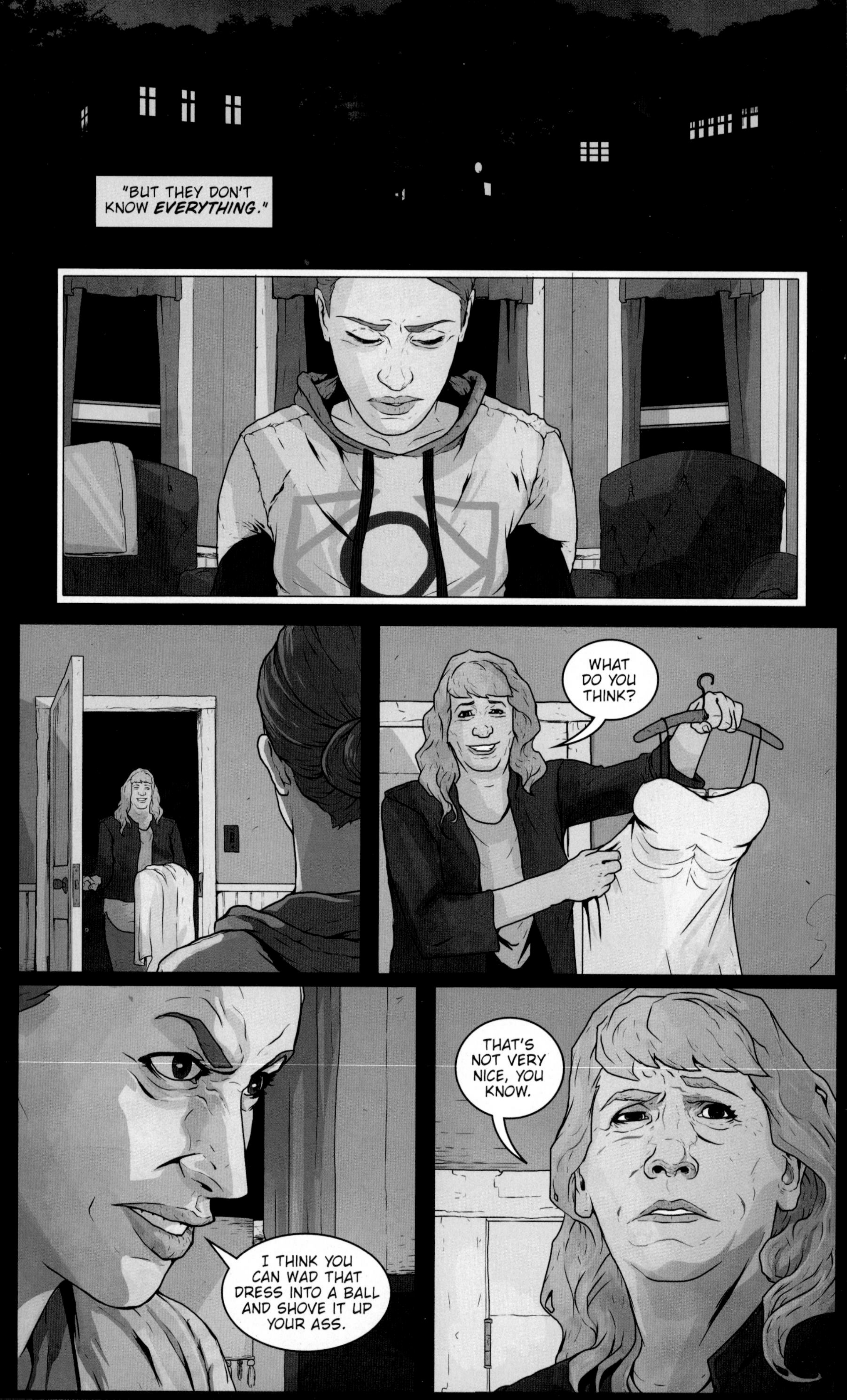
"BUT THEY DON'T KNOW *EVERYTHING*."
WHAT DO YOU THINK?
I THINK YOU CAN WAD THAT DRESS INTO A BALL AND SHOVE IT UP YOUR ASS.
THAT'S NOT VERY NICE, YOU KNOW.

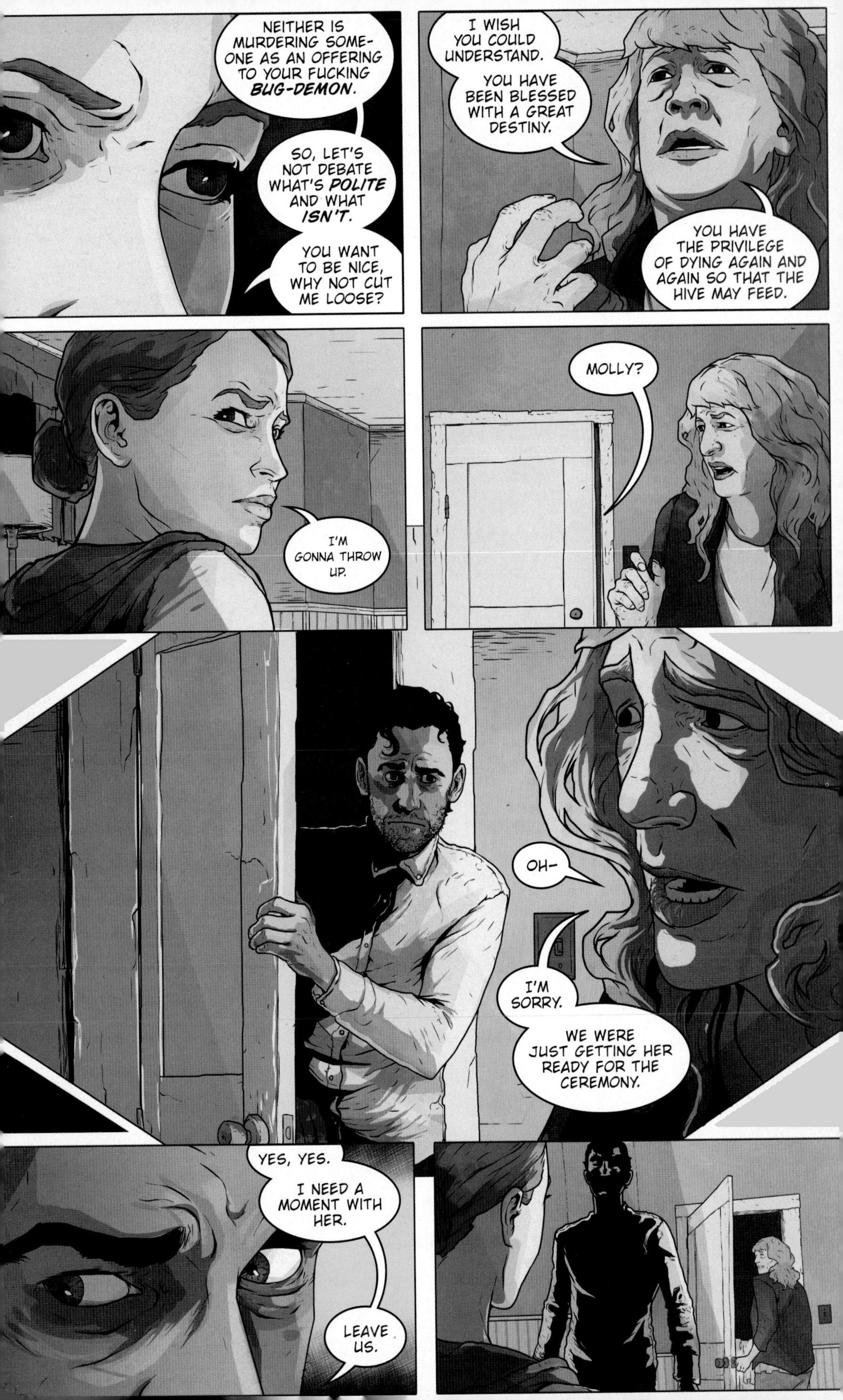
NEITHER IS MURDERING SOME-ONE AS AN OFFERING TO YOUR FUCKING *BUG-DEMON*.
SO, LET'S NOT DEBATE WHAT'S *POLITE* AND WHAT *ISN'T*.
YOU WANT TO BE NICE, WHY NOT CUT ME LOOSE?
I WISH YOU COULD UNDERSTAND.
YOU HAVE BEEN BLESSED WITH A GREAT DESTINY.
YOU HAVE THE PRIVILEGE OF DYING AGAIN AND AGAIN SO THAT THE HIVE MAY FEED.
I'M GONNA THROW UP.
MOLLY?
OH-
I'M SORRY.
WE WERE JUST GETTING HER READY FOR THE CEREMONY.
YES, YES.
I NEED A MOMENT WITH HER.
LEAVE US.

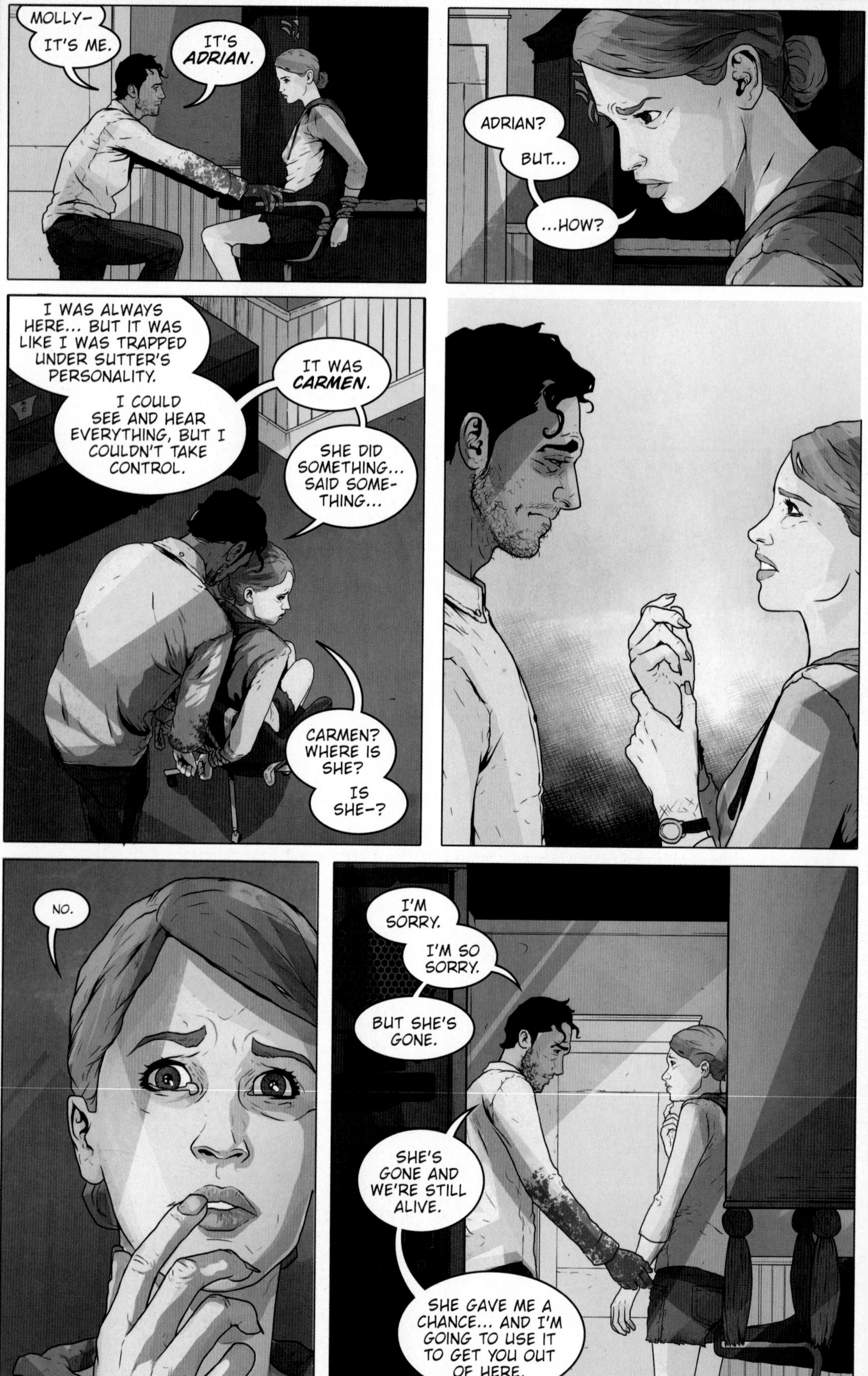

MOLLY–
IT'S ME.
IT'S *ADRIAN.*
ADRIAN?
BUT...
...HOW?
I WAS ALWAYS HERE... BUT IT WAS LIKE I WAS TRAPPED UNDER SUTTER'S PERSONALITY.
I COULD SEE AND HEAR EVERYTHING, BUT I COULDN'T TAKE CONTROL.
IT WAS *CARMEN.*
SHE DID SOMETHING... SAID SOME-THING...
CARMEN? WHERE IS SHE?
IS SHE–?
NO.
I'M SORRY.
I'M SO SORRY.
BUT SHE'S GONE.
SHE'S GONE AND WE'RE STILL ALIVE.
SHE GAVE ME A CHANCE... AND I'M GOING TO USE IT TO GET YOU OUT OF HERE.

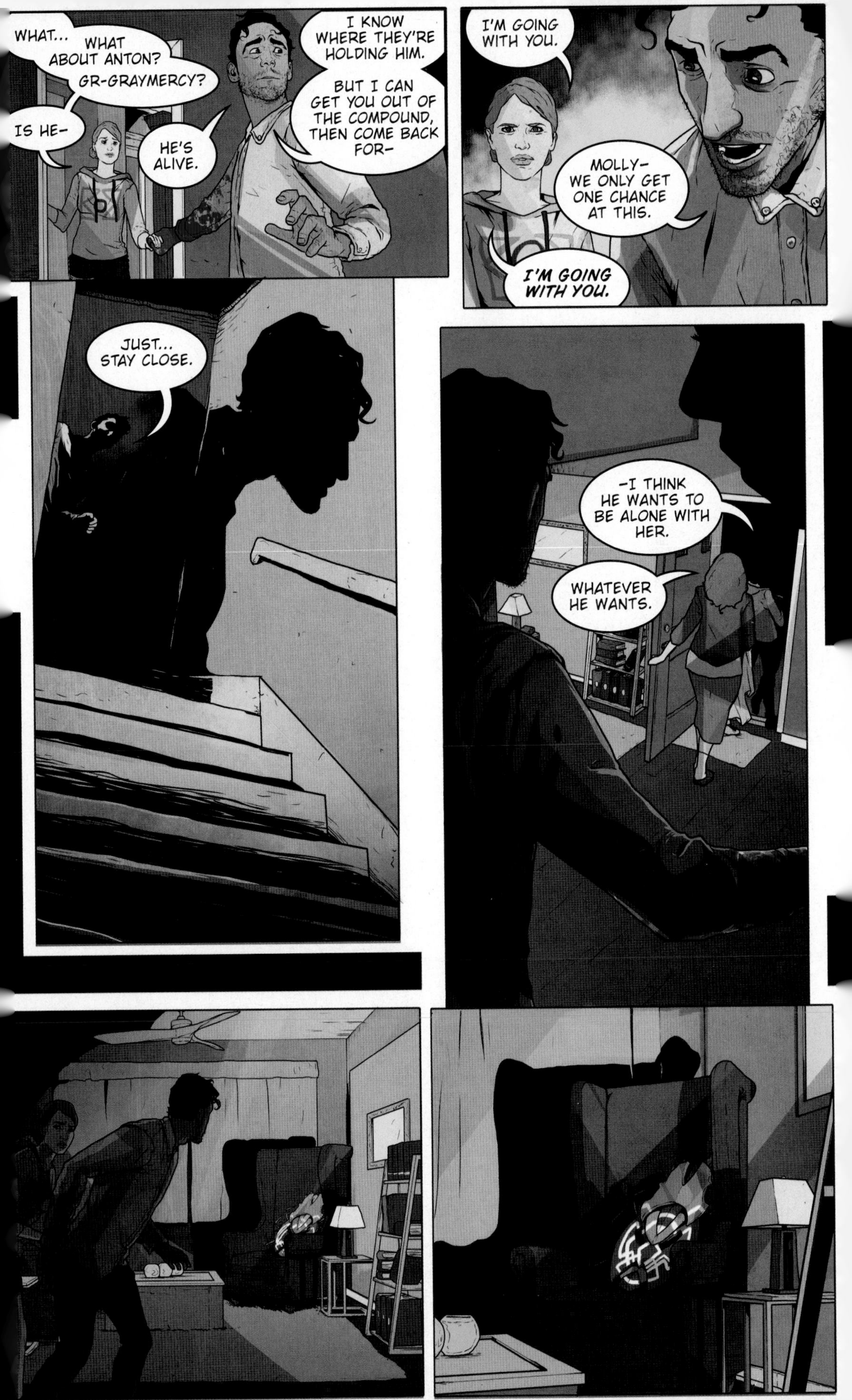
WHAT... WHAT ABOUT ANTON?
GR-GRAYMERCY?
IS HE-
HE'S ALIVE.
I KNOW WHERE THEY'RE HOLDING HIM.
BUT I CAN GET YOU OUT OF THE COMPOUND, THEN COME BACK FOR-
I'M GOING WITH YOU.
MOLLY- WE ONLY GET ONE CHANCE AT THIS.
I'M GOING WITH YOU.
JUST... STAY CLOSE.
-I THINK HE WANTS TO BE ALONE WITH HER.
WHATEVER HE WANTS.

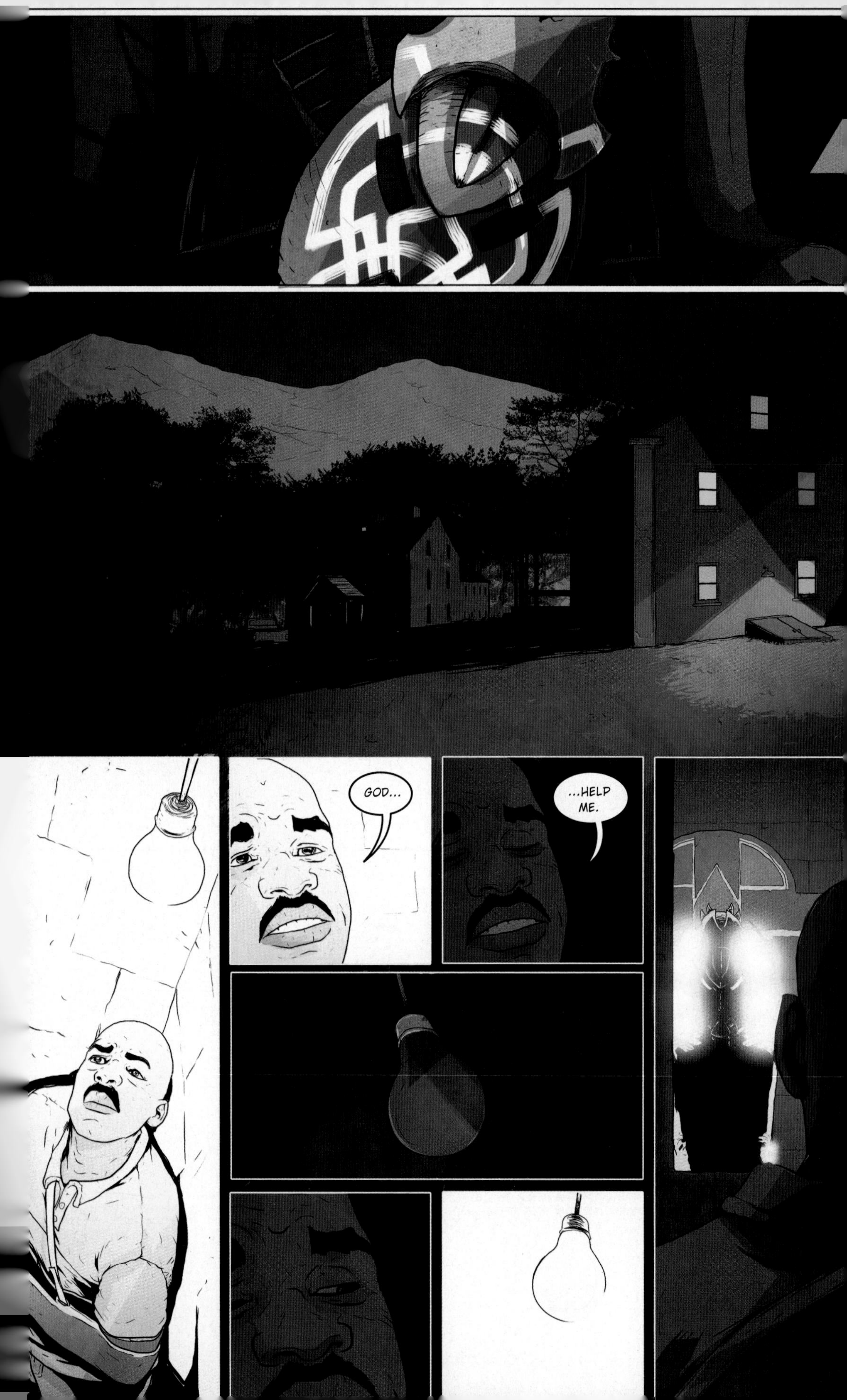
GOD...
...HELP ME.

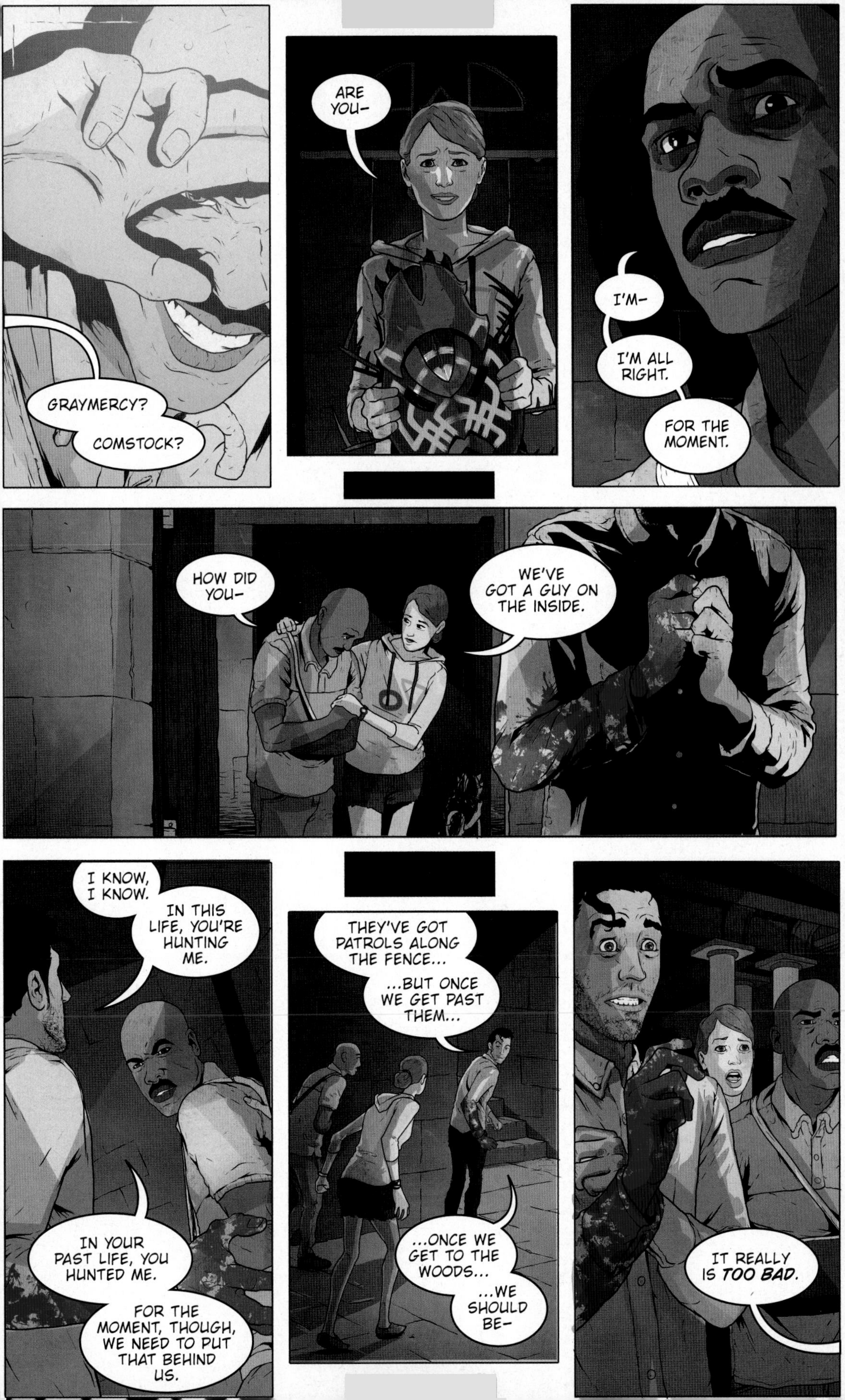
GRAYMERCY?
COMSTOCK?
ARE YOU-
I'M-
I'M ALL RIGHT.
FOR THE MOMENT.
[redacted]
HOW DID YOU-
WE'VE GOT A GUY ON THE INSIDE.
[redacted]
I KNOW, I KNOW.
IN THIS LIFE, YOU'RE HUNTING ME.
IN YOUR PAST LIFE, YOU HUNTED ME.
FOR THE MOMENT, THOUGH, WE NEED TO PUT THAT BEHIND US.
THEY'VE GOT PATROLS ALONG THE FENCE...
...BUT ONCE WE GET PAST THEM...
...ONCE WE GET TO THE WOODS...
...WE SHOULD BE-
IT REALLY IS *TOO BAD*.

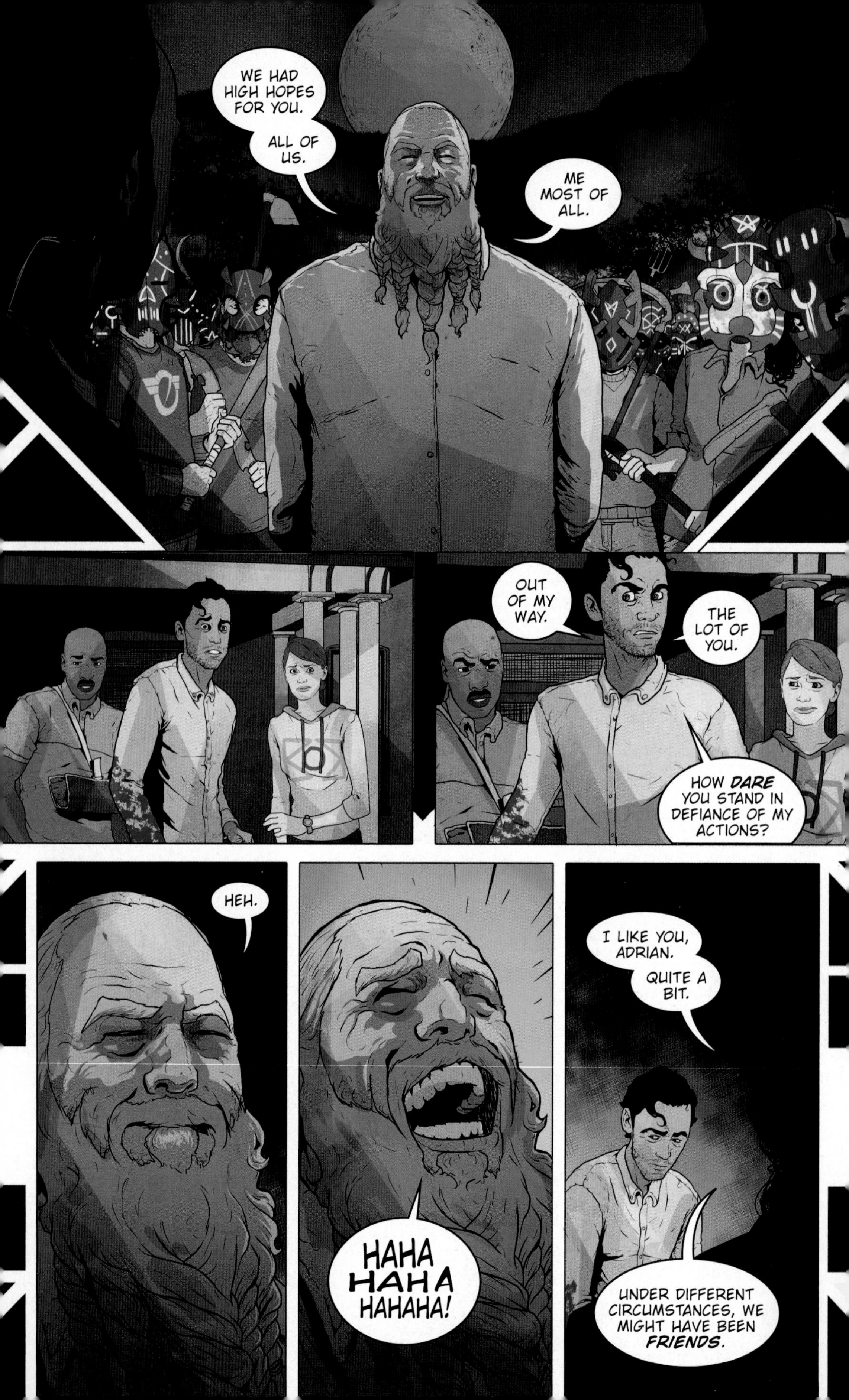
WE HAD HIGH HOPES FOR YOU.
ALL OF US.
ME MOST OF ALL.
OUT OF MY WAY.
THE LOT OF YOU.
HOW DARE YOU STAND IN DEFIANCE OF MY ACTIONS?
HEH.
HAHA HAHA HAHAHA!
I LIKE YOU, ADRIAN.
QUITE A BIT.
UNDER DIFFERENT CIRCUMSTANCES, WE MIGHT HAVE BEEN FRIENDS.

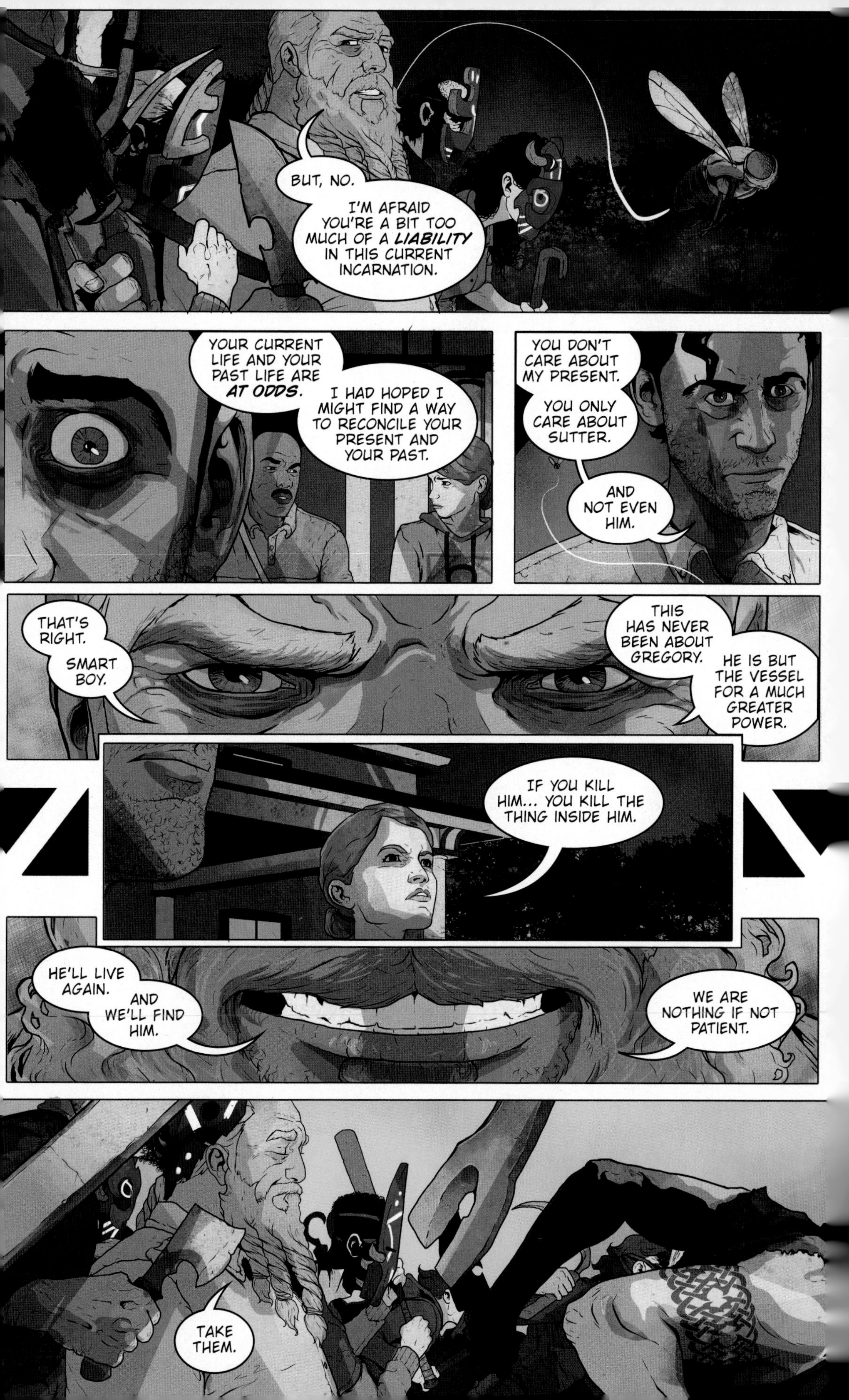
BUT, NO.
I'M AFRAID YOU'RE A BIT TOO MUCH OF A LIABILITY IN THIS CURRENT INCARNATION.
YOUR CURRENT LIFE AND YOUR PAST LIFE ARE AT ODDS.
I HAD HOPED I MIGHT FIND A WAY TO RECONCILE YOUR PRESENT AND YOUR PAST.
YOU DON'T CARE ABOUT MY PRESENT.
YOU ONLY CARE ABOUT SUTTER.
AND NOT EVEN HIM.
THAT'S RIGHT.
SMART BOY.
THIS HAS NEVER BEEN ABOUT GREGORY.
HE IS BUT THE VESSEL FOR A MUCH GREATER POWER.
IF YOU KILL HIM... YOU KILL THE THING INSIDE HIM.
HE'LL LIVE AGAIN.
AND WE'LL FIND HIM.
WE ARE NOTHING IF NOT PATIENT.
TAKE THEM.

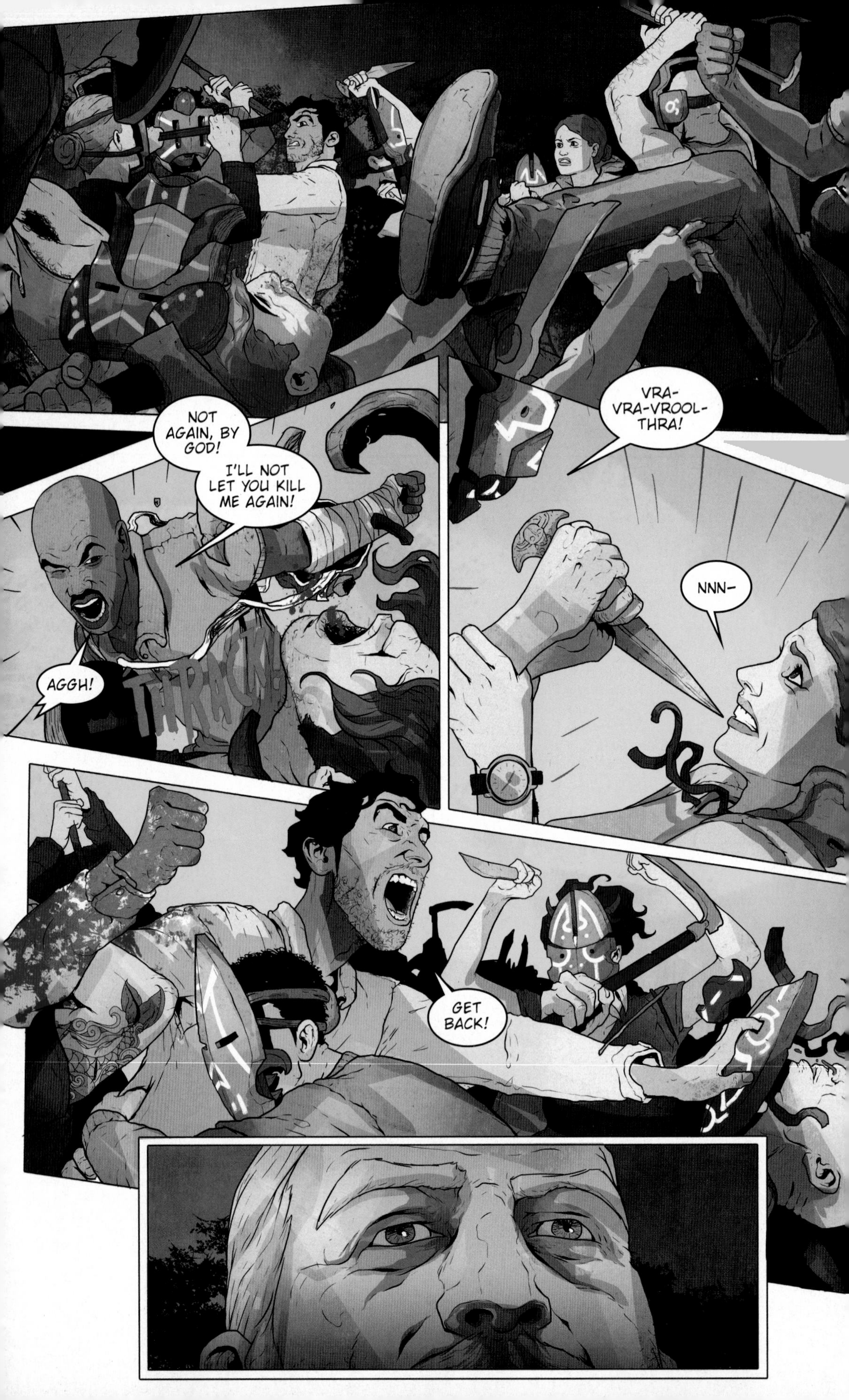
NOT AGAIN, BY GOD!
I'LL NOT LET YOU KILL ME AGAIN!
AGGH!
THRACK!
VRA-VRA-VROOL-THRA!
NNN-
GET BACK!

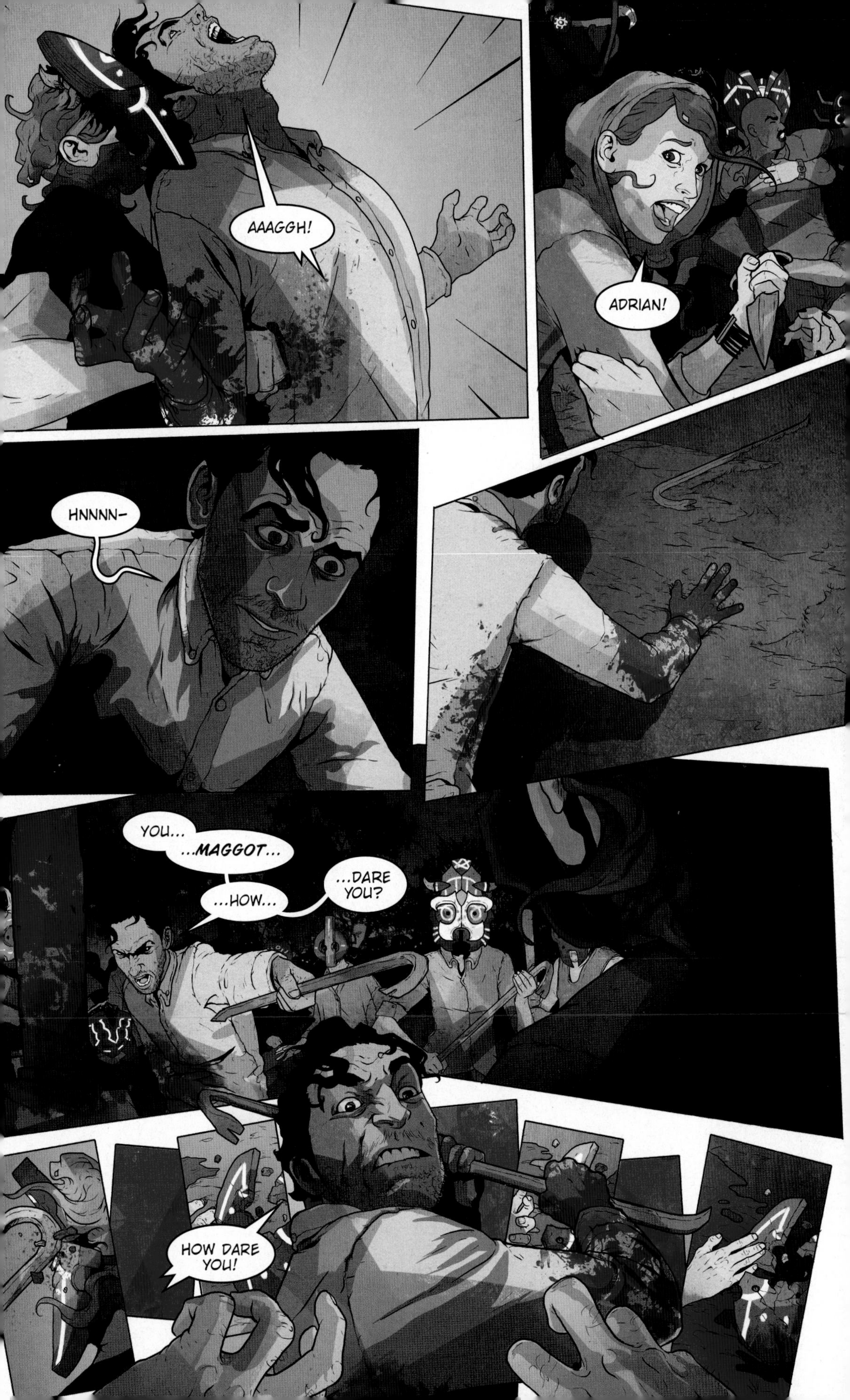
AAAGGH!
ADRIAN!
HNNNN-
YOU...
...MAGGOT...
...HOW...
...DARE YOU?
HOW DARE YOU!

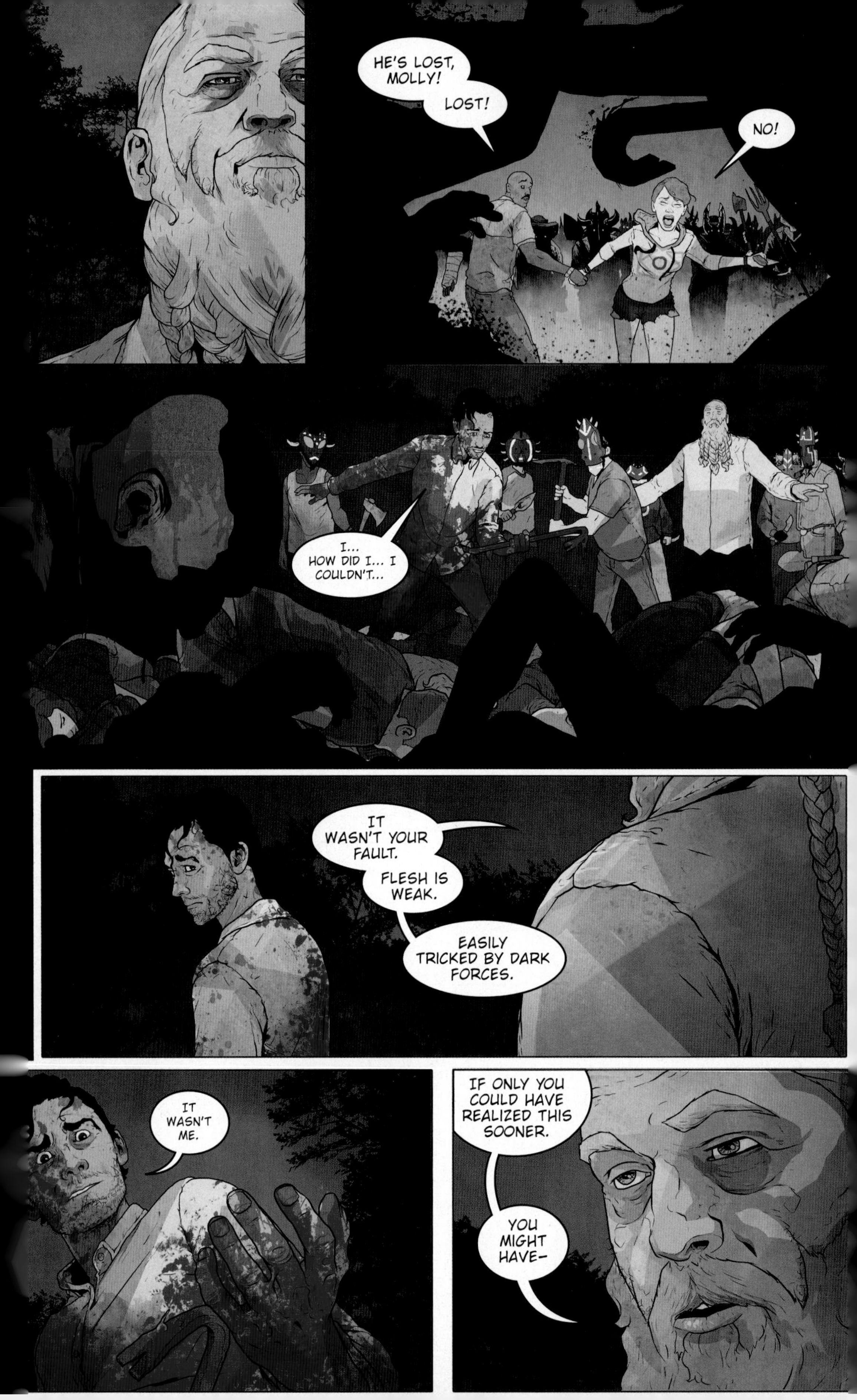
HE'S LOST, MOLLY!
LOST!
NO!
I... HOW DID I... I COULDN'T...
IT WASN'T YOUR FAULT.
FLESH IS WEAK.
EASILY TRICKED BY DARK FORCES.
IT WASN'T ME.
IF ONLY YOU COULD HAVE REALIZED THIS SOONER.
YOU MIGHT HAVE-

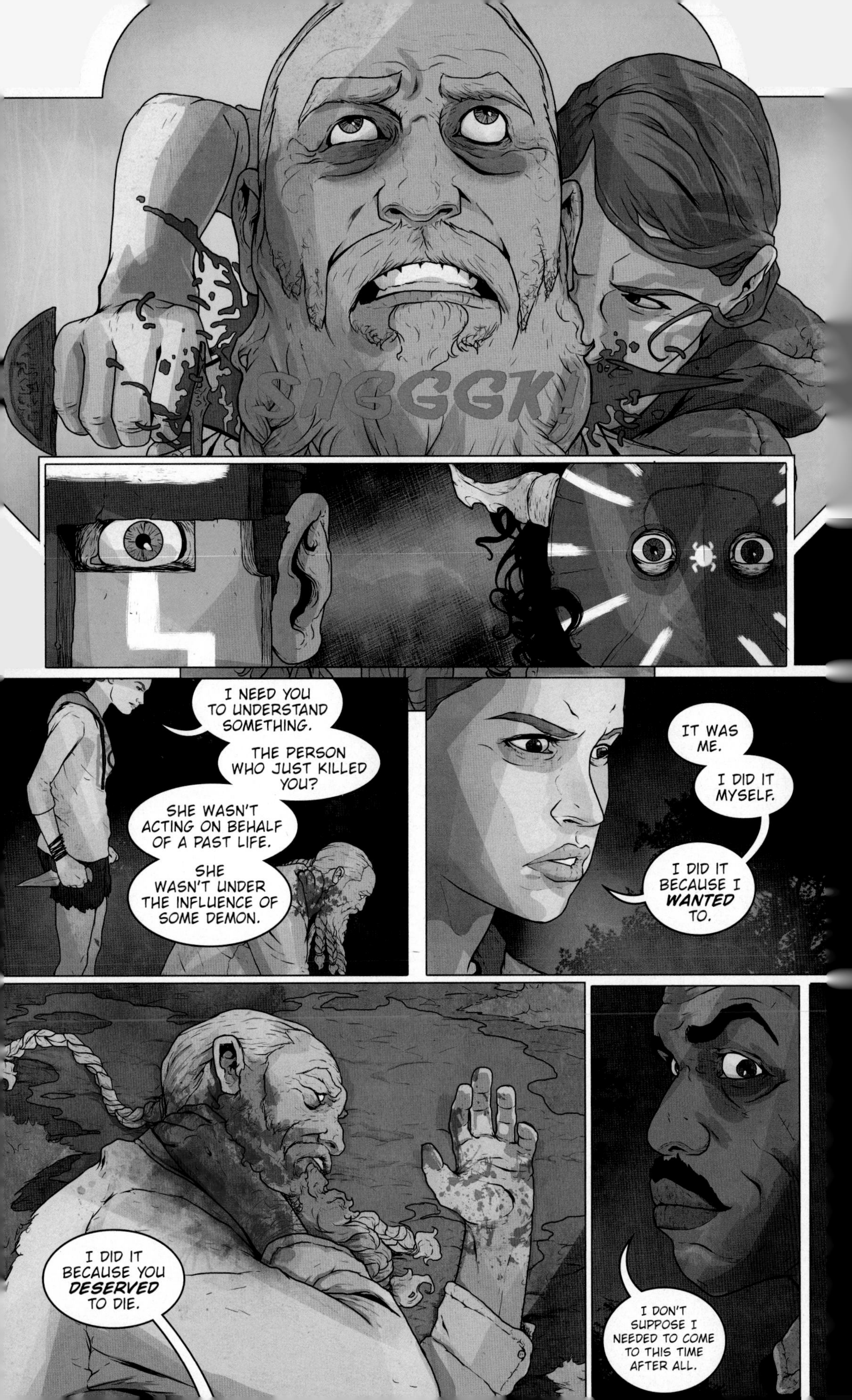
SHGGGK!
I NEED YOU TO UNDERSTAND SOMETHING.
THE PERSON WHO JUST KILLED YOU?
SHE WASN'T ACTING ON BEHALF OF A PAST LIFE.
SHE WASN'T UNDER THE INFLUENCE OF SOME DEMON.
IT WAS ME.
I DID IT MYSELF.
I DID IT BECAUSE I *WANTED* TO.
I DID IT BECAUSE YOU *DESERVED* TO DIE.
I DON'T SUPPOSE I NEEDED TO COME TO THIS TIME AFTER ALL.

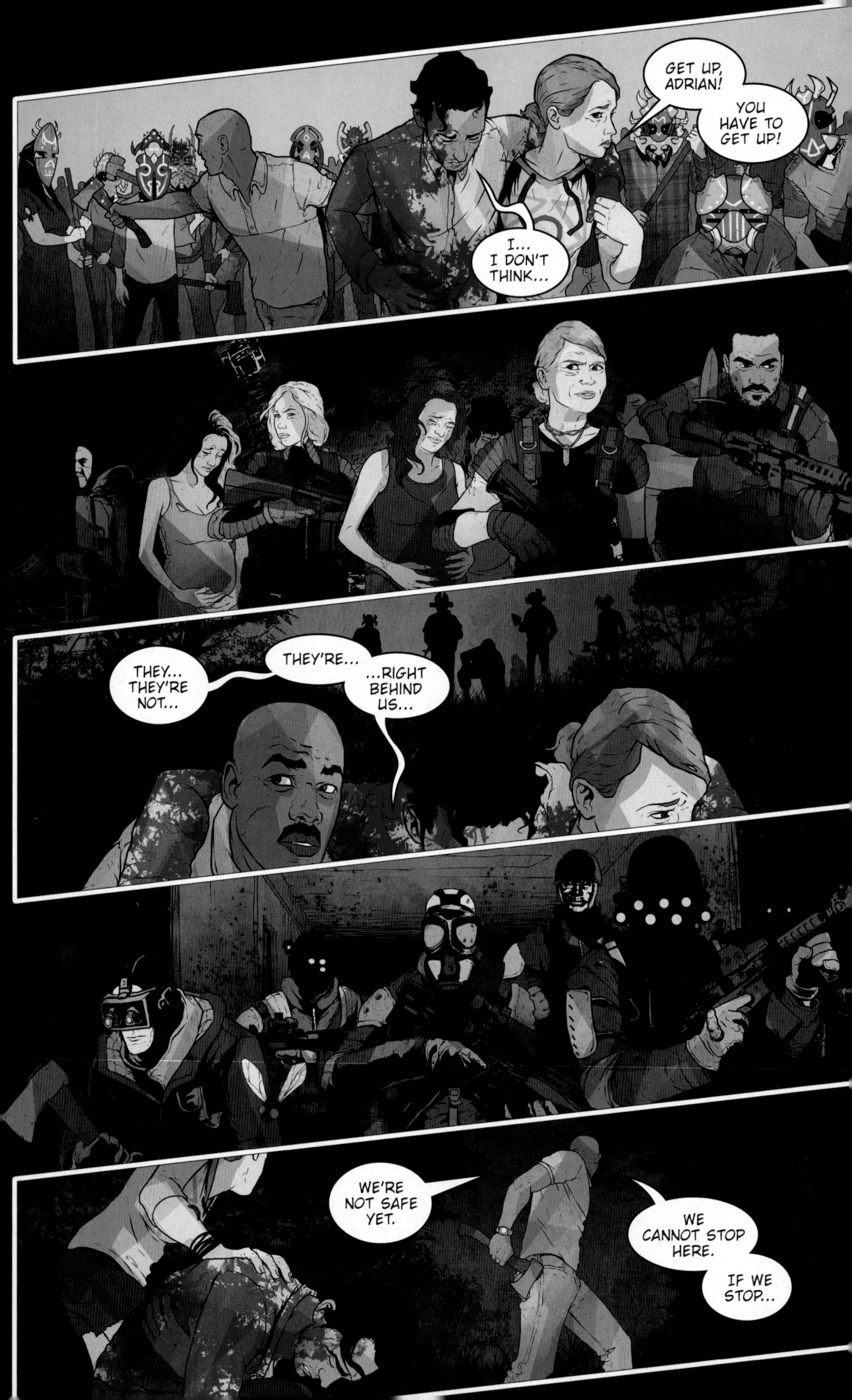
GET UP, ADRIAN!
YOU HAVE TO GET UP!
I... I DON'T THINK...
THEY... THEY'RE NOT...
THEY'RE...
...RIGHT BEHIND US...
WE'RE NOT SAFE YET.
WE CANNOT STOP HERE.
IF WE STOP...

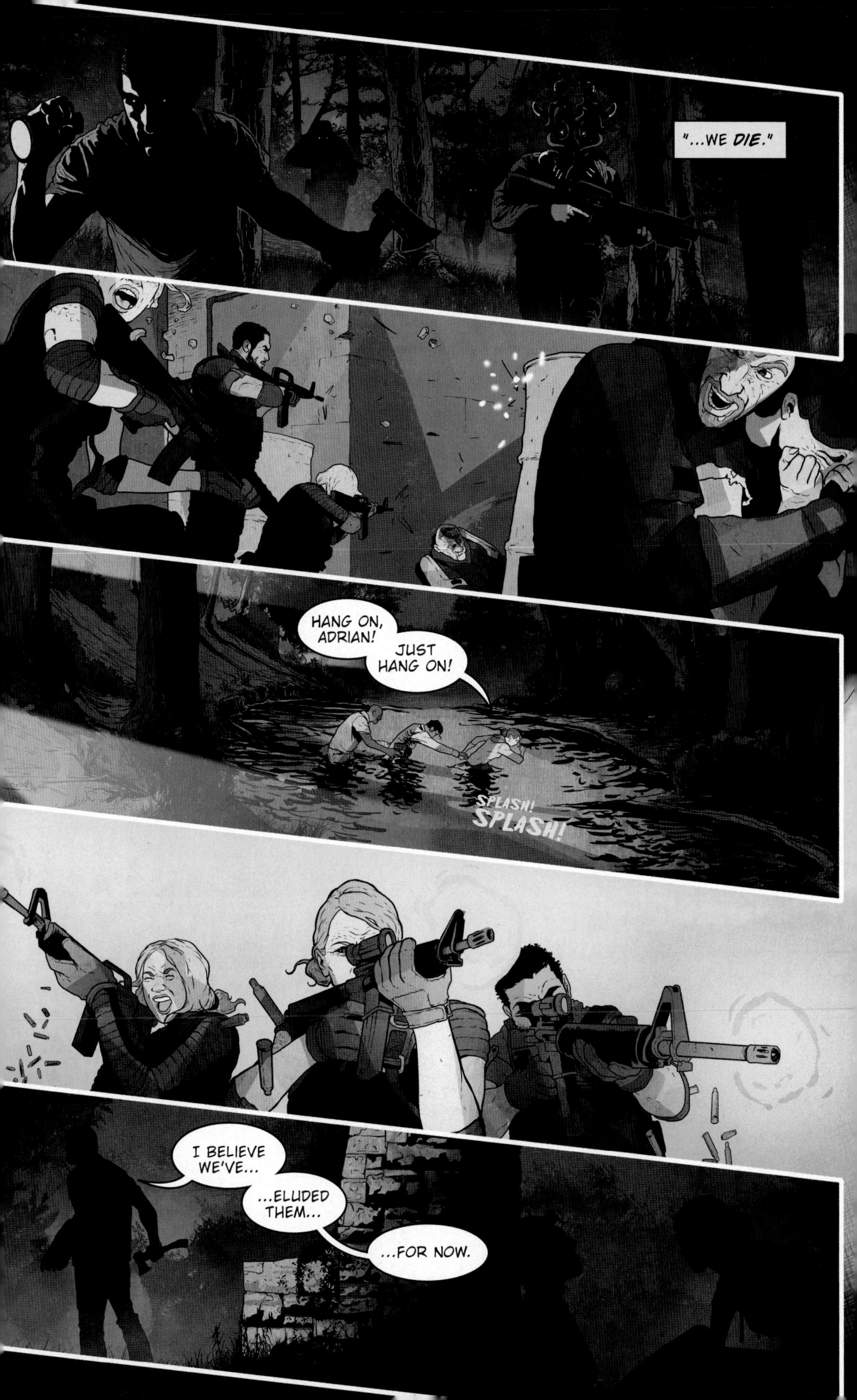
"...WE DIE."
HANG ON, ADRIAN!
JUST HANG ON!
SPLASH!
SPLASH!
I BELIEVE WE'VE...
...ELUDED THEM...
...FOR NOW.

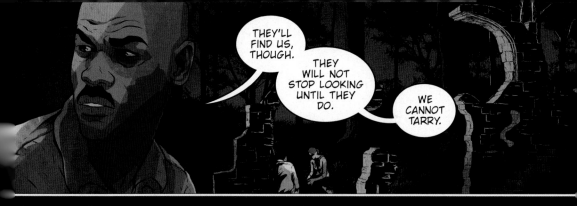

THEY'LL FIND US, THOUGH.

THEY WILL NOT STOP LOOKING UNTIL THEY DO.

WE CANNOT TARRY.

D-DID HE SAY... ..."TARRY"?

IT'S A LONG STORY.

I THINK I GOT THE GIST OF IT.

PAST LIVES.

THEY'RE A BITCH.

PRETTY MUCH.

C-CAN'T WAIT TO SEE WHAT'S NEXT.

DON'T SAY THAT, ADRIAN.

WE'VE COME THIS FAR.

YOU CAN'T JUST GIVE UP NOW.

YOU CAN'T.

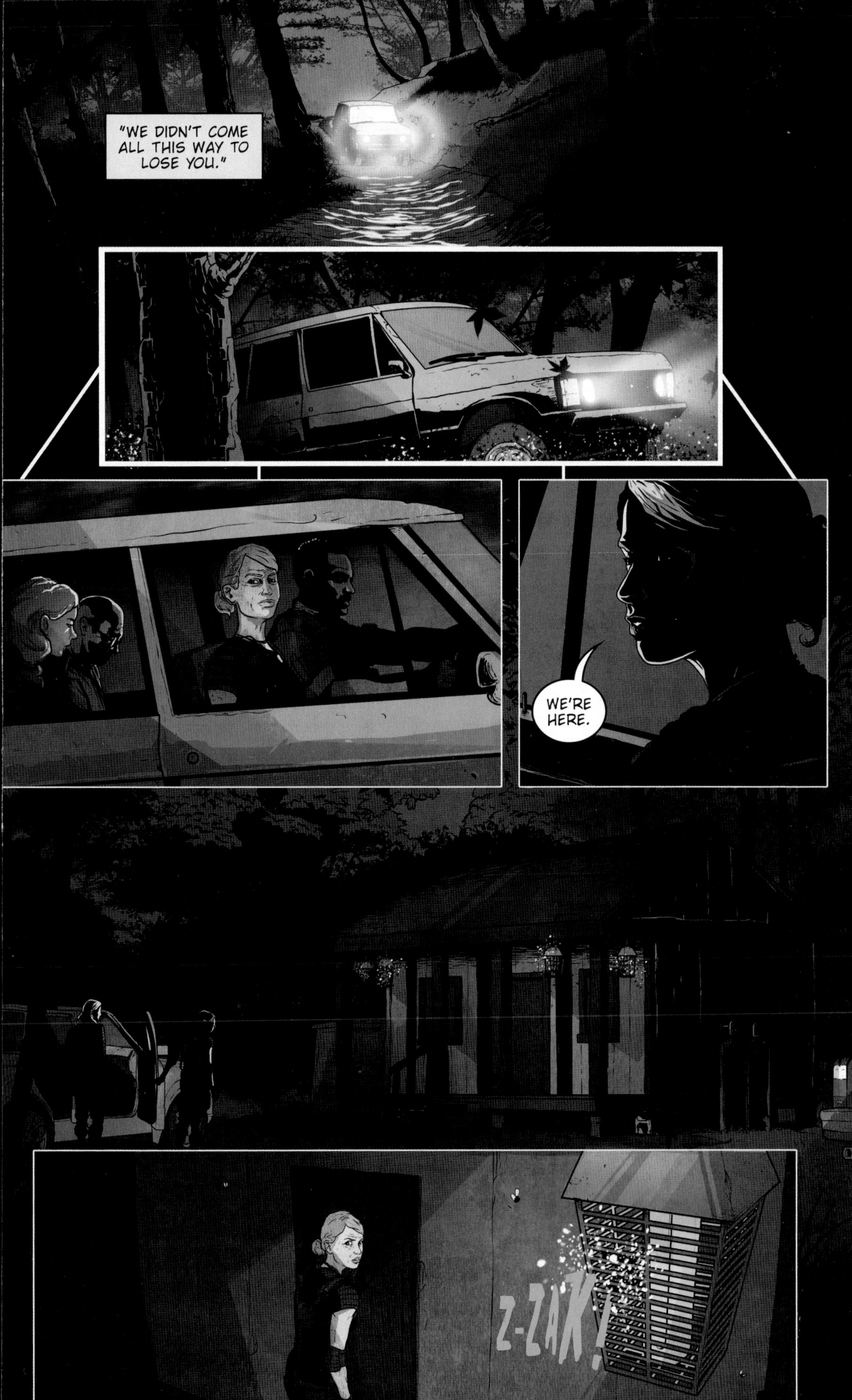
"WE DIDN'T COME ALL THIS WAY TO LOSE YOU."
WE'RE HERE.
Z-ZAK!

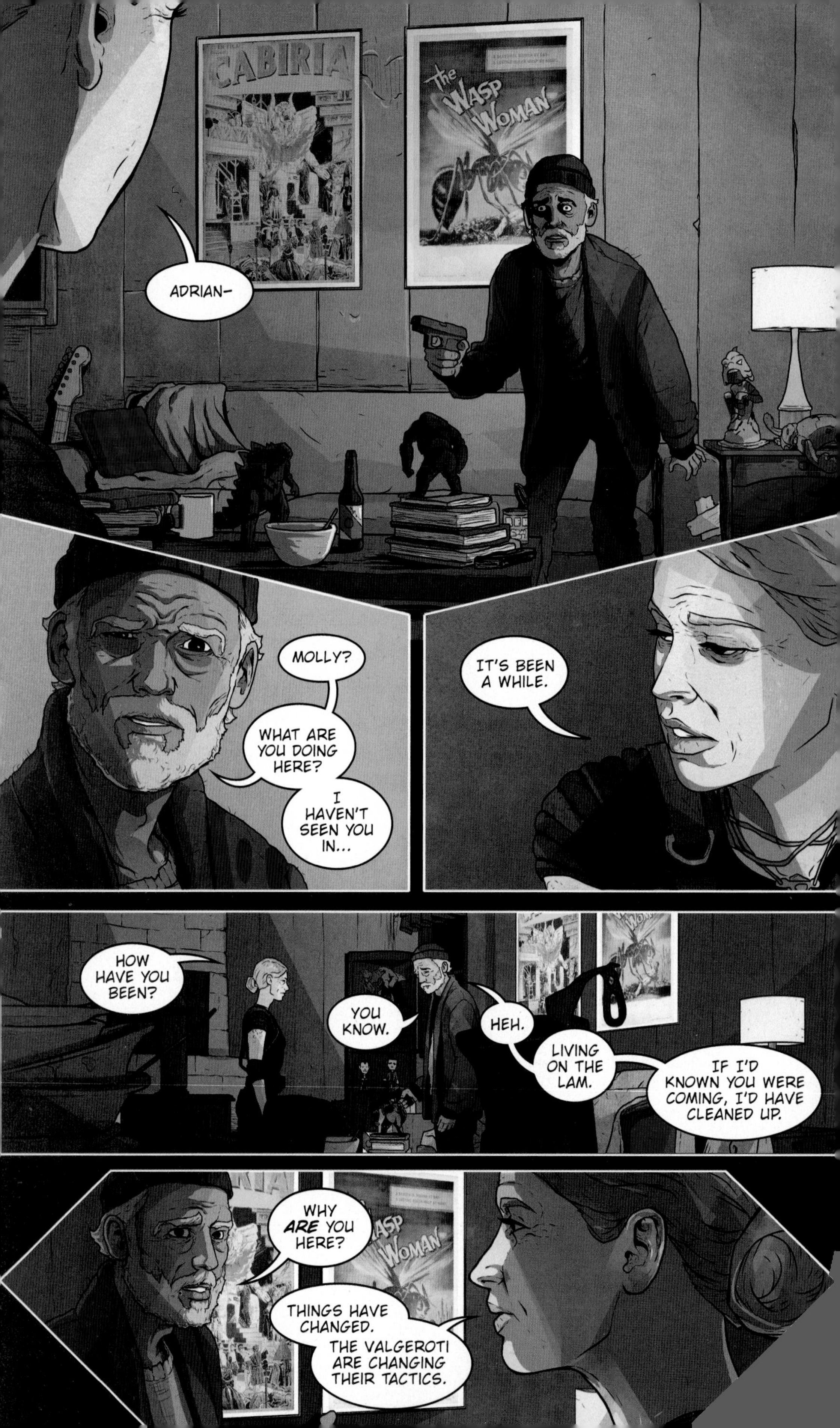
CABIRIA
The Wasp Woman
ADRIAN-
MOLLY?
WHAT ARE YOU DOING HERE?
I HAVEN'T SEEN YOU IN...
IT'S BEEN A WHILE.
HOW HAVE YOU BEEN?
YOU KNOW.
HEH.
LIVING ON THE LAM.
IF I'D KNOWN YOU WERE COMING, I'D HAVE CLEANED UP.
WHY *ARE* YOU HERE?
THINGS HAVE CHANGED.
THE VALGEROTI ARE CHANGING THEIR TACTICS.

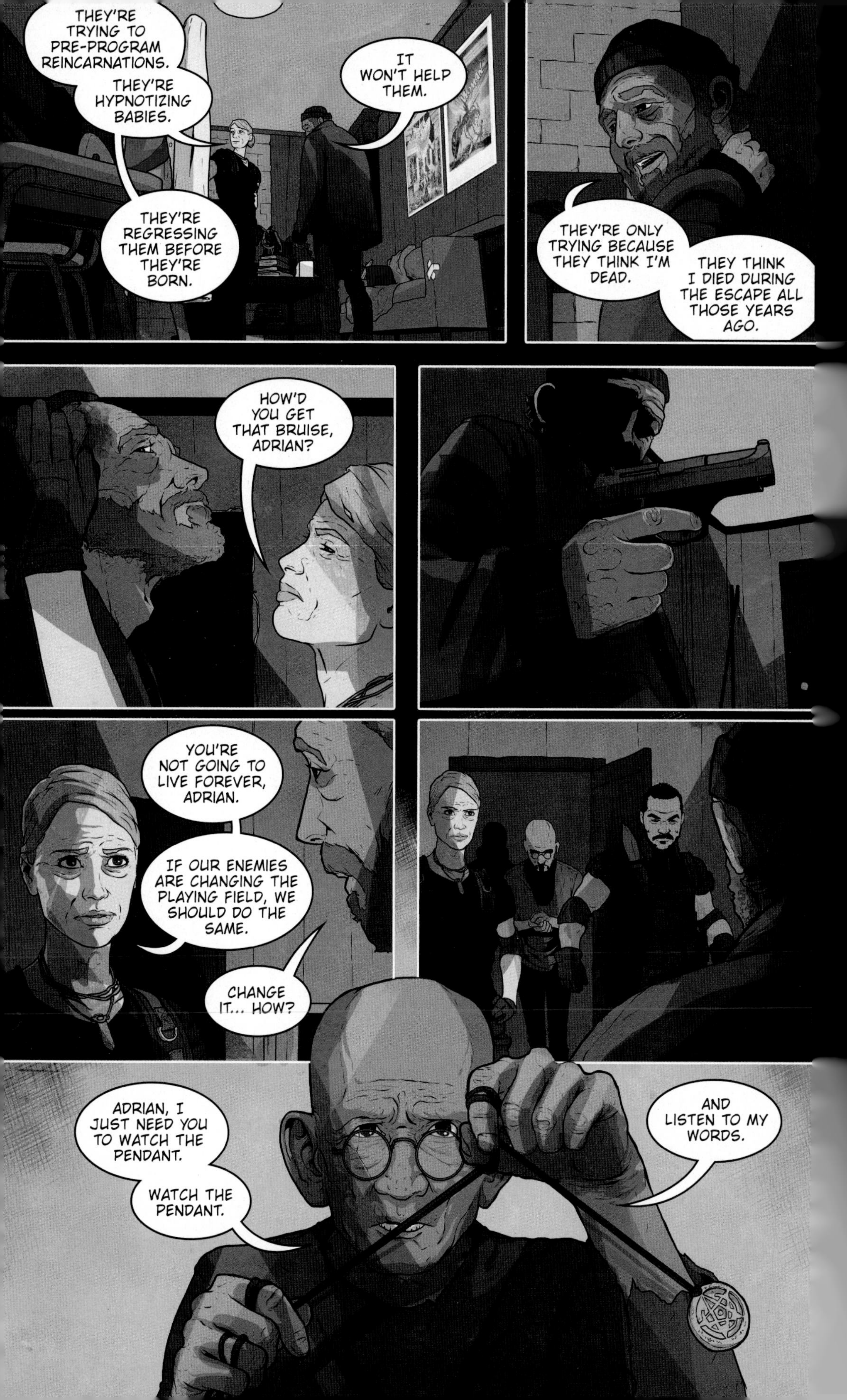

THEY'RE TRYING TO PRE-PROGRAM REINCARNATIONS.
THEY'RE HYPNOTIZING BABIES.
THEY'RE REGRESSING THEM BEFORE THEY'RE BORN.
IT WON'T HELP THEM.
THEY'RE ONLY TRYING BECAUSE THEY THINK I'M DEAD.
THEY THINK I DIED DURING THE ESCAPE ALL THOSE YEARS AGO.
HOW'D YOU GET THAT BRUISE, ADRIAN?
YOU'RE NOT GOING TO LIVE FOREVER, ADRIAN.
IF OUR ENEMIES ARE CHANGING THE PLAYING FIELD, WE SHOULD DO THE SAME.
CHANGE IT... HOW?
ADRIAN, I JUST NEED YOU TO WATCH THE PENDANT.
WATCH THE PENDANT.
AND LISTEN TO MY WORDS.

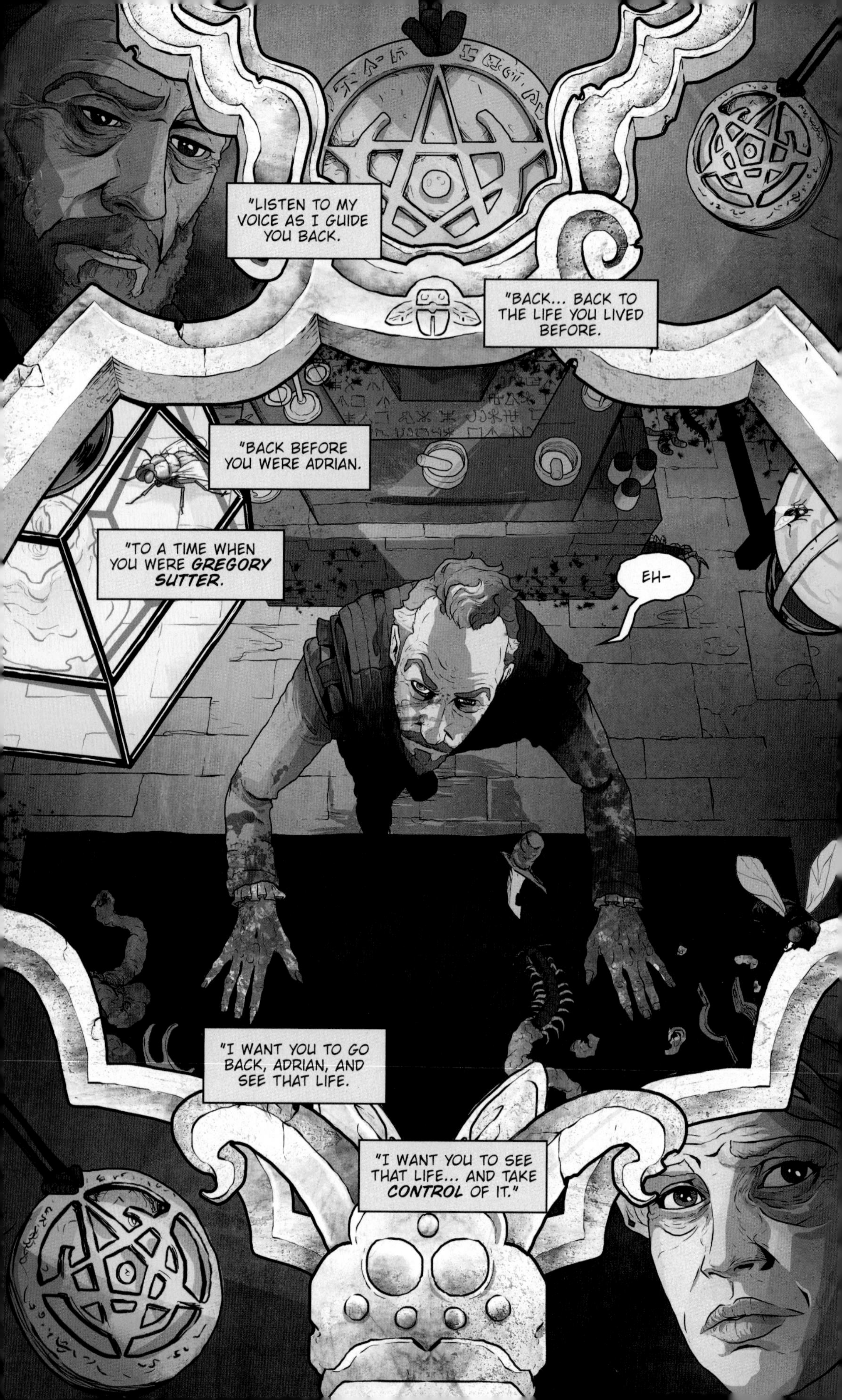
"LISTEN TO MY VOICE AS I GUIDE YOU BACK.
"BACK... BACK TO THE LIFE YOU LIVED BEFORE.
"BACK BEFORE YOU WERE ADRIAN.
"TO A TIME WHEN YOU WERE *GREGORY SUTTER*.
EH-
"I WANT YOU TO GO BACK, ADRIAN, AND SEE THAT LIFE.
"I WANT YOU TO SEE THAT LIFE... AND TAKE *CONTROL* OF IT."

FIFTEEN

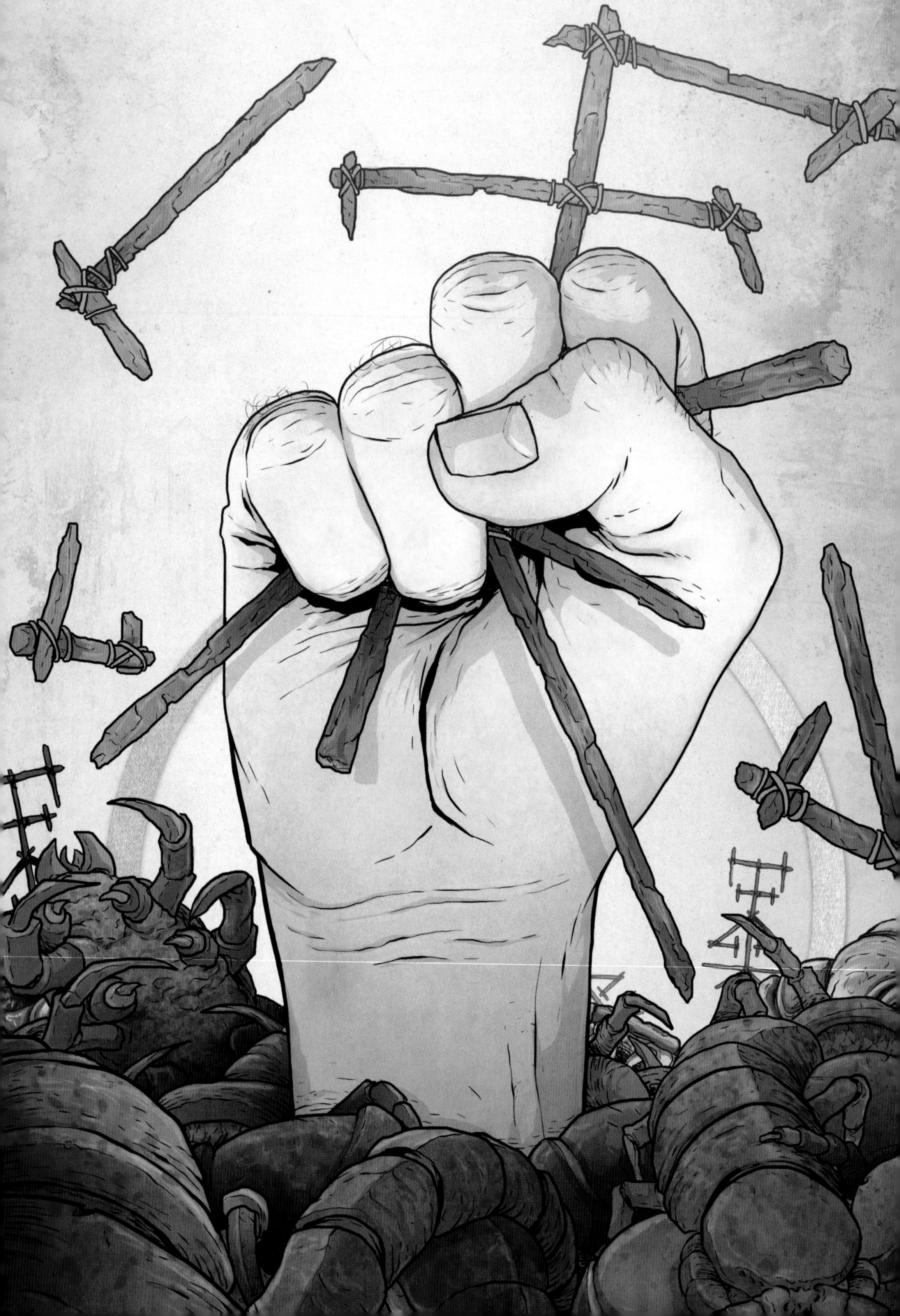

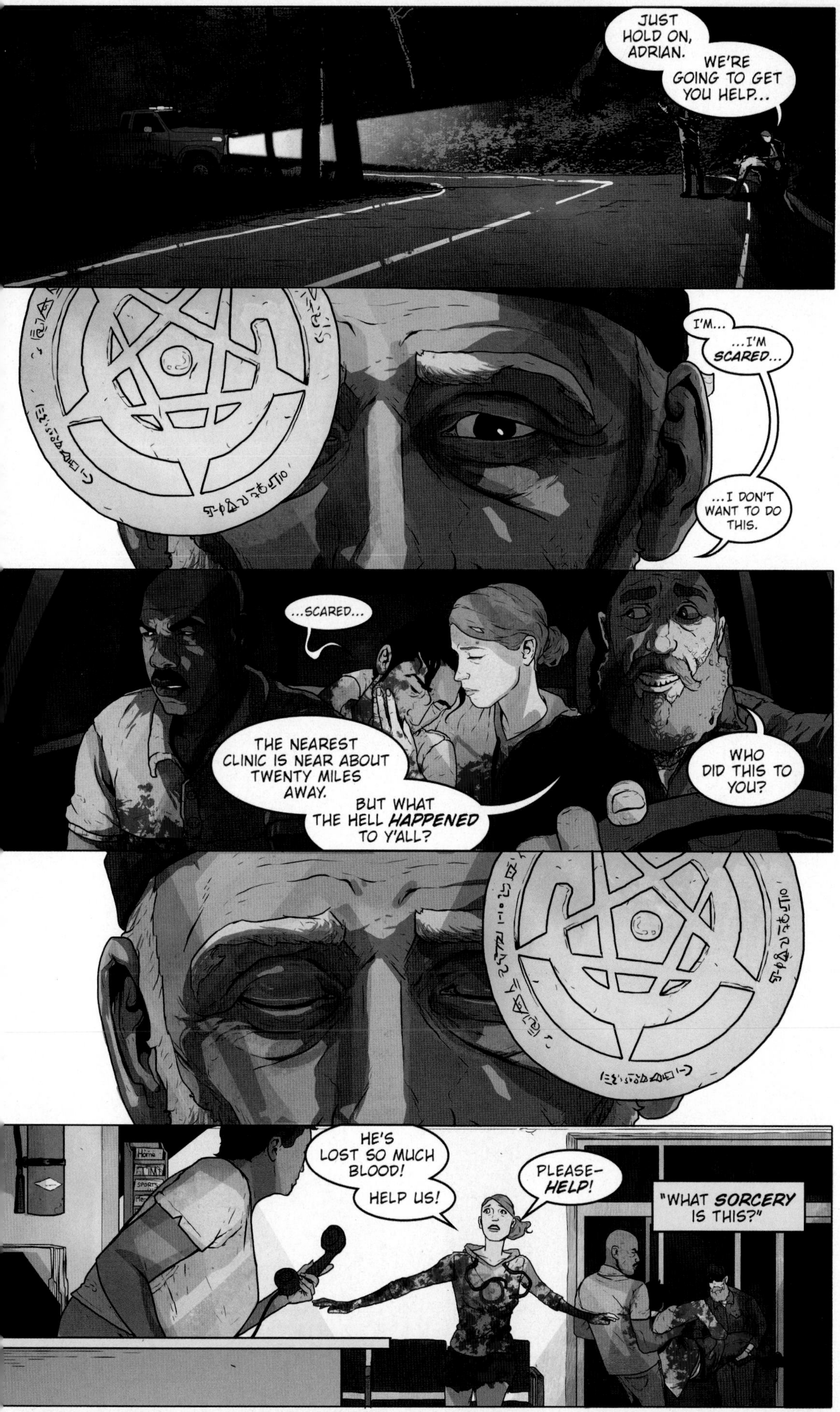
JUST HOLD ON, ADRIAN.
WE'RE GOING TO GET YOU HELP...
I'M...
...I'M SCARED...
...I DON'T WANT TO DO THIS.
...SCARED...
THE NEAREST CLINIC IS NEAR ABOUT TWENTY MILES AWAY.
BUT WHAT THE HELL HAPPENED TO Y'ALL?
WHO DID THIS TO YOU?
HE'S LOST SO MUCH BLOOD!
HELP US!
PLEASE- HELP!
"WHAT SORCERY IS THIS?"

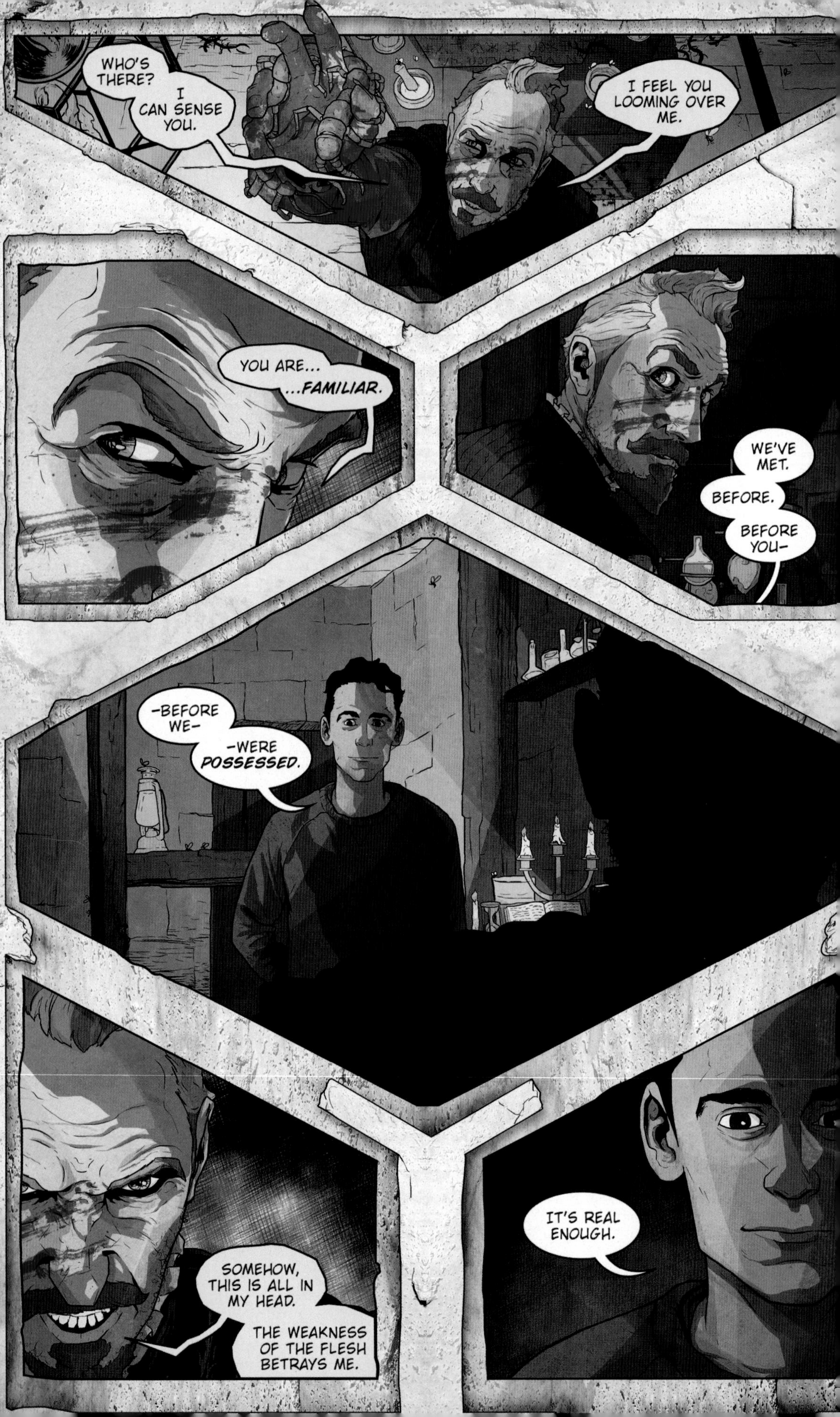

WHO'S THERE?
I CAN SENSE YOU.
I FEEL YOU LOOMING OVER ME.
YOU ARE... ...FAMILIAR.
WE'VE MET.
BEFORE.
BEFORE YOU-
-BEFORE WE-
-WERE POSSESSED.
SOMEHOW, THIS IS ALL IN MY HEAD.
THE WEAKNESS OF THE FLESH BETRAYS ME.
IT'S REAL ENOUGH.

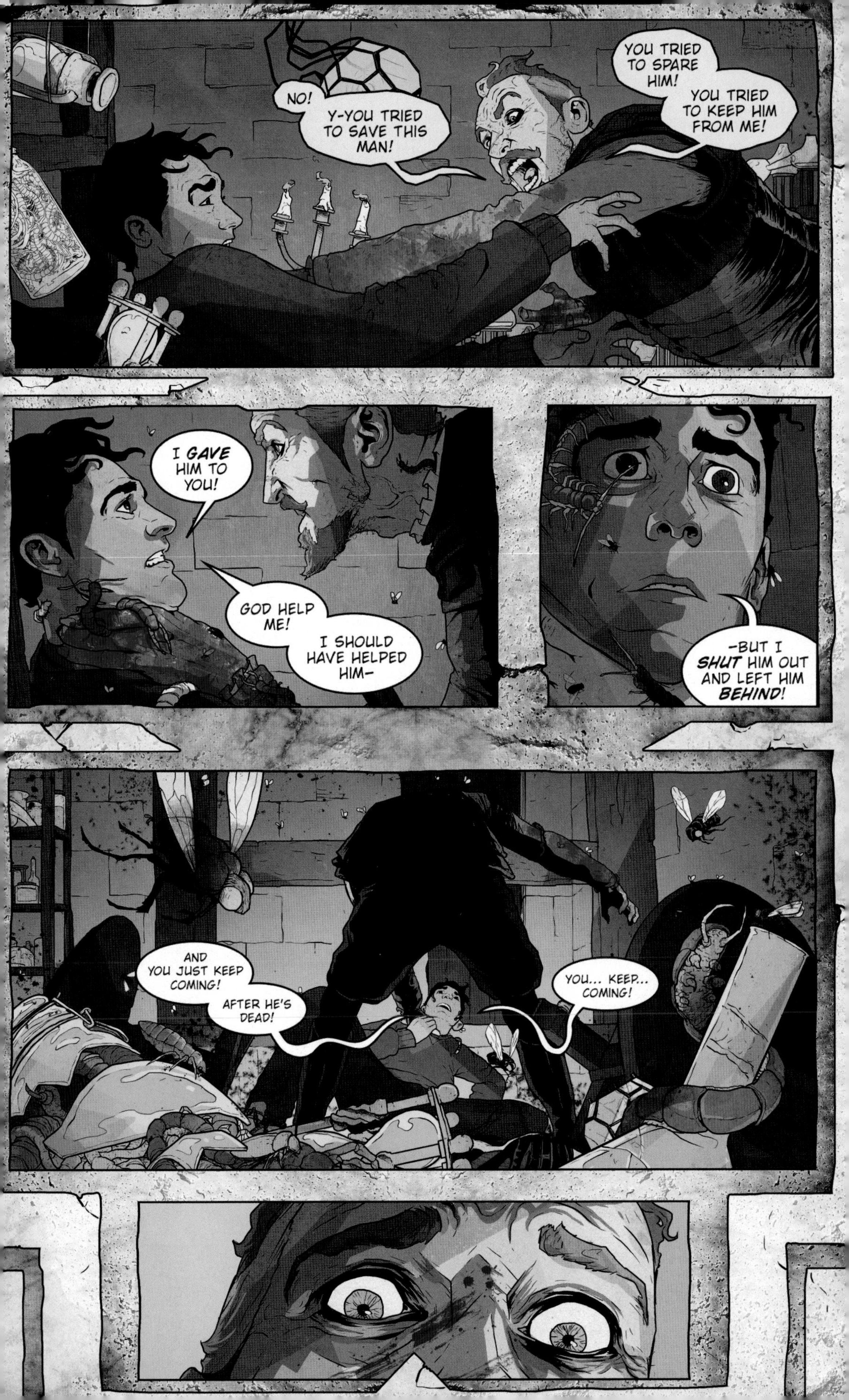
NO!
Y-YOU TRIED TO SAVE THIS MAN!
YOU TRIED TO SPARE HIM!
YOU TRIED TO KEEP HIM FROM ME!
I GAVE HIM TO YOU!
GOD HELP ME!
I SHOULD HAVE HELPED HIM-
-BUT I SHUT HIM OUT AND LEFT HIM BEHIND!
AND YOU JUST KEEP COMING!
AFTER HE'S DEAD!
YOU... KEEP... COMING!

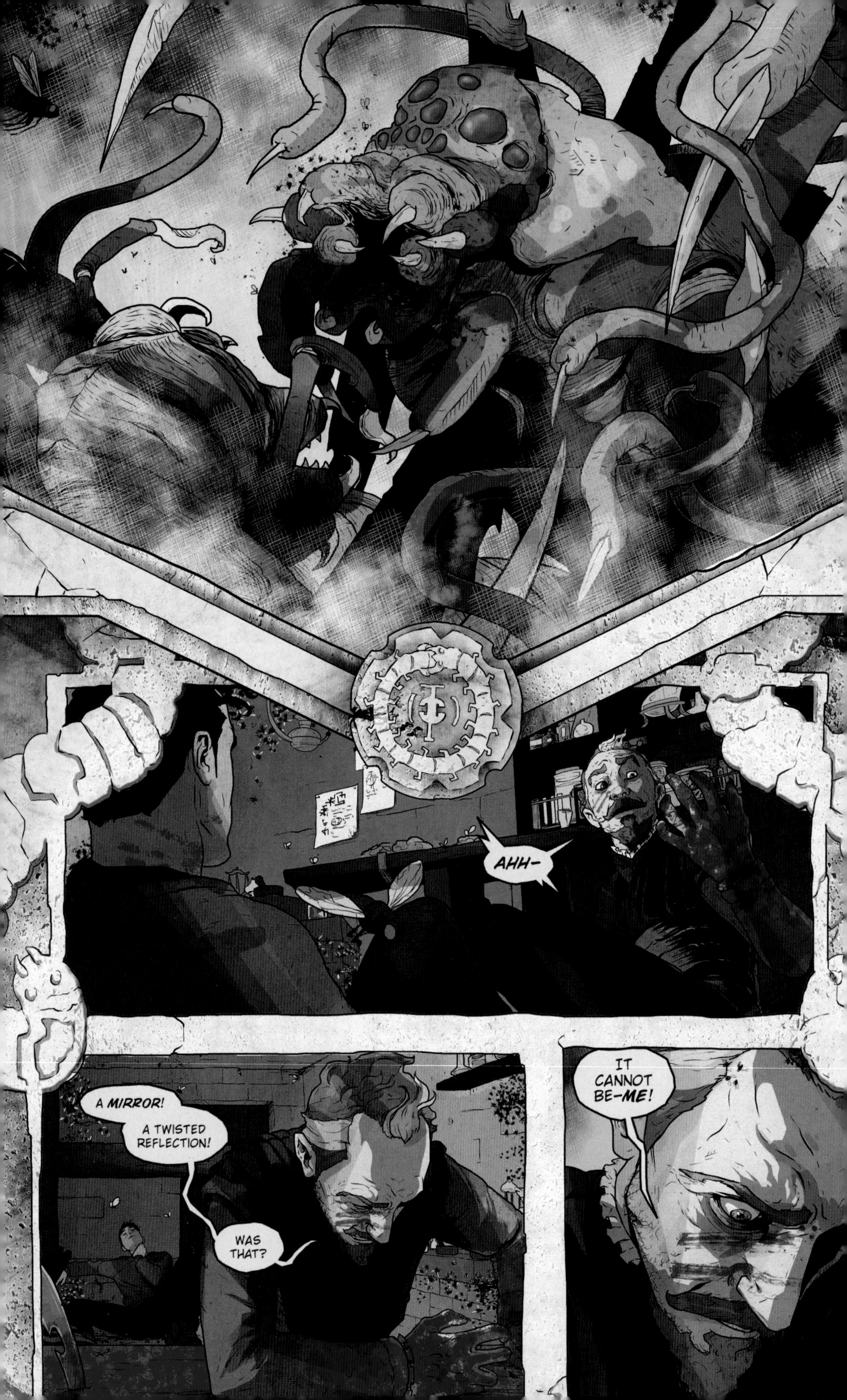
AHH-
A MIRROR!
A TWISTED REFLECTION!
WAS THAT?
IT CANNOT BE-ME!

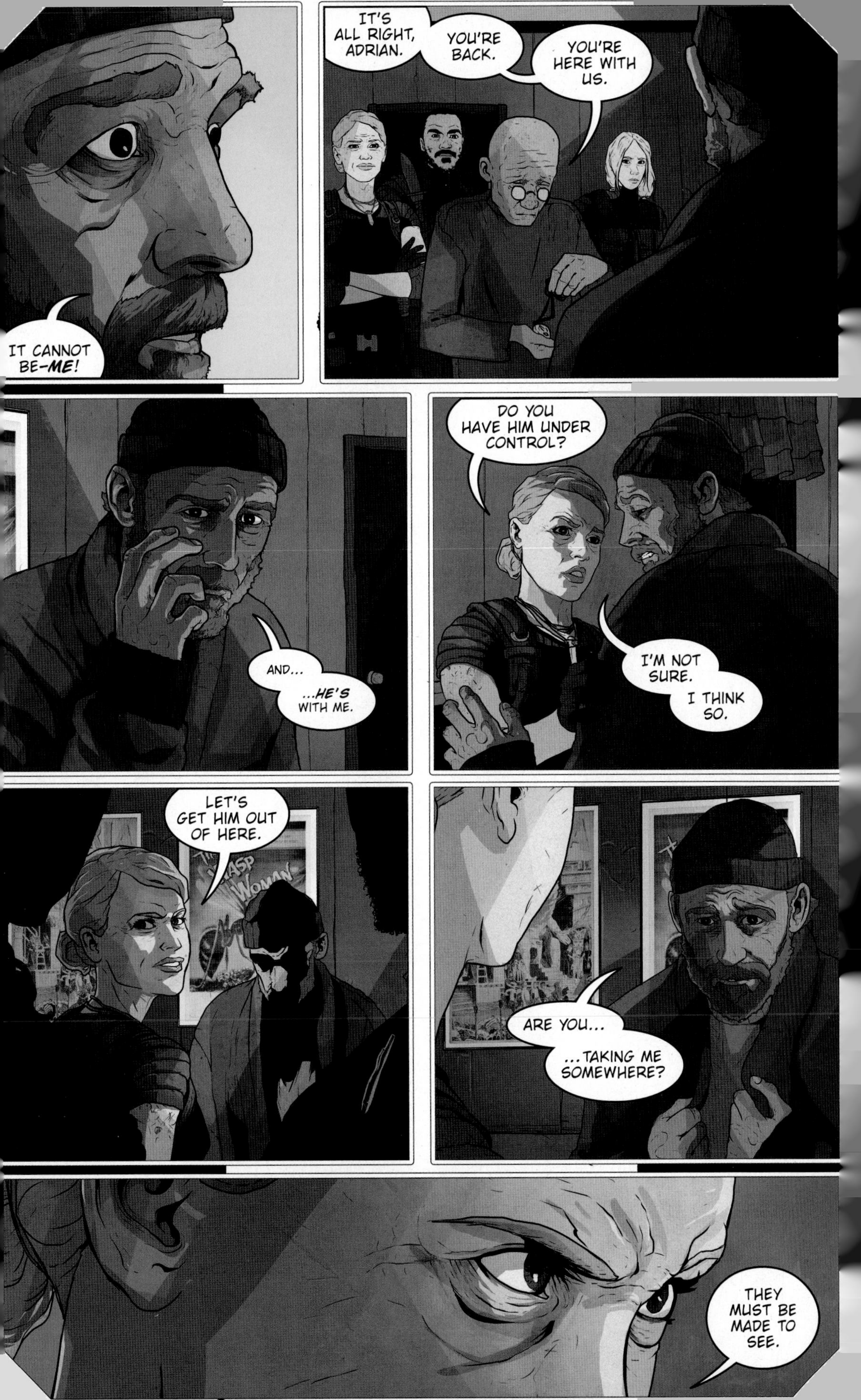
IT CANNOT BE–**ME**!
IT'S ALL RIGHT, ADRIAN.
YOU'RE BACK.
YOU'RE HERE WITH US.
AND...
...**HE'S** WITH ME.
DO YOU HAVE HIM UNDER CONTROL?
I'M NOT SURE.
I THINK SO.
LET'S GET HIM OUT OF HERE.
ARE YOU...
...TAKING ME SOMEWHERE?
THEY MUST BE MADE TO SEE.

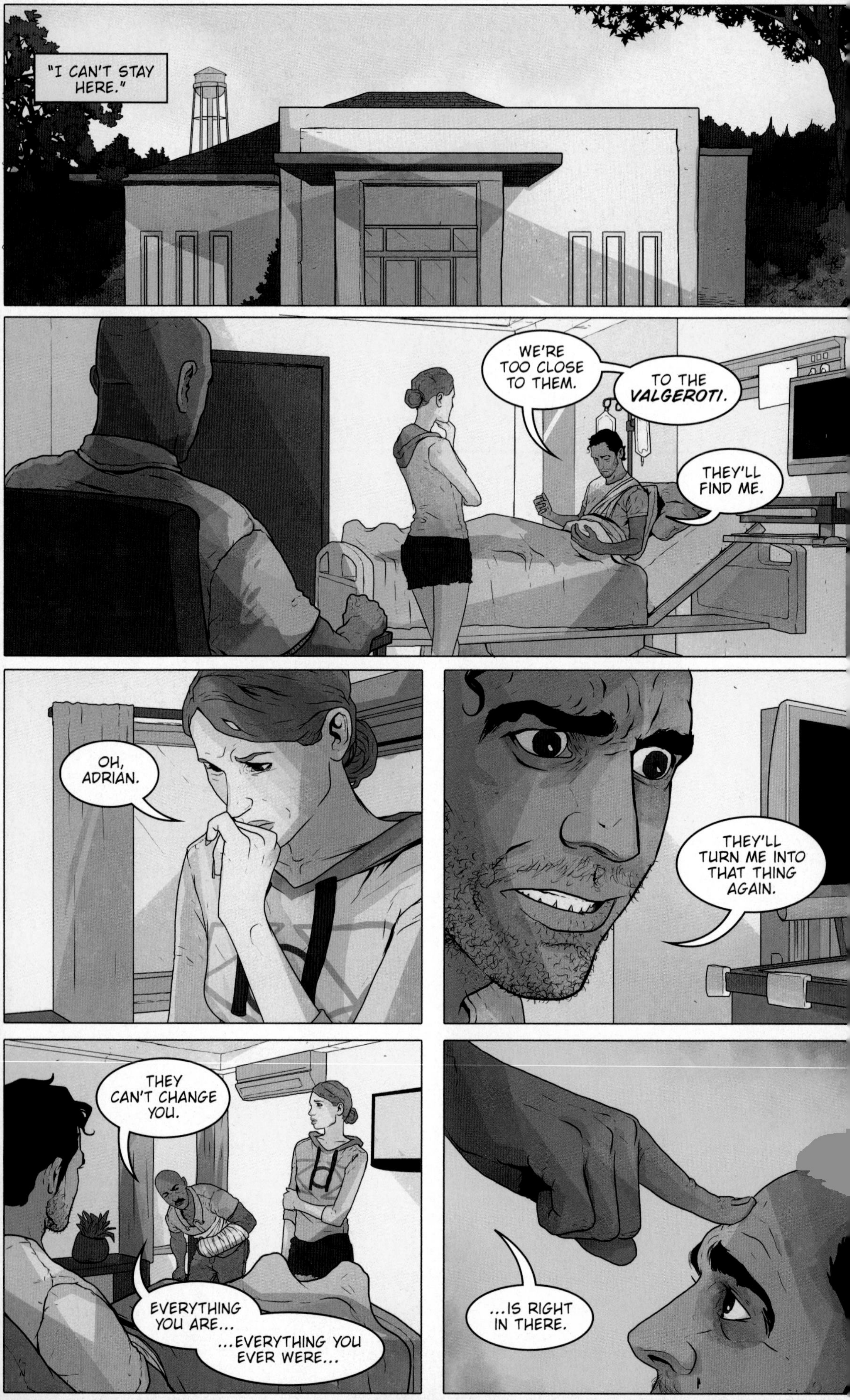
"I CAN'T STAY HERE."
WE'RE TOO CLOSE TO THEM.
TO THE VALGEROTI.
THEY'LL FIND ME.
OH, ADRIAN.
THEY'LL TURN ME INTO THAT THING AGAIN.
THEY CAN'T CHANGE YOU.
EVERYTHING YOU ARE...
...EVERYTHING YOU EVER WERE...
...IS RIGHT IN THERE.

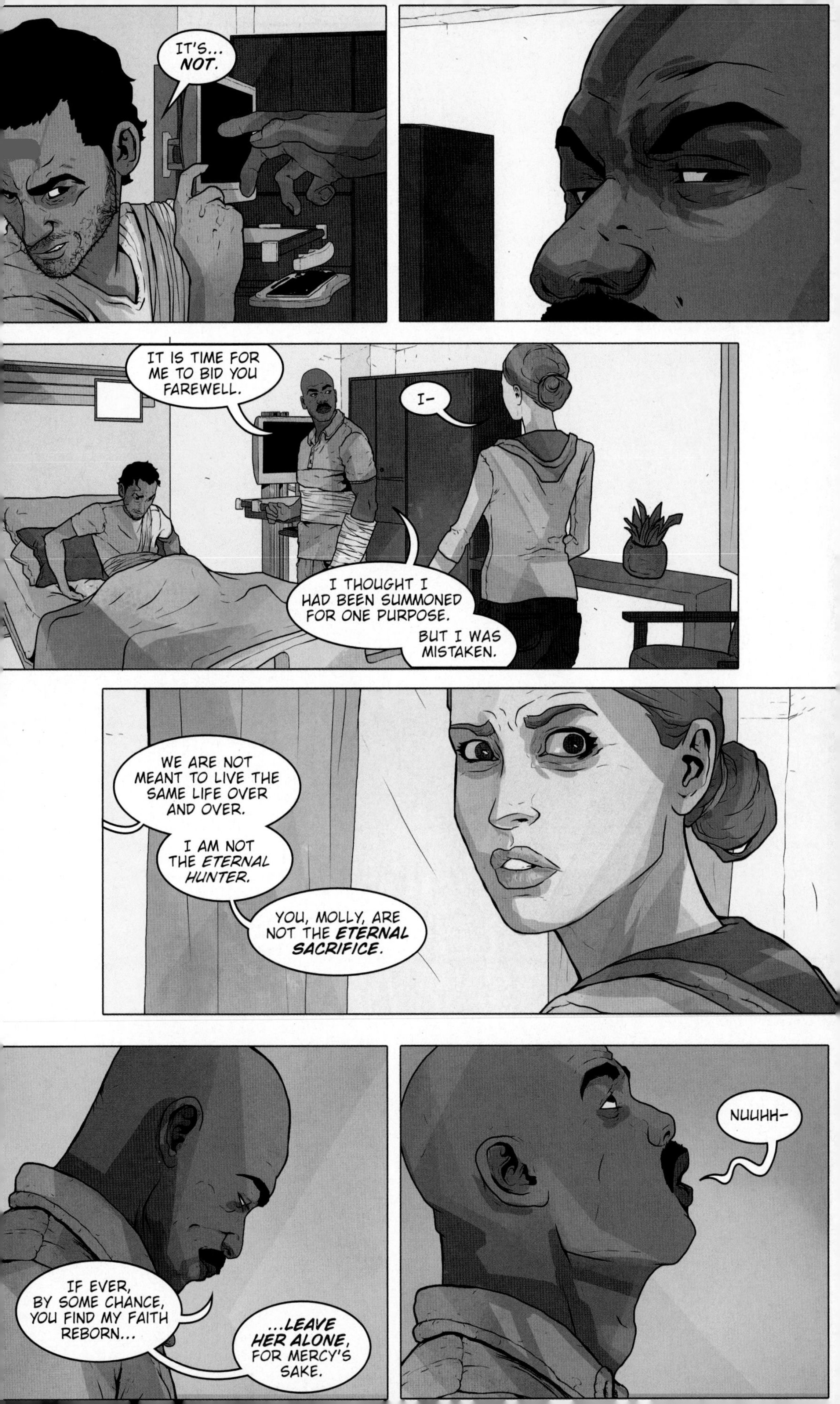

IT'S... NOT.
IT IS TIME FOR ME TO BID YOU FAREWELL.
I-
I THOUGHT I HAD BEEN SUMMONED FOR ONE PURPOSE.
BUT I WAS MISTAKEN.
WE ARE NOT MEANT TO LIVE THE SAME LIFE OVER AND OVER.
I AM NOT THE ETERNAL HUNTER.
YOU, MOLLY, ARE NOT THE ETERNAL SACRIFICE.
IF EVER, BY SOME CHANCE, YOU FIND MY FAITH REBORN...
...LEAVE HER ALONE, FOR MERCY'S SAKE.
NUUHH-

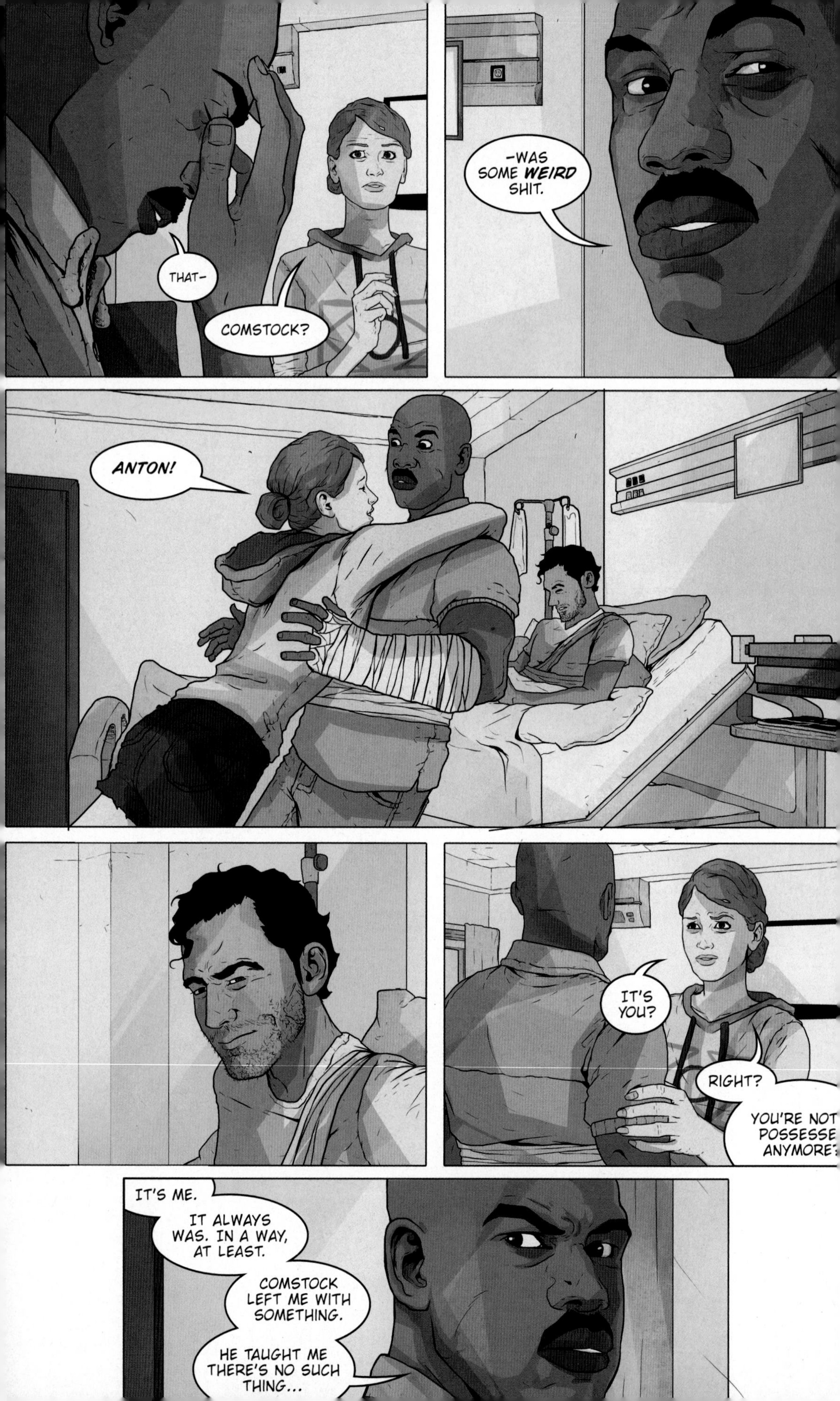
THAT-
COMSTOCK?
-WAS SOME WEIRD SHIT.
ANTON!
IT'S YOU?
RIGHT?
YOU'RE NOT POSSESSE ANYMORE?
IT'S ME.
IT ALWAYS WAS. IN A WAY, AT LEAST.
COMSTOCK LEFT ME WITH SOMETHING.
HE TAUGHT ME THERE'S NO SUCH THING...

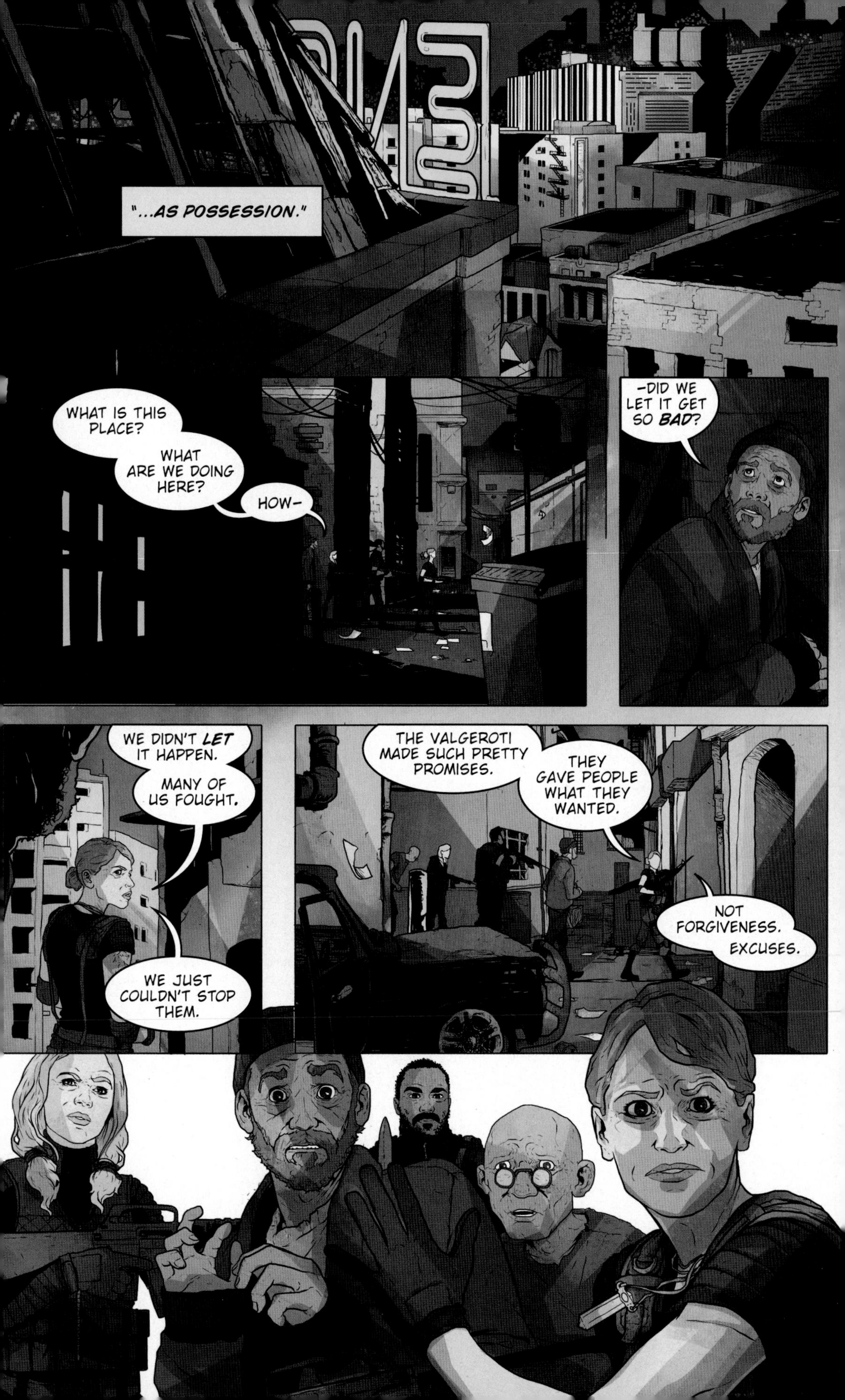

"...AS POSSESSION."
WHAT IS THIS PLACE?
WHAT ARE WE DOING HERE?
HOW-
-DID WE LET IT GET SO *BAD*?
WE DIDN'T *LET* IT HAPPEN.
MANY OF US FOUGHT.
WE JUST COULDN'T STOP THEM.
THE VALGEROTI MADE SUCH PRETTY PROMISES.
THEY GAVE PEOPLE WHAT THEY WANTED.
NOT FORGIVENESS.
EXCUSES.

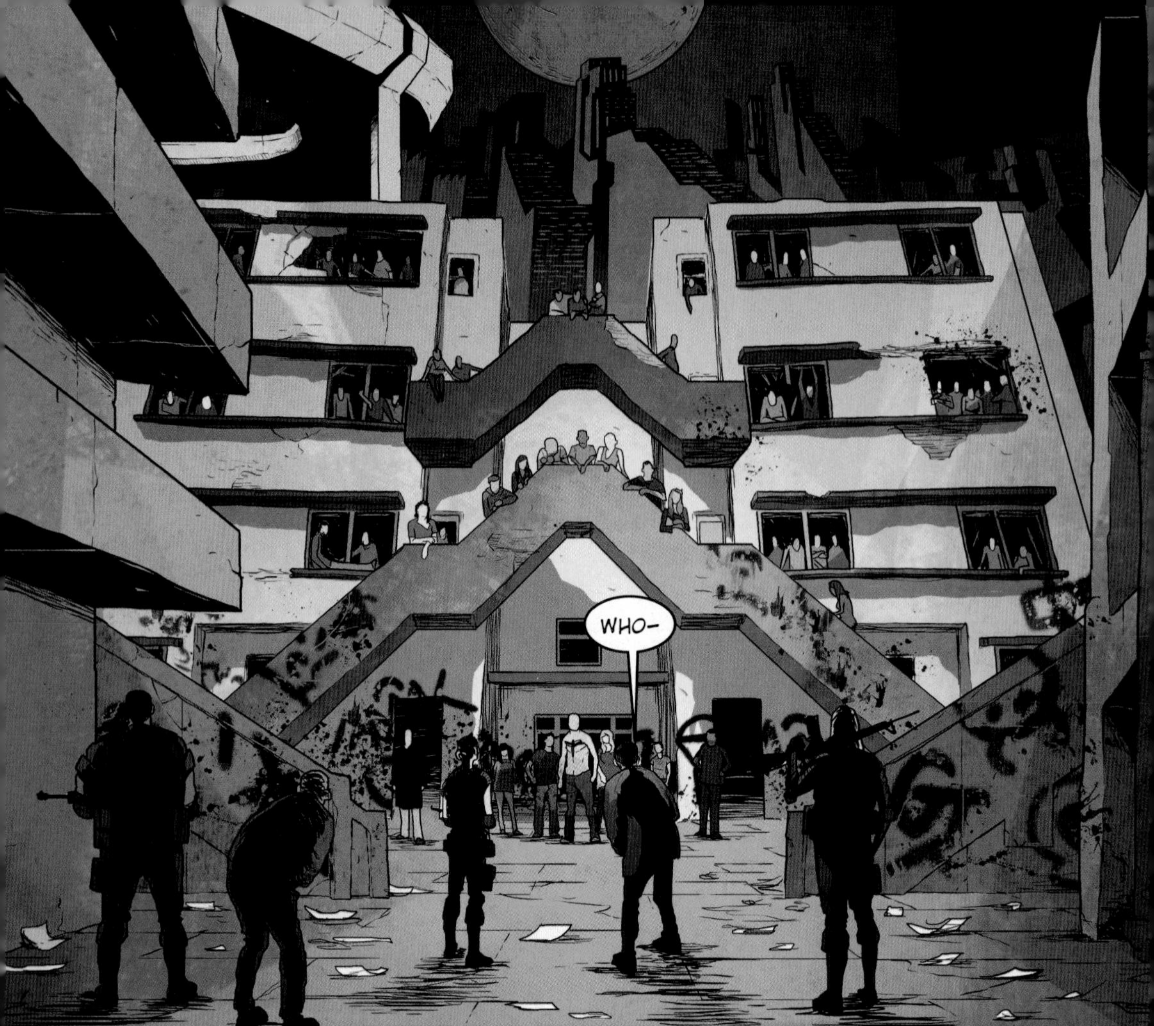
WHO-
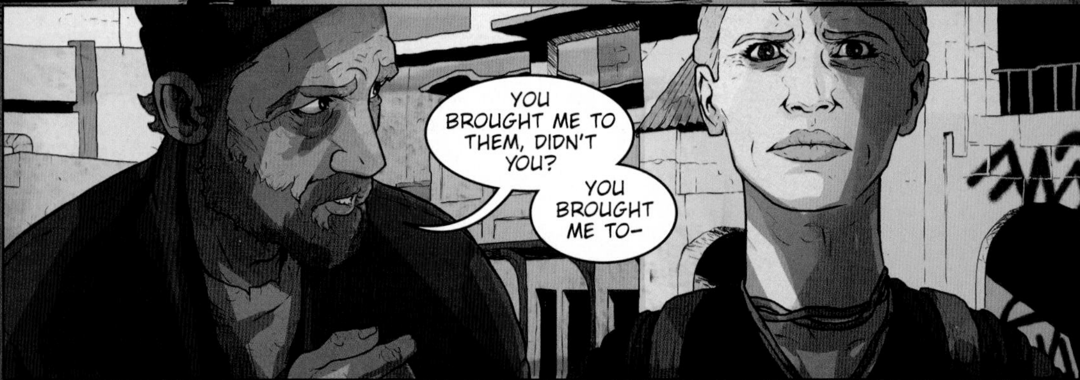
YOU BROUGHT ME TO THEM, DIDN'T YOU?
YOU BROUGHT ME TO-
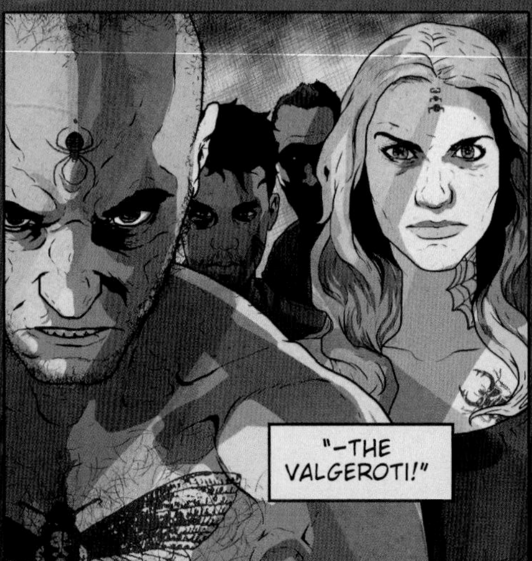
"-THE VALGEROTI!"
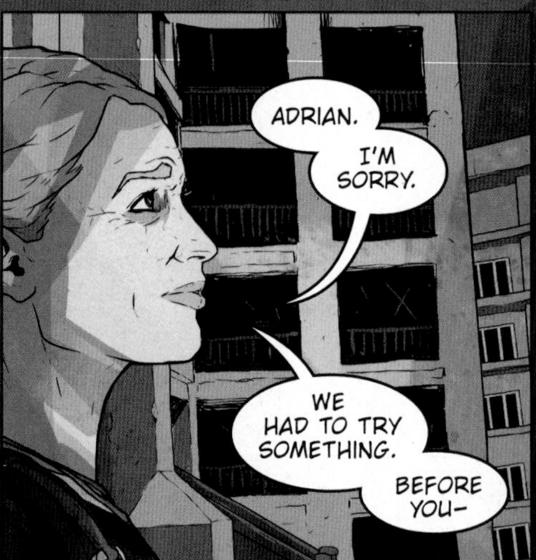
ADRIAN.
I'M SORRY.
WE HAD TO TRY SOMETHING.
BEFORE YOU-

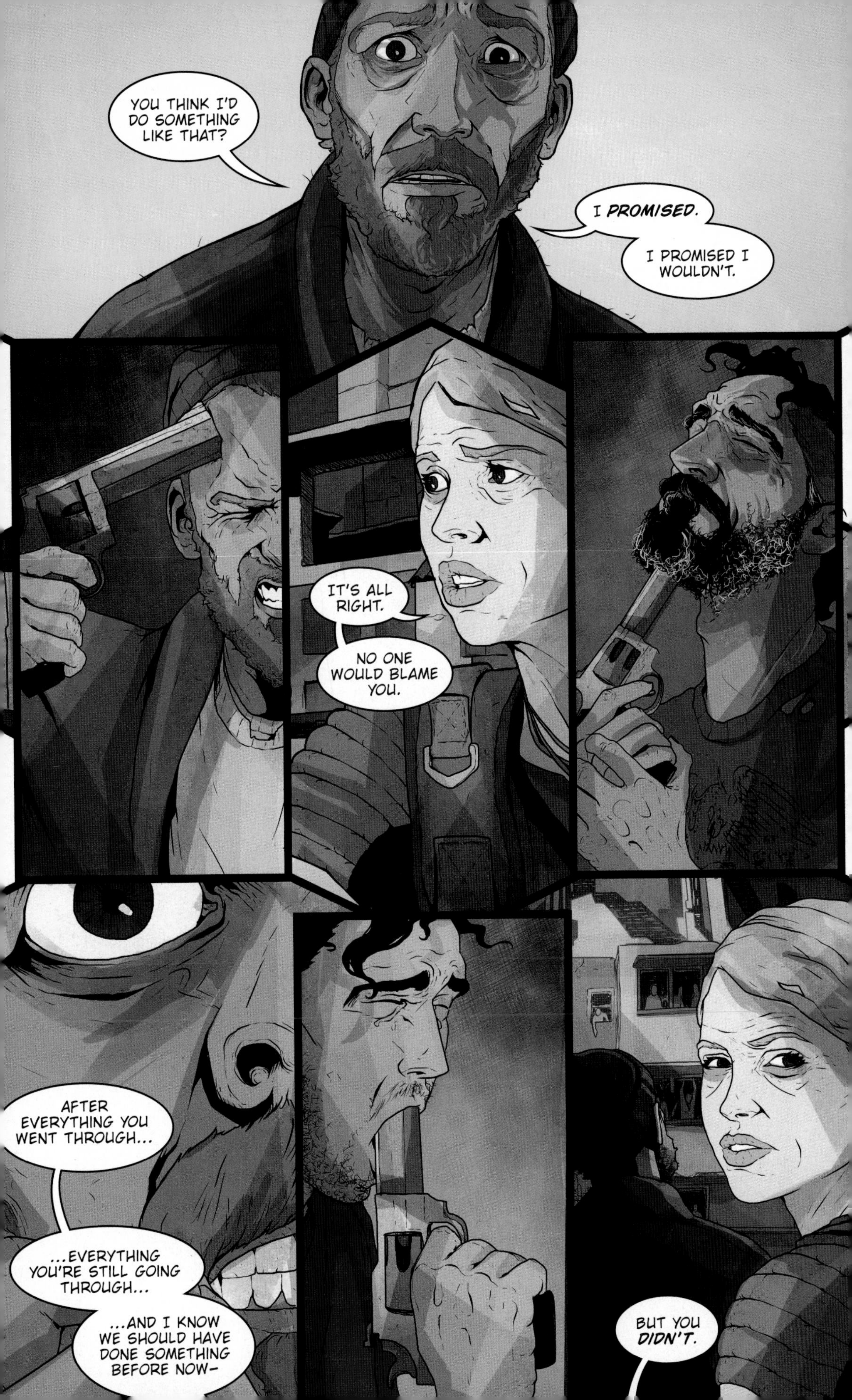
YOU THINK I'D DO SOMETHING LIKE THAT?
I PROMISED.
I PROMISED I WOULDN'T.
IT'S ALL RIGHT.
NO ONE WOULD BLAME YOU.
AFTER EVERYTHING YOU WENT THROUGH...
...EVERYTHING YOU'RE STILL GOING THROUGH...
...AND I KNOW WE SHOULD HAVE DONE SOMETHING BEFORE NOW-
BUT YOU DIDN'T.

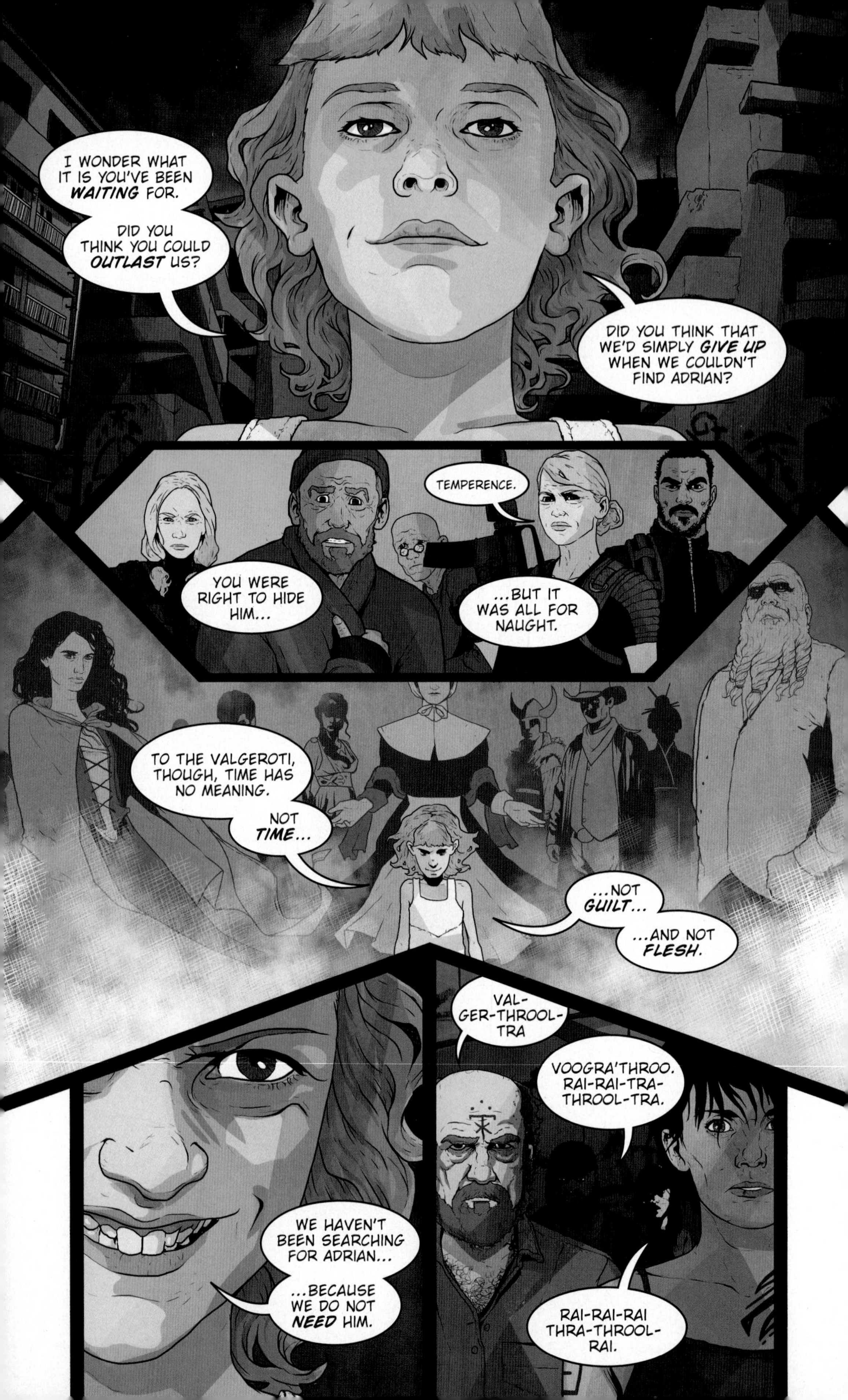
I WONDER WHAT IT IS YOU'VE BEEN WAITING FOR.
DID YOU THINK YOU COULD OUTLAST US?
DID YOU THINK THAT WE'D SIMPLY GIVE UP WHEN WE COULDN'T FIND ADRIAN?
TEMPERENCE.
YOU WERE RIGHT TO HIDE HIM...
...BUT IT WAS ALL FOR NAUGHT.
TO THE VALGEROTI, THOUGH, TIME HAS NO MEANING.
NOT TIME...
...NOT GUILT...
...AND NOT FLESH.
WE HAVEN'T BEEN SEARCHING FOR ADRIAN...
...BECAUSE WE DO NOT NEED HIM.
VAL-GER-THROOL-TRA
VOOGRA'THROO. RAI-RAI-TRA-THROOL-TRA.
RAI-RAI-RAI THRA-THROOL-RAI.

I'M ALMOST ASHAMED THAT WE DIDN'T THINK OF IT SOONER.

I SUPPOSE WE, LIKE YOU, WERE TOO FOCUSED ON ADRIAN— ON SUTTER— HIMSELF.

WE FORGOT ONE OF OUR MASTER'S FIRST LESSONS.

"THE FALLACY OF FLESH.

"IF FLESH HOLDS NO SWAY... IF TIME MEANS NOTHING...

"...WE CAN GIVE BIRTH TO OUR MASTER..."

WE CAN *WILL* HIM INTO EXISTENCE.

WE CAN RAISE HIM UP WITHIN ALL OF US.

WE CAN USE WHAT HE LEFT BEHIND.

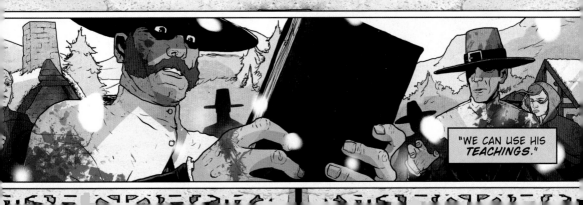

"WE CAN USE HIS *TEACHINGS*."

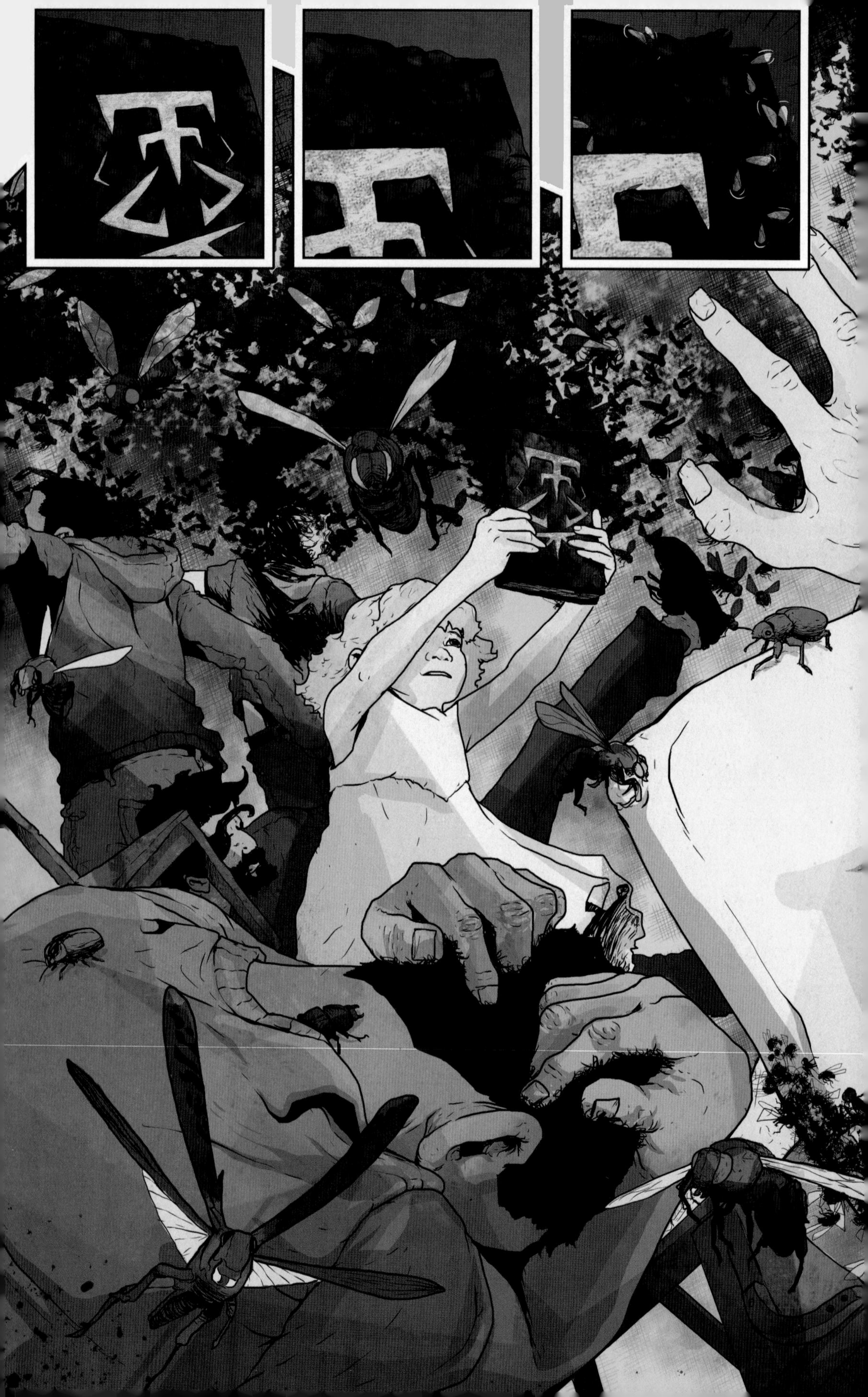

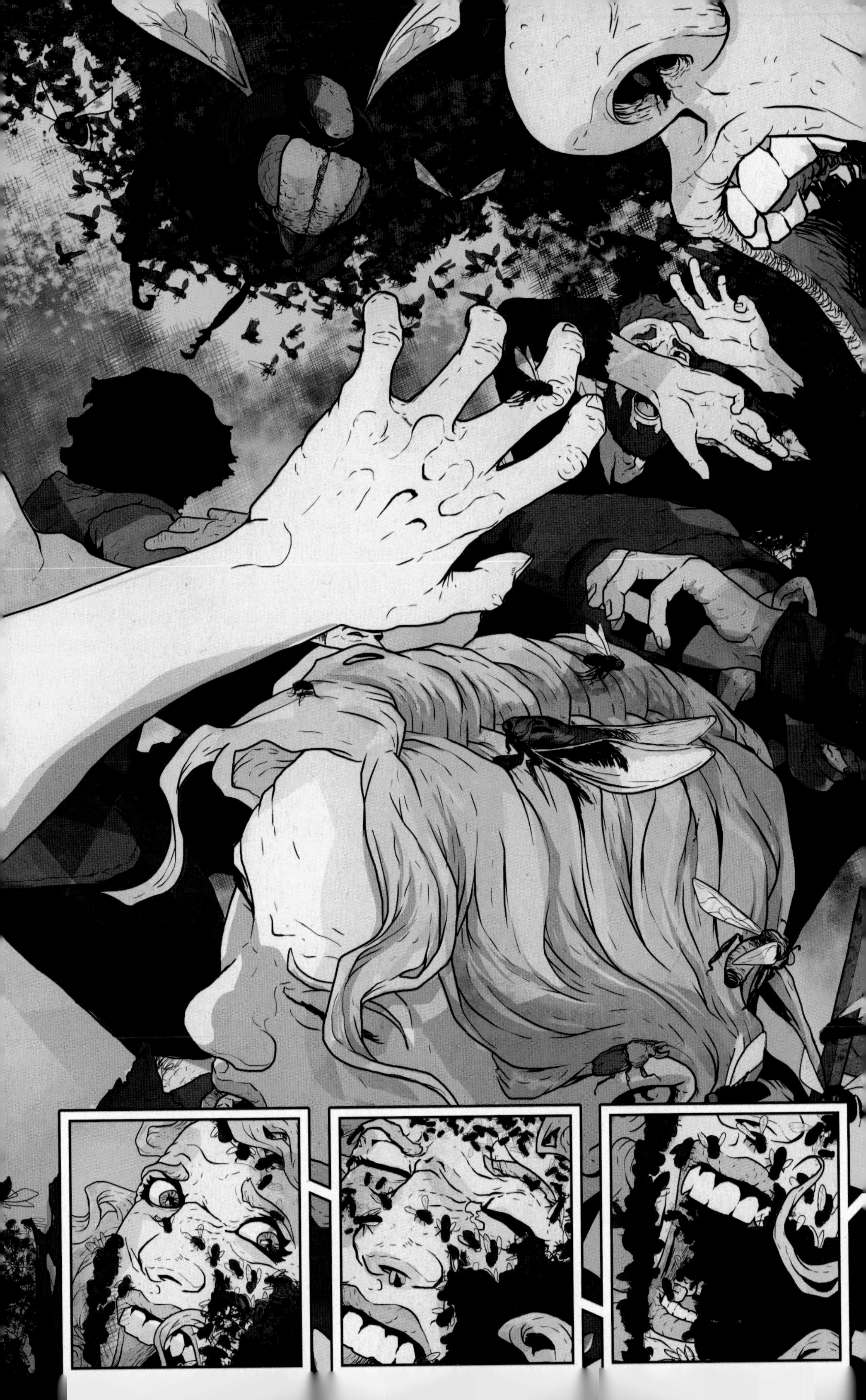

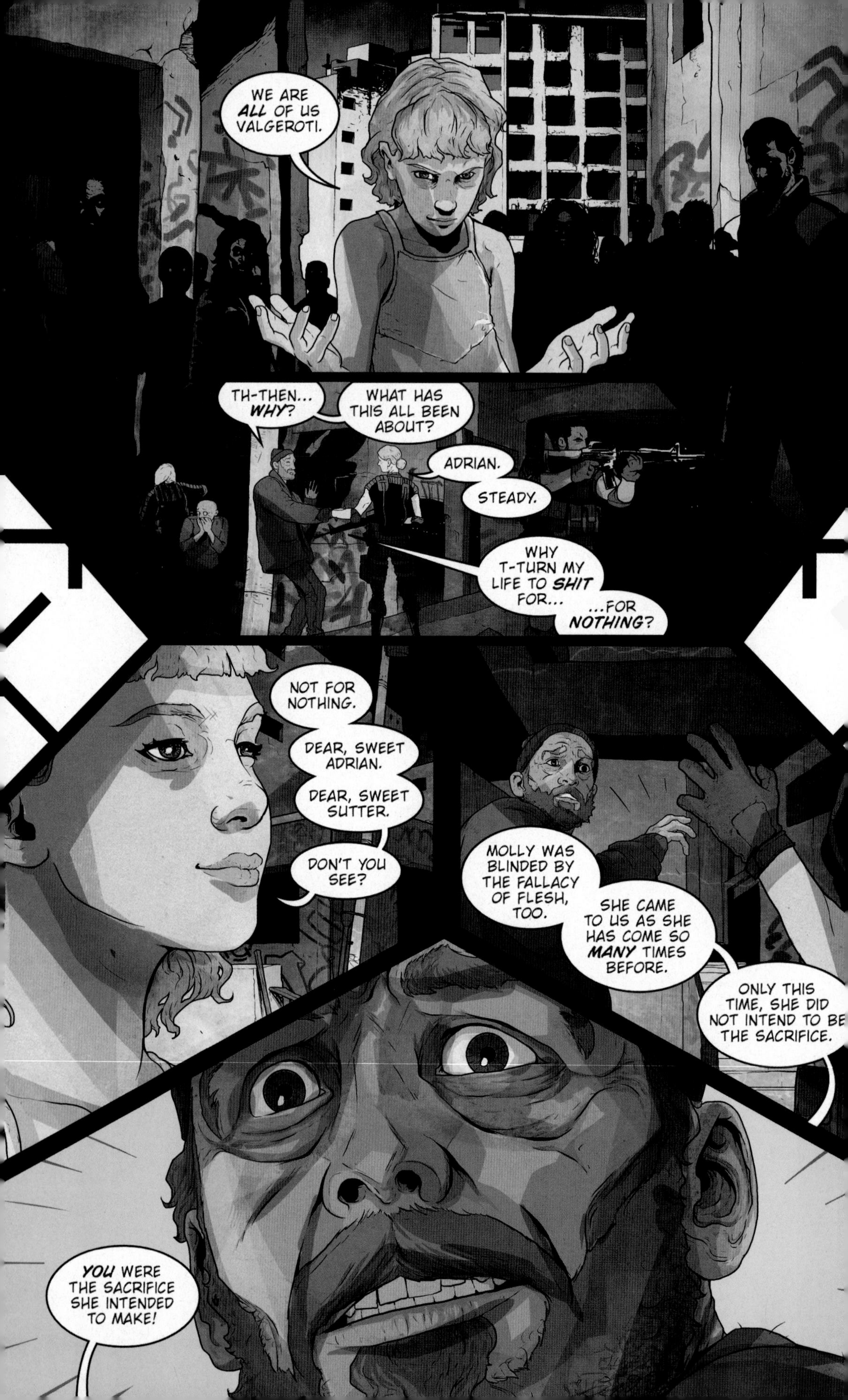
WE ARE ALL OF US VALGEROTI.
TH-THEN... WHY?
WHAT HAS THIS ALL BEEN ABOUT?
ADRIAN.
STEADY.
WHY T-TURN MY LIFE TO SHIT FOR...
...FOR NOTHING?
NOT FOR NOTHING.
DEAR, SWEET ADRIAN.
DEAR, SWEET SUTTER.
DON'T YOU SEE?
MOLLY WAS BLINDED BY THE FALLACY OF FLESH, TOO.
SHE CAME TO US AS SHE HAS COME SO MANY TIMES BEFORE.
ONLY THIS TIME, SHE DID NOT INTEND TO BE THE SACRIFICE.
YOU WERE THE SACRIFICE SHE INTENDED TO MAKE!

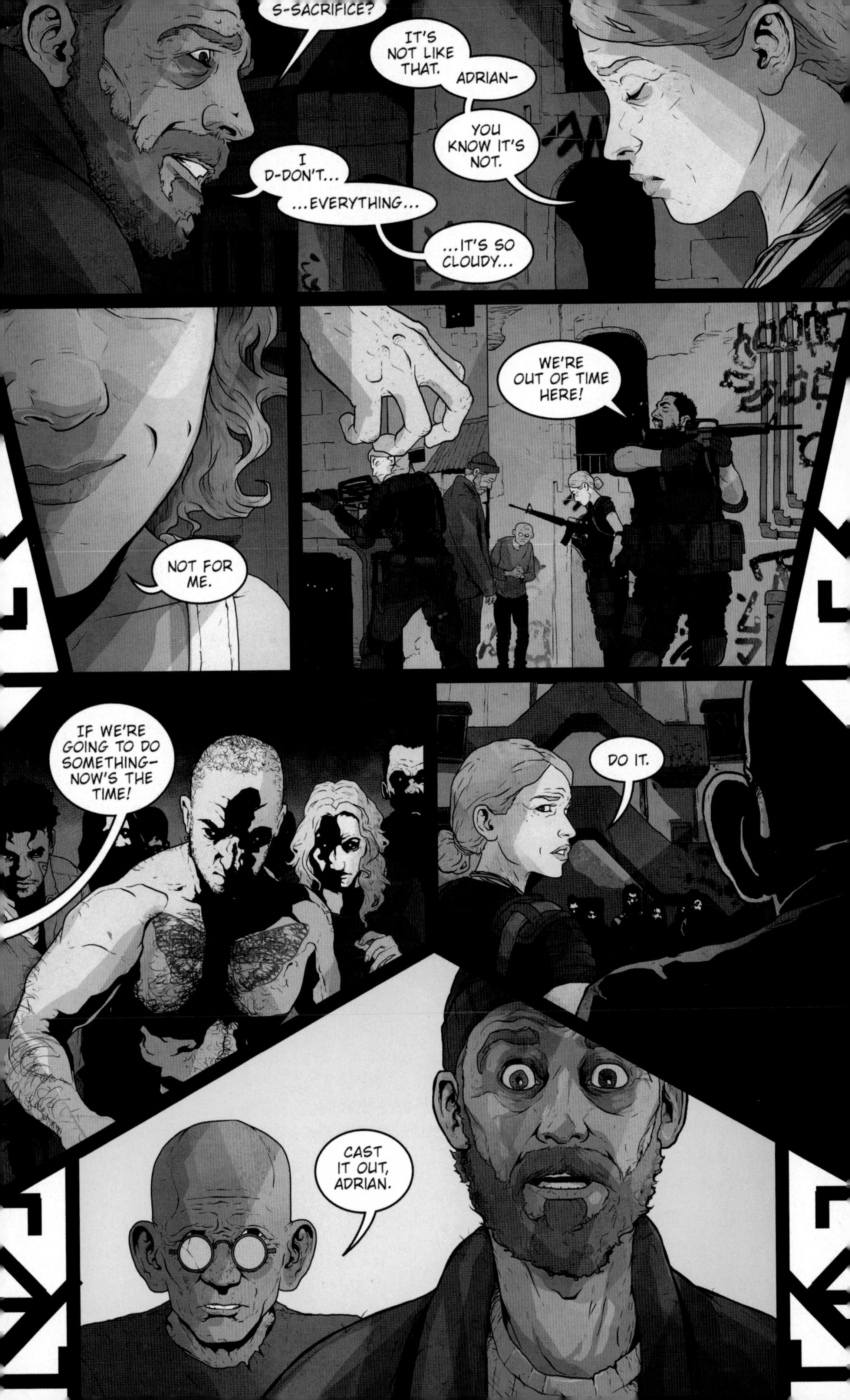
S-SACRIFICE?
IT'S NOT LIKE THAT.
ADRIAN-
YOU KNOW IT'S NOT.
I D-DON'T...
...EVERYTHING...
...IT'S SO CLOUDY...
NOT FOR ME.
WE'RE OUT OF TIME HERE!
IF WE'RE GOING TO DO SOMETHING- NOW'S THE TIME!
DO IT.
CAST IT OUT, ADRIAN.

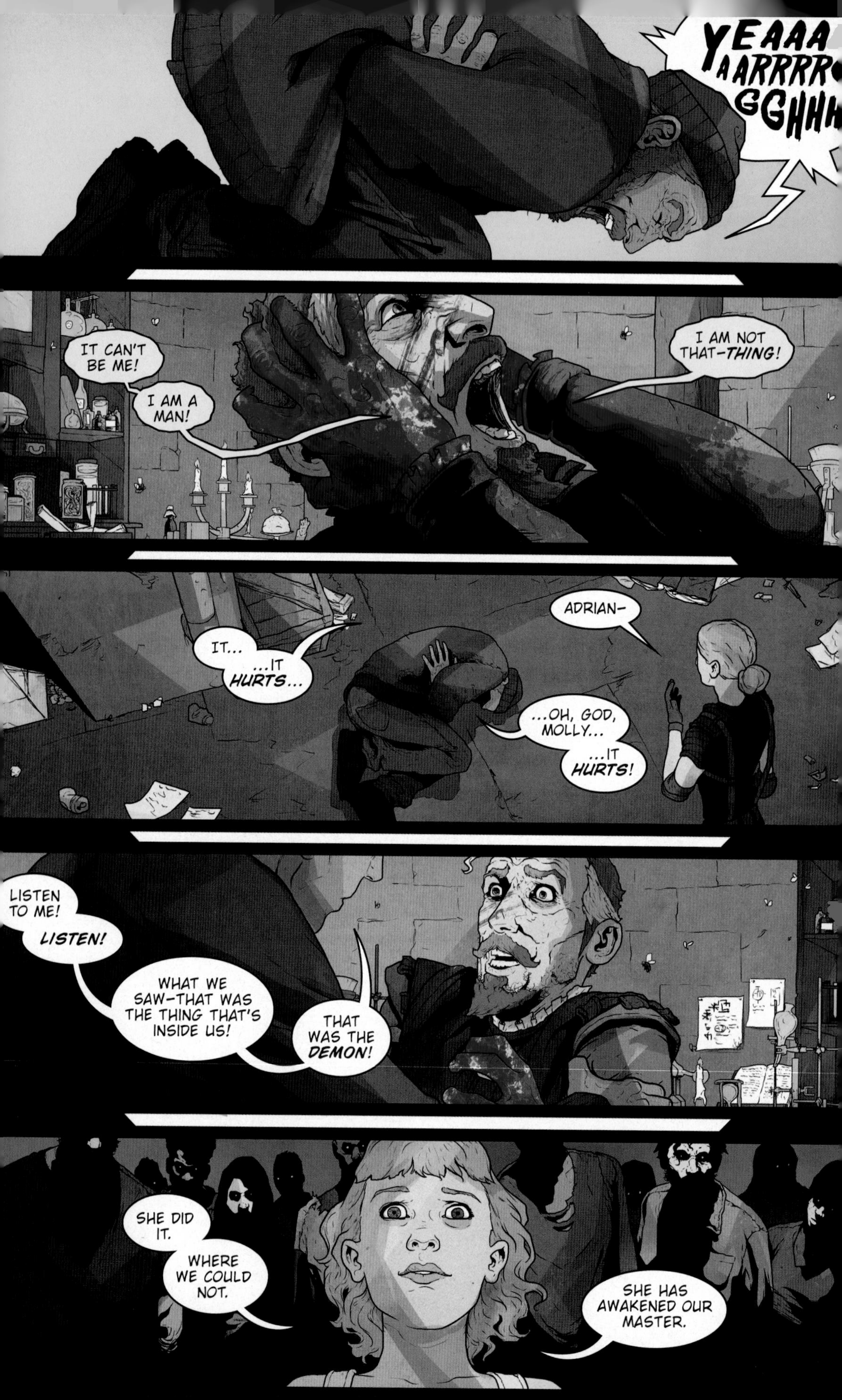
YEAAAYAARRRRGGHHH
IT CAN'T BE ME!
I AM A MAN!
I AM NOT THAT-THING!
IT... ...IT HURTS...
ADRIAN-
...OH, GOD, MOLLY... ...IT HURTS!
LISTEN TO ME! LISTEN!
WHAT WE SAW-THAT WAS THE THING THAT'S INSIDE US!
THAT WAS THE DEMON!
SHE DID IT.
WHERE WE COULD NOT.
SHE HAS AWAKENED OUR MASTER.

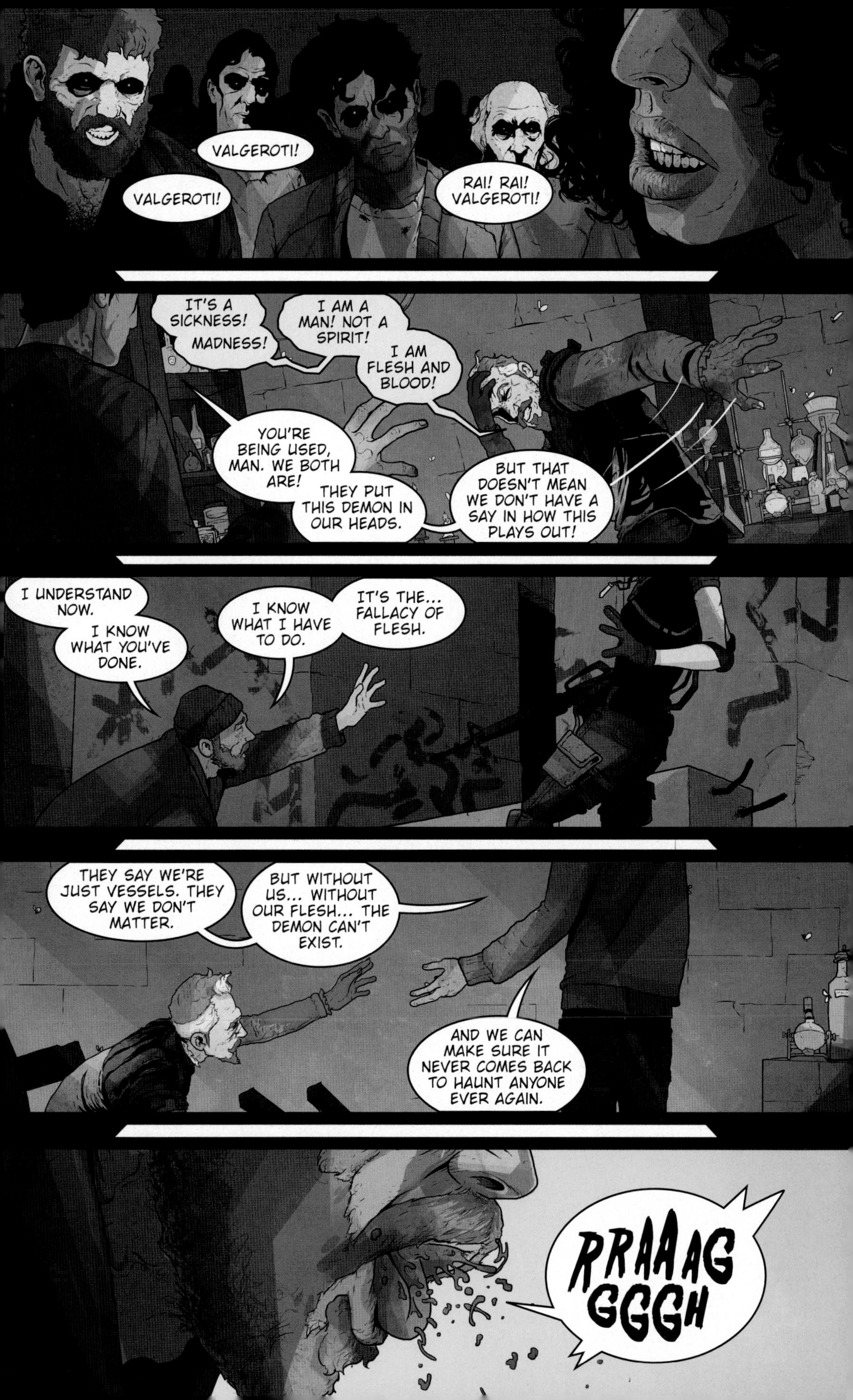
VALGEROTI!
VALGEROTI!
RAI! RAI! VALGEROTI!
IT'S A SICKNESS!
MADNESS!
I AM A MAN! NOT A SPIRIT!
I AM FLESH AND BLOOD!
YOU'RE BEING USED, MAN. WE BOTH ARE!
THEY PUT THIS DEMON IN OUR HEADS.
BUT THAT DOESN'T MEAN WE DON'T HAVE A SAY IN HOW THIS PLAYS OUT!
I UNDERSTAND NOW.
I KNOW WHAT YOU'VE DONE.
I KNOW WHAT I HAVE TO DO.
IT'S THE... FALLACY OF FLESH.
THEY SAY WE'RE JUST VESSELS. THEY SAY WE DON'T MATTER.
BUT WITHOUT US... WITHOUT OUR FLESH... THE DEMON CAN'T EXIST.
AND WE CAN MAKE SURE IT NEVER COMES BACK TO HAUNT ANYONE EVER AGAIN.
RRAAAG GGGH

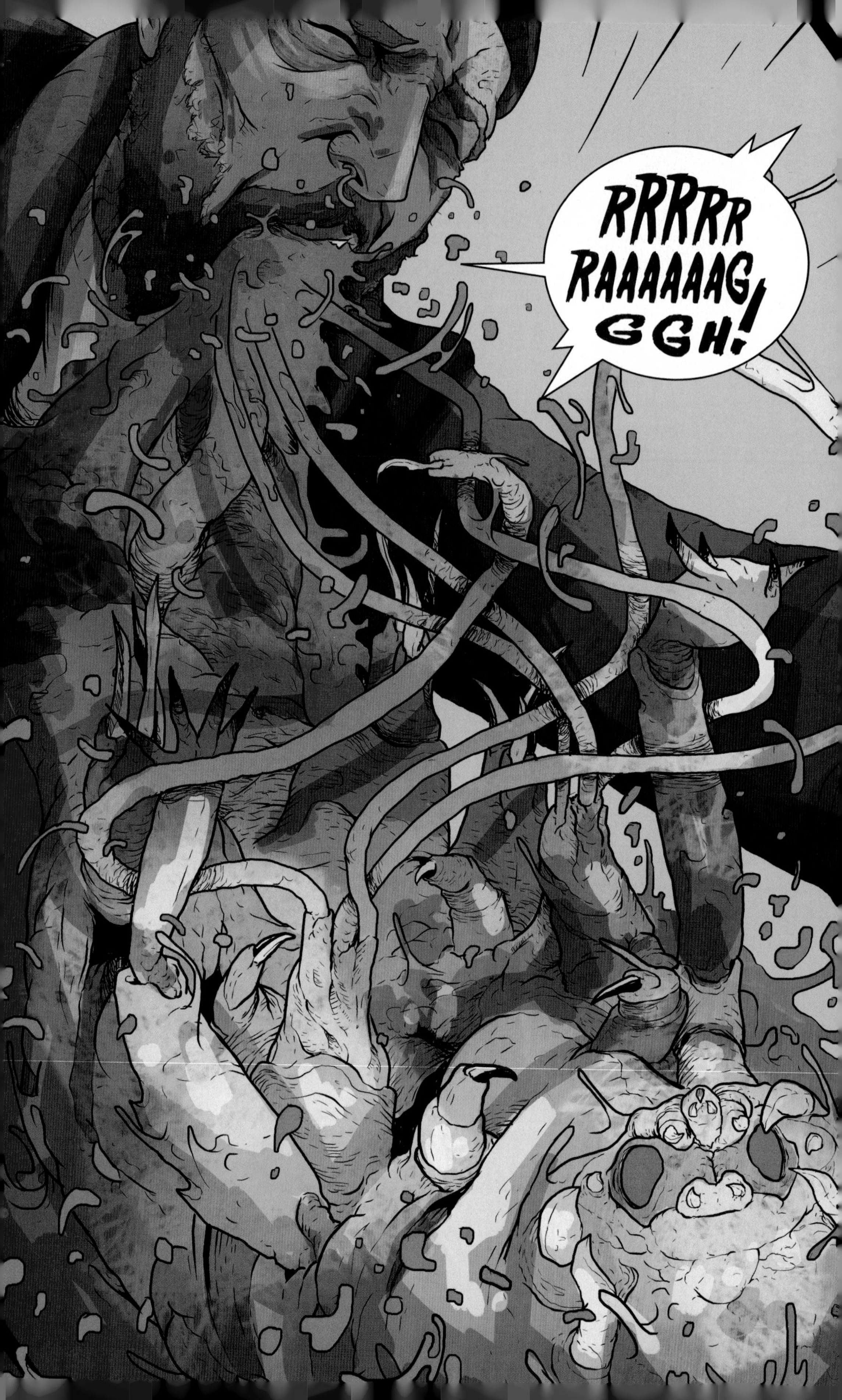
RRRRR RAAAAAAGGGH!

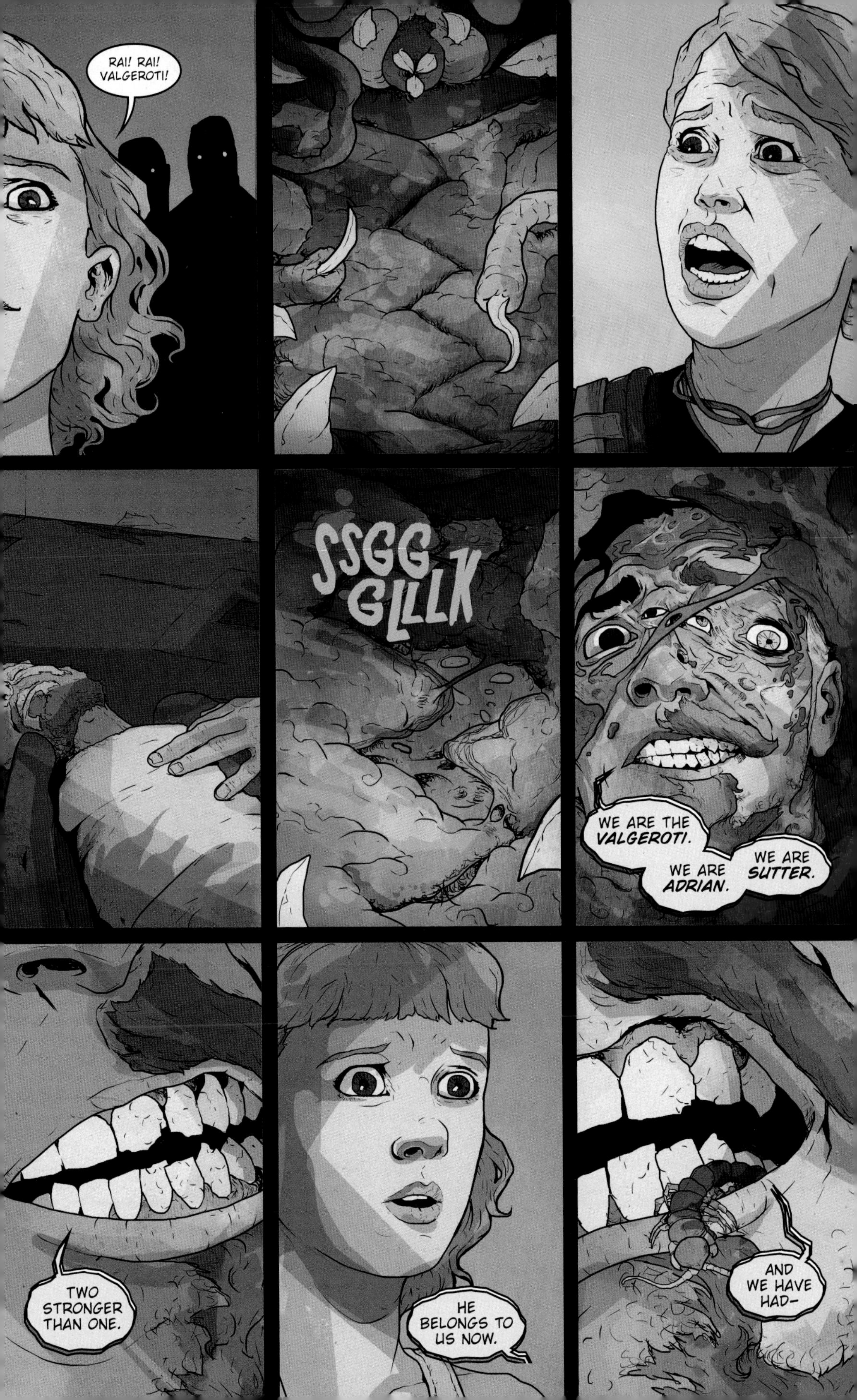
RAI! RAI! VALGEROTI!
SSGG GLLLK
WE ARE THE VALGEROTI.
WE ARE ADRIAN.
WE ARE SUTTER.
TWO STRONGER THAN ONE.
HE BELONGS TO US NOW.
AND WE HAVE HAD-

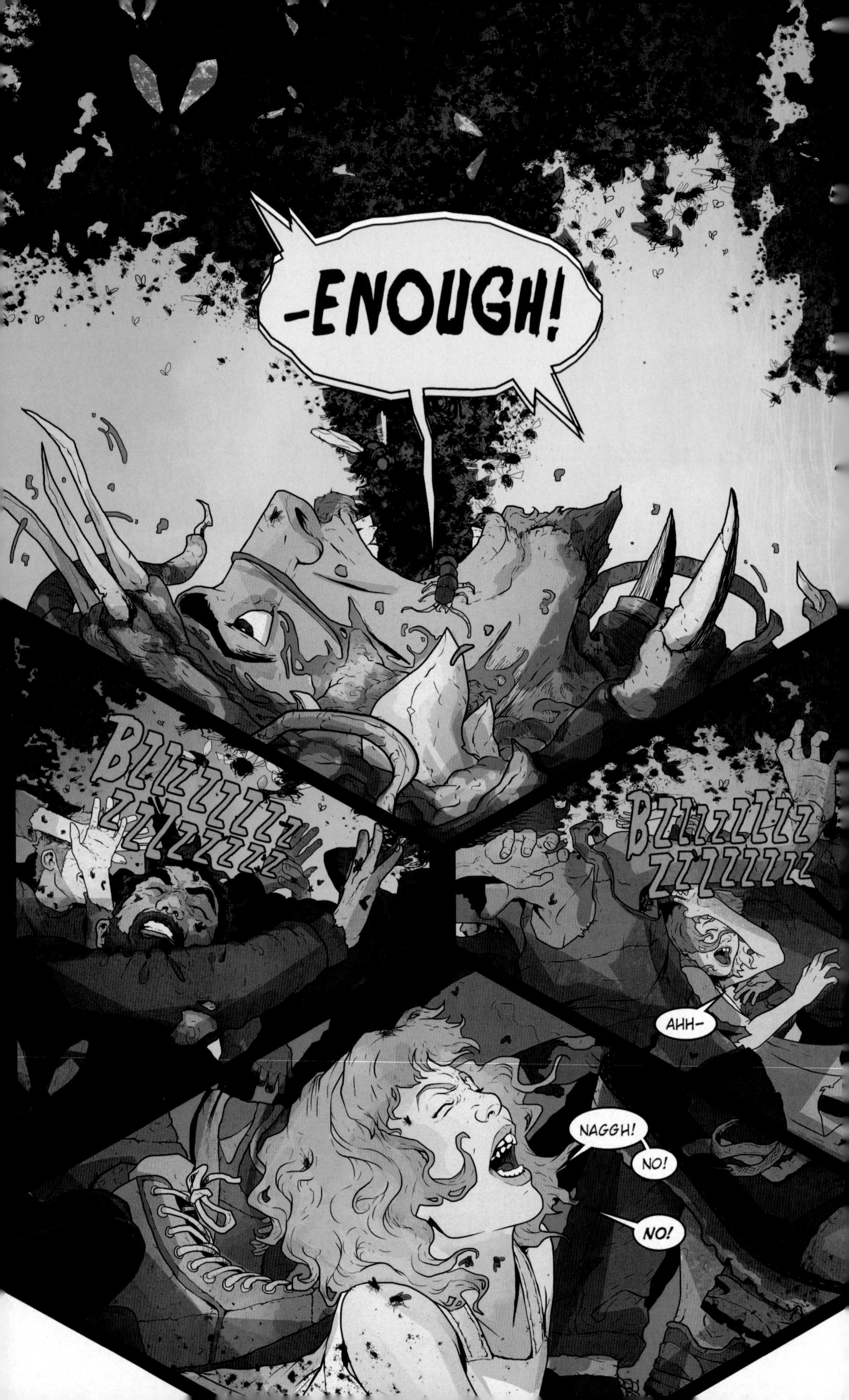
-ENOUGH!
BZZZZZZZZZ ZZZZZZZZZ
BZZZZZZZZZ ZZZZZZZZ
AHH-
NAGGH!
NO!
NO!

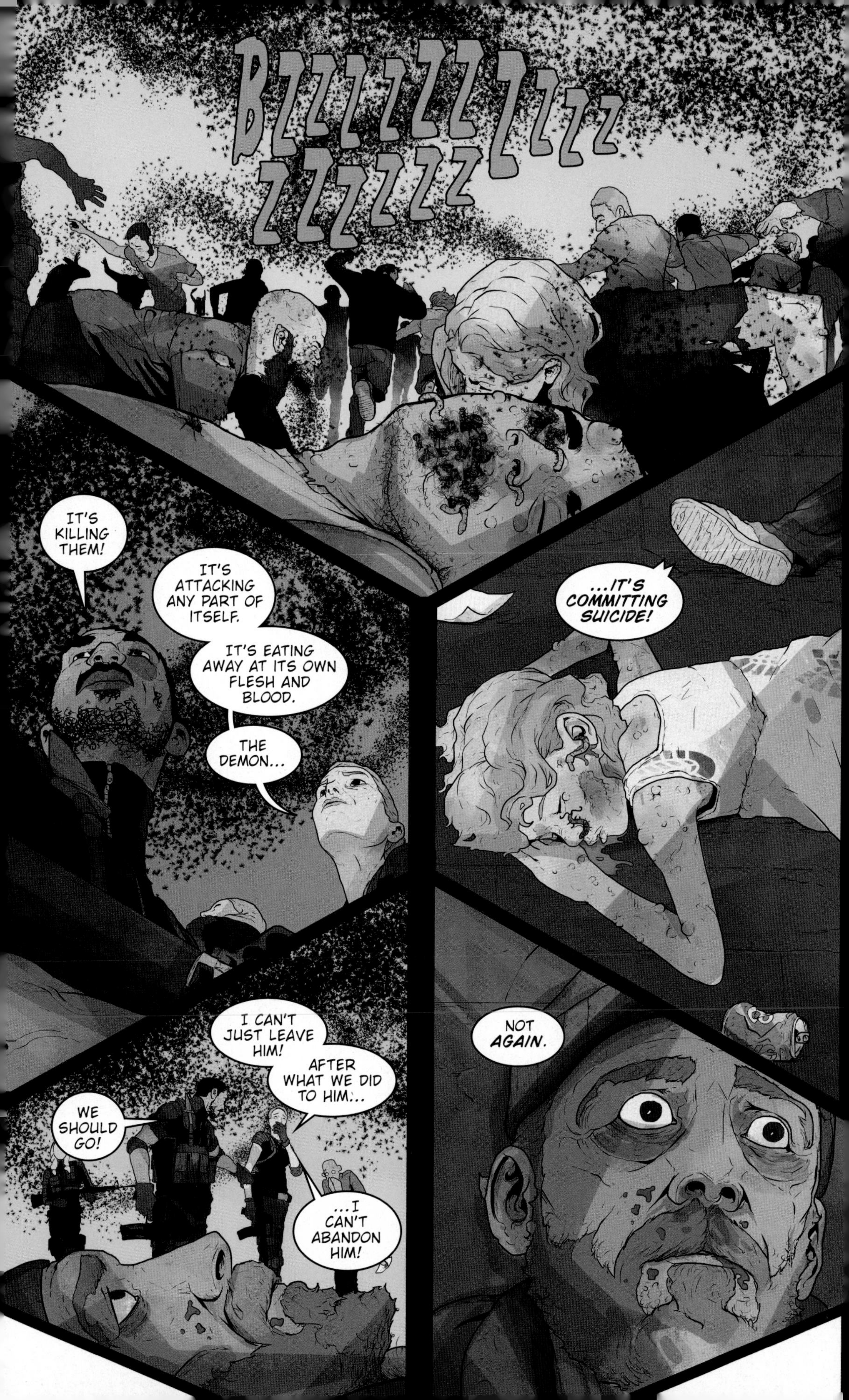
BZZZZZZZZZZZ ZZZZZZZ
IT'S KILLING THEM!
IT'S ATTACKING ANY PART OF ITSELF.
IT'S EATING AWAY AT ITS OWN FLESH AND BLOOD.
THE DEMON...
...IT'S COMMITTING SUICIDE!
I CAN'T JUST LEAVE HIM!
AFTER WHAT WE DID TO HIM...
WE SHOULD GO!
...I CAN'T ABANDON HIM!
NOT AGAIN.

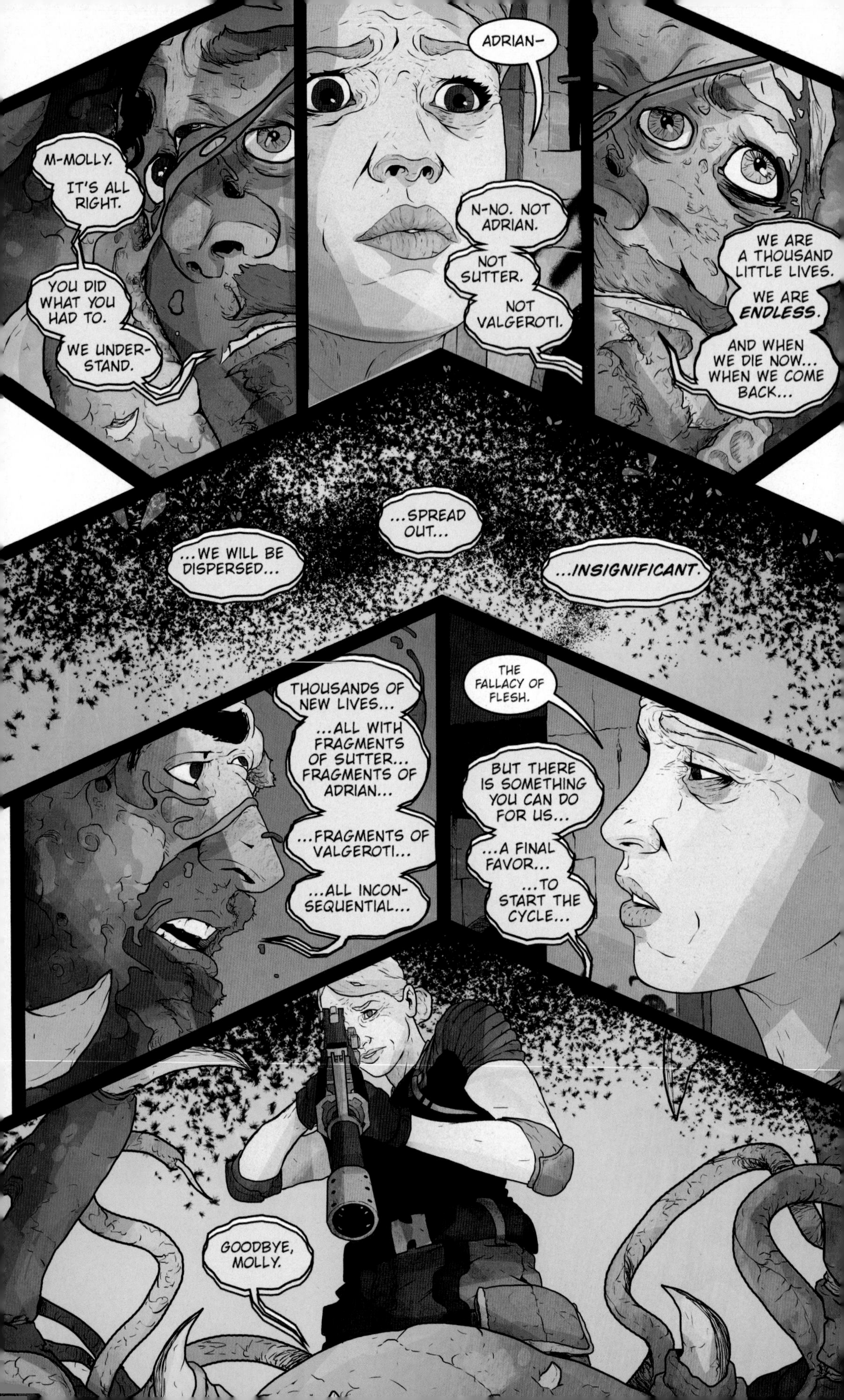
M-MOLLY.
IT'S ALL RIGHT.
YOU DID WHAT YOU HAD TO.
WE UNDER-STAND.
ADRIAN-
N-NO. NOT ADRIAN.
NOT SUTTER.
NOT VALGEROTI.
WE ARE A THOUSAND LITTLE LIVES.
WE ARE *ENDLESS*.
AND WHEN WE DIE NOW... WHEN WE COME BACK...
...WE WILL BE DISPERSED...
...SPREAD OUT...
...*INSIGNIFICANT*.
THOUSANDS OF NEW LIVES...
...ALL WITH FRAGMENTS OF SUTTER... FRAGMENTS OF ADRIAN...
...FRAGMENTS OF VALGEROTI...
...ALL INCON-SEQUENTIAL...
THE FALLACY OF FLESH.
BUT THERE IS SOMETHING YOU CAN DO FOR US...
...A FINAL FAVOR...
...TO START THE CYCLE...
GOODBYE, MOLLY.

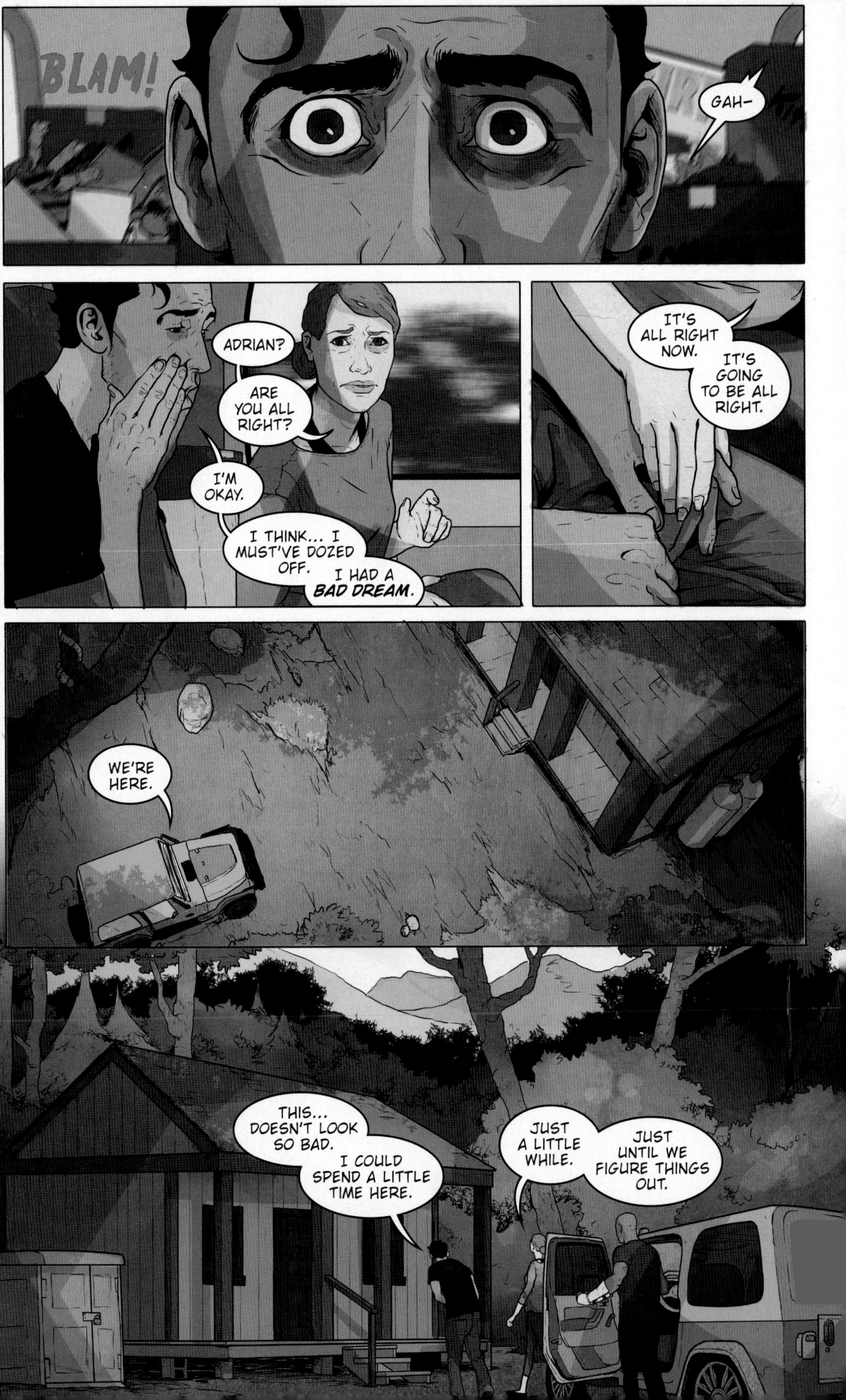
BLAM!
GAH-
ADRIAN?
ARE YOU ALL RIGHT?
I'M OKAY.
I THINK... I MUST'VE DOZED OFF.
I HAD A BAD DREAM.
IT'S ALL RIGHT NOW.
IT'S GOING TO BE ALL RIGHT.
WE'RE HERE.
THIS... DOESN'T LOOK SO BAD.
I COULD SPEND A LITTLE TIME HERE.
JUST A LITTLE WHILE.
JUST UNTIL WE FIGURE THINGS OUT.

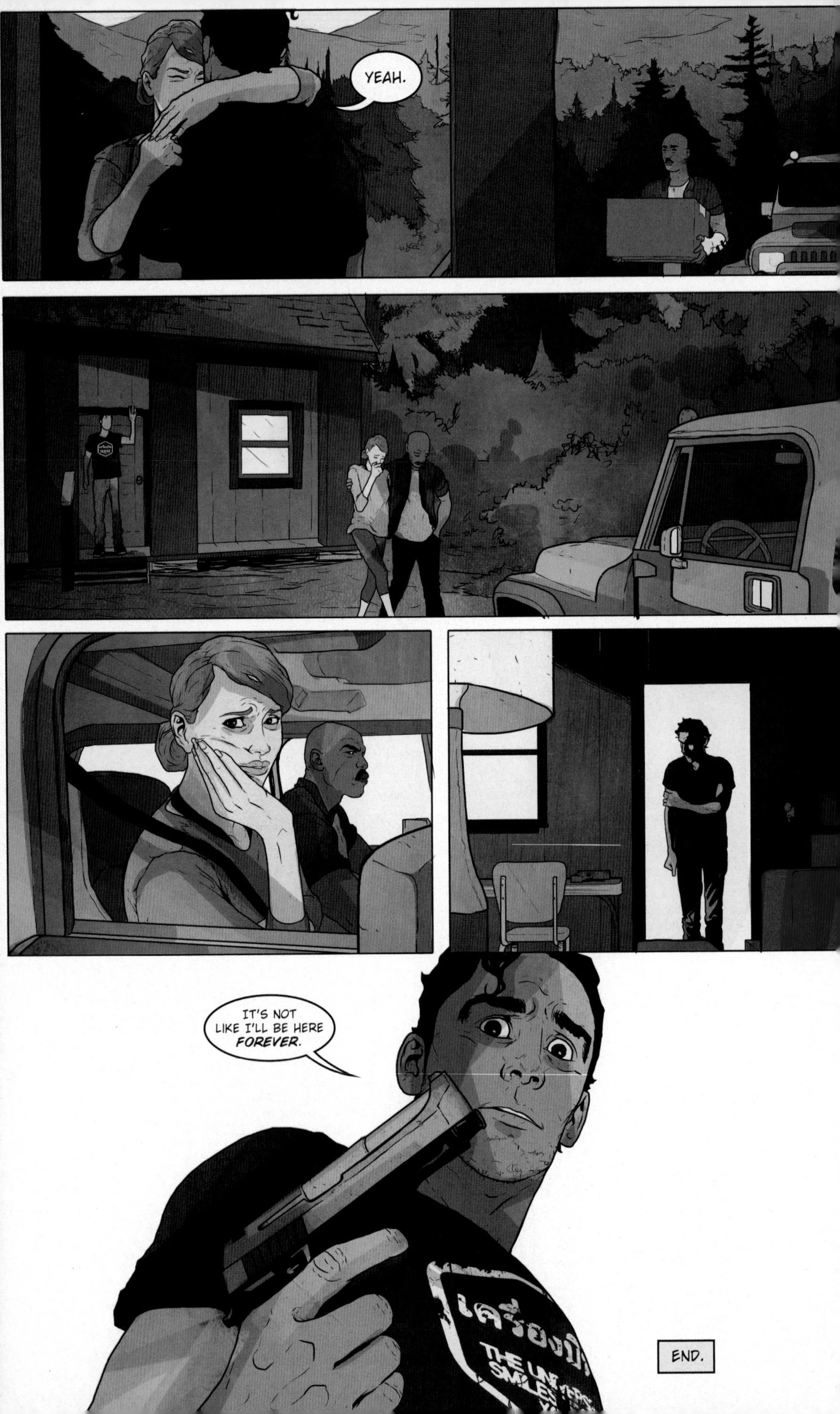

YEAH.
IT'S NOT LIKE I'LL BE HERE *FOREVER*.
THE UNIVERSE SMILES
END.